Herbie's Game

Also by Timothy Hallinan

The Junior Bender Series
Crashed
Little Elvises
The Fame Thief
Herbie's Game

The Poke Rafferty Series
A Nail Through the Heart
The Fourth Watcher
Breathing Water
The Queen of Patpong
The Fear Artist
For the Dead

The Simeon Grist Series
The Four Last Things
Everything but the Squeal
Skin Deep
Incinerator
The Man With No Time
The Bone Polisher

Herbie's Game

A Junior Bender Mystery

TIMOTHY HALLINAN

HERBIE'S GAME

Copyright © 2014 by Timothy Hallinan

Published by Soho Press, Inc.
853 Broadway
New York, NY 10003

Library of Congress Cataloging-in-Publication Data
Hallinan, Timothy.
Herbie's game : a Junior Bender Mystery / Timothy Hallinan.
HC ISBN 978-1-61695-429-1
PB ISBN 978-1-61695-540-3
eISBN 978-1-61695-430-7
1. Thieves—Fiction. 2. Private investigators—California—
LosAngeles—Fiction. I. Title.
PS3558.A3923H47 2014
813'.54—dc23   2013045393

Interior design by Janine Agro, Soho Press, Inc.
Illustration by Katherine Grames

Printed in the United States of America

10 9 8 7 6 5 4 3 2 1

For
Munyin Choy
creator, scorekeeper, and team captain of
Munyin's Game
which I have played happily
for thirty years

o o o

Herbie's Game

PART
ONE

"So you see, kid," Herbie said, "we're like Robin Hood. We steal from the rich and we give to the poor."

"How do we give to the poor?" I asked.

"I said we were *like* Robin Hood, not a slavish *imitation* of Robin Hood."

"So we're *sort* of like Robin Hood," I said.

"Yeah," Herbie said. "If you squint."

1

Ur-Hamlet

Eighteen minutes in—just two minutes short of my limit—I was ready to write the place off.

It was a very nice house in a very nice part of the Beverly Hills flats. A very nice car was usually standing in the driveway, a BMW SUV so new the odometer hadn't hit the hundreds yet, and I could smell that canned new-car fragrance through the closed windows. The locks on the house's doors, it seemed to me during my week of taking the occasional careless-looking careful look, would yield to a persuasive argument. No bothersome alarm tip-offs. Inside, I was sure, would be a lot of very nice stuff.

And I was right: there *was* a lot of nice stuff, although most of it was too big to lift. A European sensibility had expressed itself in a lot of stone statuary, some of it very possibly late Roman and some of it, for variety's sake, Khmer, plus a gorgeous polychrome German Madonna in painted linden wood, possibly from the sixteenth century. As tempting as these pieces were, they were all too heavy to hoist, too bulky to carry, and too hard to fence, especially since my premier fence for fine art, Stinky Tetweiler, and I were on the outs.

So I was adjusting to the idea that the evening would be a write-off as I went very carefully through the drawers in the bedroom, putting everything back exactly where I'd found it and counting down the last ninety seconds. And, as is so often the case, the moment that I gave up was also the moment that fate, with its taste for cheap melodrama, uncoiled itself in the darkness, and my knuckles bounced off one of the things that sends a little sugar bullet straight through a burglar's heart: a jewelry box. It was cardboard, not velvet, but it *was* a jewelry box, and it rattled when I picked it up.

Ever since my mentor, Herbie Mott, taught me the rules of burglary, I've practically salivated at the sound of something rattling in a small box.

But . . . the lid was stuck. It felt like it hadn't been popped in years, and the accumulation of humidity and air-born *schmutz* had created a kind of impromptu mucilage. The word *schmutz*, I reflected as I ran a little pen-knife in between the box and the lid, had entered Middle English via Yiddish and German, where it meant, as it means now, *dirt*, specifically, a kind of sticky, yank-your-fingers-back-fast dirt.

The top pulled free from the box with a faint sucking noise, like an air-kiss. I shook out one—no, two—objects and aimed my little penlight at them.

And heard the hum of an engine: a car, coming up the driveway.

Hurrying will kill you more often than taking your time will. I looked at the two objects closely, listening for the motor to cut out, listening for the slam of a car door.

One of the pieces I recognized immediately, a glittering little slice of history and bravery—valor, even—in platinum, rubies, sapphires, and diamonds. It looked real, it looked fine, it looked like about $12,000 from a good fence.

The brakes let out an obliging soprano note as the car stopped, and the engine cut out.

The other piece, well . . .

The other piece looked like something that had been made in the dark by someone who was following directions over the radio or some other medium with no REPLAY button. Slap it together from whatever was at hand, don't make a second pass, don't look at it too closely. It bore a sort of *ur*-resemblance to the $12,000 one, in the same way that a supposedly crude revenge play that scholars call the *ur-Hamlet* is thought to be the direct ancestor and inspiration of Shakespeare's greatest hit, but this piece wouldn't have fooled an inanimate object at forty paces.

A car door closed. Then I heard another.

The two pieces were in the same box for a reason. I replaced the lid, slipped the box into my pocket, put the drawer back in its original order, and let myself out the back just as the front door opened.

2

The Only Piece of Paper That Could Kill Him

Wattles once told me he was always happy in the morning because he hadn't hurt anybody yet.

So it's easy to imagine him singing something late-sixties/early-seventies—"Take It Easy," maybe, or "Born Free"—as he clumped out of the elevator in the black-glass, medium-rise office building where he did all the bad things that comprised the business of Wattles, Inc. Easy to imagine him, sport-jacketed and red-faced, following his beach-ball gut down the hall, dragging his left leg behind him like a rejected idea and looking, as he had for twenty years, like he'd be dead in fifteen minutes.

His hair would still be damp. His shave would be aggressively successful. He'd reek of Royall Lyme aftershave, forty bucks a bottle, with the little lead crown on the cap. As he would say, class stuff. Taken together, then: all these characteristics identified Wattles as he undid the cheap locks on the outer door to his office.

Identified him externally, that is. Wattles's interior landscape, a column of dark, buzzing flies looking impatiently for the day's first kill, was tucked safely out of sight.

Tiffany, the new receptionist, was, as always, at her desk, wearing her permanent expression: pretty in kind of a plastic way, happy, perpetually surprised enough at something to be saying, *Oh!* A brunette this week, she was wearing her LaLa the French Maid costume, although Wattles actually preferred Nurse Perky. Still, change was good. He'd had to replace his first receptionist, Dora, when a truly lethal crook named Rabbits Stennet had nearly discovered her secret, which was that she had been modeled on his wife, Bunny, about whom Rabbits went all Othello whenever anyone even looked at her. Rabbits had once backed his car over a parking attendant at Trader Vic's because the man had taken the liberty of turning on Bunny's seat-warmer.

So Dora had been hastily shredded in bulk, all two hundred of her, and replaced by Tiffany: same latex blow-up doll, different nose, different eye color, different wigs.

Wattles had probably squinted at Tiffany as he went to the office's inner door and its array of very *good* locks, because she was sagging a little. He might have heard the soft hiss of a leak, which meant that he would have to find the little battery-powered pump and top her off.

Or maybe just pop the valves and let her deflate, replace her with another one. After all, there were more than three hundred and fifty of her boxed up in the closet, waiting for the mail-order lovers who were the clientele of Wattles's one legitimate business. $89.95 a pop, although Wattles wasn't sure that was the best way to put it.

All the blow-ups leaked sooner or later, thanks to the low manufacturing standards of the Chinese factory where they were produced, which Wattles hadn't complained about because it ensured re-orders. Maybe he'd put a new one at the desk. Nurse Perky again. Or maybe Venice Skater Girl, although that was kind of informal for the office, and the shoes were expensive.

So he was probably singing, full of illegal plans, thinking about blowing up a new Tiffany, and smelling all limey when he tried to stick a key into the first of his *very* good inner locks and couldn't. It wouldn't go in. He leaned down, grunting a little as the movement squeezed his gut, and saw that the inner tumbler was upside down.

So were the others.

The door had been opened, and whoever had undone those very good locks hadn't even taken the trouble to lock things up again.

He went inside, leaving Tiffany to hiss in desolate solitude, and got the TV remote that opened the panel in the wall opposite his desk, but when he turned to aim it, he put it back down. The panel was open. So was the door of the safe behind it. He didn't even bother to go look.

The one thing that was sure to be missing was *absolutely* going to be the piece of paper that could kill him.

He wheeled his chair over to the window and plopped down, watching the San Fernando Valley work up its daily output of smog. Wattles knew whole battalions of crooks, but he could only think of one person who knew where his office was, could pop those particular locks, and was also enough of a smart-ass to leave them popped.

He could also only think of one person who could help him figure out whether he was right.

Problem was, they were the same person. And this, unfortunately, was where I came into the narrative, because both those people were me.

3
Always Do the Hard Thing First

Trying to ignore all the birds on the wallpaper, I looked at the bird in the brooch with the kind of regret a farmer might feel just before he beheads the chicken his children have named Pookie. It was going to be hard to part with it.

While platinum has been the top of the hill for jewelers for decades, giving the ultra-rich an opportunity to sneer at gold, it's still a relative newcomer to the vault. Unlike gold and silver, which have dangled from wrists and ears since the dawn of the two-syllable word, platinum didn't become available in quantity until the early 1900s. In fact, when the Spanish conquistadors discovered lumps of it in the gold they were ripping from the earth of what is now Colombia, they tried to melt it and failed, and then tossed it away as a nuisance. They called it "platina," meaning "little silver," and one theory was that it might be unripe gold. In the nineteenth century, Lavoisier conquered the metal's high melting point by using oxygen, which, conveniently, he had just discovered. So, by the end of the nineteenth century, there it was: an increasing supply of this beautiful, high-luster metal, brighter than silver and harder than iron, and no one knew what to do with it until Cartier, founded in Paris in 1847, figured out how to use it to support precious stones.

And boy, did they figure it out.

The object in front of me, perhaps an inch and a half in height, blazed with fifty to seventy tiny diamonds, rubies, and sapphires. The stones decorated the platinum body of a bird—the rubies on the breast and the sapphires on the wings, with the diamonds adorning the head. The bird perched behind a graceful, curving grid of platinum in the form of a bird cage.

Which meant that I was experiencing one of those head-on environmental and temporal collisions that frequently remind me that every moment I live contains all the others I've experienced or even read about. I was sitting, surrounded by wallpaper birds, in a feverishly avian room—bird bedspread, bird lighting fixture, bird knickknacks, actual, somewhat depressed-looking birds caged glumly in the corner—in Bitsy's Bird's Nest, certainly the north San Fernando Valley's most obsessive motel—and staring at *another* caged bird, this one made of precious stones and platinum on a royal-family-quality brooch crafted in the late 1930s. I was also smelling nail polish, which I always associated with my mother, from a brush wielded by Ronnie Bigelow, who was emphatically not my mother. Ronnie, her knees tucked to one side, was adding production value to the almost-king-sized, almost-functional Magic Fingers massage bed labeled THE BIRDY RUB, its coverlet decorated in printed parrots the color of healthy lung tissue. Ronnie's eyes took bites out of the brooch as she smoothed a tiny brush over the nail of her right baby finger.

"Why the cage?" she asked.

"It represents the imprisonment of France by Germany," I said. "It's liberation jewelry from World War II. The red, white, and blue bird stands for France, and the cage symbolizes the Nazi occupation. Cartier made these and sold them in Paris under the noses of the Nazis, which was pretty brave, considering the famous Nazi sense of humor." I held it up to the light from the window, and the stones caught fire. "Imagine a willowy French socialite with one of these gleaming on the shoulder of her gown, making small talk as she dances with some Heinrich from the Gestapo. After the war, Cartier changed the design by putting the bird on top of the cage. *Voilà*. Freedom."

"How do you know she was willowy?" Ronnie said. "Socialites eat pretty good, and French socialites probably get their pick of the day's baguettes." She squinted at the brooch again and then held out a hand, elbow straight, to look at her nails. "I could wear it better than she did." The sight of the hand prompted a frown. "The right hand is the one I always screw up."

The late-morning sunlight was discovering 24-karat gold in Ronnie's hair, which was in the kind of multidimensional tangle predicted by chaos theory, like a foam of whipped Mobius loops.

"If you always screw up the right," I said, "then why start with it?"

"Always do the hard thing first," she said.

"Whatever happened to warming up?"

"So, as I was saying, it would look better on me."

"It won't get a chance to. It's going into Rina's college fund. If I can figure out how to sell it."

"Rina's thirteen."

"And?"

The tip of her tongue clamped between her teeth, she started to paint the thumb of her right hand. "Okay," she said. "Rina's college fund is not negotiable. Why don't you sell it to that awful man with the teensy nose up in the hills?"

The awful man she meant was Stinky Tetweiler, one of LA's prime fences for connoisseur goods and generally the first place I'd take a piece like this one. But Stinky had tried to have me killed a few weeks earlier, and while I don't generally get personal about business, I wasn't giving him anything as good as this brooch.

"It's too nice for Stinky. Cartier made these things and brave women wore them while the Gestapo basements were squeezing out screams all over Paris."

"What's it worth?"

"Twenty, twenty-five K. At the burglar's rate, I might get twelve." I'd probably get more from Stinky, but the hell with him.

"Was it the only thing you got last night?"

"No," I said. "The other thing is kind of weird."

"Thing, singular? You go to all the trouble to break into that house and you only take two—?"

"What's the first rule of burglary?"

"Don't get caught." She was staring at the partially painted hand as though she was having second thoughts about the color.

"And how do we avoid getting caught?"

"Oh," she said. "Yeah."

"Herbie's Rule Number Three. In and out fast, right? Every minute over twenty or twenty-five that you're in the house—"

"I know, I know. Get out fast. But still, only two—"

"That's why junkies get caught. They take everything. The mark gets home and the whole house is missing and the TV is in the front yard, and he calls the cops and, junkies being junkies, the guy who hit him is probably nodding out at the wheel of his car two houses down."

"Junkies might as well be furniture," she said.

This was new ground. "Do you have personal experience with junkies?"

"No," she said. "I watch the Heroin Channel."

"You haven't mentioned a junkie in the rich and unreliable narrative of your life."

"If my life is a house," she said, "you haven't even gotten to the living room."

"You're just grumpy because you can't remember which town you told me you were born in."

"So, not to change the subject, what's weird about the other thing you took?"

I gave up. Morning chats with an attractive and potentially consenting member of the opposite sex always make me shift focus to one of the lower chakras, and getting Ronnie mad would lessen the chance of that chakra being allowed to go out to play.

"Here," I said. I got up from the chair and went to the bed. "Lift the brush so you won't yell at me when you paint your knuckle." When she did I plopped onto the bed. "Look. This is the Cartier. It's perfect. Immaculate artistry: rubies, diamonds, platinum, the whole shmear. And then there's this." I held out my other hand. In it was a brooch, of a kind, with an irregular birdcage made of bent wire to house a carved wooden bird, clumsily painted red, white, and blue. The whole thing had been glued to a piece of low-budget metal which had, in turn, been glued to a rusty safety pin. The metal of the cage was tarnished and corroded, an uneven spiral that looked like it might have begun life as a watch spring. There was a hair in the glue, and the colors of the paint had faded. Neither the carving nor the painting of the bird was exactly skillful, but it had a certain raw attitude, an improbable vitality.

She touched the tarnished cage and the bars wobbled. A self-respecting parakeet could have busted out in seconds. "Why would you take this?"

"They were together in the box. I thought I'd take them together, try to figure it out."

"I like it better," she said. "Want to give me this one?"

"Would it affect the way we spend the next ninety minutes?"

"Naw. You've been good enough. And, although I'll deny this if you tell anyone I said it, we women experience the occasional

meat-dance urge, too, when we're in the company of a compe-
tent but not too dominant male who smells good and has nice
manners and a knack for abstract thinking. In a pinch, forget
the thinking. Let me look at that for a minute while my nails
dry." She extended her right hand, the one she'd done first, palm
up, and I put the handmade birdcage into it. She brought it up
close to her face, looking down at it, and said, "The fancy one is
pretty. But this one is beautiful."

"You've got a fine eye."

"I already told you I'd honor your ticket."

"I need to get someone to look at it. Someone who's not
Stinky."

"Oh, just take him some flowers."

"He hired a guy to *kill* me."

"Orchids, then."

Somebody knocked on the motel room door. Not aggressive,
but confident. I snatched the homemade brooch from her hand
and dropped both of them into the jewelry box, which had a label
from a chain of budget stores on it, and motioned to Ronnie to do
one more button on her blouse, not because she really needed to,
but because I wanted to watch. When the show was over, I went
to the closet and got my Glock out of the holster that was dangling from the coat hook on the inside of the door. Then, holding
the gun in the hand I kept behind the door, I pulled it open and
felt my stomach sink.

4

Like Something Dreamworks Burped

"Junior," Wattles said in that voice of his, a torn speaker at the bottom of the sea. He looked out of place in the sunlight, like an animal that's been unexpectedly yanked inside-out. What with his bum leg and us being on the third floor, his forehead and upper lip were beaded with sweat. If the color of his face was an accurate indication of his blood pressure, it was a miracle he hadn't exploded.

"Wattles," I said in welcome. "How the hell did you find me?"

"Aaahh," he said. "Lemme in."

I stepped aside and he pushed past me, short and tilting left, giving me a birds-eye view of a sparse floss of hair that was no advertisement for his colorist. It was a shade of orange a bee would scorn.

"Didn't know you had company," Wattles said. "Pretty little thing, ain't you?"

"Oh, thank you, sir," Ronnie said, tilting her head to the right and touching an index finger to her cheek, *Sunnybrook Farm* style. Then she put the top on the bottle of nail polish and gave all her attention to screwing it on.

"Listen, Junior—"

"As I said, how the hell did you find me?" My monthly motel moves have been keeping me alive for more than a year now, but people have been tracking me down lately with distressing frequency.

"Junior," he said. He glanced around the bird-saturated room, and his eyes doubled in size, making him look like a man who had gone to sleep in Pittsburgh and awakened in the Emerald City. "Jeez," he said. "Does the restaurant serve anything but eggs?"

Ronnie said, "Restaurant?"

I said, "How did you—"

Wattles made a sound I would, if pressed, spell *tchssssss.* "Awww, come on. There's other people and then there's Wattles. The day I can't find you I should close my office. What's that?" He was limping toward the table with the jewelry box on it.

"Junk," I said, zipping around him and picking it up. I put it into my pocket. "I'd be embarrassed to show it to you."

"You don't usually got junk," Wattles said. "Lemme see. And why the gun?"

I looked down at the Glock. "This is in case someone undesirable knocks on the door. And speaking of that, what do you want?"

"Look at this place," Wattles said. "Looks like something Dreamworks burped."

"This may be difficult for you to believe, but I've got a day in front of me."

"So here you are, with a beautiful girl, way too good for you, and you're grumpy?" He put his hands in his pockets. All the cheer left his face, and Ronnie sat back on the bed as though Wattles had suddenly sprouted spikes. "Junior," he said, "when was the last time you were in my office?"

"Whatever it is, I didn't do it."

"You need to convince me of that," Wattles said. He went back to the door and opened it to reveal a six-foot-three skeleton of a man in a black suit and a pair of thick, crepe-soled work boots. The stovepipe pants had a thrift-shop shine on them, and their legs were far too short; white socks glimmered above the black boots. His narrow, bony face was asymmetrical and the color of old envelope glue, but the most disconcerting thing was that the whites of his eyes were the cheap, vivid blue of mouthwash. He'd trained dead-black hair down over his forehead and pasted it there, like Hitler's. His shoulders were hunched, painfully and, it looked, permanently, up near his ears. The suit hung on him like it was waiting for someone to join him inside it.

"Hey, Bones," I said.

Bones was looking at the floor about halfway between him and me, and he didn't acknowledge the greeting.

"Close the door," I said to Wattles. "He sucks light out of the room."

Wattles pulled his right hand out of his jacket pocket and handed four or five red and blue capsules to Bones. "Have a party, but don't invite no one," he said, closing the door.

"*Tuinal?*" I said. "Rainbows? I thought those were outlawed decades ago."

"Not in India," Wattles said. "Ranbaxy Pharmaceuticals, stepping into the void between Tuinal junkies and the danger of waking up."

"So you made a point of showing me Bones, and since you're carrying his pet treats around, I suppose he's working for you. I wasn't in your office last night."

"Did I say anything about last night?"

"No. But here you are, eleven-thirty on a beautiful Monday morning if you don't count Bones, and you're trying to push a burglar around. Sounds like something happened last night."

"I gotta sit down," Wattles said. He turned to Ronnie. "If I sit on the bed with you, you gonna bite me?"

"You wish," Ronnie said.

"I love the smell of nail polish," he said, sitting down. He released an enormous whoosh of air and began to rub the small of his back.

"Let me," Ronnie said, and she began to work his back with her feet. Wattles emitted a humid-sounding sigh, like an old steam radiator, and closed his eyes. "Why haven't I got one of you?" he asked.

I said, "Can you just leave Bones out there in the sun? Won't he melt?"

"He don't know where he is. He could be at the bottom of the pool and he'd be okay." He opened his eyes and glanced back at Ronnie. "I don't get it, Junior. You're an okay-looking guy, or you would be if you cut your hair, and you always got fine, fine trim—no offense, Miss, just a figure of speech. Old Janice, you remember Janice, she thought birds flew out of your butt."

Looking at me, Ronnie said, "Janice?"

"A go-between," I said. "Works for Wattles."

Wattles said, "Thought birds flew out—"

"Yes, we've heard that part. And no," I said to Ronnie, "she and I never—"

"They didn't," Wattles said. "Janice has a boyfriend who breaks noses."

"And then there was me," I said, "not chasing her or anything."

"Someone was in my office last night," Wattles said. "Waltzed through my inner locks like they were bobby pins."

"What are those?" I said. "A Rabson, a Heilmacher, and—"

"A Steenburg. And that kind of smart-ass attitude is why I thought of you."

"Not the talent?"

"He didn't bother to re-lock anything."

I said, "Oh," not liking the feeling in the pit of my stomach.

"And just in case it *is* you and you're shitting me," Wattles said, "there's Bones out there."

"Sort of cut-rate for you, isn't he?"

"Don't take a high IQ to pull a trigger."

"At the rate he processes information, I could shoot him five or six times before he remembers where his gun is."

"Yeah," Wattle said, "but he wouldn't notice."

"Well, I didn't do it. I know that's a cliché in our trade, but it's true."

"Fine. I believe you. Find out who did."

"You believe me?"

Wattles said, "Who gives a shit? You either took it or you didn't. I'm offering you money to get it back to me either way."

"How much money?"

"Ten K."

"Gimme."

Wattles leaned back to get into his pocket, and Ronnie lifted her feet in the air and rolled onto her side, knees drawn up in her favorite sleeping position. My lower chakra gave out a whimper of denial.

"Here's five," Wattles said. "Five more when you deliver it."

"You have no idea," I said, "how reluctant I am to take this."

"Yeah, but you're crossing the room. You got your hand out."

"Don't push it," I said.

Ronnie said, "You don't know what he's giving up to do this for you."

"Maybe not," Wattles said, "but there's Bones out there, too. Gotta have some weight in your decision."

I took the money from his hand and made a big show of

counting it. Then I counted it again as Wattles fidgeted. After I'd folded it and put it in my pocket, I said, "What'd they take?"

Wattles glanced over at Ronnie, who was reading the label on her nail polish bottle, and leaned toward me. In a very low voice, he said, "My disconnects."

I said, and I'll admit it was the stupidest thing I'd said in days, "Disconnects are people. How could—?"

After two false starts and some lip-licking, Wattles said, "I wrote them down."

"You wrote them *down*? Your *disconnects*? On *paper*?" All those italics are justified, because this went to the very heart of what Wattles did. He liked to describe himself as a full-service crook, but what he was, really, was a contractor. He'd arrange anything, from a cautionary faceful of knuckles or a modest supermarket fire all the way up to a whack, for the right fee. The art of what Wattles did was what he called *disconnects*—a chain of intermediaries between him and the crime.

Let's say you paid Wattles to hit someone and sponge up afterward. Wattles would put together a chain of disconnects— all crooks of various kinds—and he'd use a go-between, usually, the very Janice we'd just been discussing, to pass a big thick envelope to the first disconnect in the chain, who, having no idea who Janice actually was, didn't know she'd been sent by Wattles. Disconnect number one would take the money inside and pass a somewhat smaller envelope, still sealed, to the disconnect to whom the envelope was addressed, who hadn't even seen Janice, so he or she was one more step in the dark from the point of origin. This little relay would continue, a smaller sealed envelope at each link in the chain like Russian nesting dolls, until the smallest one reached the far end of the chain: the talent, who would know nothing about who hired him or why—nothing at all, in fact, but the name of the corpse-in-waiting. Each envelope was complete, including payment, for the person whose name was written on it, and the guarantee that each disconnect would pass along the ones inside, without opening the others and pocketing the cash, was that old underworld standby: pure, cold fear. Wattles knew who they were, but all they knew about him was that he was someone who had people killed. By the time the hit was carried out, there was no way in the world to connect it to Wattles.

Unless, of course, all the disconnects in the chain were all written down on a piece of paper somewhere.

"I had to write it down," Wattles said. "Something goes wrong, I need to know which disconnect to finger. I need to know who paid who what, you know?"

"Holy Jesus," I said. "I can see needing to remember it. But on paper?"

He said, looking shame-faced, "I'm getting old. Memory's not what it used to be."

"The disconnects aren't going to be happy about this."

"They're never going to know, because you're going to get it back again."

"Even if I can figure out who the burglar was, so what? You know he stole it for a client, and that client will have it by now. So how the hell am I supposed to get it back?"

"*Here's* what you need to know." Wattles leaned forward and his red face went into the tomato zone. "If you bring it back, *I'll never ask you* how you got it."

I didn't reply.

"And if you don't," he said, "There's Bones."

I felt my own face go red. "Don't lean on Bones too much," I said. "He's a slender reed."

Wattles said, "He is what he is."

"Listen, why not do this the easy way?"

"What's that? And hey, if there's an easy way and I take it, I want my five K back."

"We'll split it. Fifty-fifty."

He said, "It better be *really* easy."

"Call off the hit."

"How do you know it's a—?"

"Because of how upset you are. Just call it off."

"May sound easy to you," Wattles said, "but that's 'cause of what you don't know, which is the guy's been dead for three days."

5

An Established Burglar of Spotless Repute

David Copperfield, with an assist from Charles Dickens, began his life story this way: *Whether I shall turn out to be the hero of my own life, or whether that station will be held by anybody else, these pages must show.* If I were ever sufficiently misguided to write my own life story, the hero of most of Act One would be a burglar named Herbie Mott.

Stuck behind the wheel of my invisible white Toyota, America's most common car, as I joined the slow line of traffic up the Pacific Coast Highway toward Herbie's Malibu condominium on a hot September Monday morning, I had lots of time to think about him. In fact, I hadn't been able to think about anything else since Wattles shared the informaton that the inner door of his office had been left conspicuously unlocked.

Herbie was an established burglar of spotless repute and zero arrests, with a terrific trade in psychiatrists' houses. Some shrinks practice at home and others take their records home, thinking anyone who breaks into a house is only looking for cash or diamonds. And they're right, ninety percent of the time, although some of us specialize in one thing, say, Meissen china or historical documents. But for Herbie, psychiatric case notes were the jewel in the crown. A really incendiary set of case notes on even a D-list celebrity or a reality TV freak were solid gold. Shrinks make a lot of money, and they'll yield up large quantities of it to get their notes back. Best of all, they never, *ever* go to the cops. The whole point of paying Herbie to get those notes back is to keep it secret from the client that they were ever out of the good doctor's possession.

So there Herbie was, committing burglary with a twist—not taking something from the mark, but selling something back to him or her. And that meant announcing to the mark that he'd *been* burglarized to get his internal thermostat set firmly at panic before calling the mark and setting a price. Leaving the place *looking* burglarized. Same setup as at Wattles's place.

Herbie had been with me—or maybe it's more correct to say I'd been with Herbie—practically from the beginning, from when I was seventeen years old and began breaking into houses in earnest.

I'd commmitted my first illegal entry at the age of fourteen as a way of making a point to the man who lived next door to us, a miserable son of a bitch whose idea of a good time was quietly opening the gate to our backyard and letting out Chowser, our big dumb mutt, and then calling animal control to come and get him. One day while he was at work, I'd gone in through an open window, switched all the herbs and spices into new bottles, swapped the salt and the sugar, put a few ounces of plastic-wrapped animal waste in his refrigerator, and moved everything I could lift to a new and inconvenient location. I superglued all of it in place.

It took him weeks to discover all of it, and every time I heard him shouting or swearing, I'd run next door, ring the bell, and ask whether there was anything I could do to help. The fourth or fifth time, I could see the change in his eyes, and from then on, Chowser stayed in our yard.

After that, I became a theoretical burglar to whom any empty house represented a challenge that I sometimes accepted, thrilled with the sheer effrontery of breaking and entering, minus the breaking, which was for thugs. I never took anything; I was just sharpening my skills. I practiced on an enormous collection of locks for hours at a time; I taught myself how to tell when a house was really empty; I learned how to avoid the kind of behavior that draws attention from the neighbors. When I went inside, it was mainly to wander through the little museums people create as the setting for their lives. Sometimes a house reflects its occupants, but just as often it's wishful thinking: it's the kind of place a person puts together because it would appeal to the person he pretends to be. Or because it would impress the visitors he or she imagines entertaining.

Houses can be sad, happy, manic, dysfunctional, serene, frantic. Once you learn how to look at them, they reveal the strength and fault lines in a relationship. By the end of that summer I flattered myself that I could tell when a marriage was in trouble within five minutes in a house; I had a whole checklist of indications. I was pretty pleased with myself.

Except that I missed those same changes in my own house over the next three years, as my parents' marriage frayed in slow motion and then snapped. And all that smugness went out the window, along with the marriage, the summer I was seventeen.

That was the summer my father drove away for good in order to move in with his secretary—or, as my mother called her ever after, "Your father's tramp." Before that, there had been three of us, and now there were two, and the one who was missing was the one who had always reigned me in. As though his departure had set me free, I got serious about my hobby and started working it into something approaching obsession.

And I had learned, the hard way, something I wouldn't fully appreciate for years: that it's always good to be brought up against the limitations of your talent. It's the only way you learn that it needs expanding.

So I broke into more houses and better houses, and began to refine my interests. There was, for example, the endless fascination of what people find valuable. I'd been in a house where thousands of dollars were scattered like leaves on top of a dresser and a triple-keyed safe held four well-worn pairs of women's shoes. Or where good second-class jewelry was jammed into cheap boxes in plain sight while, hidden in a bundle of sheets in the dryer, was a first edition of William Gaddis's *The Recognitions*, with the author's spiky signature. *The Recognitions* would later become the first of several novels I would use as the basis for my self-education. If I saw a signed copy today, I'd snatch it and run, but at the time, it was just a thick book with no quotation marks to indicate the dialogue and, on the title page, an angular autograph, and I put it back. Back then, it was worth maybe $1,500, but it would go for $7,500 to $10,000 today. If I had one, I'd hide it better than that guy did.

By then, I was figuring out, without actually stealing much of anything, some of the logical rules of intelligent burglary. One of them, I thought, was to delay as long as possible the moment the mark realizes that his stuff has been boosted. But Herbie, whom I would meet, taught me the exception to the rule, the times you actually *want* the theft to be noted instantly—when, in fact, an immediate reaction is part of the plan. He even had a name for it; he called it "leaving tracks."

The person who burglarized Wattles's office had left tracks.

At the end of September in the year my father left, I was a seventeen-year-old kid taking advantage of a moonless night to do a shrubbery creep on a house just below Mulholland on the Valley side. I'd had my eye on it for a couple of weeks because one day there had been three copies of the *LA Times* inside the gate. Since then, I'd driven past it a dozen times at all hours, never seeing a car, and no lights other than the same five, one over the front porch, one in the living room, and one each in three rooms upstairs. They went off at different times, but like clockwork: living room, 10:27; left bedroom, 10:44; and so forth. Timers, in other words.

Whoever owned the place had enough money to buy a couple of lots on either side and the one below, and enough disregard for the neighbors and their micro-managed lawns to let the vacant lots revert to the indigenous San Fernando Valley snaggle of chaparral, creosote, puncherweeds, and those semi-invisible dirt-brown, ankle-high grasses that propogate by sticking the tufted, sharply barbed, one-way-only seeds called foxtails into the weave of people's socks. As I eased my way closer to the house, I was feeling a swarm of them trying to work their little points into the skin of my ankles.

It was burglar-dark. All the lights in the house had gone off right on schedule. I was thinking about a bathroom window I'd seen that didn't seem to have alarm tape running around the perimeter of the glass. As I pushed aside some shoulder-high ornamental bamboo to take a closer look, a hand fell on my shoulder, hard enough to bring me to my knees.

I managed to turn my head and found myself inches from a face not much higher than my own even though I was kneeling. It was decked out in a Lone Ranger mask. A pang of shamed discovery went through me: as ridiculous as the mask was—he looked like a crook in a comic book—I'd never given a moment's thought to hiding my face. I said, "Cool mask."

"Forget it, kid," the masked man said. He was *really* short. "There's nothing in there you want."

"How do you know what I want?"

"Lemme rephrase," said the masked man. "There's nothing in there I wantcha to have."

I said, "And I'm supposed to care?"

"Well," the masked man said, "if it comes to that." He stepped back and pulled out a short black gun, and I experienced a paralyzingly intense need to go to the bathroom.

"Got it," I said. "Just back up and point that at the sky, and I'll be on my way."

The masked man scratched his chin with the barrel of the gun, and my heightened senses perceived a tiny, molded seam running up the underside of the barrel. Then he leveled it at me again. "Not so fast," he said.

I said, "That's a squirt gun."

"'Course it is," the masked man said, looking down at it. "You know what you get if they catch you going in strapped? It's like life, even if you live as long as Noah."

I got up, which made me considerably taller than he was. "Then who are you to tell me to go away?"

"Who told you to go away?" the masked man said. "I said, *Forget it*."

The difference in our height and the water in the gun made me get a little lippy. "Kind of a fine distinction."

"Not so fine. You go away, you get nothing. You do what I tell you, you get five bills."

"How much is a bill?"

"Jeez," the masked man said. "What is this, something you have to do for a Boy Scout badge? A bill is a hundred bucks."

"So . . ."

"One times five, okay? Five hundred."

"For what?"

He sighed. "Here's what. Go get in your car, and park it at the intersection with Coldwater, since that's where anyone who's heading home would have to come from. You see a black Lincoln Town Car—you know what a Lincoln Town Car—"

"Yes," I said. "Like a Kmart Limo."

"You follow it in, go around the circle once, and honk one time as you leave. That's it."

"Five hundred? For honking?"

"Yes, no, up to you. If you're waiting out at the intersection when I come out, I'll give you the five whether anyone's come home or not."

"Um," I said. "What are you going in to get?"

For a moment, I didn't think he'd answer, but then he said, "Oh, why the hell not? Porcelain dogs, from China. Maybe seven hundred years old."

"That's all?"

He raised the barrel of the squirt gun in the air like a finger. "Rule Number One—no, no, not yet. You do this, kid, and we'll maybe get to know each other better. I been looking for someone to pass things on to. My kid will never do it, which is, I gotta tell you, like a stone on my heart." He tapped his chest with the gun, in the general region of his heart. "You know, you get to be my age, you got a rich backlog of experience—like a tapestry, but without the unicorns. Seems like a shame I should die and it should get rolled up and dropped in the grave, a couple flowers and a handful of dirt, and everything I learned is down there with the worms."

"You've been doing this how long?"

"Uhhhh." He put a finger inside the mask and rubbed his nose. "Nineteen years."

"Have you been caught?"

He said, "Surely you jest."

"And you'd teach me?"

"What I said."

My heart was on a pogo stick, bouncing so high it was bumping my vocal cords. "Keep the money," I said. "Just teach me."

"Okay," he said. "Here's Lesson Number One. It's not Rule Number One, it's Lesson Number One. Never, ever say, *Keep the money*."

That night, with five hundred-dollar bills in my pocket for the first time in my life, I followed Herbie down the hill to the Du-par's restaurant at Ventura and Laurel Canyon, open all night and deserted. Feeling like everyone behind the counter knew what we'd just done, with my heart rate at about 140, I let him lead me through the bright lights inside to a back booth. Over quarts of coffee and many slices of lemon meringue pie, I got the first of what I later came to think of as the Herbie Lectures, ten brilliantly organized disquisitions on the history, importance, economics, and aesthetics of burglary. At the end of the talk, he asked me five questions, sort of a pop quiz, and I got them all right.

The man who faced me across the table looked out from bright blue eyes set into a face crowded to the margins by a nose that looked like it had been stolen from a much larger man. His hair was in retreat, I thought, although over the decades it never seemed to recede much further, and it was an odd color, neither red nor brown, a sort of genetic indecision. He looked at me for a minute, as though trying to see in the skinny seventeen-year-old the seed of someone who might turn out to be a reliable adult, and apparently he saw it, because he finally said, "You might do."

Feeling like I'd just gotten a job, I said, "Thanks."

"Why do you want to do this?"

"I need it."

"What does that mean?"

"I see everyone doing things they hate. My mother works

part-time in a restaurant and hates it. My father—" I stopped talking and rubbed my eyes. The restaurant was too bright.

"Your father."

"My father is a full-time asshole. And he hates that, too. His friends hate what they do, the way they are. They get drunk on the weekend and talk about when they were young and free and then go back to sucking it up on Monday. I'm not going to live that way." My eyes were still bothering me, and I rubbed them again. "I want to feel alive. It's like you've got the map to a place that's a long way away from my parents' world. And you're offering to guide me, and I'm going to do whatever I have to that will convince you to do that."

"Let me tell you something," Herbie said. "Two somethings. First thing, this can turn into a job, same as anything else. The people who need it to be a thrill for a long time are the people who get caught or killed." He put both hands flat on the table and raised his eyebrows, waiting until I nodded to confirm that I'd gotten the point. "Second thing, don't think you know everything about your father. You loved him at one point, I can tell, because you wouldn't be so angry now if you hadn't. Well, the father you hate now is the same person as the one you loved. Just don't—put people in boxes like that. You have no idea whether you really know someone. You got all that?"

I said I did, although I hadn't really listened to anything he'd said after the word "father," and three nights later I served as his lookout again and earned another five bills and the second lecture. Ten days after that he took me into the house of a best-selling female writer with a fondness for expensive costume jewelry and gave me my first lesson in sifting the wheat from the chaff. I picked it up quickly.

It was years before I got over hating my father. But in the meantime, I had Herbie.

6

A Middle D

The broken glass door told me everything I didn't want to know.

It was a slider, and Herbie, like all good burglars, had put a steel rod in the track on the inside to prevent some amateur from jimmying the lock and trying to slide it open. Like all *very* good burglars, he'd also had the door triple-paned, but that hadn't worked either. The large landscaping stone in the middle of the dining room floor, maybe 150 pounds' worth, had gone through the three layers of glass as though they'd been wet Kleenex.

I knew what I'd find, but I had to go in anyway. I pulled off my shoes and slipped my feet into jumbo-size baggies, put on a pair of disposable food-handling gloves and tucked the Glock into my pants. I barely paid attention to the broken glass beneath my feet until I heard Herbie's voice in my ear: "Don't forget, kid, they got that DNA now."

Out loud, I said, "Thanks, Herbie." My voice was hardly shaking at all.

The glass door was at the back of the unit, where I'd gone when he didn't answer the bell, and it opened into a dining room with a highly polished bamboo floor, in the center of which, like some interior decorator's attempt at Zen, was that large smooth stone. At 1:30, the sun was angling in at about seventy degrees to illuminate the floor, and it bounced in bright fragments off the shards of glass to make sharp shapes on the ceiling. My earliest memory is of rainbows on the walls of the room in which I slept, rainbows made by the sun breaking itself into colors through the cut-glass vases and goblets my mother put on shelves just inside the window. The reflections off the broken glass on Herbie's floor brought that memory back for a moment, but then it was swept away by the smell of blood.

I stopped dead in the middle of the room, closed my eyes, and did what I should have done first. I listened.

What you're listening for in a house when you don't know whether it's empty are short-lived or uneven sounds, sounds of irregular volume, sounds that begin and end sharply or arrive disjointedly: someone moving, the creak of a door, a quick breath. You tend to tune out sounds that are constant, sounds that flow from one moment to the next without variation; those are the sounds you're trying to listen around. So it took me a minute or two—probably two—to hear the low, soft, unvarying whistle.

It was a middle D, I noted automatically. No tremolo, no dynamic variations: just someone with infinite lungs playing a soft, sustained middle D on a flute, a couple of rooms away.

I didn't even know what caused the sound yet, but it made the hair on the back of my neck bristle.

The condo was one story: entrance hall, living room, dining room, kitchen, guest bath at one end and then a corridor leading to the so-called private areas: three bedrooms, one of which Herbie used as an office, and two more bathrooms.

The flute was coming from the far end of the corridor.

I took the gun out, wishing I'd racked it outside to put a shell in the chamber but unwilling to make that noise now. Holding it barrel-up in the approved movie-cop position, I started down the hall.

Herbie's possessions, some of which I'd known for seventeen or so years, transformed the anonymous geometry of the rooms into a kind of album of things we'd done together, things we'd acquired together, things he'd taught me: a huge Navajo rug stolen from a mansion in the Hollywood hills, where we came in after some kind of fearsome scene had gone down, and we had to roll the body of a one-time TV cowboy across the room to get at the rug, which was worth it. A beat-up old hat that had been autographed by practically every major silent-film star, the only thing we took from the home of a faded B-list actress who'd spent her life savings scouring Hollywood for every piece of movie-related memorabilia she could find in the hope that one day she'd open a museum. We'd felt too sorry for her to take anything else. A painting of a seedy New York street, complete with a burlesque house, by John Sloan, the greatest artist among the New York Ashcan School, the first group to set up their easels on urban, working-class American streets. I loved the Sloane, and Herbie had promised me he'd will it to me. The rooms held dozens of things, all of them with Herbie imprinted on them.

Except for Herbie's things, there was nothing of interest in the first two bedrooms. Just that fucking flute, playing its unchanging, impossibly sustained D, getting louder as I neared the master bedroom. And the smell was growing stronger along with the flute: damp and rubbery, and a little like meat. It took everything I had to keep me walking to, and then through, that door, and it took even more, pulled up from some unsuspected reserve, to keep me in the room.

Herbie was facedown and spread-eagled on the canopy bed, his legs wrenched wide and tied to the posts at either side of the head of the mattress. He'd been yanked so that he was draped over a corner of the bed at a diagonal, his head hanging down, his hands dangling in big yellow rubber gloves. I knew those gloves; I have gloves like them. Herbie taught me to take meticulous care of my hands, pampering them, moisturizing them, using the finest sandpaper on the fingertips to increase the sense of touch, and protecting them from things like soap and hot water. When I had lived with my ex-wife, Kathy, and my daughter, Rina, I washed dishes, thanks to Herbie, using those very same gloves.

The flute sound was coming from the cap of a whistling teapot, sitting atop an electric hotplate that Herbie would use to melt wax so he could make impressions of keys. The hotplate had been turned low enough to keep the sound from getting too shrill, but not so low that the water wouldn't boil.

As I worked up the courage to look at what remained of Herbie, I picked up the teapot—the handle was so hot I almost dropped it—and shook it. It was light. Most of the water had either been used on Herbie or had boiled away, but one way or the other, I hadn't missed them by much. That thought was enough to take me out of the bedroom again and through the entire house, gun in hand, opening every closet, sliding aside every bath curtain, checking the garage, which opened into the kitchen and peering through the front windows at the curb for an idling car. I looked at the street for three or four empty minutes, just trying to locate the strength I needed, and then I went back into the bedroom.

What they had done to Herbie had been simple, brutally, heartlessly effective, and even creative, making improvisational use of things they'd found in the condo. They had simply forced the rubber gloves onto Herbie's hands, hung him over the edge of the bed like a sack of oats, and filled the gloves with boiling water. I took a closer look, but it didn't last for more than a couple of seconds.

I was suddenly aware of black flowers blooming in the air in front of me, like the malign blossoms that erupt on motion-picture film just before it burns. The next thing I knew, I was sitting on the carpet, which was wet even six feet from the bed. They must have filled the gloves to overflowing many times. At some point during the questioning Herbie'd had a nosebleed, and the water had thinned the blood to a pink blush, like a watercolor wash, on the white carpet all around the bed.

At God knows which refilling of the gloves, he also appeared to have had a heart attack. There weren't any bullets, no head trauma, nothing.

So there was one slender comfort. Herbie, as always, had followed Rule Number Three: He'd gotten out fast.

There's no way for me to know how long I sat there in that rose-pink, stinking damp. I don't even remember getting up. By the time I was back inside myself again, I was driving south on Pacific Coast Highway with the hard blue line of the sea to my right, threading my way automatically between cars filled with beach-goers: bathing suits, beach-towel shawls, women in straw sun hats. It wasn't until I turned left onto Topanga Canyon Boulevard that I realized I was still wearing the disposable plastic gloves, and when I saw them, I screamed.

7
We Tend to Die Early

I pulled into the little shopping center where Topanga and Old Topanga intersect, ordered a pizza at Rocco's, and let it cool. It was hot in the Canyon, and the sun sifted itself through the leaves of the sycamores, carving biblical beams in the dusty air.

The pizza sat in front of me, neglected, as I tried to put myself back together.

Crooks aren't like orchestra conductors; we tend to die early. I'd personally known half a dozen criminals, including a couple of friends, who no longer walked among us—I'd actually directed one of them to the exit—but this was the first time I'd lost someone who was truly close to me, crook or straight. My parents were both alive, if emotionally distant, the friends and lovers I'd kept track of were above ground, and my daughter and ex-wife were thriving without me.

But Herbie had crossed categories: he was a friend, a crook, a mentor, a surrogate father. He'd also been the first to warn me that friendships among those of us on the shady side of the street could end suddenly. He'd lost a friend to a meth addict with a broken bottle, who'd killed Herbie's acquaintance for the $400 the two of them had scored in a liquor-store robbery. Several days later, the tweaker had gone down under a car with no plates on it. *When you can't get closure*, Herbie had said to me, *get even*. I'd followed that advice once already, evening the score for a friend who got killed on a surveillance he was doing for me, a surveillance I hadn't thought could get lethal.

And now it looked like I was going to do it again. For Herbie. As soon as I could walk.

Since I couldn't manage that yet, I used the phone.

"I can't ask him anything," Janice said. "He's gone. He called to tell me the office would be locked up and that I should check his house every now and then."

I knew she and Wattles worked closely, but this suggested a new level of trust. "You have a key to his house?"

"Sure. When he's gone, I take in his paper, keep an eye on things."

"Doesn't sound like the Wattles I know."

"Is there some perspective from which that might be my problem? Or even interesting to me? Because if there is, I'm missing it."

"He says you like me," I said, since I couldn't think of an answer to her question.

"Yeah?" she said. "He told me *you* like *me*. Said you thought birds flew out of my butt."

I said, "I don't really think about your butt much, but if I did, it would probably be something like that."

"It sounds uncomfortable," she said. "Not to mention that it would ruin the line of my pants."

"So, do you?"

"Do I what?"

"Like me."

"I'm getting engaged," she said.

"Oh." Janice was, putting it conservatively, science-fiction beautiful, and even in my numbed state, I experienced the brief pang of loss most men—even men who are in love with other women—feel when there's one less really exceptional possibility out there. "Well, hell. But congratulations."

"You could have asked me out," she said.

"I did."

"Did you? Whoops. How fatally unforgivable of me."

"Come on. Make it up to me. Let me into his house."

"Pardon my mirth," she said. "Wait, I'll politely put my hand over the mouthpiece while I laugh."

"Okay, then answer three questions. First, what's with him writing down a chain of disconnects? Is he really likely to forget who's on it?"

"He's never forgotten anything that mattered in his life." She paused, and I could feel her trying to figure out how much she could tell me without violating Wattles's trust. "About eighteen months ago, something slipped his mind, one teeny detail out of the ten thousand or so he usually carries around in his head, and he completely lost it. Raving at the walls. He was certain it was the beginning of the end, you know, that his mind was going and he was months away from being totally senile, complaining about the food in the Criminals' Retirement Home. So he started writing things down."

"But you think he actually knows who all the disconnects were?"

"He knows that, how much he paid them, and when he used them last."

"Then why wouldn't he tell me their names?"

"You're out of questions."

"I'm just getting started."

"Well, the rude answer is that he doesn't trust you enough to share it with you. The more diplomatic answer is that he didn't ask you to investigate the people in the chain, he asked you to get the piece of paper back before someone used it to climb back up the chain and take him out."

"The person who stole it is dead," I said, and saying it out loud made my voice go all wobbly. "So I think it might be a good idea to see whether the chain's integrity is intact. Whether any of them might be connected to someone who would have, first, guessed Wattles would keep a written record, and second, sent someone to steal it."

"These people? Most of them have trouble finding their way home. And why would anyone they were connected with have known anything about the chain?"

"Okay," I said. "Suggest another place for me to start."

As I waited for her to make up her mind, I got up, picked up the pizza, and put it on another table. Someone might want it.

"I can tell you who I gave it to," Janice said reluctantly, and I could almost hear her wishing she could call Wattles and get permission.

"Do you know any names beyond that one?"

"Of course not. That's the theoretical point of the chain. I don't know where it's going, and the people on the other end don't know where it comes from."

"Okay. How big a job would you guess this chain was designed to fund?"

"All I can go by is the thickness of the envelope. I'd say pretty big. The thicker it is, the more envelopes, the more stops along the way, the more money for everyone. I mean, something like getting you to rob Rabbits Stennett's house, that was just Wattles to me to you. Something really big, let's say a hit or two, might be five or six links and a good chunk of money in the last envelope."

"About as thick as this one was?"

"Maybe a little thinner. I don't know."

"Let's say it was a hit."

"Let's not, at least not on the phone. Let's say it's an extremely roundabout way to buy Girl Scout Cookies."

A Topanga creek rat, one of the Canyon's rural homeless, cruised the table with the pizza on it, looking everywhere else. "What's to prevent the person who's actually supposed to get the cookies from just pocketing the money and going to the movies?"

"The knowledge that the person who sent the money for the cookies knows who he or she is and that the person who sent the money is really, really, *really* serious about Girl Scout Cookies. So serious that blowing the errand off would have consequences."

"And what if the person who's being sent to buy the cookies just doesn't want to do it? Let's say he's on a diet and doesn't want all that flour and sugar around."

"That's what the throwaway phone numbers are for. There's a different one in every envelope. He calls the number and the voicemail gives him a post office box where he's supposed to send the money."

"A PO box?"

"Rented about four days before the chain goes out and closed down immediately afterward. And opened with a really good ID, probably as good as anything you've got."

"Hmmm." Mine was pretty good.

The creek rat was back. He looked at the pizza and then at me. I shrugged, and he grabbed it and ran for the trees.

"But you know," Janice said, "when you get down to it, whoever is at the end of that chain knows there are only three or four people who might commission something like this, and most of them—if it's a hit, I mean—will be able to make a good guess who it is. The *point* of the chain, in fact, is to set up a situation in which everyone who could possibly testify about a connection between, oh, let's call him Mr. X, and the cookie buyer will be a convicted felon. And you know what defense attorneys call a case where the prosecution witnesses are all crooks, don't you?"

"No. What?"

"They call it an acquittal."

"Got it."

"So," Janice said. A moment went by. "Guess we won't be seeing each other for a while," Janice said. "What with Wattles hiding in Limpopo or wherever, and what with me getting engaged and so forth."

"Guess not."

"So you want to get together anyway? Hook up just once, just for the hell of it?"

"I'm very flattered, but I'm with someone myself now."

"Bad timing, huh?"

"I guess. I really did think birds flew out of your butt."

"Sweet mouth," she said. "I probably wouldn't have done it anyway."

I said, "Before you go. I need the name of the person you gave the big envelope to."

"Oh, yeah," she said. "An old friend of yours, in fact."

The All-Seeing Eye had set up shop on Ventura Boulevard, only about a mile east of Topanga, so the drive there barely qualified as a detour. The Eye surveyed its nominally infinite domain through a scratched reflective window in a vaguely Spanish stucco mini-mall that also housed a Mailboxes R Us, usually a sign of a dodgy neighborhood; one of those laundromats that provide brilliant lighting to illuminate the choices in your life that brought you to the point where you're feeding a year's worth of coins into machines to do your wash in front of strangers; and not one but two Thai restaurants. There are so many Thai restaurants in the Valley that it sometimes amazes me there are any left in Thailand.

The strip mall would have been short on parking spaces if it had been doing any business, but as it was, mine was one of only three cars in the lot, and the other two were parked in front of the Thai restaurant closer to the Boulevard. The shopfront that hosted the All-Seeing Eye was a melancholy three parking spaces wide and sat next to a much larger store beneath a bright yellow sign that read DIXIE'S DUDS: FUN FASHIONS FOR WOMEN AND GIRLS. It was closed for good, its windows sadly empty of fun fashions, and knowing who possessed the All-Seeing Eye at this point in its history, I was sure he missed the view through the wall into the changing rooms.

When I walked in, the opening door triggered a little soft-edged chime. I found myself in a waiting room, just big enough for a lumpy-looking two-cushion couch, a folding aluminum beach chair with faded nylon ribbing, and a Salvation Army table housing a bouquet of dusty plastic birds of paradise. Above the bouquet was a sign that said BE SEATED AND COMPOSE YOURSELF. I sat on the arm of the couch, glared at the door leading to the back of the store, and began to count to ten.

When I reached four, a voice with what might have been a Transylvanian accent said through a small loudspeaker mounted above my head, "I am sorry. You are being affected negatively by Mercury's retrograde and you are not clear enough for a reading. Please come back in three days."

I said, "Here's what it is, Handkerchief. Either you let me in right now or I squeeze Superglue into all those locks, and you'll be stuck there until you can get the door off its hinges. And Mercury's retrograde is an optical illusion."

The voice on the loudspeaker said, "Shit," and I heard the locks snapping open.

The extremely huffy man who led me to the back of the store had fine, floppy, flaxen hair and the narrow face I associate with some of the horsier members of the British nobility. If his face had been much narrower it would have been a profile even from the front. Beneath an elongated nose was an almost equally lengthy upper lip that occasionally hosted an ill-advised pencil-line mustache, now mercifully absent. Most of us who want to downplay our most distinguishing features—if only to make life a little harder for police sketch artists—know that a pencil-line mustache on a long upper lip does nothing but make it seem longer. It looks like a fifty-yard line.

He was draped in a loose, flowing white gown that looked like something Lawrence of Arabia might have worn to his prom, and his head was crowned with a complicated-looking turban. In his earlier incarnation, as one of California's premier plausibles, or con men, he'd been noted for his fine British tailoring and the accent that sometimes came with it, as well as the elegant silk pocket handkerchiefs that gave him his nickname.

But now Handkerchief Harrison was in psychic drag, and to my mind it was a big step down. I don't like plausibles—no one anywhere on the metaphorical ladder of relatively honest crooks does—but fortune tellers would have to stand on tiptoe to brush the bottom rung with their fingertips.

The passageway was swathed in black drapery. I said, "Velveteen was on special?"

"It's sensory deprivation," he said, still walking. "It distances the clientele from the distractions of the day, makes it easier for them to slip into the pool of reflective consciousness."

We entered an egg-shaped space with walls of the same light-sucking velveteen, hanging down to a paper-thin, theoretically

Oriental carpet in deep Victorian peacock-greens and blues. In the center of the chamber stood a round table about four feet in diameter, draped with yet more velveteen. Handkerchief walked around the table to put it between us, standing behind the larger of the two chairs.

I searched the room for props or other telltales. "So what's the modality?" I said. "Is that what you'd call it, the modality?"

"I'll call it whatever you'd like." Handkerchief sounded British, so he was miffed. God only knew where he actually came from, although most bets were on Pittsburgh. "I can do Tarot or the crystal ball, interpret your aura, read your palm, the bumps in your head, your tea leaves. Astrology, either Chinese or Western, dream interpretation, including Freudian and Jungian. We could break out the old Ouija Board. I can dispel or redirect a curse or summon a blessing. If all these choices confuse you, I can conjure up your spirit guardians and consult them." He sounded for all the world like a waiter who has recited the day's specials so often he's sick of them all. "I can uncover your past and reveal your future, read the color variations in the pupils of your eyes or the vertical lines in your upper lip."

"The vertical lines—?"

"In the upper lip. Especially good for heavy smokers."

"I'm impressed. These are new talents?"

"Of course not," he said, pulling an invisible cloak of dignity around his shoulders. "This is a lifetime's worth of experience."

I was ambushed by a surge of fury: Handkerchief was alive and Herbie wasn't. "And here I thought you were a con man."

"One should always have a fallback," he said, going positively Buckingham Palace. He gave me a second look and backed up a couple of cautious inches, pulling the chair with him. "Being a plausible is an ideal life when times are good, since con games are, in essence, simply low-impact ways to get those with money to part with some of it in exchange for the hope of more. But when no one *has* money, it's a bit like being a highly trained tenor in the land of the deaf. When no one has money, they're not inclined to risk the little they've got. What they want is psychic guidance, a nudge in the direction of the horn of plenty. Cynics, of which you are one, act like it's all baseless mumbo-jumbo, when actually it's as practical, as down to earth, as a pair of glasses that simply enable people to see farther afield."

"Where the answers are." It was just short of a snap.

He regarded me for a moment, and when he spoke, his voice was gentle. "Do you frequently find that the answers you need most badly are close at hand?"

"Good point."

"Thank you." He rubbed his eyes with a pianist's long fingers. Handkerchief's claim to elegance arose mainly from the fact that he was as elongated as a Modigliani. "But I'm sure you haven't actually come for a reading."

I said, "Why not?"

"Well, for one thing, you're barely holding yourself together. For another, you have a skeptic's aura, rusty at the edges."

"Rusty?"

"As an old shovel." Handkerchief gave me a tiny shrug, as though to apologize for his perceptiveness. "You're not as opaque as you fancy yourself."

"And I try so hard." I pulled out my chair, sat down, and drew a deep breath. "But I would, actually. Like a reading."

"Ahh, well." He sounded resigned. He seated himself and looked at the surface of the table as though trying to decide which piece of mumbo-jumbo apparatus would look best there, then shook his head. "Well. Well, let's keep it simple. Both hands on the table, palms up. Open your hands, open your chest area—that's right, pull your shoulders back, but don't lift them—and open the Crown Chakra. That's the one on top of your head. Keep your eyes open and look into mine."

I did everything I could manage. My control of my Crown Chakra comes and goes.

Handkerchief looked directly into my eyes for a long moment and then his eyelids fluttered rapidly several times. He reached across the table and pressed his fingertips into the mounds at the base of my thumbs, and something like a jolt went through me. When I looked back up—I'd dropped my eyes to his hands when he touched me—his gaze was steady. He shook his head and pulled his hands back and folded them on the velveteen tabletop.

"You have suffered a loss," he said.

"And what tells you that?"

"Someone close," he said, ignoring my question. "And recently."

"See," I said, growing angry again, "this is where I get confused. The psychic tells me something I already know, and I'm not sure whether to applaud the parlor trick or ask for some information that might actually be *valuable*, you know? Like how to deal with it, how to get past it, stuff like that."

"You're obviously thinking," Handkerchief said comfortably, "that I can read you like this because of a *lifetime* spent reading people to find ways to part them from their money, and you're right, in a sense. Few people are more sensitive than con artists. But that begs the question, doesn't it? Did I learn how to read people by being a con artist, or did I become a con artist because I could always read people?" He tented his spidery fingers and regarded them with satisfaction, like a good third draft. "But how you should *deal* with it, how you should get over it? That's in your territory. You're a fully formed personality, Junior, some might even say over-formed. No matter what

I say to you, you'll deal with it your way." His eyebrows drew together questioningly. "Something paternal? Not a father, but something on that order."

All traces of Great Britain had vanished from his speech; he sounded as American as a hot dog. He put his hands flat on the table, and all the communion between us vanished. "What actually brings you here?"

"Do you know someone named Janice?"

"No. Can't say I do."

"Middle twenties, a knockout, shoulder-length brown hair, square glasses with black plastic frames."

Handkerchief pursed his lips. "Mmmm, might. Hard to say, from that descrip—"

"You saw her just last week."

He wasn't looking comfortable. "A client?"

"No, not a client. Now come on, I know you can give her a name."

"Mollie," he said. He looked at the center of the table and said, more softly, "Mollie."

"Good, Mollie. And your relationship with Mollie is—"

"I have no idea what you're getting at, old bean," Handkerchief said, imitating someone who was thinking hard. "None at all."

"Let me put it into a context," I said. "Did you hear ever the phrase, *Tinker to Evers to Chance*?"

He relaxed slightly. "Can't say I have. Rhythmic, though, isn't it?"

"It's from a poem, actually, a baseball poem by an early twentieth-century newspaper columnist, Franklin Pierce Adams. Tinker, Evers, and Chance were double-play artists, three-quarters of the infield of the Chicago Cubs way back there in the nineteen-teens—"

"The things one learns," Hankerchief said, linguistically edging back across the Atlantic.

"Adams, as a New Yorker and therefore a Yankees fan, hated the Cubs, but even so, 'Tinker to Evers to Chance' was essentially shorthand for the perfect double-play—you did learn in England, didn't you, what a double play is?"

"Something about two outs, isn't it?"

"So, even now that you know who, say, Tinker was, you might not know *which* Tinker someone is referring to, minus the rest of the phrase, which is to say, 'to Evers to Chance.' It's like a chain. See what I mean?"

"Not at all."

"Well, my fault for not completing the chain. That name, Mollie? You might not recognize the name's significance, distinctive though it is, stripped of the whole double-play parlay, which is *Mollie to Handkerchief to X.*" One of Handkerchief's eyelids had drooped in anticipation of the coming punch, but I gave him a two-penny smile in encouragement.

"To X?" I watched as the confusion cleared miraculously from his eyes, replaced by a dawn of false recognition—pretty well done and, I figured, pure habit since we both knew he was lying through his teeth. "*Mollie,*" he said at last, as though correcting my pronunciation. "Yes, of course, Mollie. Lively girl, probably quite attractive to the susceptible. Wears those awful glasses. Mollie, yes, Mollie."

"Gave you something."

He swallowed loudly.

"An envelope. With your name on it. With another envelope inside it. To give to X. Who is X? To whom, Handkerchief, were you supposed to give the envelope inside yours?"

He was already shaking his head. "No idea, no idea where you're taking this."

"Handkerchief. Your nose, unlike most, is long enough to break in multiple places."

A sort of cold front slid in behind his eyes, and I reminded myself that Handkerchief was reputed to be quite skillful with a knife. He let me look at the dip in temperature for a moment and then said, "What's today?"

"The All-Seeing Eye doesn't know what—?"

"All time for the All-Seeing Eye is the present."

"The present's name is Monday."

"I saw Mollie last Tuesday."

"What was the deal?"

"The usual. I've done this before."

"I know," I said.

"Well aren't you the smarty boots. She'd already called to make sure I was at liberty."

I said, "To do . . ."

"To be part of a chain. Of disconnects. To give me an envelope that I could give to someone who would give it to someone else."

"And one more time, to whom were you supposed to give it?"

He gave it a half-second, probably to consider and reject a lie. "Do you know Dippy Thurston?"

"I've seen her, but we haven't met." Dippy Thurston was a close-up magician who worked minor lounges in Las Vegas a few months a year and, the rest of the time, picked unusually full pockets in elaborate setups. She was famous for one stunt in particular, a little dazzler in which she would chat with three people for less than two minutes, and at the end of the talk they'd all be wearing one another's wristwatches. "Did you give it to her?"

"That same day."

"Tell me about the envelope."

"The usual size. Manila, ten-by-twelve, pretty thick, sealed quite decisively."

"So you were to call Dippy, meet her, give her the envelope, and *not* tell her you got it from Mollie. And you did all that."

He watched me as though to make sure there wasn't more to the question, then nodded. "And she wouldn't tell whomever she passed it to that she'd gotten it from me."

"Had you given envelopes to Dippy before?"

"I had."

"And did Dippy ask where it came from? This time or any time in the past?"

"Of course."

"And you told her?"

"This is good money for doing essentially nothing," Handkerchief said. "Why would I endanger it?"

"Because Dippy's cute."

"She's not *that* cute. In this economy, no one is that cute."

"So did you open the envelope?"

"Junior," Handkerchief said, wrapping the word in aggrieved patience. "It was unopenable. I mean, obviously, it *could* have been opened, but Dippy would have spotted it."

"Sealed how?"

"Glue, fibertape that had been wrapped around the envelope three times before a big letter M had been embossed into it, through the tape and both sides of the envelope. Staples in four places, that I would literally have had to put back into exactly the same holes, even if you could manage to get the fiber tape off without shredding the envelope, melt the glue, and then re-seal and rewrap it somehow with the same fibertape so the M was aligned exactly with the impression on the envelope. Plus matching up the staples. Impossible."

"So you opened the envelope. How would you know otherwise that the fiber tape was three layers deep?"

Handkerchief pressed the side of his right index finger against his upper lip, a little mopping-up operation. "Suppose," he said, "someone was hiring someone to remove *me* from the scene. Suppose whoever started the chain decided the view would be better without me and part of the joke was to make me part of the chain."

"What was in it?"

"What you'd expect, given the nature of the dodge. Another envelope, smaller but still thick, and a wad of money for Dippy—more than I got, I'm sorry to say—plus a note with that same big M pressed into it, telling her how much she should find in the envelope." He sniffed. "As though he thought I wasn't trustworthy."

"She pockets the money and delivers the envelope to who-ever's name is on it, and then he or she does the same."

"I assume. I didn't open the other envelope. It presented dif-ficulties of another magnitude entirely."

"But you remember who it was addressed to."

"Let's slow things down for a moment." He tapped his robe, on the left side of his chest. If he'd been wearing his usual duds, the gesture would have been a checkup on his handker-chief. He did it when he smelled money. "What's your interest? You wouldn't be bobbing if there wasn't an apple. How big an apple?"

"It's personal."

Eyebrows lifted in ninth-generation, well-bred skepticism. "Not pecuniary?"

"Not a penny's worth."

"But there must be a value, or you wouldn't be here."

"If you tell me, I'll give you five hundred—"

"Peh."

"—and if you don't, I'll tell the person who initiated the chain that you opened the envelope."

"Oh, dear," he said. "You see, it's not a name that is likely to go down easily."

"Try me."

"First name, Monty," he said. "As in Monty Python. Last name, Carlo."

I nodded, thinking about picking up the table and hitting him with it. "Monty Carlo."

"I told you it wouldn't go down easily." He tidied his nonexistent handkerchief again.

"It's too stupid for you to make it up." I got up and reached into my pocket for the money. "But just so we're clear, Handkerchief, if it turns out that Monty Carlo is, let's say, an improvisation on your part, you'll be hearing from the man himself, or maybe from a guy named Bones, who's running his errands these days. You know Bones?"

Handkerchief said, "I," swallowed, and said, "do."

"Well, if Monty Carlo turns out to be your idea of a joke, you might want to keep the All-Seeing Eye on full scan for the next week or two."

8
Herbie's Game

I made a right on Ventura and then the next right. The street was lined with old pepper trees, green, cool, and lacy, gracefully drooping their bright little pepper-spheres almost to the ground. There used to be thousands of pepper trees, lining streets all over the Valley, but they're mostly gone now, traded for wider roads, uglier for their absence. I parked in the shade and sat there, waiting for the tears that had been threatening to make me a lot less intimidating during my last five minutes or so with Handkerchief. I'd been feeling the tightness in my chest, the pre-sting in my eyes, and I'd really thought I was going to lose it.

And now that I was alone, now that I *could* lose it, it wouldn't come.

I worked on it. I summoned up Herbie's face, I listened to his voice in my ear, I remembered times when we'd laughed till we couldn't stand up, times we'd been certain we were both dead—on one memorable occasion, on the same night. I ran over the phrases from his lectures, phrases that came to me almost every time I was in an empty house, almost every time I decided to take this instead of that. I knew so many of Herbie's lines by heart that he'd become a burglar's Kahlil Gibran, but funnier.

I did everything I could think of to break my heart.

But all I did was get mad.

So I decided that the thing to do was follow Wattles's start-and-stop trail as best I could and then, when I got to the end of it, kill someone.

There was a green pepper-tree dangle resting on my windshield, the little peppercorns proudly displaying their pastel colors beneath the frilly green leaves. The air stirred the branch, so I put down the window to feel the breeze, which turned out to be 102 degrees.

A pigeon landed on the hood of my car.

So. Next steps.

The pigeon looked at me sideways.

I turned my head and looked at the pigeon sideways.

The pigeon winked at me, although it might have been a blink since I could only see one eye.

I took out my phone and looked at it, not actually having the energy to push the buttons. Instead, I put the window back up. That required only one button.

The pigeon had walked up the hood of the car to the windshield and was really working its neck, giving me alternate eyes as though trying to figure out which one I looked better through. I wondered if pigeons divided other pigeons, and maybe people, for that matter, into left-eye and right-eye. Like, *She's a right-eye knockout, but left-eye, she's all beak.*

What I wanted to do was go to Bitsy's Bird's Nest, crawl beneath the parrot-festooned bedspread, and assume the fetal position until Ronnie came home from wherever she went in the daytime and decided to make me feel better. The other thing I wanted to do was go to my old house—not far away—where my daughter, Rina, lived with my former wife, Kathy, but they could both read me too well for that. Plus, Kathy had fifteen years' worth of resentment filed under Herbie's name because, in her version of our lives together, Herbie had led me astray, in spite of the fact that I'd followed him so eagerly. She'd be tiptoeing around in sensitive mode, trying not to say something negative about Herbie, and I'd probably end up having a fight with her.

Herbie had referred to burglary as "the game." When you're in *the game*, he used to say; those of us who are in *the game*; you gotta learn the rules of *the game*. The game demanded fair play, at least from Herbie's perspective. Don't steal from the poor. Don't take everything that matters from anyone. Always leave something on the table, something the mark values. "You gotta leave them their heart," he used to say. "What you want is the 'At least they didn't take *that*' reaction. They can live with it, especially if they've got plenty of other stuff."

My life, it suddenly seemed to me, was an extension of Herbie's Game.

Among the possible next steps, what I *most* wanted to do was fly away with that pigeon and check out the world from alternate eyes. If you looked at something bad through only one eye, would it be only half as bad?

What I did was call Ronnie, to hear her voice and get some sympathy, which she provided in full measure. Then I grabbed two huge breaths and called Louie the Lost.

Louie had managed a career as a getaway driver for several years, until his nonexistent sense of direction caught up with him and put him at the wheel of a stolen Cadillac that was stranded in traffic in downtown Compton with four jacked-up jewel thieves in the front and back seats, a pound of diamonds in the trunk, and half the people in the street peering in through the windows while the crooks screamed four-part harmony at Louie. So the phone had stopped ringing with getaway offers, and he'd become a telegraph instead, scooping information up every-where and parceling it out to those who could afford it.

He was also the closest friend I'd ever had in the, um, crimi-nal underworld.

Except for Herbie.

The thought of Herbie made me say, "*Fuck*," just as Louie said, "Hello."

"Yeah, sure," Louie said. "Go ahead, just spit it out, don't nurse it or it'll give you ulcers. I'm sure I did something to deserve it. Hold on, it'll come to me. Nope, nothing. Fuck you." And he hung up.

I dialed again. "Sorry," I said. "That wasn't directed at you."

"Hope to hell," he said. "Two weeks you don't call, the Mis-sus is asking, *Hey, did you miss that nice young man's funeral?* and I'm saying, naw, naw, he just made new friends he likes better than me."

"Lots of them," I said.

"Ouch. And here I been faithful to you."

"So what's happening?"

"You know, same stuff. Just pisher stuff, all the real action's in Washington. Nine-figure, ten-figure crime, and they get to wear such nice suits. Boy, I gotta tell you, if I had it all to do over, I'd get elected to something, just belly up to the public trough—hey, is that pronounced *troff*, to rhyme with *cough*, or *tro* to rhyme with *though*?"

"Hell, I don't know. Could be *troo*, like *through*, or *trow*, like *plough*."

"Or *truff*, like *rough*."

I said, "I don't think it's *troo*. Pull up to the public *troo*? Uh-uh."

"Well," Louie said. "Good to have that settled. So why the sudden call? Get tired of your new friends?"

"What would it feel like," I asked, "to have your eyes on the sides of your head, like a pigeon?"

"Am I supposed to be billing you for this information? Because if I am, I think you maybe oughta call the Smithsonian."

"No. I'm just getting the eye, and I mean that literally, one eye, from a pigeon."

"I woulda come over," Louie said. "You don't have to hang with *pigeons*."

"First, Wattles," I said. "He's disappeared, within the past few hours, and nobody, by which I mean Janice, knows where he is. Second, Dippy Thurston."

"Nice kid, but keep an eye on your wristwatch. What about her?"

"Where is she?"

"Probably home. Encino, I think. Hang on a minute."

"Before you go," I said. "Monty Carlo."

"In Monaco. That poor Princess Grace."

"No, it's a person."

"Gambler?"

"Good idea. Maybe."

"I'll ask around. Hold on while I get Dippy's address."

The pigeon had gotten bored with me and waddled back down the hood. I wondered why it pushed its head forward every time it took a step and how it saw the world in three dimensions when it could only look forward with one eye at a time. It seemed like being able to see in three dimensions would be important to a bird, what with flying and landing and all.

"Damn, I'm good," Louie said into the phone. "Encino. Got a pencil?"

I wrote it down—a surprisingly nice area for a pickpocket, south of the Boulevard, next door to the sitcom second bananas and the bank branch managers and the cameramen and the mouse-level Disney execs: ivy and ice plant, rambling one-story houses set far enough back from the street to make mowing the lawn something to dread. I knew this from personal experience, since I'd grown up mowing lawns about three blocks from *Chez* Dippy.

"So," I said, putting the pen away, "Wattles and Monty Carlo."

"Got it."

"Wait. Have you heard anything lately about Herbie?"

"Pretty much retired," Louie said. "Up in Malibu or something, got his toes in the sand. Why would anybody want his toes in sand?"

"Listen, be a little careful about checking on Wattles and this Carlo guy. I think Herbie may have done a job on Wattles's office, and he's dead."

Hearing myself say it out loud again really sealed it. I lost whatever Louie was saying for a moment or two. When his voice finally came through, he was saying, "—killed?"

"Not quite. He, uh, he died of a heart attack, is my guess. But they were working him over, and as far as I'm concerned that's what did him in."

"Well, you know," Louie said, "not to sound cold or nothing, but do you think they got what they wanted out of him?"

"No," I said, recognizing the conviction as I said it out loud. "If he'd told them what they wanted to know, they would have killed him."

9
Elfin

I had an index finger extended to ring the bell when the door was yanked inward and a short thick man, a cross between a fireplug and a football center, barreled through it, shoved me to one side, and shouted over his shoulder, "When I'm finished with you, you won't be able to get a booking on an *Indian reservation.*" He gallumphed across the lawn and got into a very nice-looking black BMW sedan and took off, leaving about forty bucks' worth of rubber on the street.

As I turned back to the open door, something whistled past my nose. It hit the lawn and tumbled a couple of times, and when it came to rest, it turned out to be a Plexiglas case with a trophy in it.

"I'm sorry about this welcome," a female voice said from behind the door. "Could you get that for me, please?"

I said, "Sure," and went after it. It was a bowling trophy, a woman holding a bowling ball to her chest with a look of severe concentration and that ten-mile stare you see in old Chinese propaganda posters. "The case is cracked."

"Did it hit him?" the woman said.

"Not even close."

"Oh, well, he'd just have sued me. Can you bring it in?"

I said, "I thought you'd never ask." I toted it up to the porch, and the door opened the rest of the way.

The word that came to my mind when I saw Dippy Thurston up close for the first time was *elfin*. She looked like a new human-pixie hybrid, a genetic shuffle that might get patented and bred commercially for its cuteness quotient. Her eyes were uptilted and greenish-hazel above fine, angular cheekbones, and she had a tiny nose, not much bigger than Stinky Tetweiler's, although this one looked like it might be its original size, unlike Stinky's, which surgeons had been planing down for decades. Add a short, raggedy haircut pulled into a careless ponytail, and you had an elf, Southern-California south-of-the-Boulevard style.

She gave me a smile that melted my socks with pure, unadulterated adorableness, and said, "My trophy, please. Do I know you?"

"Just barely," I said, handing it to her. "We have friends, or at least acquaintances, in common."

She put the trophy on a table near the door, where it would be handy the next time she wanted to throw it, and tilted her head winningly. "I didn't hear our mutual acquaintance's name."

"Well, that's the problem," I said. "Handkerchief Harrison."

The eyes got a bit more alert and the smile went a little stale. "And would you describe him as a friend?"

"If it would clarify things, I just finished threatening him."

She pulled her mouth an inch or so to the left, not an expression of unreserved approval. "That helps a little."

"How about Louie the Lost?" I said.

"Oh, *well*," she said. "Come on in." And she opened a drawer in the table she'd put the trophy on and pulled out an adorable little automatic, the kind of thing Gangsta Barbie might pack. She tucked it into the pocket of her cut-off jeans. "Don't take the gun personally," she said. "But also, don't assume I can't get to it whenever I want to. Is that going to stifle your spontaneity?"

"Not at all. If you're keeping one hand on the gun, my watch is probably safe."

She said, "That old thing?" without even glancing at it and shut the door behind me.

We were in a spacious, arched entry hall, saltillo tile studded here and there with smaller tiles of a saturated blue deepened with just a hint of gray. I said, "Delft?"

"Sorry? Oh, the tiles, yes, Delft. You've got a good eye."

"I'm a burglar."

"And an interesting-looking burglar at that. How come Louie hasn't introduced you to me? He knows I'm usually looking. Come on in, I've just made some lemonade."

After the conversation about birds and butts, I was primed to notice her derriere, and it was, well, elfin. I followed it through a shadowy living room, pale gray drapes shouldering aside the sun's heat, then a dining room centered on a hand-planed hardwood table that looked like it weighed a thousand pounds, and into a bright, butter-yellow kitchen. The perfect California swimming pool gleamed a perfect California blue through the window. By that time, I was no longer studying, or thinking about, her butt. Something about the whole place was stirring ripples in my already agitated emotional state.

"So," I said, pushing it aside, "who was the guy who just left?"

"He used to be my manager. Lemonade?"

"Until when?"

"Just before you arrived." She leaned against the counter, and I observed neutrally that her legs were tanned and very muscular, and that she was barefoot.

"You really made lemonade?"

"Sure," she said. "Too wholesome?"

"No, it's just—" I realized what it was, and why the house was troubling me. "I grew up near here, with a pool outside the kitchen window, and we had a lemon tree. On a day like this, my, um, my father always made lemonade." I smiled, just a general, all-purpose, budget smile, and looked around the kitchen. "Sorry, skip it. I'm having kind of an emotional day."

"I'm not, except for Frank, who just left," she said, "and he's more than enough. I hope it doesn't sound unfeminine if I ask you to keep the emotion to yourself."

"Lemonade would be fine," I said. "I'd love some lemonade."

"Attaboy. You like my legs, or what?" She went to the refrigerator and pulled open the door.

"The light didn't come on."

"And it shouldn't," she said. She pulled out a big pitcher, using two hands, and kicked the door closed. "Suppose there's someone out there with a gun in his hand. Suppose I get up in the middle of the night and want a drink, and there I am, in the spotlight."

"Hadn't thought of it that way." She put the pitcher on the counter and turned her back to open a cabinet. She went up on tiptoe, revealing a set of highly developed gastrocnemius muscles. "About your legs," I said. "You've done a lot of work on them."

She twisted around, one heel still in the air, and looked down. "Too much? Getting a little prison-yard?"

"No, just very nicely toned."

"I run eight miles a day and do an hour in the pool with a kickboard. I should have used them to kick Frank."

"What was the problem?"

"He was getting fifteen percent of me, and he wanted all of it."

"Well, he's lost a good client. I saw you perform once, in Reno at the Four Aces."

"Yeah? What did you think?" She was pouring into two thick French water glasses.

"I thought you were great. I especially liked the trick where the playing card some woman had signed wound up in a sealed envelope in her husband's wallet."

"I liked that one, too. Can't do it any more, though. The hotel told me, nothing involving the customers' wallets."

"Really."

She picked up the glasses and handed one to me. "They said they were worried about some mug saying there had been a couple of thousand bucks in his wallet, and after the trick it wasn't there. Insurance problem, according to them."

"Well, maybe—"

"Come with me," she said. "We'll sit in the dining room." She kept talking, without looking back, as I tagged along into the room with the giant table in it. "What I figure is that the LA Sheriffs, who can be very Chatty Cathy, told the Reno cops that I'd once been stopped with quite a lot of property that wasn't exactly mine, according to the traditional definition."

"Cops can be stuffy," I said. I sat at the table, the top of which was about ten inches thick, and looked for a coaster.

"Just put it down. This wood has more marine varnish on it than the *Queen Mary*. Listen, you're a very interesting-looking burglar, but you came looking for me, and that can't be a hundred percent good, right? And the person you mentioned when I asked you who we both knew was Handkerchief. Double notgood, since he couldn't tell the truth if he'd had a year of lessons. Drink your nice lemonade and tell me what you want."

The lemonade was cold but way too sweet. "Handkerchief gave you something last week."

"I take it back," she said. "He can tell the truth, at least when he shouldn't." She looked at her glass and then brought her eyes up to mine. "You're not supposed to know about that."

"How often have you been a disconnect in one of these chains?"

"Chains?" She lowered her head a bit, giving me the uptilted eyes from what she probably knew was their best angle. It made me think for a second about my pigeon. Then she said, "Well, fuck a bagful of Handkerchief Harrisons. You stay where you are." She got up and went to the double doors that opened from the dining room onto the backyard. She shoved one of them ajar, sat on the step, and fished in her blouse for a second. Then she came up with a pack of Marlboro Reds and fired one up. She blew smoke out her nostrils and waved it away from the dining room. "This shit is supposed to be secret."

"One reason I'm here is to tell you to find somewhere else to be, because this one has gone wrong. The guy who started the chain has taken off, and he's hard to scare."

"I was gonna have my floors redone this week."

"They look fine. You've got to think about this. This chain probably ended in an order for a hit, and here I am, asking you about Handkerchief. Maybe the hit went wrong, or maybe the hit went right, and either way the hittee's friends are trying to climb the chain."

She said, "Oh, *man*."

"How many of these have you done?"

She squinted at her cigarette as though it had challenged her. "Five? Six?"

"Who recruited you?"

"Girl who said her name was Laurel."

"Dark hair, shoulder length? Square black glasses? Kind of a head-turner?"

"Yeah."

Our girl Janice. I said, "I think she's rolling the sidewalks up behind herself, too. She told me she just got engaged and they were going on a trip together."

Dippy said, "I knew it was too easy."

"How thick was the envelope you passed on?"

"Compared to what?"

"Compared to the other times."

"Jeez." She took a drag off the cigarette and studied the coal as though to make sure it was burning evenly. "A little thicker than usual. Given what my own envelope felt like, I'd guess there were three inside the one I passed along. Maybe two if one of them was really thick."

"And did you pass it on?"

"I did."

"To whom?"

She looked at me over a ribbon of smoke. "Do you really need to know that?"

"Let me give you a hint," I said. "Monty Carlo." She just kept looking at me, as though she was trying to X-ray my clothing for weapons. "If you're worried about me, call Louie and ask him if I'm dangerous. The point is, this isn't the secret you thought it was, and you might be in the way of some people who are really, really pissed off."

She looked at me and then past me, and then down at the cigarette, all the while chewing on her lower lip. Then she said, "Okay, okay. He's a—a wirehead. Never washes his hair, looks like he lives under a grow-light. Got tats all over his arms, but they're like algebra and that other thing, with co-signers or whatever they are."

"Cosines? You mean, algorithms? Calculus?"

"I guess, yeah, sure. Calculus. And he's strange. Like Doctor Forgetto or something, the absent-minded braniac."

"And he's a crook?"

"I don't know. I didn't get his bio, I didn't look him up on IMDb. But he's in this chain, right? So he's probably not, like, an insurance salesman. I'd guess he's a techno-crook. Computers, coding, puzzle stuff. You know, some crooks, some dips especially, they're like magicians? Pickpockets, magicians, techno guys, they're always working a trick in their minds. Look right through you, thinking about some palming move or a new way to travel a card to the top of the deck. Techno guys, they've got the same thing. But Monty, I mean, he's not weird compared to magicians." She shrugged. "Nobody is."

"So other than Handkerchief and Monty Carlo, you don't know any other links."

"Well, that's the point, isn't it? I knew it was coming from Hankie and I was supposed to give it to Monty, but other than that . . . no, no way I'd know them. It's like a party I wasn't invited to."

"Where does Monty live?"

She shook her head, her lower lip poked out. "Uh-uh," she said. She dropped her cigarette to the pavement, leaned over it, and spat on it to put it out. When she straightened up, she had the little gun in her hand, aimed at the pocket of my T-shirt. "For that, I think I need to check you with Louie."

Three glasses of lemonade later, the last two of them enlivened with a moderate shot of vodka, I was back in the car, which was pulled to the curb about two miles from Dippy's house. The last hour or so of our conversation had been a lot more relaxed than the first one. Through my windshield the houses' shadows stretched into the middle of the street, so with Daylight Savings Time in effect, it was getting late, a little after seven. I had the address where Dippy had left the envelope for Monty

Carlo—she claimed they hadn't actually met this time—and the note that had been in Dippy's envelope, which contained the phone number she had used to reach Monty.

The day felt twenty-four hours long, even though it had only been eight hours since Wattles had barged into Ronnie's and my room, interrupting what had looked like a very promising day. Since then, I'd driven probably sixty miles and found my adoptive father dead.

Marking, I supposed, the end of one phase of my life.

I was on a street only a few blocks away from Kathy and Rina's house—once mine, too. If this was an appropriate time to think about the phases of my life, I was in an appropriate place to do it, because that house, so close and so unrecoverable, encapsulated one phase, maybe the happiest. The way I saw it, sitting there, my life had gone through four phases, with the fifth beginning with the discovery of Herbie's body: first, a generic childhood, just freckles and stepping barefoot on sharp stuff, like everyone else; second, the development of my career, when I broke into the house next door and later met Herbie and began to get good at Herbie's Game; third, the years when Kathy and I were in love and trying to make it work—she trying harder than I, I'm afraid—culminating in Rina's birth and the first ten years of her life, the only perfect thing I ever had a part in. Fourth, the Unhappily Solo Years, after Kathy and I gave up in despair. That period finally culminated in my shuttling from one temporary uncomfortable bed to another, recently while holding hands with Ronnie; and now, the Post-Herbie period, which had dawned, as far as I was aware, a little after one that afternoon.

Even though I hadn't seen much of Herbie lately—an omission that sat on my conscience like a weight—life without him was feeling pretty damn empty. It felt empty enough to draw me close to Kathy's house because I derived a kind of dull comfort from being in the neighborhood, even if I couldn't actually see her and Rina. So it was almost a woo-woo moment when the phone rang and the display said RINA.

"Hi, Daddy," she said as my heart filled with helium and floated to the top of my chest. "Can you come by? Some messenger just dropped something off for you."

Kathy had met me at the door, taken one look at me, and said, "What's wrong?" and I'd told her, and she'd thrown her arms around me and said, "Come in, come in. You poor thing."

I'd underestimated her again.

Now I was in the living room—a room I hadn't sat in since the day I toted my suitcase to the car—and Rina was at the other end of the couch, her hands clasped, palm to palm, between her knees, a glass in front of her. To my amazement, I'd been invited to dinner. Kathy was rattling things in the kitchen, refusing offers of help so Rina could work her magic on me, and I'd already blinked away tears twice.

"Aren't you going to open it?" Rina said. In front of me, on the marble-topped coffee table, was a thick envelope made of a heavy, creamy paper so swell that trees probably competed to be pulped for it. The upper left-hand corner proclaimed in incised type that the envelope had sailed proudly into the world from the offices of Wyndham, Twistleton, & Pine, Attorneys at Law, in Century City.

"No hurry," I said. "Lawyers, even lawyers named Wyndham, Twistleton, ampersand Pine, never send you good news. Jesus, I wonder which of them wears the whitest shoes."

Rina said, "I just read a book in which a poor young girl gets a letter from a lawyer telling her she's inherited half the world and a castle, too."

"The castle is a nice touch."

"It's a dumb book. But it's got a kindly lawyer in it. Sort of grandfatherly, but not like my grandfathers." Neither Kathy's father nor mine was likely to be shortlisted for Grandfather of the Year.

"That's a fictional lawyer. They're different from real lawyers."

"How?" She was drinking something made with tomato juice. I averted my eyes because tomato juice has always given me the creeps. It's just too arterial.

"Let's say you've been hurt," I said. "A fictional lawyer, say a TV lawyer, would comfort you, maybe fold his suit jacket under your head as a pillow and murmur eloquent encouragement to keep you going until the ambulance comes. A real lawyer would represent the ambulance company when it sues you for payment."

"You think that might be a little sweeping? People say bad things about burglars, too."

I said, "And they're right."

A brief pall settled over us. Rina dispelled it by asking, "How's Ronnie?"

I looked around my old living room, everything pretty much where I'd left it three years earlier, although the pictures had changed. I wasn't in them. "You want the truth? I have no idea how she is."

"How who is?" Kathy had a Bloody Mary in her hand. More tomato juice.

"His friend," Rina said.

"Miss Motel?" Kathy sat in the chair she always sat in, which I noticed had been reupholstered in what had undoubtedly been sold as natural leather, as though nature was rife with powder-blue animals. She put her Bloody Mary on the little square mahogany table that had belonged to her mother and said, "Sorry sorry. I'm sure she's a very nice person."

"She is," I said. "And the motels are one of the things I like about her. Her name is Ronnie, by the way."

"Short for Veronica," Rina put in.

"I know, dear." Kathy said with just a tiny edge. "And what do you mean, the motels are one of the things you like about her?"

"She doesn't have to live in them. She's got a perfectly nice apartment in West Hollywood, big and airy and full of books—"

"What does she read?" Rina said. Rina wanted to know what everybody read.

"Mostly history. A little science."

"So she has an apartment," Kathy prompted.

"Right. And she never goes there unless it's to pick up some books or some new clothes." I looked at their tomato juice and wondered why I wasn't drinking anything and then remembered the vodka at Dippy's house. "I mean it's a really nice place, and this month she's sleeping at Bitsy's Bird's Nest. A few months back, it was Valentine Shmalentine."

"It *wasn't*," Kathy said.

"Afraid so. Before that, the North Pole. I don't know why she does it."

"Daddy," Rina said, "it's because she likes you."

"I suppose," I said, trying not to sound morose.

"You know what it is?" Kathy said. "You know why she likes you?"

I said, "Um."

"I can say this because I was married to you," Kathy said, with the certainty of someone who'd been asking herself a question for a long time. "It's because you're decent."

"Me?"

"I?" Rina corrected me, making the lifetime Grammar Gotcha score 1,139 to one in my favor.

"That's what it is," Kathy said. She sometimes shook her head side to side, in the negative, when she was saying something positive, and she was doing it then. "There aren't that many decent men around. Nice men, sure, funny men, always. You've got some of those things, too."

Rina said, "Even hot men. There are plenty of hot—"

"Lots of them," Kathy said, "even if so many of them are stupid. But decency, it's something people don't think about. The people who have it usually don't even know it. You know if you're smart, you *definitely* know if you're handsome, but if you're decent you never give it a moment's thought. And you know why?"

It wasn't a rhetorical question, so I said, "Why?"

"Because decent people assume everyone else is decent. They don't see it as anything special. Just like liars always figure everyone is lying."

"No shit, Mom," Rina said. "I mean, that's totally true."

"You've got it, too," Kathy said, "despite your language. That's one of the ways you're his daughter."

"I don't know what to say," I said. "But thanks."

"So if you don't have any idea how—Ronnie—is doing, what do you think that means?"

"Oh. I don't know." I sat lower. "I'm just sour today."

"Well, you've got a reason," Kathy said. "But don't duck it. You're the one who opened the box."

"We don't seem to be *going* anywhere," I said. "I don't even know where she comes from."

Kathy lowered her drink and shrugged. "Who cares?"

"Yeah, but you know, it's sort of fundamental, like whether

she's right- or left-handed." I couldn't believe I was talking about this with Kathy, but there was no stopping now. "If she can't even tell me where she comes from, what else can't she tell me?"

"Well. Apart from your conviction that she's—I don't know—keeping secrets from you about the past, and I can think of *lots* of reasons for that, how are things from day to day?"

"It's—nice, okay? We get along, we like each other, we can be together in small rooms without bumping into each other or carefully stepping around each other. We *amuse* each other."

"That's important," Rina said. "Tyrone can always make me laugh."

"Doesn't sound very thrilling, though," Kathy said.

"You know, I've stopped asking for thrilling." Kathy was looking straight at me, and I had to lower my eyes to continue. "I think *thrilling* is pretty exclusive to the first few months. After that, I'm happy with comfortable. And happy, I'm happy with happy."

"And are you happy?

I had an overpowering urge to leave the room. Still, I'd started it. "It just doesn't seem to be *going* anywhere."

"You already said that," Kathy said. "Who's at the wheel?"

"Sorry?"

"She's abandoned her nice apartment and she's living in these dumps with you. Sounds to me like she's given you the wheel. Maybe she's waiting to see where you want things to go. When we were married—"

Rina said, "Mom."

"He knows what I'm talking about, sweetie. Don't you?"

"I know exactly what you're talking about. But when we were married, it wasn't so much that I wouldn't take the wheel. It was that I wouldn't steer it where you wanted me to."

"Where you should have wanted to go, too." She blew out

and waved her hand side to side, like someone dispelling smoke. "I didn't say that. Getting back to you and Ronnie, which is probably safer than you and me, maybe what you're seeing is an enormous amount of patience, someone who has faith that you're not going to be content to float aimlessly through space with her, like a couple of marooned astronauts. Maybe she preserves the quaint idea that a woman should give the man a chance to define how the relationship is going to be, even if it's only because it gives her a clearer negotiating position."

Rina said, "I am so going to write that down."

"Ease up, Rina. And maybe, Junior, she's the same species as you are, and I don't intend that to sound mean. You and I, we were different sides of a coin, do you know what I mean? If one of us was up, the other one had to be down. But maybe you and her—"

"She," Rina said. Then she said, "Sorry."

"You and she," Kathy said. "Maybe you and she are more natural partners than you and—you and I were."

I said, "I've always loved you." Out of the corner of my eye, I saw Rina look down at her lap.

"I know that. But it's not enough, not when we'd be on opposite sides of any fight in history. I mean, if you were a cowboy, I would have been a sheep-herder." She laughed and touched her index fingers to her eyes. "Maybe you and she are more like each other. Maybe even each of you is a little better than the other, in, in different ways, so you can—I don't know—improve each other."

"That's my mom," Rina said.

"And he's your dad, and he's half the reason you're who you are, and don't you forget it." She knocked back a good whack of her drink and sniffled and said, "So take the lead, for Christ's sake. *Push* her a little. What's the worst that can happen, that she'll leave you? If things don't get better, you'll leave *her*."

"When a man needs help with a girlfriend," I said, "he doesn't usually think about going to his ex-wife."

"If you'd done it yesterday, when you weren't in such a sorry state, I probably would have cut your head off. Speaking of knives, let's eat dinner."

To: Mr. Junior M. Bender

If "Junior M." strikes you as odd, the "M" stood for Merle, my father's name. He'd wanted to name me after himself, but by the time I was born he'd had thirty-two years of telling people that, no, Merle wasn't always a woman's name, and would you like to talk about it outside, so he named me Junior and squeezed Merle into the middle, where it could peek safely from around an initial, and then he abandoned my mother for another woman and left me, middle name and all, with my mother.

From: A. Vincent Twistleton, Wyndham, Twistleton, & Pine
Re: Herbert Arthur Elgar Mott, Deceased

Dear Mr. Bender

Unfortunately, it falls to me to inform you of the death of Herbert Arthur Elgar Mott, who has been a client of this firm (and, I may add, something of a personal friend) for many years.

I write to you in accord with two instructions given to me by Mr. Mott several years ago. The first of these is to inform you that you are a legatee in Mr. Mott's will and to invite you to the reading of that document, which will take place this coming Saturday, September 22, at four P.M. in my office, the address of which will be found on this letterhead. I add a formal request that you either attend the reading in person or arrange to meet me face-to-face in the near future, as your bequest comprises a substantial portion of Mr. Mott's estate, and I would be reassured to confirm that this letter has found its way into the correct hands.

It causes me some pain to explain to you why I must carry out the second of Mr. Mott's requests. At the time he last revised his will, he gave me the enclosed envelope and instructed me to put it into your hands with all haste in the event that he should not pass away from normal causes. So it's necessary for me to tell you that I learned less than an hour ago that Mr. Mott died either directly or indirectly at the hands of others.

On a closing note, please let me say that lawyers meet a great many people from all walks of life, and I have been a lawyer for a long, long time, but I never met anyone like Herbie Mott, and he led me to believe that you felt much the same way I do. You, like me, were fortunate to have him in your life.

I look forward to meeting you and I am deeply sorry to be the one to give you this news.

Best personal regards,
A. Vincent Twistleton

He'd signed it, "Vincent," and beneath his signature, he'd written "Courage!"

"I take it all back," I said to Rina. "There *are* some good lawyers."

"Some good burglars, too," she said.

"He sounds like an okay guy," I said. "Herbie wouldn't have a jerk lawyer. Boy, Herbert Arthur Elgar Mott. No wonder he changed his name all the time."

"Do you want me to leave? While you read his letter?"

"No. In fact, I'd rather you stay right where you are."

"Here I am," she said.

The envelope had two of those stiff cardboard button-things on it, one on the flap and one on the body, and a length of string that you wound in figure eights around the two buttons to fasten it. Very nineteenth-century. As I tugged at the string, I saw that my fingers were trembling. I said aloud, "Breathe deeply," and unwound it the rest of the way.

The letter was printed in a sans-serif font on heavy paper, probably two sheets of the bond paper Twistelton printed his letterhead on. It had been folded twice and was written only on one side, although it was single-spaced. For some reason it was in italics, which gave me a vague image of Herbie writing it fast, before someone else came into the room.

Hey, Junior:

If your reading this, somebody got me. I hope the news got broke to you gently, although your a pretty tough kid.

Sometimes I'm sorry that I helped you get into this business. You could have had a good life on the straight. But, you know, guys like us have to come from somewhere. When I took you down to Du-par's that night I was going to give you a lecture and get rid of you. Sort of catch-and-release, like fishing. But you were already smarter than I was, and the only way for any game to get better is if it attracts smarter players. You probably know what I mean. So if your life hasn't worked out the way you thought it would, I'm sorry. Maybe it would have been better if you hadn't met me.

Also I want to say that you've got the greatest eye I ever saw in fifty years. You can look at ten pieces of jewelry when one is worth more than all the others put together and you'll pick that one every time. Not bringing you in would have been a waste of talent.

But I'm sorry about your wife and kid not wanting any of it. Boy, do I know how that can hurt.

Look, there are two things I need to say. First is, if it isn't obvious why I got killed, I mean, if I didn't get killed for something I did just before it went down, there's a guy who would kill me seven days a week if he could ever find me, and if your reading this, maybe he did. He's the main reason I disappeared like I did. His name is Ruben Ghorbani. He's a knee-breaker who worked for a while for Trey Annunziato's dad, the one she killed. I think Wattles may have used him some, too, and old Burt the Gut used him for collections back when Burt was making loans. So Ghorbani went after a friend of mine who owed Trey's dad a bundle and my friend was flush so he paid it all in cash and Ruben stomped him really bad and pocketed the cash and told my friend he'd be back to get it again. He broke both of my friend's arms at the elbow and told Trey he'd taught my friend a lesson and that she'd get her money real soon. So I got Harmon Huss, I think you met Harmon, he used to wrestle pro, and we grabbed Ruben and took him up to the Angeles Forest, and Harmon held him down while I took a ball-peen hammer to his nuts, one for each of my friend's arms he broke. I guess it hurt pretty bad because he threatened to kill me once he could walk again, and a couple of people have told me that he looks for me every now and then, so he might have found me.

So Ghorbani is half Persian and half Mexican. He's got dark skin and black hair, a lot of it on his arms, and a square face with a flat nose that looks like a cricket's and green eyes. About your height but twice as wide because he's bulked up. And he chews steroids for the muscle, so he gets angry kind of fast. Please don't take this as an order or even a suggestion, but if it turns out Ruben is the one who did me, and you can either put a bullet through him or get someone else to, well, it would make an old man happy wherever he is.

But I mean this, only if you can do it easy and get away with it. Otherwise, walk away. It's not like it's going to bring me back above the ground.

Second, and this isn't an order either, but second, I've got a son. His name is Edward Mott but he goes by Eddie. He lives straight. My ex-wife just hated me and she made sure that Eddie did, too. I've tried to talk to him a hundred times, but he won't say a word to me. I just want someone to tell him his father wasn't a total asshole. Mostly an asshole, maybe, but not total.

I don't know what Eddie does now but he lives in the Valley, I'm pretty sure, and last I knew he was selling Hondas in Van Nuys. You'll probably meet him at that thing where they read the will because your both in it. I left you the John Sloane picture, which you obviously shouldn't let the LA Times take a picture of.

So that's it, Junior. Kill Ruben for me, if he's the one who did me, and you got some free time, and try to make my kid think a little better about me. If you can only do one of those things, try to find Eddie. Somebody will get Ruben sooner or later anyway.

If I fucked up your life, I'm really sorry. But I'm proud of you.

Herbie.

"Can I read it?" Rina asked.

"I'm not sure that would be—what's the word?—appropriate. No, I'm pretty certain it wouldn't be appropriate."

"Is it going to get you into trouble?"

"If I'm not careful, it might."

"And will you be—oh, forget it."

"Rina," I said, "I love you and your mother more than

anyone else in the world. If I did anything right in my life, it was fathering you."

"Then try not to orphan me, okay?"

"I'll do that. And tell your mom it was just a goodbye letter, okay?"

She leaned over and kissed me on the cheek and said, "Like I know anything different."

11

It Can Be a Dolphin If It Can Do the Job

As I pulled away from the house and made the left onto the long straightaway down to Ventura, a car pulled out behind me. That wouldn't have engaged my attention for more than a second or two, but it didn't turn on its headlights until I'd gone half a mile downhill.

That engaged my attention.

A little street called Santa Rita came up on my left, and I signaled and took it about two blocks east and then turned left again, into a little four-house circle. I made the half turn in the circle and sat there, facing out.

Fifteen seconds later, a dark Nothingmobile, a generic sedan that might have been a Ford or a Kia or a Flahoolie for all I could tell, drove straight past me without even slowing. I gave it thirty seconds and then pulled out behind it, in time to see it belching smoke to accelerate away. I stomped the accelerator, and the 300 horsepower of Detroit iron that Louie the Lost somehow jammed under the hood of my Toyota punched me halfway into the backseat. But the other driver had already floored it and he'd reached the next cross street, where he swung left, almost losing the road, and I could hear the engine's roar all this way, even over the noise of my own.

If you're chasing someone, the problem with the Tarzana/

Woodland Hills area is that word "hills." The roads have to get around the hills, which means that straightaways like Santa Rita are rare among the east-west streets. Most of them fork and circle around and join up again like spaghetti on a plate, following the ghost-impressions of the streams and arroyos carved into the landscape to provide footpaths for the Chumash Indians during the thousands of years when they had Southern California to themselves. I was planning to accelerate left onto the cross-street, hoping I didn't spin out, but at the absolute last moment I saw the headlights coming up from the right and I hit my brakes. As I lurched to a stop I saw the car I'd been chasing make another left, into what I knew was an absolute snarl of streets, the kind of convoluted knot you'd probably have to cut out of your hair. I remembered that the driver hadn't actually followed me into the circle, so my bet was that he was using a GPS unit and already had a route mapped out.

A silver Rolls Royce, maybe twenty years old, glided by at the pace of a Rose Parade float, well below the 25-mile-per-hour speed limit, probably with five or six miles per hour to spare. This person knew where he or she was going, was in no hurry to get there, and had bought a living room on wheels to enjoy the trip. There was probably a hot tub in the back seat. As I made my left I considered chasing and passing it, but by the time I got up to the *next* left, the other car could already have looped around and be heading back north to any of a number of streets, toward Ventura.

It could be taking Vanalden or Tampa or Topeka or Shirley, any of which would take it straight north to the Boulevard and into the 260-square-mile maze of the Valley. Or, if the driver was willing to run a couple of unpaved patches, he or she could follow Vanalden all the way up to Mulholland and, from there, go pretty much anywhere in North, Central, or South America.

Hopeless.

The Rolls honked elegantly, a contralto protest, to tell me I was tailgating. I gave up, pulled over, felt my pulse beating against the side of my throat for a moment, and hit speed-dial for Louie.

"Back so soon?"

"I need someone you'd trust to defend you personally, and I need him sitting in front of Kathy's house within thirty minutes."

"Can it be a chick?"

"It can be a dolphin if it can do the job."

"Got it. Thirty minutes."

"Call me back and give me a description of her car so I don't kill her by mistake."

"A red little whatsit, one of those things that runs on sunlight and happy thoughts. A Leaf, that's it."

"A red Nissan Leaf."

"That's what I said."

"Tell her the guy in the white Toyota is me."

"Sure. She drills you, how you gonna pay me?"

"Thirty minutes." I cranked the wheel around and headed back to Kathy's to wait for the gun to show. Twenty-two minutes later, as a red Leaf took the corner and blinked its lights at me, I left my *real* home to head for tonight's home.

12

How to Look Like You Admire Stupidity

The question was, where had they picked me up?

I hadn't been paying much attention to anything in the first hours after finding Herbie's body. Which meant I could have been followed that whole time by someone who saw me come out of the house. So if whoever killed Herbie had been behind me ever since Malibu but had nothing to do with Wattles's chain, well, that gave me one possible individual, or pool of individuals, to worry about. If, on the other hand, whoever killed Herbie *did* have something to do with Wattles's chain—or if the follower had picked me up at Handkerchief's or Dippy's—that gave me a different individual, or pool of individuals, to worry about. In short, related to Wattles's damn chain, or not?

It would be nice, I thought, as I hauled myself up the stairs to our room at Bitsy's Bird's Nest, to figure that out as soon as possible.

Bitsy, or some demonic carpenter who worked for Bitsy, had built little pressure switches into some of the stairs, and when you stepped on one, it produced a bird call. When I found the place, I thought, cool, I'll always know when someone is coming, but the bird calls proved to be so irritating that I'd already tuned them out. Wattles must have set off a whole aviary of squawks, whistles, chirps, trills, honks, and caws as he and Bones climbed the stairs, but I hadn't heard a thing.

The stairs that chirped and nattered had been chosen at random, and in the twelve days we'd been there I still hadn't found the pattern. So I just tweeted my way upstairs, feeling heavier, sadder, and more useless with each cheerful chirp. By the time I opened the door, it was all I could do to smile at Ronnie, looking expectantly up from her book on the parrotscape of the bedspread.

"Oh, baby," she said. She dog-eared the book—a habit I'd failed to break her of—and got up and crossed the room and wrapped long arms around me, giving me the warmth of her body and the faint fragrance of the lavender-scented face cream she used (she said) to delay the day men would stop bothering her on the street. "I've been worried about you ever since you called."

I put my arms around her and closed my eyes and let her just draw the sadness out of me. After a minute or two, I blew out a huge sigh, unwrapped her, and followed her, like a puppy, over to the bed.

I said, "Did you eat?"

"I always eat. What about you?"

"At Kathy's."

She plumped up one of the pillows she'd brought from her apartment and put it on top of one of the bran sacks or whatever they were that Bitsy put on the beds. "What did she fix?"

The moment my head hit the pillow, the iron bar in my neck melted. "I don't remember."

"Sure, you do."

"Some kind of meat. One of the tough cuts, cooked for a long time. With, you know, stuff."

"Did you like it?"

"Sure," I said. "Don't take this wrong, but it tasted like home."

"I'm not going to take it wrong. I sneaked back to West Hollywood tonight and ate at the French Marketplace. First real restaurant I ever ate at in LA, a friend of mine who ate there seven days a week took me when I'd just gotten here, and that's what tastes like home to me, the French Marketplace."

"That's kind of sad," I said.

"Aaaahhh," she said. "Toughen up."

"I don't feel very tough."

"I know. Losing a parent, even a symbolic parent, can do that to you."

"I need to talk to you."

"Do I get to answer?"

"Yeah. I mean, ideally, it should be a conversation."

"Okay." She began to knead the muscle at the top of my shoulder nearest to her. "Will this distract you?"

"From what?"

"Very funny."

I said, "I have no idea how to put this."

She got a thumb under the muscle and pushed up and it hurt really great. "Just dive in."

"I don't feel like we're going anywhere." She stopped massaging me. "And I'm wondering whether it's my fault."

"Where are we supposed to be going?" She went back to work on the shoulder.

"I don't know. But it's feeling—static."

"Do you still like me?"

"Of course."

"Do you like me more, less, or the same?"

"More."

"What does that mean?"

"Everybody's asking me that tonight. It means I know you better than I did three months ago, with some exceptions—"

"Aahhhh," she said. "The exceptions."

"Wait. It means, even *with* the exceptions, the better I know you, the closer I feel to you. I've given you ample opportunity to bore me, and you never have, and I don't seem to bore you. It means—"

"Are you falling in love with me?"

"Jesus," I said as an ice cube slid up my spine. "Is that what this is?"

"I can't answer that for you." She folded her hands over her stomach and lay back against the pillows. "It would be presumptuous."

"Okay, okay. Let's put love to one side for a minute."

"Oh, let's."

"Let's look at the small picture and work our way up to the big stuff."

"That sounds safe."

"The way we live, for starters. I've been kind of dragging you from place to place—"

"And what places."

"And all the while, you have a really nice little apartment over in WeHo, and I—I haven't even asked you whether me hauling you around like this is—is—"

"This is very sweet," she said. "But you have to trust me to complain when I feel like it." She rolled over on her side, facing away from me. "But then, you don't know what I'd be likely to complain about, do you? Because you don't know who I was before I met you. The exceptions we were just talking about."

I put a hand on her shoulder, and she put one of hers on top of it, but she didn't turn to face me. "I'm going to take a deep breath here and then make a short speech, and if you're not totally tone deaf, you'll let me finish it." She took a deep breath, as promised. "I *do* realize that I haven't told you much about myself, and I know it bothers you. There are things I can't talk about. I don't even talk about them to myself. It's not that I did horrible things," she said. "It's that some horrible things were done to me and they didn't make me a better person. That is *not* a play for sympathy."

I said, "Want me to rub your shoulders?"

"You lack talent." She squeezed my hand. "Okay, counting down." She took another breath. "When I was seventeen I stopped secretly cutting slices into the skin on my forearms and began to behave in a way that a shrink would describe—*has* described—as 'acting out.' Running away from home, getting involved with the wrong guys—crooks, some of them violent crooks. When you leave a violent home and hang with violent guys, you develop a set of skills. You learn how to laugh at things that don't amuse you and how to look like you admire stupidity, you learn that no argument, no matter how good, is going to open a closed mind. You learn how to get way down into your center and hide there in a little ball while things happen to your body. You learn how to find the place in the room where you'll be least conspicuous." She licked her lips. "You learn, eventually, how to get even." She rolled onto her back, sat forward, took one of the pillows that had been behind her, and hugged it to her chest. She leaned back against the headboard, but immediately sat up again. "Are you using that pillow?"

"My head is."

"Well, give it to me anyway. Your head has been through worse."

I rolled over and she snatched the pillow, put it behind her, and resettled herself. "Better. Do you know how old I am?"

"Twenty-five."

"I'm twenty-seven. I even lied to you about that. From seventeen to about twenty-three, I just hung with wrong guys. I was on the sidelines of some pretty bad shit. It scared me senseless, but not bad enough to go home again. Whatever I was going through, home scared me more. When I was twenty-three, someone offered me a job tending bar. I grabbed it. I worked there every hour they'd let me, stealing a little every night, until I had enough to get out of Trenton or Albany and get a job where nobody knew me. You still with me?"

"Sure. Wherever you were."

"Atlantic City. By then, it was Atlantic City. People who come to Atlantic City carry a lot of cash and they gave me a bunch of it as tips. I bought some of the books I'd refused to read in high school. I read all day and I worked all night. When we first met each other, you and I, once I got past the way you look, I watched the way you studied my bookshelves when you didn't know I was watching. If you hadn't looked at them that way, we probably wouldn't be here." She looked into my eyes and gave me a smile that was more thought than anything else. "So I read and read. I got a little less crazy, I stopped looking behind me all the time and jumping at every noise. I read some more. I still went out with bad guys because bad guys were what I thought I deserved, if that makes sense. And I got better in a lot of ways, although every time somebody would slap me around or punch me in the mouth I'd go right back into the *what did I do to deserve this* mode. Until one night I asked myself why the fuck I accepted it. And that was a real light bulb moment, you know? I'd kept getting hit without ever asking myself why, I'd kept climbing into the ring when there were perfectly good seats on the other side of the rope. And that was when I decided to come out here where the sun shines and I could take a shot at being somebody else, and I hooked up with those guys who brought me here in stages."

"As I remember, a car thief, a dope dealer, and a journalist."

She laughed. "Boy, does that sound bleak. But you know, they were all okay, except for the journalist, and he was the one who looked best on the surface." She broke it off and rubbed her eyes with the heels of her palms. "So I'm telling you all this because it's like an imitation of being intimate. It's about as close as I can get to it right now, and that's probably one reason things feel static to you. But this is the deal: I met you, I fell for you, and I've gone wherever you went and I've appreciated it that you haven't told me to get lost—wait, it's not as abject as that. Let's take your first question at face value, shall we? Would I rather be in my sunny little apartment with all my books than in this—this *aviary*, or whatever it is? You bet your ass, I would. But would I rather be there without you or here with you? Well, hell, you know the answer to that."

"But should you have to? I mean, thank you for what you just said. It's, um, it makes me feel good for the first time in a really bad day. But shouldn't I have asked you where you wanted to be? Shouldn't I—"

"Maybe," she said. "But you know what? Who gives a damn? Maybe you could be marginally more sensitive, but you know, one of the things about this relationship is that we know how to leave each other alone. We're not always touching each other's moist noses to double-check whether every little thing is all right."

I said, "No."

"So, what I asked you before. Is this—this thing we're doing—is it going, as far as you're concerned, in the direction of love?"

"Hell, yes."

"Then I don't care," she said, and she rolled over and put her hand on my cheek. "We can sleep in the fucking car as far as I'm concerned."

She had six little moles on the side of her neck that looked a little like the Big Dipper, which is to say they looked slightly more like the Big Dipper than they didn't. I traced the dipper with my forefinger for the hundredth time and said, "I'm getting off too easily."

She pushed her shoulder into me, just getting closer, and said, "I tell myself that every day."

PART
TWO

I asked, "But how do you learn to tell good stuff from bad stuff?"

Herbie hit a key on the piano. "What's this?"

"It's a G."

"And this?"

"B-flat."

"And this?" He hit three keys.

"B-minor chord."

"Okay." He hit a bunch of adjoining keys with his fists. "What's this?"

"Garbage."

"Good," he said. "Now learn to do that with everything."

The next morning—the beginning of my first full day in a world without Herbie in it—Wattles was still unfindable and Janice had apparently followed him. I wondered how Limpopo was this time of year.

It had to be better than the Valley, which was suffocating. It couldn't have been hotter if the sky had been a big brown electric blanket set to high—brown because the inversion layer, which I understand intermittently, had slammed its lid on top of the mountains, sealing in the hydrocarbons and the stench and the little quick-shimmy cough-ticklers that smog plants in the back of your throat. It wasn't that long ago that the Valley was all blue skies and orange trees and red tomato plants, but progress had had its way with us, and now for consolation we had a lot of pavement and a system of alerts to reassure us that suffocation was safely months away.

Louie had replaced the gunperson on Kathy's street with another one, who would be replaced after six hours by yet another. They would park within fifty or seventy-five yards of the house, facing it, with the gun no more than a few inches from their preferred hand.

"Got you a bargain," he said. "You know who's out there right now? Debbie Halstead."

"It better be a bargain. Debbie gets five figures, and the first figure is usually a seven."

"One-eighty an hour, she said, special for you," Louie said. "Girl last night was one-ten, but Debbie, Debbie could shoot out every other eyelash at fifty paces."

"Well, say hi to Debbie for me." Debbie was a hitperson with a big smile and an infectious laugh who cozied up to targets and stuck a tiny .22 into the nearer ear. She'd essentially saved my life eight to ten months ago. No, not *essentially*. She'd saved my life, period.

"Will do," Louie said. "I think girls are a good idea in that neighborhood, whaddya think?"

"I agree, but I wish you'd stop calling them girls."

"What're we, on PBS? Haven't got anything yet on the guys you asked me about. Nobody seems to have heard of Monty Carlo, and I can't find anyone who's heard from Ruben Ghorbani in a couple, three years."

"Maybe he's dead."

"Uh-uh. Somebody would know. There'da been parties. People would have bought gift ribbon, shot off fireworks."

"Well, keep looking. I'll come by later today and give you a wad of cash."

"I can front you for a couple days."

I was touched. Among crooks, this is the next thing to a proposal. "I'll get it to you today, but thanks."

"Yeah, yeah. Burt the Gut, he's retired now, but I got his address and talked to him, and he'll be looking for you in, say, forty-five." He gave me the address, which almost made me whistle. Burt the Gut had matriculated from the Valley to Hancock Park, home of some of Los Angeles's very best houses, and he was on Hudson, my very own personal favorite street. In my infrequent mental fast-forwards to my Golden Years, should

I reach them, I'm spending them in a 1932 Moorish castle of about 5500 square feet on Hudson. I break into it every now and then just to make sure the owners are taking care of it.

Burt the Gut lived half a block from my castle, not bad for a guy who started out running a small betting parlor, turning two competing mobs against each other so he could do business among the falling bodies in the war zone, expanded into the numbers game, and then went into the kind of high-interest, short-term money-lending that no one but the very biggest and most prestigious banks can do legally. Burt, as Herbie once explained to me, had three rules: interest would compound daily, collateral would be worth triple the loan, and pain would be inflicted upon the careless and the tardy. And when pain was the mode *du jour*, Burt turned to Ruben Ghorbani, a man who apparently felt about hurting people the way Ronnie felt about chocolate, although from what I'd heard about him, she controlled her craving better than he did.

I coasted past my castle, noted with distaste the new color of the trim, a sort of Postal Service bad-meat green, and pulled into Burt's curving, sun-dappled driveway. Judging from the eye-ringing emerald hue of the lawn, the grass had never endured a dry minute since it was planted, about forty-five minutes ago. There are two schools of thought associated with good lawns: the British approach, which says you simply plant it and roll it for several centuries, and the Los Angeles nouveau-riche view, which says you just put in a new one whenever the old one gets a little ratty.

Burt's place was a hulking, broad-shouldered white Mediterranean with a red-tile roof and a front door twelve feet high. The woman in gray sweats who opened the door was a premature victim of plastic surgery; she looked to be in her early thirties, but she already had plump pillows of what might have been blancmange floating above her cheekbones and chin to reshape her face, and her eyes had that wind-tunnel pull at the outer corners that said *facelift* in every language on earth. Her hair had been bleached to fiberglass. Confronted in a mirror with the face she'd had at twenty, she probably would have burst into tears.

"You're that guy," she said. "Ten-thirty."

"I am," I said, but she had already turned her back and was heading for a curving stairway. Without looking back, she pointed to her left, toward an arch, and said, "It's in there" rather than "*He's* in there," and did the stairs two at a time, her body young and lithe and individual, a terrible contrast with the mass-produced, department-store face.

In there was the living room, vast and vaulted, with a stone floor and a beam ceiling. It was stuffed with bulging, over-dressed furniture of vaguely Eastern European origin, enough for three rooms of its size. On the biggest couch, wearing a massive white bathrobe at 10:30 in the morning with the assurance of a guy who plans to wear it all day, was a powerful-looking, surrealistically tanned individual who had to be Burt the Gut. I'd been expecting stomach, but what I got was all of it: from his big square head to his shoulders to his bare feet, everything was outsized. He had to be pushing eighty, but there was none of the dwindling I sometimes associate with age. The leathery brown skin was firm, the body intimidatingly chunky, the hair as black as shoe polish. He looked like he could crack walnuts with his teeth, chew the shells into a paste, and glue somebody to the wall with it.

"You meet Seven?" he said without getting up. He had his right hand jammed into the pocket of the robe, which made me a little nervous.

"I guess."

He shook his head in what seemed to be commiseration. "Talk your arm off?"

"You must pay her by the word."

"Heh," he said. He squinted at me as though I were standing in front of a spotlight. "Why am I seeing you?"

"I haven't got any idea," I said. "I'm seeing *you* because I'm looking for someone."

"Oh, yeah. Ruben." He used the hand that wasn't in his pocket to indicate an armchair big enough for two. "Sit. I got a stiff neck."

I sat. The chair was upholstered in something prickly. "Is her name really Seven?"

"Don't be silly. How many people you know named Seven? She's my seventh wife, right? And I'm old enough and rich enough that I can call her what I want. Let me give you a tip. If you're going to marry a lot of women, make sure they all got the same name. Otherwise, some night at one of them intimate moments when you're expected to say something like, 'Oh, Maria,' sure as shit her name won't be Maria."

"Not a problem I'm likely to face."

"You never know. So, like I said, I ain't seen him."

"Ruben? You haven't actually said that."

"I said it to your travel agent, whoever it was that called to ask if you could come."

"Louie."

"Him. I told him. Told him I ain't seen Ruben for two, maybe three years."

Burt's right eye was off-center, wandering over my left shoulder, and I kept feeling like I should lean over to meet it, but then I wouldn't be meeting his other eye, so I stayed where I was. But then I found myself wanting to look back over my shoulder. I said, "What was he doing, last time you saw him?"

"Why would I know? I didn't hoist shots with the guy. He was busting heads, right? Somebody needed his head busted, I called Ruben. He didn't come over after and watch the game or nothing."

"So after you stopped using him, you never saw him again?" He opened his mouth, and I said, "Or heard from him?"

"Had a couple calls. Nothing much. Looking for work."

"Hear anything *about* him?"

This time, both eyes were looking over my shoulder, and I gave up and turned around.

Seven was leaning up against the side of the archway as though it took the entire resistance of the house to keep her upright. "I'm going to the cheese store."

"Stop the presses," Burt said.

She gave the keys in her hand an impatient shake. "You want anything?"

"The cheese store? Gee, I don't know. Cheese?"

Seven said, "I don't know why I bother," pushed off from the wall, and turned to go.

"Go over to Viktor Benes, get me some alligator."

"That's not on the way."

"What's not on the way? Santa Monica Boulevard, for Chrissakes."

The skin over her plumped-out cheekbones turned dark red. "Century City, I'm not going into Century City."

"Then don't fucking ask," Burt said. "Just go get your fucking cheese."

Seven flipped him a finger, shook her head, wheeled, and disappeared. A moment later, the door was closed with some force.

"Don't get married," Burt said.

He didn't seem like the kind of person to discuss my failed marriage and my daughter with, so I just said, "You were going to tell me whether you heard anything about Ruben after you stopped talking to him."

"Yeah, yeah, yeah." He took a couple of breaths and focused one of his eyes on me. "Last I heard, he beat the shit out of some priest, some kind of pastor or something, in the Valley. That's the kind of story that gets around, beating on a priest."

The hand in the pocket of his robe was clenched into a fist. I kept my eyes on it and said, "A priest. Why would he punch out a priest?"

"The 'roids," Burt said. "He took them like a kid chews gum. Lotta coke, too, didn't make him any easier. This is a guy, tore one of his shoes apart with his teeth when a lace broke. Did it in my living room—another one, not this one. A real leather shoe, just sank his teeth into it like it was roast beef and ripped a big chunk out. While it was still on his *foot*. Spit it on my carpet. Practically dislocated his own leg, hauling his foot up to his mouth like that. Damnedest thing I ever saw. So no, I wasn't hanging with him when I didn't need him."

"Do you remember the priest's name? The church? Anything?"

"No. But I can call somebody maybe. Gimme an email address."

I tore a sheet off the little pad in my wallet and wrote my email address on it and leaned forward to hand it to him. He pulled the hand out of the robe's pocket and then looked down at it and tried to hide what was in it. He jammed it behind him and took the note. If he hadn't been so tanned, he would have been blushing. He looked up at me and said, "Aaahhh, shit," and reached behind him, and took out the toenail clippers and put them back in his pocket. "Gotta take care of my feet," he said. "Even though I can barely reach them. *She's* not going to do it."

I got up. "So that's it, right? You haven't seen him, you heard he beat up a priest, you'll email me if you learn anything."

He blinked a couple of times and said, "You gotta go?" He hiked up the sleeve of his robe and looked at a big gold watch. "Not even eleven. Want some coffee? I could make some coffee."

The house was soundless. It could have hidden twenty people, but I knew, from decades of expertise in empty houses, that he and I were the only people in it. "Seven will be back soon," I said.

"No, she won't," he said. "Cheese store, my ass."

I had nothing to say, and I didn't say it.

"Lemme tell you something," he said. "You're a young guy, a nice-looking guy. Things pretty much okay with you?"

"Pretty much."

He raised both hands, palms facing me, and then let them fall onto his thighs with a *smack*. "Well, appreciate it while you got it. Just say *thanks* all the time. 'Cause you know what? It'll average out. Every day you stay lucky, every day you stay happy, your personal supply of bad luck gets bigger. It's like a rock hanging over your head, the luckier you are, the bigger and heavier it gets. Listen, things go a little wrong? You got some problems? Your teeth hurt? Say thanks, because that's whittling away at the rock hanging above you. Me, I went years and years, everything fine, lots of money, no real work, cops left me alone, I had a great time with One through Six. Happy as a pig in shit because I didn't know." He raised his hands again, palms toward the ceiling this time, elbows bent, Atlas waiting for the world to be lowered into his grasp. "Every time I found a four-leaf clover, that thing up there got bigger and colder and heavier. And then, here I am, eighty, and *bam*—" He brought his fist into his palm with a sound like a pistol shot. "—that fucker falls on me and everything turns to earwax. Just, you know, take it easy with the good times and say thanks for all the good stuff and the not-so-good stuff, too, 'cause otherwise that shit's gonna land on you like Mount Everest."

I said, "This is all Seven?"

He said, "Biggest mistake ever. It'll be night forever. Never be happy again."

"It can't be that bad."

"You think eighty sounds like fun?"

"Not particularly."

"You think it would be more fun to be eighty and married to someone who hates you, who won't divorce you, who knows so much about you that you can't divorce *her* without spending your final decade in the jug, who's going out to the *cheese store* or the *nail parlor* every day, who's just waiting for you to die?"

"No," I said. "Doesn't sound like fun."

"Come on," he said. He tried to get up and failed. Put both hands under him to try again. "Just one fucking cup of coffee."

Most of a cup of very strong coffee later, he said, "You like this house?"

"It's a swell house," I said. "I've always wanted to live on Hudson."

"I'd give it to you in a second," he said. He extended his arm and moved his coffee cup left to right in a long arc to take in all we could see of the house. "All of it, furniture and all. I'd move to whatever dump you live in—you live in a dump, compared to this?"

"That's a safe way to describe it."

"Got a girl in it?"

"It does."

"I'd take her sight unseen," he said.

I said, "She's not available."

"You know what I mean. I'd take the dump you live in, take the girl without even looking at her, give you this place, my bank account, Seven, whatever you want. Just to be your age. Shit, to be halfway between my age and your age. You could have the pool, the fucking Mercedes, everything."

"Yeah, but neither of us could deliver."

He screwed up his face in concentration. "Dog years, you know dog years?"

I drained my cup, feeling my heart accelerate to keep up with the caffeine. "I'm familiar with the concept."

"I used to think dog years was a way to, you know, figure how old a dog is in human years. But now I think dog years means how many more dogs I got years for. I figure right now, if I get a dog that dies young, I got a little less than one dog year left."

I'd seen nothing in the house that indicated that a dog was present, and like all burglars, I'm keenly attuned to dogs. "You like dogs?"

"Not much," he said. "But if I did, and if I got one, it would outlive me. Maybe I should do it, let it fight with Seven for a piece of the will."

"What's with the plastic surgery on Seven?"

"Oh," he said. "Yeah, well." He looked down into his cup. "Might have been a mistake. I wanted her to look more like One, so I paid for a little work. Doesn't look so good, does it?"

"Might just conceivably be one reason she's so pissed at you."

"The first time was good," he said, sounding defensive. "She didn't have no more chin than a goldfish, so we fixed it, and it looked okay. Then we did some more and it kind of went down-hill. It was like, you know, when you're cooking something, and you put too much of one thing in, like salt, so you figure add sugar or something, balance it out. And it just tastes worse and worse, but you keep trying. Like that."

"So," I said, unkindly, "does she look like One now?"

"You kidding me? One was beautiful."

"And Seven?"

"Seven looks like one of them wooden puppets used to sit on a voice-thrower's knee. More coffee?"

"Sure," I said, and he pulled the pot off the burner. "I'd give you a hard time myself if you did that to me."

"Look at me," he said, pouring. "It ain't like she fell for me at first sight. It was a deal. She marries the old guy, she does what he wants for a few years, he dies, she's rich forever. No more cheese stores, she can have the boys brought in, in threes and fours if she wants. We just hit kind of a bad streak with the surgery."

All I could think of to say was, "Strong coffee."

"Why drink it," he said, "if it don't get your attention?"

"Did you ever meet a burglar named Herbie Mott?"

He didn't give it a second's thought. "I don't mess with burglars. The more stuff you got, the less you like them."

"In the old days?"

"Nope." He sniffed his cup but didn't drink. "Hey, you wanna be careful with Ruben. This is a guy who eats shoes—"

"You told me."

"I did? Oh, yeah, I did." He put the cup down. "Wish we could make that trade," he said. "Listen, I didn't tell you this before, I think, but Ruben did some hits. Not for me, 'cause it's bad strategy to kill people who owe you money, but he did for other guys. I put him in touch with a couple of guys who needed somebody done."

"Who?"

He made a sound that might have been a scoff, if I'd known what a scoff sounded like.

"Thanks for the tip," I said. "You haven't asked me why I'm looking for Ruben."

"Why would I? I told you, we ain't friends."

I said, "Right."

"But here's a favor you could do me," he said. "If you find Ruben and, you know, there's anything left when you're through with him and if he's not as crazy as he used to be, tell him I said hi. Tell him he might drop around some day." He pushed the cup aside and looked around his kitchen. "Have a cup of coffee or something."

14
Wasted Love

It was past noon and I was buzzing like a bag of hornets as I backed out of Burt's driveway. I had the kind of caffeine high that replaces my normally orderly, even somewhat stately, mental processes with something I call the Flip Book, based on the old kids' toy in which the reader fans through the pages to make a little animated dog run or dance or, I don't know, lift weights. But when I get the Caffeine Flip Book, the pages speed up and slow down at random, whole groups of pages are missing or upside down or sideways, and what should be a progression turns into an uncontrollable stutter, skipping important connective material and slowing over the painfully obvious, as my little cartoon dog becomes a dwarf with a shovel over his shoulder, a rhinoceros, a spreading oil slick, finally resolving into those little airborne drops of water cartoonists sometimes use to indicate extreme anxiety. When I found myself wondering what the War on Drugs was for if Burt's coffee was legal, and all the places I had to go seemed equally urgent and equally pointless, I called a time out.

Paying very close attention to what I was doing—*check the mirror, turn the wheel, don't hit the parked car*—I pulled over to the curb, sat back, and did some deep, slow breathing as I watched dark sedans drive by with Koreans in them. Koreans *like* Hancock Park, in part because some of them can afford it, in part because it's minutes from Koreatown, and in part because *Hancock* sounds like *Hankook* or *Hanguk,* which is what South Koreans call South Korea and—when the North Koreans aren't looking—North Korea, too. So people from Hankook have moved into Hancock and have taken remarkable care of the houses they bought.

Here I was, on this side of the hill for a change. The "hill" is the long line of highly flammable dirt mounds officially known as the Santa Monica Mountains, except in Hollywood, where they're called the Hollywood Hills because Hollywood, being Hollywood, just needed its own mountains. Whatever they're called, they divide greater Los Angeles from the southern edge of the valley, and "over the hill" means, essentially, whichever side you're not on at the time you say it. Right now the Valley was over the hill, and on this side of the hill were the China Apartment Houses and my ultimate hiding place.

On March 9, 2001, a Korean plausible named Winnie Park came face to face with the rapidly changing emotional landscape that always results when someone who has given all or most of his or her money to someone else realizes that he or she has bought real estate on Mars. In this case the he or she was a he, and he was armed. Winnie was great with blue-sky—she could have sold Bibles to the Taliban—but her people-reading skills weren't as highly tuned as Handkerchief Harrison's. The sucker Winnie was working was a former LAPD cop who'd made a fortune on the take before getting ever-so-discreetly fired, and he'd entrusted most of it to Winnie on the promise of a sixty-percent profit in eight weeks. When the ten-pound penny had dropped, he'd thrown down on her, and he'd had big hardware. I'd been in the room, not entirely innocently, and since he was less angry at me than he was at Winnie, I'd succeeded in talking him down over the course of ten very sweaty minutes. A week later, he was looking for both of us, and Winnie was in Singapore, where she was promptly caught and then jailed for a con scheme. She still faced seven more rent-free years in the tropics before she could hit the street again.

Before she left, Winnie had paid me for my services by taking out a lease on Apartment 302 in the Wedgwood Apartments, once one of the art-deco glories of Los Angeles, and turned it over to me, with my name nowhere on it. Once the luxurious residence of directors, almost-stars, screenwriters, and mistresses, the Wedgwood and its sister buildings, the Lenox and the Royal Doulton, had seen property values plummet in the forties and fifties as money and the people who earned it moved west, toward Beverly Hills and Brentwood and the sea.

The buildings, called the "China" apartments because each of them was named after a manufacturer of fine china, had peeled and leaked and opened their arms to rats and roaches until they were bought, all in cash, by a somewhat mysterious syndicate of Korean businesspeople. The syndicate had restored the apartments inside the buildings to their former glorious luster, while adventurously distressing the exterior walls and the corridors. The palatial spaces inside these three paint-peeling eyesores today housed some surprisingly wealthy and almost uniformly shady occupants, mostly people with several names, who made their payments in cash and parked their nice cars in the anonymity of the giant, connecting underground garage that stretched beneath all three of them. Since the China apartments were on a corner, that meant I could pull into the garage of an apartment house on one street and drive out of the garage beneath a different apartment house on a different street entirely. Crook's paradise.

Apartment 302 was my end-of-the-world hidey-hole, the

place no one knew about, not even Rina and Kathy. Well, one person did. The world's oldest still-dangerous mobster, Irwin Dressler, had found out about it by accident—he'd had a friend, a one-time starlet named Dolores La Marr, who had occupied the entire top floor. But I was on Dressler's very small good side for the time being, and my secret felt reasonably safe.

Still, I'd driven the smoggy, eye-stinging streets, taking my habitual evasive moves and making needless stops, all with one eye on the mirror. And after I'd ridden up in the battered elevator and paced the dingy third-floor hallway, when I undid the superlative locks in the cheap-looking door (thin, brittle fiberboard over half an inch of iron), I entered the world of gracious living and Gloria Swanson, fourteen-foot ceilings and built-in bookcases, silver nitrate film and Barrymores, the age when orange blossoms dappled the trees behind the silent-film cameras while, just out of shot, high, squarish cars spooled billows of red dust from the unpaved surface of Hollywood Boulevard. A world that had a lot of injustice and inequality in it, but also a world filigreed with touches of grace that we'd tossed overboard as we sailed through time. We had, however, retained the injustice and inequality.

The Wedgwood cleaning crew, required by the building's owners, had buffed everything to a high gloss since I'd been there last, and as the door closed quietly behind me, I let out the sigh the place always seems to wring from me. The building's walls are three feet thick. The city would have to be on fire for it to get hot inside my living room.

I went into the kitchen and filled a very nice Baccarat glass with ice water and carried it into the big living room, with its art-deco windows that faced east toward downtown. The window framed only a fragment of the usual view, since the top floors of our relatively small collection of skyscrapers disappeared abruptly into a line of yellow-brown smog as hard and sharp as the stripe on a shirt. I had a three-person leather couch pulled in front of the window, with its back to the rest of the room since I was the only person who was ever in it, and I sat there and just looked at my city.

Yesterday it had had Herbie in it, and now it didn't, but it didn't look any different. It was too big to cry. What it looked like was a good idea gone wrong over time, a metropolitan version of Seven's successive plastic surgeries, created too fast and without any kind of long-term plan, nothing more forward-looking than *put something shiny here*. Seventy or eighty years later, most of the shine was gone and instead of a Paris or a Vienna, where some sort of shared fundamental aesthetic had shaped the city's growth, what we had was a crow's nest, where a thimble was next to a piece of tinfoil for no reason except that they had both briefly appealed to a crow.

It was, however, a good city for burglary. People with money didn't live in high, guarded apartment houses; they had big houses with lots of space and greenery shielding them from the presumably nosy neighbors. Once on the property, you could poke around for hours without getting spotted. Los Angeles people bought and trusted their insurance. There were several police forces, who weren't always eager to share information. Lots of money, lots of easy doors and windows, lots of small, movable, shiny things to line the rich people's crow's nests.

I used to like the city more than I did right then.

Okay, drink some water. Think about Herbie and Wattles's chain of disconnects.

First item on the Herbie list—find Ruben Ghorbani. Louie was working on it, although it was odd that he hadn't found even a scrap of information. Maybe Ghorbani *was* dead. But Louie would keep throwing out lines and tugging on them—and,

I realized, it could give Rina a chance to exercise her online investigative skills.

Hey, I texted, my thumbs way too big for the microscopic keyboard on the phone's screen, fnd out about a clergyman, dont no wht denom, beat up bad in Valley, 2-4 yrs ago. I thought for a second. Also, guy nmed edwd mott, in valley. Gd to C U last nite. We text tatters to each other. I pressed SEND, or probably SND, and envisioned my daughter hearing her father beep at her in the middle of English class or Environmental Studies class or Inter-Species Sensitivity or whatever damn class she was in. I paid her twenty bucks an hour when I needed her, and she went for it because she enjoyed it and because she was enough like me to be fond of money and to know how it worked, whereas Kathy genuinely believed that $19.99 was less than $20 and that used-car salesmen worked to give you the best possible deal. So Rina would find both that battered clergyman, denom unknown, and Herbie's unfilial son. She had billable-quality search skills.

Another thought: Ruben had worked as a hitman. Ask someone else in the business. I pulled up a number on my phone, listened to it trill a couple of times, and then Debbie Halstead said, "Nothing happening, Junior."

I checked my watch. "You still there?"

"The girl who's taking over was in Solvang when Louie reached her. Imagine carrying a gun in Solvang. Probably made of gingerbread. She's on her way. Anyway, your daughter got picked up at seven thirty this A.M. by a tall, skinny, *extremely* handsome black kid—"

"That's her boyfriend, Tyrone."

"Well, with a face like that, Tyrone is going to be dodging women right and left until he gets married, and maybe after, too."

"Oh, good. Something else to worry about."

"I don't mean to stir you up. Kid looked really *upright* even from here, maybe minister material."

I laughed, I hoped, just enough. I sort-of-almost liked Debbie, but it wouldn't do to forget that she pushed gun barrels into people's ears for a living. When I had allowed my mirth to subside appropriately, I said, "Did you ever hear of a guy named Ghorbani?"

"Iranian?"

"And Mexican. First name, Ruben. Mostly supplied muscle for loan sharks, but every now and then he did a hit, for variety, I guess."

"Got kind of weird eyes?"

"Green, I think."

"I met him, once. At a party."

"Party full of hitters? What was that like?"

"Not much dancing. Pickup lines were kind of grim. I only talked to him for a couple of minutes and then I just backed away, all the way into the next room. Didn't seem like much of anything was holding him together. You ask Wattles about him?"

My ears pricked up. "Why would I?"

"Well, Wattles hires out hits once in a while. If you're looking for a shoe salesmen, you check shoe stores, right?"

"Right. Wattles isn't available right now. He's taken himself off the board."

"Isn't that interesting? And I'll bet you know all about it. Whoops, here comes the Missus."

"Toward you?"

"No, getting into her car. Nice-looking woman. Her, Ronnie. You do okay, Junior."

I got up and went back into the kitchen. Just moving through the large, cool rooms calmed me. I said, "It's my character," and poured some more water. "Is that it? About Ghorbani? Any idea who used him?"

"Not that comes to me. You know, he was the wrong kind of person for this job. He had emotions. He looked like he might enjoy it. Those things'll get you killed. If he's not around, maybe he's dead. There she goes, the Missus, driving right past me without so much as a glance. Why do they make it so easy for us? Don't they know we're out here?"

"Not usually," I said. "Not till it's too late."

"I could ask a few of my employers whether they've heard anything about him. What do I tell them when they ask me why?"

"That he's inherited a million dollars, and—"

"You going to kill him?"

"I don't really kill people."

She didn't say anything, which was tactful of her. I wandered into the library, maybe fifteen hundred books on the dark teak shelves, my favorite chair in the world in the corner with a beautiful art deco floor lamp from the mid-twenties standing behind it. Threw a nice yellow light, just like reading lamps are supposed to, not the vein-popping, iris-shriveling, soul-shrinking glare of the ones that are saving the world this year until it becomes public information that they're full of mercury and people in China who live near the factories are developing Mad Hatter-disease delusions. I had a hundred now-illegal incandescent bulbs for my lamp, and I'd buy a hundred more in a minute if I knew where. The bulbs are jammed into my linen closet. See, the apartments in the Wedgwood had *linen closets*. And cold pantries. More lost filigree.

I said, out loud, "Why don't I just stay here?"

Debbie startled me by saying, "Stay where, Junior?"

"Where I am right now, someplace where no one would ever find me, where I could just read Proust or whoever the hell I want for the rest of my life."

"Proust?"

"He's a lot funnier than people expect, once you get past his not being able to sleep for sixty pages."

"Well, I'll put it on top of both the books in my house. So I shouldn't ask anyone about Ghorbani? I can't unless you give me some kind of reason."

I sat in the chair and looked at the books. A wall of books makes civilization seem real, despite all the evidence to the contrary. "No, forget it. If I think of anything good, I'll call you."

Debbie said, "Junior? Are you okay? You sound down."

"Me? What have I got to be down about?"

"Fine," she said crisply, backing right up. "We all chatted out here?"

"Listen," I said. "Did anybody talk to you about a job lately? A job in Malibu?"

The silence stretched out as I turned my head sideways and read the titles of eighteen or twenty novels whose authors' names began with G. I had reached Graham Green's *The Comedians* when she said, "That's over the line, Junior."

"I wasn't asking whether you were *involved* in the job. But you know, it's a pond of a certain size, that world is, and I was wondering whether you'd felt the wake. So to speak."

"Here she comes," Debbie said. "My replacement. Is Louie going to have my money?"

"Sure."

She hung up. Cell phones have robbed an entire generation of the pleasure of slamming down the receiver, but she managed somehow.

One more friend for life. I realized, in the wake of my apparent insensitivity, that Debbie had always been almost oddly nice to me. For a hit woman, I mean. I hadn't been paying attention.

I looked around the perfect room again: the polished floor, the high ceiling, the orderly ranks of books, obeying the rules of alphabetical order and letting the ideas that filled them permeate the air like the fragrance of intelligence. Herbie, I realized, had never been here.

The thought made me feel like crying. I hadn't really cried for Herbie yet, and I felt like I owed him that. But, knowing Herbie, he'd prefer it if I found whoever poured that hot water into those gloves and tattooed him or her with an acetylene torch for an hour or two before carving him like an Easter ham. So if I had all this grief-energy, Herbie would say, turn it into something useful, like fury.

. . . If you can't get closure, get even.

Right. And get moving. I stood up, went into the living room, and reached up into the chimney above the generous fireplace to retrieve the flat metal box I kept on the recessed niche I'd carved there. I found the key where I always hid it, and no, I'm not going to say where that was, and unlocked the box. Beneath my best fake ID—passport, driver's license, bankbooks, active credit cards—I pulled out some rubber-banded wads of cash. I counted out $5,000 for Louie and then thought better of it and took another $2,500. With the $5K Wattles had given me, I should be okay for a bit. Taken as a group, hired guns are reluctant to extend credit. Even the ones who might like you.

Why would *anyone* like me?

I put everything back and stood in front of the fireplace, blinking back tears and fighting down one of those dreadful moments when my life looked like one long dirty smudge on the surface of the world, just darkness and breakage behind me, thievery, dishonesty, broken promises, betrayed relationships, wasted love. Love, I mean, wasted on *me* by people who had the right to expect something in return, something I wasn't able to deliver. This vision of myself is always tiptoeing along just behind me, but most of the time it's as faint as my shadow on a cloudy day. As long as I keep moving forward, the attention that requires prevents me from looking behind me for too long, catching a glimpse of the past from the wrong—or perhaps, the right—perspective. Wasted love. Wasted love is the heart-breaker.

Moving right along, moving right along. Wattles's chain: Wattles to Janice to Handkerchief to Dippy to Monty Carlo to whom? How many *whoms* after Monty Carlo? One? Two? Three? Which one of them was the one with the gun?

Just to do something, I checked my voice mail. Nothing from Monty Carlo, whom I'd called twice at the number that Dippy gave me. I thought about seeming pushy by calling him again and decided I could risk it.

I once again got the worst robotic voice in the world, the audible equivalent of one of those old ransom notes in which all the words were snipped from different magazines and books. Not just every word, but even the occasional single syllable, was said by a different voice. On my first two listens I'd recognized, provisionally, James Earl Jones, Arnold Schwarzenegger, Hilary Clinton, George W. Bush, and Margaret Cho imitating her mother. This time, I spotted Rihanna (singing) and what sounded like a bad impression of James Franco and Anne Hathaway, done by the same person. Listening to the message unspool felt like being in a small room in which 27,000 ping pong balls were bouncing at high velocity between the walls. It said:

You may or may not have reached the right number. Do we even know whether the number we actually mean to dial is the right number when looked at from a broader perspective? Is it perhaps a good thing that we're thwarted so often when we try to exercise free will? I will either call you back or not. If you wish to pursue this further, speak after the collision.

Tires squealed and at least two cars crashed, head on, from

the sound of it. I said, "It's Junior Bender again. Do you know that three of the people who were in the chain that led Dippy Thurston to hand you that envelope have gone into hiding? If you'd like to confirm that, try to get in touch with Dippy. In the interest of self-preservation, you might want to talk to me about it. You may call me back after the cough." I coughed into the phone and disconnected.

My phone rang.

"My little thief," Ronnie said. "What time are you going to be home?"

"By *home*, you mean Birdie's?"

"Bitsy's. No, I mean, let's have dinner together. Someplace nice."

The tightness in my chest loosened. "That's a great idea. Where?"

"Why not meet me at my apartment? I'll do some laundry and pick up a few books, and we'll go to the French Marketplace."

"I'm on that side of the hill," I said, and then figuratively kicked myself. Ronnie knew nothing about the Wedgwood.

But she let it pass. "Seven sound okay?"

"Absolutely."

"Did you take the thingamabob with you?"

"The—"

"You know. The bird. I mean, the birds, remember the birds?"

I touched my front pocket, just checking. "Yeah. Yeah, I've got them."

"Well, do something about them. I'm curious. Go see the awful man."

"How do you know he won't shoot me?"

"Duck," she said. "People always duck in the movies."

"If it doesn't work, you'll be eating dinner alone."

"I did that last night," she said. "It was okay." She hung up.

I was surprised to find myself back in the kitchen. I washed the glass and dried it, then put it back into the cupboard. Everything ship-shape. Why, I asked myself, didn't I just live here?

Because eventually I'd get careless, I answered myself, and someone would find it. By going to it only after a precautionary sequence of double-backs, around-the-blocks, waiting at curbs, and other dodges, I had a chance of its being here if I ever *really* needed it. If, for example, a gorilla, or several gorillas, ever wanted to kill me.

Ducking doesn't actually work.

15

And Then You Find Out You're a Radish

Through the chain link fence, I watched eight women in their fifties and sixties, all wearing big-brimmed hats and flowing scarves against the whiskey-colored afternoon sun, looking like figures on some Impressionist's beach. They moved across an acre or so of dark earth ribbed with straight, almost military, lines of green, dawdling between the plants and stooping every now and then to pull a weed or sniff something or whisper encouragement. Beside each woman, as though tethered to her by an invisible cord, was a smaller figure, a girl of eight or ten, her face shaded by the bill of a baseball cap. The girls were narrow-shouldered and slight, their arms bare to the sun. When the women stooped, the girls stooped, too.

"That's kind of pretty," I said.

"I got no argument," Louie said. We were in the car he liked best—the black Caddy, buffed to showroom perfection—and the laughter of the little girls poured in through the open windows. They laughed quite a lot. Louie had an unlighted cigar between the fingers of his right hand. "First time Alice told me about it, about the garden, I mean, I thought, oh, yeah, it'll be like the pots. You remember the pots?"

"Vaguely. Which one is Alice?"

"Who can tell?"

"Well, what color is she wearing?"

"A regular color," Louie said. He lifted his chin in the general direction of the field. "Maybe that one. Anyway, the pots, Alice and her women's group were throwing pots, you remember, and you probably also remember that when people throw pots, it's not what it sounds like, it's not like anger management or anything, it just means they're making pots. Problem with Alice's group is that they start things and then drop them because— well, pots, for example. You can only throw so many pots before it's pretty clear that some people are a lot better at throwing pots than other people, and at that point a lot of them don't want to throw pots any more. The way Alice put it, she said she'd Achieved Her Potential in throwing pots. And I figured with this thing here, you know, the field and the little girls, some people's beans wouldn't come up, and it'd be over." He looked longingly at the cigar. It was part of his routine, a prolongation of desire before the physical act. "You bring my money?"

I'd wound up trekking back over the hill to the Valley to give him the $7,500 because I didn't think it was fair for him to be fronting money for me, and also because I had a half-formed intention of dropping in on Stinky, not far from here, and risking my life to show him the birds. I said, "Seventy-five hundred."

"Don't forget to give it to me. So I figured this would be the same as the pots, but with beans, but I was wrong, you know why?"

"The little girls," I said.

"The little girls," he said, as though I hadn't spoken. "When it was just Alice and her group, it was all about them and whatever they were doing, their pots or whatever. Now, it's about the little girls. They all just love the hell out of these little girls. It's like they get a chance to be mothers again, even if it's only two days a week. Except Alice. Alice never had a kid, so this means extra to her." He sat forward and pointed a stubby finger through the windshield. "*There*, the one with her arm in the air, that's Alice. Nice-looking woman, huh?"

"She sure is. Where do they get the girls?"

"Hell do I know?" he said. "Little Girls R Us, maybe. But they're all from places where they don't have dirt, just pavement, or if they have dirt they grow, like, tin cans on it. Old tires and used needles and things. They don't get to play in the dirt much."

"Louie," I said, "they're not playing in the dirt. They're *growing* things."

"Yeah. The little girls just wait for this all week, Alice says. Well, almost all week. They get Tuesdays and Fridays out here. It's been going on for a couple months now, and no one has dropped out. I mean, they lost a couple of the kids, they had to, jeez, I don't know, go to work or something, but they got replaced like next day and all the women are still out there, getting dirty."

"I think it's great."

"Softie," he said. "You know what those tall green ones are, third row away?"

"No idea."

"That's broccoli." He nipped off the end of his cigar, spat it out the window, and watched it fall. "I thought broccoli was a root vegetable."

"Any word about Ghorbani?"

"I got the name of someone who hired him for a hit. But I *really* had to pull on a string to get this, so you got to make sure you make a good impression."

"And the name?"

"Well, yeah. Problem is, you know her."

"She?" I said. "Trey Annunziato? I'm not sure I can make a good impression on Trey. She's not a fan."

"No, you kind of screwed her over." Trey Annunziato was the boss of one of the biggest criminal families in the Valley, although she'd been working for a year or two on taking it straight. I had let her down rather decisively the only time I'd met her.

I parked the thought of Trey for a while as Louie fished out his lighter and resisted the impulse to kiss it, and then said, "Listen, if Alice ever wants some advice about this garden, here it is. Have these kids grow radishes. Radishes could grow on the moon. They could grow in a working microwave oven, on the downslope of a volcano. You don't fertilize them, they grow. Plant them where there's no sun, they grow. Don't water them, and they cough all night until you get up and turn on the hose. They're going to win, no matter what."

"Imagine that," Louie said. "You hang on and fight for life like that for months and months, just trying to make it outta the dark and into the world, and then you find out you're a radish." He lit the cigar, and I rolled down my window.

"Are you allowed to smoke near these kids?"

"There's a fence." Louie said. "So you want me to talk to Trey for you, set it up, or you want to do it yourself?"

"I'll handle it." I added her to my mental list. Then I crossed her off my mental list. Life was too short to meet with Trey.

"Good. She gets mad at you, I'd just as soon not be involved."

"Who told you Ruben had done a hit for her?"

He shook his head. "Don't ask. It cost me eight-fifty, which I'll take out of the money you're not going to forget to give me, but you don't need the name. That's the only thing this guy knows about Ruben."

"You know, the problem with all this is that people *don't tell me names.* You won't tell me who told you about Trey, Debbie Halstead won't tell me who might have hired a hit done in the last week or so, and Wattles won't tell me who got hit on the end of the chain I'm supposed to be following."

"Ask him again."

"He's in Limpopo."

"Why you asking Debbie who mighta hired a hit? If Wattles started the chain," Louie said, "*he* ordered the hit."

"Yeah, but who paid for it? Wattles doesn't take things personally. He wouldn't arrange a hit for himself, someone he's got a motive for. He'd hire someone like him to set it up."

Louie took a big drag on the cigar and looked at it like it was the female cousin he'd been dreaming about since they were both eight. "Yeah, yeah, that's right," he said. "You know, if Wattles took off, there's something with real big teeth out there. It's not like he scares easy."

I'd been thinking the same thing, but the phrase *real big teeth* brought it into sharper relief. "Just keep the women with the guns at Kathy's house. I'll worry about myself."

"You thinking about when they're not at the house? Rina's going to school. Kathy's going shopping or whatever she does."

"This is a problem," I said, waving smoke back at him. "I can't hire a whole platoon of armed women to gather outside the house all night and then split up whenever one or both of them go anyplace. Sooner or later, Rina, or maybe Kathy, will notice."

"Lookit this," he said, pointing through the windshield with his cigar.

The women in the hats and scarves were moving between the rows of plants to the far end of the field, their charges in tow. The girls called back and forth to each other in a mixture of Spanish and urban English, and one of them took her baseball cap off and sailed it high into the air, then ran after it, skillfully jumping over the row of broccoli to catch it. Both the girls and the women laughed and applauded, and the girl took a sweeping bow with the cap in her hand, and Louie said, "Babies," in the tone a sugar addict might use for *chocolate*.

"How did you know she was going to do that?"

"I didn't. *This* is what I wanted you to see."

At the end of the field, each of the women bent and picked up a long, shallow basket with a big woven loop to pass an arm through, and handed it to the nearest girl. "This is the best part," he said. "They're going to pick stuff. They wait all day for this, just all together out here picking food right out of the soil." He sniffed, once, and his eyes were a little bright.

The girls had separated, each to a different row with a woman beside her, down on their knees, studying the plants. They only seemed to take anything off every third or fourth plant, and once in a while one of them looked up and I heard a sharp interrogative and the nearest woman would reply, and the girl would pick something or move on.

Two of the girls began to sing, and others joined in. Why can most girls sing so sweetly?

"They'll remember this their whole lives," I said.

"Probably. You want me to ask who got hit in this past week?"

"Didn't I already ask you to do that?"

"How much do I forget?"

"Okay, okay."

"So I'll do it," he said. "And you might want to think about doubling up on Rina and Kathy," he said. "You'd only need two more girls. One could wait near the house with the other one on the next block. When Rina goes out, the one watching the house follows her to school and the other one pulls into the spot the first one just left and waits for Kathy."

"Make it so," I said sonorously.

Louie said, "I fucking hate *Star Trek*."

"Yup," I said, "that's a problem, all right."

The sun was at a pretty good slant now, and the women and girls were lined in gold as they moved between the plants. The light picked out the colors of the women's scarves and made them glow like scraps of sunset. "What's this field doing here in the middle of the Valley?"

"It's part of the junior high back there. It'll be a couple of buildings in a year or so."

"Too bad." We watched the harvesting girls and women for a minute or two, and I said, "Louie. Why are you here?"

"What? Whaddya mean?" He sounded defensive. "We been looking at this for—"

"I mean, why are you here in your car? In *this* car? Alice can drive, Alice has a car."

"Yeah, but, come on, look at her, she's squirming around in the dirt. She gets all muddy and, and crappy. She doesn't want to track it into her car."

I said, enjoying myself for the first time that day, "So you drive her here and wait for her and let her get *your* car all dirty, and—"

"It's a *guy's* car," Louie snapped. "Guys don't care about things like that."

"No," I said. "I forgot. You don't care about your cars. And Alice is the only one who wishes you'd had kids. You don't care at—"

"Awww, come on," Louie said, sounding like he'd been kicked in the stomach. "Why're you busting my balls? You're a father. You know that every grownup's gotta do something to make things better for some kid. If you don't have kids, then you go get some other kids and do it for them, 'cause otherwise, what're adults for? I mean, we're useless right?" He pointed with the cigar again, so vehemently it looked like he was going to stub it out on the inside of the windshield. "Just *look* at that."

I looked at Louie instead, and the affection I felt for him brought Herbie back again, yanking the ground from beneath my feet and leaving me suspended over something dark and deep and starless. I said, "Do you ever regret the way we live?"

He drew on his cigar. "Whaddya mean, regret?"

"Lying all the time, keeping so many secrets. Being in the game. Being, you know, a crook."

"Is this a joke?" The words came out in a cartoon dialogue balloon of smoke. "You're kidding me, right? *Lookit* that," he said, nodding at the field. "Gorgeous afternoon—little smog but that's okay, it's a regular calendar shot—a bunch of beautiful women and girls just over there, playing farmer while we sit here looking at them, and ninety-five percent of the people within two hundred miles of here are stuck someplace they don't want to be, surrounded by people they don't want to be with, doing something they don't want to do. Selling their lives an hour at a time and getting shortchanged on payday. One day at a time, day after day after fucking day, until they're too old to do anything, and then what they get is poverty and doctors' bills and worse places to live in and their backs hurt and bad eyes."

I looked back at the field and said, "I'll take that as a no."

16

Hi, Girlfriend

"I am either in a meditative state or helping someone penetrate the veil," Handkerchief said. "But your problem is as important to me as it is to you. Please leave a number, and I'll be with you as soon as we're on the same plane of existence. And don't forget, if you're tight for time, our telephone readings are quick and relatively inexpensive. Or, in an emergency, write your question on a piece of paper and send it to me mentally, and then burn it. When the answer arrives in your mind, a check for thirty-five dollars will clear the karmic imbalance. The All-Seeing Eye is as close as your ear." There was a beep, and I disconnected.

The school where Louie and I had met was only a few miles from the All-Seeing Eye, and I had about ninety minutes before I was supposed to meet Ronnie in West Hollywood, so I tabled the idea of seeing Stinky about the birds and pointed the car in Handkerchief's direction. I was feeling guilty that I hadn't been more emphatic about the precariousness of being a part of Wattles's latest chain.

I'd dialed Hankie, as Dippy had called him, the moment I wheeled out of the parking lot and this was my second try, so the obvious conclusion was that he was scanning someone's palm or putting her in touch with the Egyptian princess she'd been back in the days of King Tut. Or maybe, I thought a bit self-critically, just demonstrating the kind of sensitivity and perception he'd shown me.

But way down deep inside, I didn't think he was. Perhaps it was something I'd picked up from him, a kind of spiritual contact high, but I didn't like it at all. I was getting a kind of formless dark thing, a psychic ink spot as amorphous and as potentially toxic as an amoeba, that had crowded into the space between my lungs, and it was changing shape and weight as I drove.

I tried to push it away with good, old-fashioned cynicism, since I definitely didn't believe in any of it, but it sat there, sloshing around unevenly and uncomfortably, and just when I thought I'd finally dismissed it I found myself shouting and pounding my steering wheel and trying not to accelerate straight through the driver in front of me, who waited the duration of a long red light before flicking on his turn indicator. The fact that I didn't believe in woo-woo of any kind didn't mean I could fight the conviction—carried through the air like a djinn on some evil wind from the *Arabian Nights* to take up residence in my chest—that something had gone badly wrong for Handkerchief Harrison.

It was close to six, and traffic was clotting in all directions by the time I got to Ventura and made the right that would take me to Handkerchief's awful little mall. As it was, I got there in time to see the red lights flashing, the police cars and the yellow tape and the waiting ambulance. The blue cluster of cops drinking coffee in a formal-looking semicircle around the wide-open door. I pulled past all of it, past the All-Seeing Eye and the first Thai restaurant and Dixie's Duds, swearing silently at myself. In the empty Thai restaurant at the rear of the mall, I ordered a Thai iced coffee at a table by the window, and before I could take the first sip they wheeled out the gurney with the body on it, oddly collapsed and diminished beneath the blanket that draped it from head to foot.

I called Louie, and the instant he answered I said, "Put the two new girls on Kathy and Rina right now," and he was saying, "But wait a—" and then the phone buzzed for a call waiting, and the display said RONNIE, and I hung up on Louie and answered it, and she said, "Junior, someone is following me," and then the phone buzzed again and I put Ronnie on hold because the display said RINA, and when I answered it, she said, "Daddy, somebody's following me."

To Rina, I said, "Where are you? Are there cars around? People?"

"We're on Reseda Boulevard, heading toward home."

"You and Tyrone?"

"*Daddy*, he got his learner's permit."

"*Are you with Tyrone?*"

"Yeah, sure."

"Okay, keep driving. Hold on a second." I put her on hold. "Ronnie, where are you?"

"On Fountain, in Hollywood."

"Keep driving. Stay on busy streets. I'll be right back to you." Switching lines, I said, "Rina?"

"I'm here."

"How far back is the car?"

"Two cars. But it's been with us for a while. Tyrone's not supposed to drive without somebody with him, somebody with a license? so he's always checking the mirror for cops."

"Still back there," I heard Tyrone say.

"Is there a police station anywhere near?"

"A police station? Tyrone's on a *learner's* permit."

"Look, stay calm. Look for a McDonald's, this time of night they'll be jammed. Go in, order something, and stay there, inside, under the nice fluorescent lights. Do you know where there's—?"

"One coming up," she said.

"Well get your asses inside. See what the car does when you make the turn, check what make and color it is, and see if you can get the beginning of the license plate. And *don't leave that restaurant* until I'm there, got it?"

"Okay." She sounded younger than usual. Fear will do that, strip right away all our imitation of maturity and misplaced certainty that the world is actually safe.

"Ronnie," I said, "where are you now, and where's the other car?"

"We're just cruising down Fountain. Fairfax is coming up. He's a couple, three cars back."

"Turn south. Go down to Cantor's Delicatessen and pull into the parking lot. Then go inside and stay there until I call you back."

"Who do you think it is?"

"Someone who might want to get at me."

"You, you, you," she said. "Everything's about you." She laughed, but it didn't have much support.

"I'll call you right back."

I hung up and sat motionless until, in my mind's eye, they were all in their respective restaurants. Then I called Louie back.

"I already did it," he said, before I could even say hello. "I put the second girl on them, before I even asked you."

"Well, thank you. Call and see whether one of them is following Rina right now."

"I just did, and she is. Says Rina's with this great-looking black kid, and—"

My lungs practically collapsed, and all the breath I hadn't known I was holding rushed out of me. "Good, good, good. Who is it?"

"Debbie."

"I thought she was mad at me."

"Junior, she *kills* people. They don't get mad the same way we do. They save it up until they need it. It's like an anger piggy bank."

"Well, tell her to stay with them. Rina and Tyrone are in McDonald's. In fact, tell her if she's hungry to go in and say hi, have a burger with them."

"Sure, whatever you say. Your daughter and Debbie, having a burger."

"Thanks again, Louie. Thanks a lot."

I did the call-shuffle again and said, "Rina, the person who's following you is okay."

"What do you mean he's okay?"

"I mean, first, he's a she, and second, she's there because I sort of asked her to be. She may be coming in and sitting with you—really, really cute-looking woman in her mid-twenties. Her name is Debbie Halstead."

"Is she nice?"

How was I supposed to answer that question? "She's on your side."

"On my side against what? Am I in a fight of some kind? What's the other side?" She covered the phone and said something to Tyrone, and she came back, she said, "Is this something that's going to piss Mom off?"

"I'll tell you in an hour or so. At the house. Just eat and go home. Let Debbie follow you home." I hung up and dialed Louie. "I need to hire you as a driver. Somebody's following Ronnie, and I've got her sitting at a table in Cantor's waiting for someone to come and get her out of there."

"And you're going to *pay* me for this."

"That's what I just—"

"Fuck you, I'm your friend, remember? Where am I supposed to take her?"

"To Kathy's place."

"Can I go in with her?" he asked.

"Why would you want to?"

"I don't know. I just never seen anyone commit suicide before."

Handkerchief had been a plausible, and most crooks—as I think I already said—don't really like plausibles. Burglars, car thieves, even hitters—whatever their dealings with the straight world, they tell the truth to one another, probably about as often as orthodontists and cosmeticians and insurance actuaries do. But plausibles never tell the truth, at least not on purpose. Their skill in creating a successful con is based not only on assuming a plausible identity, with a persuasive and harmless-sounding agenda, but also *believing* it, and Handkerchief believed it all the way to his bones. I once heard it said about English people that if you woke them up in the middle of the night, they'd talk like the rest of us. But I knew a burglar who'd surprised Handkerchief, then in his tweedy Antony Mosely-Fenwick role, in a dark and supposedly empty house in the middle of the night, and the burglar said that Handkerchief, terrified or not, sounded like Winston Churchill.

So we didn't like them much, we relatively truthful crooks. They always make me think of how Superman—who, despite all the super-powers and that little curl on his forehead, must have had a sad and freakish inner life as a teenager, with no one to confide in, no one to jump tall buildings at a single bound with—how Superman, as I was saying, felt the first time he came up against the Bizarro Superman. I'd give odds that his immediate thought, when he saw that fractured, crudely assembled, bad-geometry reflection of himself, was, "That's who I *really* am." A lot of us—we *relatively* truthful crooks who lie all the time to the cops, to the straight world, and to the people we love—we secretly feel the same way about plausibles. They're a bad-day reflection of ourselves, and it makes us uncomfortable. They provide yet another unflattering angle, as if we needed one, on Herbie's Game.

I was feeling deeply ambivalent about Herbie's Game. Despite Louie's pep talk, those of us who chose Herbie's Game faced a lifetime of wearing a mask, of lying, of making—sooner or later—the kind of decision that had cost me my wife and daughter. I probably hadn't even figured out yet all the things that choosing Herbie's Game had cost me.

So maybe the main reason we relatively honest crooks looked down on plausibles was simply that we needed to look down on *someone* in order to feel better about ourselves. Had Handkerchief, with the empathy that made him a good plausible and an effective fortune-teller—the empathy that had shown him, in my eyes, the loss of a father-figure—known how I and the other relatively honest crooks felt about him? If so, he'd been nicer, more gracious, about it than I would have been, if I'd been in his empathic, intuitive shoes.

I felt like I could devote a little time to Handkerchief right then, I felt like I needed to. There was nothing I could do to deal with the emergency of the moment except wait for Rina to get home and Louie to get to Ronnie, so I sat and watched the ice melt in my coffee while I gave ten silent minutes to the passing of Handkerchief Harrison. There'd been something brave and a little sad in the way he'd flaunted those awful, cheesy handkerchiefs.

Maybe heaven for plausibles is a place where they're always believed, where the purplest lies, the most desperate flights of fancy, land in the other person's ears like the Testament they feel closest to. Or maybe heaven for plausibles is a place where there's never a reason to tell a lie at all, where their *bona fides,* the people they actually are, are always good enough for everything. Where you could pass the brightest of lights straight through them, and it wouldn't pick out a single area of darkness, not a shadow anywhere.

And it struck me that, all of a sudden, I was watching people die.

What they do in an ambulance after they load the meat into it is a mystery to me, but Handkerchief's last ride was still sitting there with him in it when my phone rang and Kathy said, "Would you like to explain all this, Junior?"

It took her a full minute to answer the door, and I had a vision of her stopping to choose and then reject something to throw at me. She was wearing the reserved expression that she usually offered me, but a *lot* more rigid, and her hair, normally abjectly under her control, had gone kind of fly-away so that two long, slightly curling wisps hung over her forehead. Not a good sign.

"You have someone following my daughter," she said, without actually inviting me in.

"Our daughter," I said.

A totally strange woman just ushered her and Tyrone through my own front door—and don't you *dare* say 'our' front door—as though I had no say whatsoever in whether she could come in."

"Speaking of which—" I tried to move forward.

She stepped to the side to block my way. "Do you remember what—whoever it was—said? That the only people who feel at home everywhere are kings and whores?"

"I do, and she's neither. I'm coming in."

"What is she? Who is she?"

"She's a professional trick shooter," I said. "In a lot of demand, too. Listen, as bad as the last twenty minutes have been for you, that's the way the whole day has been for me, so why not just let me come in?"

She blew one of the wayward wisps from her forehead and gave the door a little lick with the side of her foot. "As though you have nothing to do with how bad your day has been, as though that bad day was just floating around, looking for someone to land on, and it picked poor blameless, spotless you."

I said, "Do you know this house has been under guard since last night? Do you want to know *why* I was having Rina followed?"

She lowered her head to look up at me, and the wisp fell back where it wanted to go. "What do you mean, under guard?"

"You've driven past them several times."

"I don't believe it. And how could I possibly know why you were having Rina followed?"

"Well, if you don't let me in, I'm not going to tell you."

"Will it frighten Rina?'

I gave it a moment's thought. "I think it's more likely to frighten you."

She stood aside. "Come in, but keep your voice down."

"Where is she?"

"In her room with Tyrone and—that woman."

"Debbie. Her name is—"

"I don't care what her name is. In the living room." She held the door for me and then, when I was through it, shoved it shut and stayed on my right as I moved so I couldn't make the turn up the hallway to Rina's room. As we passed the hall, I heard Rina and Tyrone laughing.

"She sounds okay."

"She's a *child*, Junior. It's all a movie to her."

I went to the couch and sat down for the second time in two nights. Kathy sat in her special chair and said, "I'm waiting."

"And I'm thinking. Did you know she was driving with Tyrone, and he's only got a learner's permit?"

"Are you seriously suggesting that her riding around with Tyrone with his permit is anything *like* as dangerous as whatever you've gotten her—us—into, with guards on the house and people following her to protect her?"

"See?" I said, "Those things are, as you said, to protect her, while letting her drive around with Tyrone—"

"Won't fly, Junior." She was picking at a button on the front of her blouse, and she had no idea she was doing it. "All this stuff, does it have to do with the death of your—your friend yesterday?"

I said, "Maybe. I can't be sure yet. Let me tell it to you my way." And she did let me, so I was able to present it all, every bit of it, *my* way: the robbery in Wattles's office, the murder of Herbie, the possible problems with Wattles's chain, the disappearance of Wattles and Janice, and the killing of Handkerchief. She listened patiently while I told it all my way, relating everything to everything else and carefully putting all in proportion, and it sounded just bloody awful. When I was finished, I said, "Maybe I should have let you ask me questions, the way you wanted to."

She nodded and turned away from, me, apparently studying the familiar objects on the mantel above the fireplace they never used. She was still picking at the button. When she'd finished her inventory of the mantel, she nodded again slowly and said, "And I know, deep in your heart, that you don't think you're to blame for any of this." She leaned back in the chair, her head back and her chin lifted, and gave me the down-the-nose gaze that had always meant that further argument was useless. "You had nothing to do with what happened to Herbie, nothing to do with that chain or whatever you called it. But ask yourself this, Junior. If you weren't a crook, would it have reached this house? Would we need guards? Would you be worrying about our daughter's safety?"

I said, "No."

"Do I get to hear any of this?" Rina said from the entry hall. Debbie was next to her, looking cute and chipper and as harmless as a hamster, while Tyrone, who had grown an inch in the month since I saw him, hung back, knowing he was in for it no matter what happened.

"I need to think about that," Kathy said, and the doorbell rang, and a lot of things happened in a very short time. Rina disappeared to the right, going to answer the door; I jumped to my feet, slapping at the center of my back, where my gun wasn't, since I'd left it in the car; out of sight, I heard Rina let out a loud gasp; Tyrone's eyes widened and his mouth dropped open, Kathy, terrified at the sound of the gasp, said, "*Rina;*" and Debbie grinned and said, "Hi, girlfriend."

And Ronnie came into the room.

17

Temporal Amber

It was fully dark outside. The day—which had seemed endless, as though maliciously preserved in some sort of temporal amber—had moved on at last, finally towing its problems to a different slice of the globe. The glass back wall of the dining room was a shining, vertical sheet of reflective black, the pool and the cabaña and Kathy's fig trees still there, presumably, but needing to be taken on faith, which was a quality I was very short on at the moment.

But I knew they were back there, just as surely as I knew that there was enough ill will in my former living room to pickle a saint's heart.

The seating chart was improbable enough to make me wish I were dreaming. Kathy was in her chair across the room, and the matching chair to her left, the one I once sat in every night, was empty, as I suspected it had been for some time except for Kathy's occasional home try-out for my potential replacement. The chair had a disconsolate air to it, like the horse in the stable no one ever saddled. I was on the far left end of the crowded couch, facing Kathy at what didn't quite feel like a safe remove. Beside me was Rina; on the other side of Rina was Tyrone, his knees jackknifed in front of him—the kid really *was* getting tall; and jammed into the end of the couch, between Tyrone and the arm, was Debbie, who had apparently used the time in Rina's room to make friends. Debbie was good at making friends. She was a terrible shot, so it was an important part of her job description.

Sitting cross-legged on the floor a discreet eight or ten inches in front of me, having chosen to sit on the floor as though she hoped the bullets would whistle over her head, was Ronnie. Claiming two wooden chairs hauled in from the dining room were Louie and a person I'd never met before, a young, long-haired Asian woman who had based her personal style on the sixties, and who obviously wasn't one to do things halfway, since she called herself Eaglet. She'd been the one sitting outside the house all afternoon, the one who'd been up in Solvang.

Seen from above by a neutral party, if such a thing existed, it would have looked like the five seated on and in front of the couch versus one in the chair, the one being Kathy, with two fence-sitters in the middle, Louie and Eaglet.

But Kathy didn't know what it was to be outnumbered. As far as she was concerned, she was wrapped in the cloak of righteousness, and, what's more, she had me dead to rights. With an audience, no less.

She'd run down the situation as I'd related it, but with a definite spin that positioned me—with some justice—as the heedless heavy, the one who had opened the door to the dark side and politely held it open to admit the orcs and gremlins who were now stalking an innocent family through the leafy streets of suburbia.

Ronnie said, "I don't think that's quite accurate."

Eaglet tugged on the one of the feathers woven into her hair and said, "We're taking care of them."

Debbie contributed, "We've got your backs."

Louie said, "These are some tough girls."

Rina said, "*Mom*," turning it into two aggrieved syllables.

Tyrone waited, long-fingered hands spread on his knees, for someone to bring up his learner's permit.

Kathy said, "*Thank* you. It's so reassuring to know that thanks to two Annie Oakleys and you," she said to Louie, "whatever you are, and my husband's paramour there, that my daughter and I are safe."

"You should *know*," Ronnie said. I squeezed her shoulder to shut her up, but she shrugged it right off. "You should know he'd never intentionally do anything to put you and Rina in danger."

"We're not focusing on *intent*," Kathy said, showing many of her teeth. "Mrs. O'Leary's cow didn't mean to burn down Chicago, either. Junior just drags this kind of thing behind him."

Rina said, "That's not fair," and Eaglet said, "Who's Annie Oakley?"

"You," Kathy said to Eaglet, "go clean your gun or something. Work on a frame of reference. And *you*," she said to Rina, "you and I will talk when all these—interesting people are gone. You *and* Tyrone."

Ronnie uncrossed her legs, got her feet under her, and said, "I'm not his paramour. I'm the person who takes care of him now, since you've decided that your marriage vows don't apply."

Kathy said, "*Hey*, you. You've got no idea, and no right, to—"

"You knew who he was when you *married* him. I mean, has he misled me about this? Did you think he was studying for the ministry?" She waited, but not long enough for Kathy to formulate a reply. "No? Then you knew he was a crook? Am I mistaken about this? And you figured he'd wear the ring around, what, his neck? And once there was a kid, you'd have him by the—"

Kathy was up. "Out," she said. "Out right now. Go back across the tracks to wherever you—"

But Ronnie was just getting warm. "Once you had him glued down, or pinned to the display case or whatever—"

"Whoooo," Eaglet said, raising a fist in the first Black Panther salute in decades.

"—you figured you could turn him into a substitute teacher or a male nurse, as though you'd promised—"

"That's it, honey," Kathy said, walking toward the kitchen.

"—promised to take in holy matrimony not *this* man, but whatever man you could turn him into. Was that the idea?"

"When I come back out," Kathy called, "I want all of you gone. That means you, too, Tyrone."

No one looked at anyone. The only sound was Ronnie's breathing.

"Golly," Debbie said. "That went well."

Rina said to me, "She's scared. She gets like this when you scare her."

I looked at Rina, seeing in her still-half-formed face the ghost of Kathy as a teenager. I sighed and got up. "I'll go talk to her."

"Won't do any good," Rina said, and Tyrone said, "You *listen* to her."

"They're both right," Ronnie said, getting the rest of the way up and following Kathy in the direction of the kitchen.

I said, "Hold it."

"What's she going to do?" Ronnie said. "Throw me out? She's already thrown me out."

"But—but what can you say to her?"

She put her hand on top of my head and pushed me back down. I hadn't even realized I was getting up. "I can remind her why we both chose you and stayed with you, for years and years, in her case. Maybe I can make friends with her."

"Let Ronnie go," Rina said.

"Like I get a vote," I said.

Ronnie said, "If I need you, I'll break a window," and followed in Kathy's tracks.

I called after her, "The door right across the hall from the kitchen." A door slammed. "That one," I said.

We lapsed into the kind of silence that can end a party in its first ten minutes. It was broken by Debbie, ever the people-pleaser, saying to Rina, "Look at you, look how lucky you are. You got the best from both parents in your face. Your mom is beautiful, and you got her eyes and that tremendous mouth, and Junior passed along his cheekbones, which are too good for a man, anyway."

"Thanks," Rina said, rubbing her right cheek. "I'll bet you look like your mom."

"Do I ever," Debbie said. "Caused problems with her, too." She broke off and fanned herself as though the room had suddenly become warm. "But you don't need to know about that."

Rina bent forward to look at her around Tyrone, who leaned back. "Sure, I do."

"Well, she drank a little. Not true, not true, she drank all the time. When I was about fourteen, she started looking at me and then looking in the mirror." Debbie glanced around the room. "Feels like group therapy. So then she'd beat me up. She said it was like the worst part of being a movie star, without any of the good things. They've always got their young faces following them, no matter how terrible they look now, and she had me, just tagging around behind her with my face on."

Eaglet said, "That's, like, tragic," and then her gun fell out from beneath the only tie-dyed cape I'd seen outside the movie *Woodstock* and hit the carpet with a thump. She said, "Far out," and picked it up, doing an automatic and very professional quick-sight down the barrel and blowing some dust off it before putting it back.

"Anybody here," Tyrone said, "*not* carrying?"

"I'm not," I said.

"I saw that," Tyrone said with a quick smile. "You slapping at your back like that."

"Luckily for you," I said, "we've got the girls."

Louie said, "I guess we could do some business, for a minute, since the kids here know what's happening. You're gonna need four more."

"I figured."

Rina said, "Four?"

"Two at a time, eight hour shifts, three shifts a day," Louie said. "I'm Louie, by the way."

"Louie the *Lost*?" Rina said enthusiastically. "Daddy talks about you all the time."

"Yeah?" Louie said. "I know enough about you, I should be your godfather."

"So what's the deal?" Tyrone said. "You got a line in, uhh, gun girls? You're like an agent?"

"That's the problem," Louie said. "I can't find that many girls."

Debbie said, "Women."

Louie said, "Yeah."

"Why women?" Rina asked.

"We thought it might go down better with the neighbors," Louie said. "Better than some hard-timer in black leather."

I held up a hand and listened. Kathy's voice was raised, but well south of the red zone.

Rina said, "I can't believe they're both still in there."

"So," Louie said, reclaiming the floor. "Whaddya think? Three girls—" He caught Debbie's eye and said, "and three boys. Sound okay?"

"I'll get some more money tomorrow," I said.

Tyrone said, "What's the hourly rate?"

Debbie said to Rina, as though no one had broken in on her original train of thought, "And you've got a gorgeous boyfriend, too."

Tyrone said, "Whoa."

"He is, isn't he?" Rina said.

"I am," Tyrone said. "And getting better."

"Rina," I said. "You're not driving with Tyrone any more unless there's a licensed driver in the car. Tyrone, if she does, I'm going to assume it's because you asked her to or because you said yes when she asked if she could, and no matter how gorgeous you are, I'll have someone steal whatever car you're driving and total it, and I know dozens of people who could do that by the time you've gotten from the curb to your front door. Do we need to talk about this any further?"

"No," Tyrone said. "That's my brother's car."

"And, Rina, you're going to be careful. Don't go places you don't need to until this is over. And don't lose your follower."

"I'm not going to follow her," Debbie said, "I'm going to drive her."

Eaglet said, "I could drive Tyrone."

"Not on my nickel. Rina, did you have time to check out that clergyman who got beaten up?"

"Got it all," she said. She stood up. "I want to know what's going on in there."

"I do, too," I said. "But what's the deal with the clergyman?"

"Achilles Angelis," Rina read off the palm of her left hand.

"*Achilles*?" I said.

"Angeles?" Debbie said. "Like the city?"

"With an I-S at the end," Rina said. "Greek, I guess. First Valley Church of the Eternal Redeemer."

"Where?"

"Sylmar, sort of. He got banged up pretty badly." She started to say something else and was interrupted by a peal of laughter from the bedroom. It was solo at first, but it quickly branched into harmony.

"'Eternal Redeemer' is a nice touch, isn't it?" Rina said, visibly relaxing. "'Temporary Redeemer' just raises a bunch of new questions."

The laughter started up again.

"Guess who they talking about," Tyrone said.

"I'm just glad they're not throwing things," I said. "I'd hate to have to protect one of them."

Rina gave me both eyes, double-barrel, and said, "Which one would you protect?"

I said, "Exactly."

18
Like Fighting With a Tulip

Ronnie and Louie were certain that no one had followed them from Cantor's, so Debbie drove Ronnie back to Fairfax to get her car and grab a couple of pastramis on rye since neither Ronnie nor I had eaten dinner.

Louie followed me down the hill from Kathy's house, both of us looking for a tag, leaving Eaglet chatting in sixties slang with Tyrone and Rina while Kathy did the suburban-mom thing and made dinner.

"Nobody," Louie said on the phone.

"Thanks. Say hi to Alice for me."

"Wanna come on Friday and watch the kids again?"

"Maybe."

"You gonna talk to Trey?"

"If I have to. Maybe I won't need to. Maybe the Reverend Achilles Angelis—"

"Guy got pounded," Louie said. "Him and Ghorbani, they're probably not playing golf on weekends."

Lights came on in a car parked a block ahead of me. "I'll do anything before I talk to Trey."

"Yeah. Well, be careful. You see that car?"

"Yeah, but I'll just turn whichever way he doesn't when we get to the Boulevard."

Louie disconnected, and the car in front of me turned left as I turned right onto Ventura, feeling like I'd spent half my life running shady errands on this ugly street. The only ray of sunshine I could locate in the entire day was that I'd gotten out of Kathy's house with all my skin. It wouldn't have been entirely unreasonable for her to have been displeased with the ex-husband who endangered both her and her daughter, hauled two contract killers into her living room, and introduced her to his girlfriend, all on the same night.

I'd underestimated both her and Ronnie. They'd come out of the back bedroom cheerful and chatting, and neither of them had even glanced at me until the evening broke up half an hour later, and there was no way to avoid polite goodbyes. Kathy even kissed me on the cheek, although she also snapped her teeth together, hard, an inch from my ear.

So I could probably be forgiven for feeling blithe enough to believe my lucky streak would hold I could just drop in on Stinky, despite our recent problems. If I'd been thinking clearly, I would have remembered what Burt the Gut told me about that big rock.

Ting Ting opened the door and gave me a wide, white, spontaneous Filipino smile. He'd lasted longer with Stinky than any of the other boys he'd plucked from the folk dance troupes he kept bringing over from the Philippines. They'd been together a year and a half now, but apparently Ting Ting didn't automatically share Stinky's grudges, which made me happy because I'd always liked him.

He put a finger to his lips, leaned forward, and said, *sotto voce,* "One minute, I think. Let me see if Mr. Stinky still want to kill you."

"Good idea."

He patted the air two-handed, meaning, *stay where you*

are, smiled at me again, and trusting me to stay put, left the door wide open. I watched a waist smaller than Ronnie's shimmer down the hall, wrapped in some sort of shiny fabric that might have been ripped from an old ABBA costume. There were two new and exquisite small drawings on the hallway wall, certainly seventeenth-century, done in silverpoint, a medium used to create miracles on parchment and paper by Van Eyck, Durer, Holbein, and Rembrandt. These weren't by a brand-name artist I could identify, but they were achingly beautiful, with the fine, fluid, precise lines made possible by a master drawing a silver wire over parchment that had been coated by a gesso. The gesso was a sort of liquid glue made from rabbit tendons, plus some whitening agent, such as chalk. After the medium dried, the silver wire made a gray line over it, but the gray eventually turned a gorgeous pale brown, the same beautiful brown you see in the splotches on a foxed book. It's a much warmer effect than gray or black; I think it's the reason some people get sentimental about sepia.

Unfortunately for me, the technique was more or less vanquished in the seventeenth century by the sudden availability of high-quality graphite, which meant that drawing pens made of fine silver wire were essentially replaced by the lead pencil, one of thousands of developments that has, in my view, made the world coarser and more prosaic every year since the Renaissance sputtered to an end. Yet more lost filigree.

I practically had my nose pressed against the surface of the smaller drawing, a middle-class matron whose every flyaway hair had been drawn individually, when Ting Ting was suddenly beside me. I hadn't heard him at all, and I hear very, very well.

"Very pretty, yes?" he said.

"Gorgeous. I could stand here for hours."

"Mr. Stinky, he see you now."

"Does he have a gun?"

"Ho," Ting Ting said, poking me in the ribs. "Mr. Stinky, he never stay mad. He has very good heart."

If he did, I thought, I'd like to know who stole it for him. But I poked Ting Ting back, getting a surprisingly hearty giggle, and he led me down the hallway.

Stinky's nickname comes from the fact that he's one of the heirs of the family who invented the perfume strip, but he turned his back on a trust fund and three quarters of an Ivy League education to become an extremely discerning fence. In part because he'd grown up surrounded by beautiful things, he has an even better nose than I do, and dealing in them illegally brought through his big house an unending parade of the best of civilization. Isn't that what art, even stolen art, is? The best we produce, minus the crap we create?

But Stinky's nose was better than mine only if we mean "nose" metaphorically, as in the sense of being able to sniff out things of real value. Stinky's *physical* nose had been sanded and shaved by a procession of plastic surgeons who had abetted Stinky in his lifelong desire to look like he was wearing a stocking mask even when he wasn't. He'd had his ears pinned back, his hairline weeded into a widow's peak, his cheekbones pared down, his skin chemically peeled and plumped. Burt's wife Seven looked as though things chosen at random in a dark room had been thrown at her face: chin, cheekbones, a jawline. Stinky's aerodynamic sleekness was the product of a decade of surgical subtraction, and what was left was the face kids put on their drawings of aliens: noseless, almond-eyed, sharp-chinned, soul-free. Maybe *soul-free* was what he'd been working toward all along.

The living room was an unpleasant surprise: the fine Early American and nineteenth-century English furniture from my previous visits was gone, and now the long, narrow room looked like it had been stolen intact from someplace deep in the heart of Texas: all heavy Western wood, massive and hand-worked, with blackened, riveted steel plates holding it together, plus more leather than a slaughterhouse, most of it rough and distressed. One couch offered that little-seen and, to me, quite alarming effect of still having its covering of short fur, in a pinto pattern. It looked like it might moo at me. As I entered, Stinky launched himself to his feet from behind the one thing in the room I might have slowed down to look at, an ornate French cylinder desk from the eighteenth century, possibly inspired (as many of them were) by the most famous cylinder desk of all, the *Bureau du Roi* made for Louis XV's office in Versailles.

"Just totally over the top, uncalled for, completely unforgivable," Stinky said, pushing his bulk around the desk. "Immature, short-sighted, inexcusable, especially between chums. *Do* forgive me." He had both hands extended, palms up, Papal style, as though I was supposed to grasp them, and he was doing British Stinky, an accent he refreshed daily with scones. Not as convincing as Handkerchief's had been.

"Forgive you what?" I said, ignoring the hands. "You mean the attempt on my life?" I laughed lightly, feeling like I was in a scene by Noël Coward. "Don't give it a thought."

"Water under the bridge," Stinky said, moving one hand to rest it over the place where his heart might or might not have been.

"The snows of yesteryear," I said.

"What's past is past," Stinky said.

"Gone with the wind," I said. "Written on water."

"Well," he said, and we stood there, breathing at each other. Now that he knew he wasn't going to get shot he remembered his manners and said, "Please, please. Sit."

"Where?" I said, looking at the couches. "I'm a vegetarian."

"Isn't it ghastly?" he said, surveying the room. "Some nights when I can't sleep I come in here and brand things."

"Nice desk, though."

"It is, isn't it? I think it's important to have at least one thing that sings of the past. Not our *personal* past," he added hastily. "But you know, the beeswax and tapestry and yellow-candle past. The past of empire, monarchy, the only really *functional* forms of government."

"How old would you say it is?"

He gave it an appraiser's scrutiny and then reached out and ran a hand over the satiny cylinder of wood, which he had drawn shut before he got up so I couldn't see what he'd been working on. The cylinder desk is the direct ancestor of the rolltop, but instead of interlocking flexible slats, the cylinder desk has a single curved piece of wood that slides up into the back of the desk to reveal the workspace. This one had been inlaid with wood of various colors, probably ash, ebony, boxwood, and sycamore, to create a formal-looking floral arrangement in the center of the curve.

"Seventeen-seventies, eighties, I'd think," he said dreamily. He looked like he wanted to lean over and sniff it.

"Definitely raises the tone of the room."

"It's the first colonizer," Stinky said. He tore his eyes from the desk and gazed unappreciatively at the other things in the room. "In a month or so, it will be the center of a chamber modeled on the better apartments in Versailles."

"What'll you do with the rest of this stuff?"

"Send it to a shoemaker, I suppose. Must be enough

leather to make boots for a platoon. I can't *imagine* what I was thinking."

"I thought maybe you'd have Ting Ting wearing chaps."

Stinky's eyebrows rose without wrinkling his forehead, but then he shook his head. "No," he said. "Not during my lifetime." He went back behind the cylinder desk and brought out a beautifully shaped high-backed wooden chair, undoubtedly made for a nineteenth-century English tearoom. "Please," he said, turning it so it faced him. "Sit. What brings you here?"

"Well, healing the breach, for one thing."

"Of course," Stinky said, thinking he was smiling.

"And, you know, shoot the shit."

"Ahhh, Junior," he said, shaking his head fondly. "You know me, business, business, business. I'm hopeless where, as you put it, the shit is concerned. Won't hold my interest, I'm afraid. No matter how vividly you present your material, I'll just wander off, and that would be rude. I wouldn't want to be rude. And I'm sure you have somewhere to go." He looked at his watch. "My, my," he said. "Past nine."

"Okay, piece of business number one. Sit down, sit down."

He pulled a delicately carved chair, undoubtedly French, from behind the cylinder desk, and sat, very carefully. It creaked once beneath his bulk, but it held.

"I wouldn't tilt back if I were you."

"Actually, you probably would." Stinky said. "Anyone who tilts back in a chair is a barbarian."

"Okay, now that we're sitting, piece of business number two. Since I've learned that you have connections in the world of commercially arranged death, I'm wondering whether you've heard of someone named Ruben Ghorbani."

Stinky didn't bother to react, just looked at me. It was one of his skills, looking at people as though they were objects of no value. After fifteen or twenty seconds, which is a long time to be looked at that way, he said, "And third?"

"Bored already?"

"I've never heard of him. Your attitude is a bit strained. Am I incorrect in thinking you're no longer holding a grudge against me?"

"*Me*?" I put my hand, fingers splayed, in the center of my chest. "Against *you*? *Zut, alors*," I said. "It is to laugh."

He pursed his mouth, about the only moveable feature the Botox had spared, and said again, "And third?"

"You're about as much fun as you always were," I said. "*Third* is more in your usual corral—sorry, this living room is affecting my word choices. What do you think of this?" I reached into my pockets and brought out the jewelry box. I opened it, holding it so that the lid hid the contents of the box, and took out the Cartier brooch.

He gave it a quick look, and then his eyes went to the box. "What *aren't* you showing me?"

"Oh, come on. You practically broke that nice desk closing it when I came in. I wasn't tiresome about that. How about you return the favor?" I held up the brooch.

He peered at it and then extended a hand. "Give."

I gave, and he turned back to the desk, slid a drawer open, and came out with a jeweler's loupe. He offered the brooch three or four unenthusiastic seconds through the loupe and said, "Very nice. Real, of course, liberation jewelry from Cartier. I assume you know the story."

"Assume away."

He gave the piece a little toss, straight up and down, and caught it in his open palm, more a way of assessing its weight than anything else. "I've seen worse and I've seen better," he said. "It's in good condition, but the value is compromised because so many of them were made. Still, for a buyer who subscribes to the emotional miniseries behind it—valiant French countesses, German dueling scars, wartime heroism, and all that—it's worth a bit."

"How big a bit?"

"If you could find the right customer, which would be difficult for someone in your position, perhaps fifteen thousand."

It was the usual Stinky lowball. "And if I sold it to you?"

He shrugged and handed it back. "I'd have to hold onto it until the right person turned up. Or—no. No, never mind."

"Or what?" I checked the brooch to make sure he hadn't worked a switch.

"Or I could sell it to a collector of Nazi memorabilia. It would interest some of them."

"Why?"

"Well, I'd have to tart up the story. Tell them it was bought from the estate of a Gestapo officer who ripped it from the bloody blouse of some brave *mademoiselle* who wore it to her execution."

"There are people like that here?"

Stinky had enough control of his mouth to produce an unpleasant smile. "Within blocks."

"I think I'd rather you didn't sell it that way."

"I haven't even agreed to buy it."

"Okay." I put it back into the box. "Nice seeing—"

"What *are* you hiding there?"

"Tell you what. Let's trade. I'll show you if you'll show me. Open the desk."

"This is the point," he said, "at which my mind begins to wander."

"Fine," I said. I got up. "If I get home fast enough I can watch *The Walking Dead*."

"Twenty seconds," Stinky said. "In each direction."

"How much would you give me for the brooch?"

"Well, since you have me at a moral disadvantage, what with my little lapse of judgment about that attempted hit, I could go seven thousand."

"Mmmm," I said. "Okay, open the desk." I went around behind it so I could get a clear shot.

"Not so *close*, not so close."

I backed up three steps. "Here all right?"

"Look." He showed me his watch, gold on a black alligator strap with more dials and wheels than a submarine. He did something to it, and it displayed a blinking 20. He pushed a button on the watch and opened the desk.

Beautifully carved ivory chess pieces, probably Chinese, a full set, on an ivory and onyx board; a small vase shaped from a single translucent piece of Imperial jade; and the thing that almost stopped my heart, a partly unrolled painting on paper, women with braided ropes of heavy black hair, sitting bare-breasted beside a stream. I said, "Is that—" and the desk's cylinder came down again. "The picture," I said, swallowing. "Is that a Hyewon?"

"Don't be silly," Stinky said. He let the silence stretch out like someone savoring a flavor. "No one can get a Hyewon. They're all in national museums."

I felt like I'd been kicked in the stomach. Hyewon—real name Shin Yun-Bok—essentially reinvented Korean painting late in the eighteenth century. "How did you—?"

"I didn't," he said, so smugly that I wanted to paste him. "You didn't see anything. Your turn."

"Forget it," I said. "What I've got is nothing compared to that."

"Allow me to judge. We had a deal, remember?"

We did, in fact, have a deal. So I backed up a few paces, opened the box again, looked at my own watch, and said, "Here," and held up the handmade brooch.

Stinky squinted and then rubbed his nose, a good, full, four-aces rub. He doesn't know he does it, and I'll kill the person who tells him. He took a step forward and I took one back. We did that several times, as though we'd been choreographed, until we were practically in the center of the room. I said, "Twenty seconds," and dropped it back in the box.

"How—quaint," he said. "You're right, of course, it's nothing much." He rubbed his nose again and then he cleared his throat. "If you want to toss it in with the other one, I'll give you eight thousand."

"Don't think so," I said.

"All right." He held up his hands in surrender. "You have me at a disadvantage, given my halfhearted attempt on your life. Ten."

I said, "Halfhearted?"

"An errant impulse," he said. A vein was beating on the side of his neck. "A two-year-old's tantrum. I don't even remember why I was so angry. Twelve."

"Good thing he missed then," I said. "Boy that'd be a load of useless guilt, wouldn't it? Sort of a *Who will rid me of this troublesome priest* situation, huh? Remember? Henry II and Thomas á Becket? A king can't even think out loud without someone leaping to follow his order. Talk about an errant impulse. A lifetime of regret, hairshirts, crawling in penance on his royal knees, and the guy he killed by mistake gets sainted. Well, Stinky old lad, I'm happy you've been spared that. It would have made me feel guilty, even in heaven." I put the box in my pocket. "Bye."

"Sell me those brooches. Sixteen. *Seventeen*."

"I think not. All I have to do is find myself a Nazi, and—"

"You're not leaving."

"It's not polite to contradict one's host, so I'll just say, 'Of course not,' and find my own way out."

Stinky shouted, "Ting Ting."

I turned back to him. "Ting Ting? You're threatening me with *Ting Ting*?"

"The brooches."

I shoved them all the way to the bottom of my pocket. "Why? You practically blew your nose, hard as that may be to imagine, on the first one. What's the deal with the second?"

"It's not my fault you don't know your business. Twenty, and that's extremely generous."

"I'll take your word," I said, and turned to see Ting Ting standing in the archway that led to the hall. He smiled at me again.

"I'm leaving, Ting Ting," I said.

He smiled again and said, "Mr. Stinky say no."

"Come *on*, Stinky," I said. "It'd be like fighting with a tulip."

"Then leave," Stinky said. "Or be smart and sell me the brooches. The sound you hear is hundred-dollar bills being fanned. Two hundred of them. Twenty thousand. You're not looking."

"I've seen money before," I said. "Move, Ting Ting."

Ting Ting said, "Nope. Cannot," and assumed the pathetic, off-balance, wide-footed stance of Bruce Lee wannabes the world around.

"I can't do this," I said.

Stinky said, "Watch his left," and I figured he was trying to misdirect me, so I watched Ting Ting's right fist and completely ignored his left foot until it flattened my nose.

Instantly, I was sprawled on my back on the floor, bleeding heavily. Ting Ting reached down to help me up, but I waved him off, pushed myself onto my hands and knees, blew blood out of my nose all over Stinky's pinto sofa, and let my emotions get the better of me. I got up and charged Ting Ting, who stepped aside with the kind of silent grace you see in slow-motion film of a hanging piece of silk evading a bullet, and then pivoted to bring his right elbow into, of course, my nose.

This time he didn't knock me down. This time I went to my knees on my own, simply lacking the energy to do anything but try not to drown in the pain, which was sort of a cross between being hit in the face by a streetcar and inhaling a nest of hornets, with just a connoisseur's hint of having bitten into something that exploded. I stayed on my knees while Ting Ting fussed over me, going *tsk tsk tsk* as I focused on the new discovery that pain could be emitted in concentric circles, like an expanding target, and that the circles seemed to be alternately red and redder, with the occasional thin, jagged perimeter of bright yellow.

"The brooches," Stinky said from across the room. He waved Ting Ting over, and with a last, anxious look at me, Ting Ting trekked across the increasingly blood-spattered carpet, and Stinky handed him the wad of hundreds. Ting Ting, not even breathing hard, brought it back and, guiltily, extended to me.

Like the seventh idiot son of a seventh idiot son, I tried to slap them away. Ting Ting reacted with what he probably thought was measured violence, bringing his knee up sharply beneath my chin. This had the effect of a) making me bite my tongue harder than I've bitten into most steaks, b) snapping my head back, the weight of which c) pulled me over onto my back, on which I lay, watching the ceiling waver through my tears and thinking about swallowing blood until I came to my senses and turned my head instead so I could spit it onto Stinky's carpet.

"Mr. Junior," Ting Ting said, "You stop, please."

I rolled onto my side to get an arm under me. Over the roar of the pain, I heard Stinky say, "Take the money, Junior, and give him the box."

It took me a long, watery minute to get to my feet. When I did, I shook my head to clear it, which had the effect of spattering blood in a nice semicircle on everything within an arm's length. Then I squinted at Stinky—I didn't have to squint much, because my eyes were trying to swell closed—and said, "You're not the only one who knows how to hire a hit. I am up to my elbows in contract shooters right now, and I swear to you, if you take these brooches you'll be dead before you go to bed tonight."

Stinky's eyes went sub-zero. "And we'd just made up, too," he said. "I'm letting you walk out of here, but don't flatter yourself that it's because I'm afraid of you."

There was a large, hard lump of sheer rage almost blocking my throat. I said, "Put your fingers in your ears, Ting Ting."

Ting Ting put his fingers in his ears.

"If I don't get an apology from you tomorrow, you noseless sociopath, you'd better hire an Israeli army unit to protect your surgically enhanced ass because I swear to you, I will bring you down."

The last thing I saw before I made an unsteady turn and wobbled down the hall was Stinky taking an involuntary step back. It wasn't much but it was my only victory of the evening. Out in the car, leaning sideways to bleed into the street, I took stock: I hadn't made any progress on Wattles's chain, Handkerchief was still dead, and I was no closer than before to the solution of Herbie's murder. On the plus side, I'd learned that my Bizarro Liberation brooch had some interest value, and a chunk had been sliced off the big black rock Burt the Gut had said was hanging over me. If the good-luck/bad-luck ratio evened out in a timely manner, I had a *great* few hours in front of me.

19

He Seemed to Have Been Born in a Dozen Places

Like a lot of former addicts, Doc stayed up late.

Addicts, serious ones, anyway, tend to fall into two categories: people who are just one step up from being an inanimate object and are looking to close the gap, and people who live at the center of a twenty-four-hour cyclone of energy and are looking for twister control. Doc fell into the second category, and since he had spent several decades as a licensed physician, he approached the control of his personal twister with a lot of pharmaceutical expertise. By mixing and modulating various controlled substances he turned himself into a functioning medical man, apparently sober, although I'd been told his verbal diagnoses sometimes wandered into unexpected areas with roots in medieval witchcraft, and a pint of his blood could probably have cured malaria throughout the world. After he lost his license and straightened himself out, he developed an off-the-record practice with a specialty in crooks' injuries, especially gunshot wounds, and a tolerance for being awake practically all night long.

I'd met Doc when I was trying to get a drug-addled former child star named Thistle Downing out of the hands of some people who wanted her to make what used to be referred to as a naughty movie; and, as it turned out in the long run, she'd needed Doc more than she needed me.

"Jesus," he said as he opened the door. His string tie told me that he still encouraged his resemblance to Milburn Stone from the old *Gunsmoke* series. "You could have warned me."

"Didn't think it would be nesheshary."

"It's a popular misconception," Doc said, "that doctors never look at an injury and heave. Come on in, unless you're still dripping."

"I've clotted."

"Good. Get in here, air conditioner's on."

I stepped into his entry hall. The last time I was there I'd shot someone, and the place looked better without him.

"Who is it, dear?" the woman I knew only as Mrs. Doc called from the top of the stairs.

"Just Junior," Doc said. "Or what's left of Junior."

"That nice boy," Mrs. Doc said with the fatalism of medical spouses everywhere. "I hope he lives. Do you want some tea, Junior?"

"No shank you," I said. My tongue felt like a loaf of bread.

"Boy howdy," Doc said with a certain amount of admiration. "Who did this to you?"

"Filipino dansher."

"Yeah, I've heard they're dangerous. Look up." I lifted my face toward the hanging fixture that illuminated the hall. He made a clicking sound with his tongue that wasn't encouraging. "Where in the world am I going to start?"

"You're ashking me?"

"Let me see that tongue." He screwed up his face as though I had a dead rat in my mouth. "That should be stitched up."

I said, promptly and quite clearly, "No fucking way."

"Novocain," he said. "Although that'll probably hurt more than the stitches."

"Shkip it."

"But it'll hurt *shorter*."

"No. Here'sh what I want. I want to know if my noshe ish broken, I want shome pillsh, and I want a casht on my left arm."

He took my nose between his fingers and wiggled it while I screamed, and he said, "Yup. Broken, but we just straightened it out. The pills, no problem. Now bend your arm." I did. He said, "Flex your wrist." I did. He said, "Rotate it." I did. He said, "Lift the arm away from your body." I did, and he said, "Am I missing something?"

"No," I said. "I jusht want a casht. I want you to leave my fashe alone and put a casht on my left arm."

Doc nodded and held his hand up. "How many fingers?"

"Five," I said, "but you're only holding up one of them."

"Well, then, why don't you tell me why you want a cast put on a perfectly good arm? You going to collect signatures?"

"I'm looking for shomeone, and I'm beginning to doubt that I have the right reshourshes to find him. Sho I'm going to get the copsh to find him for me, and firsht, I need to file a complaint."

Back at Bitsy's that night—for the first time, despite wearing goggles made of painkillers—I managed to avoid most of the steps that tweeted and whistled, so I put that fact in the otherwise-empty mental column marked PROGRESS. At the door, I tapped lightly, opened it a few inches, and said, "Prepare yourshelf."

When I stepped in, the caged birds chirped in horror and Ronnie's face more or less fell apart. She managed to keep her smile in place, but her eyes went enormous and her eyebrows leapt halfway to her hairline. "Baby, baby, *baby*," she said. "What can I do for you?"

I said, "Have you eaten my pashtrami shandwich?"

"Of course not. Do you want it?"

"No. I jusht want to watch you take a couple of bites sho I can pretend you're me."

"Do you want me to go *yum* and make noises to show you how much you're enjoying it?"

"Oh, shkip it. I'm pretty loaded, thanksh to Doc. I think maybe what I need to do is find a position I can shleep in before I fall over."

"Peeling back the parrots," she said, folding the bedspread down and plumping the pillows. "Do you need help with your clothes?"

"I thought you'd never ashk."

She managed to get me undressed, then brought over a couple of cushions from the peacock-feather couch and arranged them in the bed so I could get comfortable on my right side, which let me avoid rolling over onto the cast with my mysteriously sore ribs.

I said, "I've had it with the motelsh. They're not good enough for you. Let'sh go shomewhere better tomorrow."

"Sure," she said. "We'll see how you feel about it then." She touched her nose to my cheek and whispered into my ear, "But you know what?"

"What?"

"I really don't care where I am, if I'm with you." She kissed me lightly, just a breeze of a kiss. "Now count backwards from ten."

I was out before I got to seven. I found myself in a dark room of indefinite size, although it seemed to be enormous and also roofless. One corner, far, far away, was brightly lighted, and I waded through something thick and viscous to get to it, and when I was finally there it turned out to be Herbie's bedroom, where I spent what seemed like a very long time trying to turn off the whistling kettle until it all rippled and went away.

WOODLAND HILLS
MAN MURDERED

A Woodland Hills resident who did business as a psychic was killed yesterday afternoon at his place of business in the Vista del Cielo shopping mall on Ventura Boulevard, police said.

Two police units, responding to a call from a customer, found the body of Henry Willifer in the back room of the shop. Willifer had been beaten to death, although police declined to disclose the specific nature of his injuries.

Willifer, 53, had been convicted several times for confidence schemes under the alias Henry Harrison. Police said he was better known in the criminal world by a nickname, "Handkerchief," which was derived from his characteristic sartorial style.

"The *criminal world*," I said. "They make it sound like it's somewhere else."

Police were called by one of Mr. Willifer's clients, RuthEtta deWoskin, who said that she showed up without an appointment and heard loud voices coming from the inner room, where Mr. Willifer saw his clientele. Ms. deWoskin said she thought at first that Mr. Harrison was performing a service he called an "afterlife group session" in which multiple deceased individuals

**who influenced the client's life were called upon
to account for themselves.**

"Those could get kind of hairy," Ms. deWoskin said. "They'd get to arguing and like that. Sometimes stuff would get thrown."

"Group sessions of the dead?" Ronnie said. "He seems like someone I would have liked." She sipped her coffee, the smell of which was tying me in knots. I'd let one mouthful pass over my shredded tongue, which felt a little like gargling fire ants. My cup was sitting on the table, mocking me as it cooled. The table had a little ceramic birdcage wired to it, the circular front opening of which had been used as an ashtray by many a weary traveler, with the expected fragrant result. I'd noticed when we moved in that one of the caged birds had a cough, and now I knew why.

I stuck my finger in the coffee. Still too hot. "I probably didn't like him as much as I should have," I said. "But he just *never* told the truth."

"He and I would have gotten along fine, then," Ronnie said.

> **Ms. deWoskin said she went to wait in a res-
> taurant in the mall because she "didn't want to
> eavesdrop" and became concerned when she had
> been there more than an hour. "He kept those
> spirits on the clock," she told reporters. "They
> just toed the line for him." After another half an
> hour she called the police.**

> **LAPD sources said that Ms. deWoskin, who
> lacked a cell phone, left her table at the window
> to make the call, and they believe that was when
> Mr. Willifer's assailants left the business loca-
> tion and slipped away.**

Mr. Willifer had done business in the mall under the name The All-Seeing Eye for a little less than four months. All-Seeing Eye for a little less than four months.

I said, "Beaten to death. I wasn't all that fond of Handkerchief, but he didn't deserve that."

"It seems to be a theme," Ronnie said. She'd been reading the paper over my shoulder. "First your friend Herbie and now, uh, Handkerchief."

"Somebody wants really badly to know something," I said. "Maybe you ought to get out of Los Angeles."

"Maybe you got your brains addled. How's the tongue?"

"It hurts," I said. "But at least I don't sound like a bad ventriloquist."

"You look awful."

I said, "Good. That's exactly what I need. To look awful."

20
The Eternal Redeemer

I gave myself a parting look in the rearview mirror before getting out of the car. Everything Ting Ting had done to me the previous night had swelled, ripened, and deepened into the palette of colors that signal biological distress: grays with red beneath them, a hemoglobin purple like the blood that's pulled to the skin by a really energetic hickey, and a kind of nameless yellowish darkness like the glass a water-colorist has been dipping his brush into for days. My nose was twice its usual width, and my lips were fat enough to cushion a bumper car.

What with its grand name, the First Church of the Eternal Redeemer was a bit of a letdown. Decades ago a Los Angeles bakery called Vandekamp's built itself a chain of stores, white stucco buildings that were distinguished by having at one end a Dutch windmill, often with the blades outlined in neon. Today these buildings are architectural fossils, usually with the windmill long gone but the towers still pointing heavenward, and the First Church of the Eternal Redeemer had repurposed the tower by putting a cross on it, giving the impression of a church that baked its own communion wafers.

One story high except for the holy windmill, with a painted-over display window, the building stood in a somewhat weedy lot at the center of what, thirty or forty years ago, had been a medium-level mini-mall. The stores immediately on either side had been bulldozed and cleared away, making the church stand out like a lonely tooth, but the structures at both ends of the mall were still standing: a donut shop, a Mexican restaurant special-izing in menudo, an Army-Navy surplus store, and a shuttered, dusty shop front with the word ADULT fading from the stucco above the window.

The Redeeming, such as it was, was being done where Paco-ima shaded indistinguishibly into Sylmar, the northernmost town in greater Los Angeles. The "mar" in Sylmar is Spanish for *sea*, suggesting that the town fathers were bad judges of dis-tance, since the Pacific is at least thirty miles away and on the other side of the hill, but geography has never been allowed to get in the way of land values in Southern California.

I hurt in places where I couldn't even remember getting hit, so I was walking clumsily, but that wasn't why I turned my ankle the moment I got out of the car. The parking lot was rippled and torn from beneath by the roots of the big ficus trees that lined the street. The roots had broken right through the asphalt in places. The entire mall, the church included, had the depressive air of a property developer's tax write-off, a loss allowed to fester on some spreadsheet by way of balancing the picture for the IRS.

I was limping toward the church on my newly turned ankle when a man came out of the Mexican restaurant with a large foil tray of take-out that was almost buckling beneath the weight of the food, and made the right that put him directly in my path. He was dark-haired and buzz-cut, slight and skittery looking, a nat-ural lightweight without an extra ounce on him and the bright, deep-set eyes that often announce the furnace-like metabolism of someone who could live on donuts and not gain an ounce. This characteristic is common, I've noticed, in preachers. Since I'm an instinctive atheist, I always wonder whether they mistake their elevated internal processes for some sort of divine energy. For all I know, high metabolic processes are responsible for religion itself: the persistence of easily-available ecstasy and all that obsession with *food*—what you can and can't eat, when you can and can't eat it, the demonization of gluttony, all those starving sojourns in the desert, all that fasting to rattle up all those visions, all those holiday feasts. The man stopped, looked back to the church as though to verify that I was on a course for it, and said, "Yes?"

"Reverend Angelis?"

"I am." He blinked, but it was more than a blink. He slammed both eyes closed and then popped them open again. It was a flincher's blink. "But properly speaking, it's Doctor Angelis."

"Apologies, Doctor. I'd like to talk to you for a moment."

Two bang-shut blinks. He said, "If it's about the rent—"

"It's not. Oh, I'm sorry. My name is, um, Merle Bender." *Junior* didn't seem appropriate for a guy who insisted on being called "doctor." And I'd have to explain it to him.

"Merle," he said, going straight to the heart of the matter. Blink blink. "Unusual name for a man."

"It was my father's. You can call me Junior."

"It's hot out here," he said, "and, paradoxical though it may seem, the food is getting cold. We can talk inside."

He wheeled around and headed for the door, revealing a clearing of male pattern baldness at the top of his head that could have passed for a tonsure. I dragged myself along behind him, feeling like Igor and studying his not-very-white shirt, the frayed cuffs of his dark slacks, the rounded heels of his shoes. His gaze hadn't lingered for an instant on my face, and he'd turned his back on me with complete faith that this absolute stranger who looked like he'd bobbed for apples in a bucket of lava was harmless and trustworthy.

"The rent," he said over his shoulder. "It's always a problem. Property is expensive but God should be free."

I had no problem with the idea that God should be free, so I said, "Amen."

He didn't turn his head for a sincerity check. "And the Lord's work can run up the bills, too." He stopped at the door, which opened out. "Can you get this for me, please?"

Doctor Angelis side-stepped so I could open the door, and I followed him in.

The church's origin as a storefront was obvious. The pulpit was a plywood riser with a banged-up podium on it, stuck at a forty-five-degree angle in the far right corner of the room. Metal folding chairs had been arranged in diagonal rows but many of them had been dragged out of place to surround a long plastic table that occupied the center of the room. Around it sat nine people, all in their seventies and above. Some were *well* above, perhaps in their nineties. Sylmar and Pacoima are largely Latino areas, but only four of the people at the table looked Latino; two others were black, and three were Caucasian. They all turned to face us expectantly when the door opened.

"Felipe," Doctor Angelis called, and a slender young Latino man hurried from the back of the store to take the sagging tray and put it on the table. There was a pile of plastic utensils and paper plates at the table's center, and Felipe began to parcel them out. No one said anything, just watched Felipe's hands and occasionally glanced at the food.

"Taking a stitch," Angelis said with a touch of acid, "in the social safety net."

I said, "The deficit never seems to interfere with the legislators' food chain."

"Render unto Caesar," he said, "pretty much everything these days." He watched Felipe, who was expertly ladling the food onto the paper plates. Angelis said, "Have we said grace?"

Without looking up, Felipe said, "Not yet,"

"Well, grace," Angelis said. "Eat up, everyone." He turned to me. "And what can I do for you, Mr. Bender?"

I absolutely could not lie to this man. "I'm looking for someone."

The deep-set eyes regarded me as warily as lights in a cave. "Do you mean him harm?"

I said, "What a question."

I got the flinch-blink. "That doesn't mean it hasn't been asked."

"Let's say no."

He gave me a tight smile, astringent enough to sting the cuts on my face. "Let's answer truthfully."

"It depends on what I learn. A man has been killed, and I want to make sure this person had nothing to do with it."

"Not a conversation for this room," he said. "Follow me." I tagged behind him as he headed for the back of the store, pushing aside a dark curtain that brought back the ones I'd scorned at Handkerchief's, and then through a door into the open air.

Except for the building immediately behind us, we were surrounded by knee-high weeds, dry and dead and coated with dust, bordered by a high brick wall, over which more ficus trees spread their leaves, shading the houses beyond. Angelis emitted a sigh I remembered from when I was a smoker and pulled a pack of unfiltered Camels, kind of a butch smoke for a preacher, from the pocket of his shirt. "If this bothers you," he said, "take a couple of steps back and hold your breath." He lit up and blew the smoke away from me. "In your world, Mr. Bender, are people killed often?"

"People are killed in everybody's world. Do you feed those people in there every day?"

"Sometimes. Sometimes it's twice that many. Dinner is the big meal. Don't be Jesuitical with me. Are you in law enforcement?"

"A related field."

"A private eye?"

"Are there really private eyes? I'm on a personal errand. The person who was killed meant a lot to me, and his lawyer gave me a letter in which my friend had written the name of a person who might eventually kill him."

"How careless of the murderer, to reveal himself in advance to his victim. What was the name?"

"Ruben Ghorbani."

The response, and a cluster of blinks, came so fast I was still pronouncing *Ghorbani*. "Never heard of him."

"Really? What about the scar under your mouth? What about the skull fracture he caused? You must know that I'm not wandering around asking random people whether they know Ruben Ghorbani."

Three more blinks. "Yes, of course, that was his name. I've— I know this sounds improbable, but I think I've erased it from my memory."

I said, "Improbable doesn't begin to describe it."

He smiled, more sweetly this time. "Then let's put it in a different light. If you intend to do him harm, my telling you where he is—if I knew where he was, which I don't—would be akin to sending someone to take revenge on him, wouldn't it?"

"So you do know where he is."

"No," he said, and I could have spotted the lie from twenty yards.

"Okay," I said. "Just to be clear, if he didn't kill my friend, I mean him no harm." I reached into my pocket, using the hand that didn't have a cast right above it, and pulled out some of the money I'd taken from the box in the Wedgwood.

I got a tight, unpleasant grin. "Are you attempting to bribe me?"

"No," I said, surprised. "I'm attempting to give you some money to help you feed those people and pay the rent. How much *is* the rent?"

"Eleven-fifty."

"Jesus," I said. "Begging your pardon, but the landlord's doing okay, isn't he?"

"There's a good reason that landlords are among the first targets whenever there's a revolution." He wasn't even looking at the money; he was, instead, studying my face for the first time. "You got beaten up worse than I did."

"My skull's intact," I said. "Here's twelve hundred."

"I do hope you realize you're not buying information."

"Why did he do it? I'm not asking where he is, I just want to know why someone, anyone, would attack someone like you."

He pocketed the money and thought about the question. "He was living in hell. Do you believe we create hell?"

"Was? Is he dead?"

"I have no idea," he said. He had no talent for lying. "Do you? Believe we create hell? For ourselves, if for no one else?"

"How did he create hell?"

"He was a violent, brutal man and he took drugs that made him more brutal and more violent. So I suppose you could say he was imprisoned by genetics and dope."

"So *you* believe we create hell."

"I do. I just wonder why so few of us create heaven, either for ourselves or for the people closest to us."

"I have a related question. Well, sort of. Do you believe in luck, or do you think a stroke of luck is a blessing?"

"Luck is a tough one." He inhaled the final quarter of the cigarette, dropped the butt, and stepped on it. "What I think is that I agree with Pasteur: fortune favors the prepared mind.

Luck? I don't have any idea. Maybe it's something that kicks up spontaneously, like a breeze, and then it's gone. I'm pretty sure that every time we find a quarter, it's not a blessing in the way many people use the word. On balance, I believe that God is too busy to micro-manage, and that if you're going to give Him credit for a coin toss, then you also have to blame Him for an earthquake."

"Thanks," I said. "It's a pleasure to have met you." I opened the door and held it with my foot. "So Ghorbani was brutal by nature and dragging a bunch of drugs around. But what was the reason he went after you? The cause, right there in that moment."

He took out another cigarette and sniffed one end before slipping it back into the pack, and then he sighed. "He disapproved of the relationship between me and Felipe. He saw us together in West Hollywood, and he didn't recognize it as love. But the way he was then, he wouldn't have recognized love spelled out in blinking letters two stories high." He glanced back through the door, toward the room that had Felipe in it. "A good definition of hell, I'd say."

It was winking at me from across the parking lot as I approached, but I paid it no attention because it was obviously an optical illusion, a reflection on the windshield, since I'd locked the car. But when I unlocked it and climbed in, there it was, taped neatly to the center of the steering wheel. A small envelope, like one that would contain a greeting card.

I opened it and pulled out a sheet of paper, folded to fit. When I opened it, I was looking at laser printer output, one word and two combinations of numbers.

The word was STOP.

The numbers were 11/28/2000 and 3/12/1978.

Rina's birthday and Kathy's.

"Yeah, I seen him." The man working in the surplus store looked like a GI Joe doll, but life-size and many, many cartons of beer later. "I was watching, 'cause sometimes the little shits around here, they like to carve things on windows or key the side of the car, you know?"

I allowed as to how I knew.

"But he whipped out a keychain, popped the door, got in, and got out a minute later. Locked it again and walked away like the whole world could be watching and he wouldn't care."

"Popped it," I said. "With the key?"

"Uh-uh. A remote. Locked it the same way. Walking away, and the car beeped."

"A little shit, you said."

"A kid. Maybe thirteen, fourteen, probably Mex. Dark hair under a baseball cap. Real skinny." His eyes dropped to his paunch for a second. "You know, the way kids are."

"Did you see where he went?"

"That way," he said, pointing to his left.

When I got outside, I found that "that way" led me to a street corner. At the far end of the street, I could see a stoplight, so the street could have been the first hundred yards of a trip to anywhere.

No kid. No waiting car.

Rina's and Kathy's birthdays.

STOP.

21

An Absolute Bar Code to Designate Criminal Stupidity

I hadn't seen nearly enough of Herbie in the past few years. I'd been, I told myself, *busy*. It had caught me off-guard when people started asking me to tidy up certain kinds of situations, situations involving some kind of wrong done by a person unknown. Solving problems for people who weren't comfortable, usually with good reason, about going to the cops.

The idea of investigating crimes on behalf of crooks hadn't been mine, and much of the time it took a gun at my head, metaphorically and occasionally literally, to get me to go to work. Even though I kind of enjoyed figuring things out and it was mildly flattering to be asked, there was the drawback of my possible death every time I went to work. If I was successful in identifying the culprit, he or she might try to kill me, and if I wasn't successful, my client might kill me. Staying alive ate into my time.

And there were Kathy and Rina and Ronnie, and the business of being a careful and somewhat successful burglar. And reading and watching baseball and getting my hair cut and staying in shape and doing all the things that made it possible for me to think of myself as a reasonably successful, reasonably personable, reasonably admirable human being.

I just had *way* too much on my plate to bother keeping up

with the person who, over the course of almost nineteen years, had given me whatever I needed, within reason, without ever calling my attention to the score, which was as lopsided as the national debt. I'd known when Herbie more or less retired, I'd known when he moved to Malibu, I'd even known that he was probably lonely and bored up there. As Louie put it, why would anybody want his toes in the sand?

But I hadn't had the spare time in my crowded life to go up and ask what I could do by way of repaying some tiny fraction of my debt. Why is spare time so often the only time we have for those who have done the most for us? He'd stood in as the attentive father, and I'd stood in as the ungrateful son.

And all I wanted at that moment was to talk to him.

If he'd known what I was about to do, he'd probably have chained me to my steering wheel.

It's a terrible thing to see someone's eyes as they realize that you've registered their approaching death. It's another confirmation of what they're trying, against all odds, not to believe.

The last time I'd seen Paulie DiGaudio, a little less than six months ago, his waist measurement probably exceeded his height. The man sitting behind the table when I was led into the interrogation room in the Van Nuys police station—and whom I hadn't recognized for a blank, off-balance second that felt like taking a step down I didn't expect—was as gray as a Confederate uniform, and diminished in that terrible, deflated way that happens when someone loses fifty or sixty pounds so fast you could almost watch it come off.

The skin hung in loose folds from his face and draped his neck like a scarf. Most of his hair was gone, almost certainly burned off by the fire of chemo, and a patchy, peeling red pattern over his otherwise colorless forehead and cheeks looked like the marks of splattering hot fat. The eyes were still pure DiGaudio, the frayed, seen-it-all-and-surprised-by-none-of-it eyes you see in cops everywhere, but sharpened and focused now by something that could have been fear or rage or pain or all of them at the same time.

I said, "Jesus, Paulie."

His face went red enough for the splotches to disappear. "Since when am I Paulie, you fucking crook? And what are you doing, waltzing in here and asking to talk to me like a real person? You think people here don't know who you are?"

"I'm sorry." I started to sit, but looked at him for a moment instead and said, "And I'm sorry about—about this."

"Aaahhhh," DiGaudio said. He looked down at his lap. "I had it when we—you know, that thing with Vinnie, I had it then. But back then, they thought—oh, who gives a shit what they thought? Like they know fucking *anything*. What do you want?"

"I know what you're going to say, but is there anything I can do for you?"

"You?" he said. "Yeah, you can hop over to France, to the Loover Museum, and steal me the Mona Lisa. Give me something nice to look at. For the second time, what do you want?"

"Somebody beat me up," I said.

"No shit."

I pulled out the chair and sat down. "And he stole a lot of money from me."

"Poetic justice, is that what they say?"

"I got a really good look at him, and so did two other people."

"So?" He put both hands low on what remained of his belly, and I watched his face twist into a different face.

I said, "Should you even be here?"

"As opposed to what?" He brought his chin all the way down to his breastbone, squeezed his eyes shut, and then opened both them and his mouth as widely as he could and breathed out. "Sitting around and groaning all day?" He blotted sweat from his brow with the back of his hand, the gesture uncharacteristically delicate. "Taking my pants in? I'll tell you, since we probably won't see each other again, avoid cancer, okay? It's like target practice for poisoners. You ever watch *The Borgias*?"

"No, but I know who they—"

"They woulda gone straight to the top of the heap in a cancer hospital. Everybody mixing up poison, like kids playing with clay. 'Here, let's try this one, it'll only kill *part* of you. Whoops, wrong part.' Do *not* get cancer."

"I'm trying."

"Try harder. So, some crook ripped off the crook, huh? And we're supposed to go out and pound the pavement. Gotta right this wrong. You know what they say about two negatives?"

"They make a—"

"They make a positive. Would you want your tax dollars, assuming you pay tax dollars, spent tracking down crooks who make life rough for crooks?"

"I see your point."

"So go away."

I said, "No. I did you a favor once, and I want one in return."

"And if I don't? What, you gonna tell people I got a relative who's mobbed up? Look at me, Bender. Do you really think I give a rat's ass?"

"No threats," I said. "I'm not dumb enough to threaten you. No better way to lose the argument. It's just—I guess it's just fair play."

He winced again, pushing himself back against the chair, and then he laughed a little air with no voice behind it. "You got *cojones,* I'll give you that. Whaddya want? So I can say no, I mean."

"I want to fill out a complaint or whatever I'm supposed to do and describe him to you, and look at a bunch of likely hits on the computer and then, if I think I see him, I want to look at him in person."

"A line-up. Do you know what a pain in the ass that is?"

"If I'm right, the guy I'm looking for has been in here so often it's like going out to pick up the paper in the morning. If he starts yelling for a lawyer, we'll forget it."

"Three witnesses," he said.

"And he's a bad guy. Look at me." I stuck my tongue out, and DiGaudio recoiled. I said, "What kind of a guy would do that?"

"Are the other two witnesses crooks?"

"No. Cross my heart." I didn't.

"Well, shit." He drummed his fingers in the table. "Okay," he said. "You helped Vinnie stay outta jail, even if the rest of it didn't work out so good. I'll let you take a look and we'll see who you come up with. Then I'll think about it."

It was all on computers. I gave the guy at the keyboard the best description I could of Ghorbani and we identified what he'd supposedly done to me as assault with intent to cause grievous bodily injury and grand theft, and he did his magic.

For eight to ten minutes I looked at the worst-looking bunch of mutts I'd ever seen, a parade of dim eyes, hanging jaws, missing teeth, facial tattoos, and bottled fury, all adding up to an absolute bar code to designate criminal stupidity. All of them were photographed head-on and in profile, all of them looking straight through the camera, none of them suggesting a really high skill set, and then there he was. I flagged him and two others as possibles, and went back to the interrogation room.

"Two of them, forget it," DiGaudio said as he came back in. He walked as though the floor might ripple and pitch beneath him at any moment. "One of them is inside and the other one has disappeared. But the one with the funny last name, the one from Eye-ran or wherever, him I can bring in."

"I'd appreciate it."

"But no lineup, nothing official. I'll haul him in for questioning, and you and your witnesses can look through the one-way glass for about thirty seconds, and that's it. If he's the guy, you fill out the complaint, got it?"

"Got it."

He leveled a finger at me. It was shaking, and I watched him watch it shake. "And if you tell me he's *not* the guy, and anything happens to him—I mean anything at all, like he stubs his toe or anything—I'll have you in here so fast your shoes will still be on the pavement."

"Fine."

He sat back in the chair and trained the eyes on me. Normally cops' eyes made me feel like my skin was transparent, but this was more along the lines of an assessment than an X-ray. "So," he said, and there was a kind of reluctance behind it. "Somebody did Herbie Mott."

"Yes," I said. Hearing him say it, it felt like my heart had doubled in size.

"You guys were kinda close, huh?"

"No," I said. "Not particularly." For a quick, over-my-head moment, I wondered whether he'd clicked on the connection between Herbie and Ghorbani, but couldn't see any way it was possible.

"Not what I heard." He seemed to be thinking, and while his mind was occupied he reached into his jacket pocket and found it empty. That was where he had always kept his Tootsie Rolls. "Can't eat them anymore," he said, seeing that I was watching his hand.

"I'd think you could eat anything you want," I said.

"Just one of the bitches that come with this shit," he said. "The stuff you like best? Tastes terrible. I'm living on Asian buffets because they got so much different crap that I can usually find one thing I can swallow. Big irony, huh? Me never much liking Asians. Still don't much like Asians, as a matter of fact. But listen, I'm not trying to connect you to Mott's death. That's Malibu. Cutest cops in California, but they do their job. But I'm thinking there's probably some stuff about Herbie you don't know."

"Like I said, we knew each other a little, but—"

"He dimed you once," DiGaudio said, and then he pulled his head back the way a turtle will do and just watched me.

I said, "Sorry?"

"He dimed you." He chewed on the inside of his cheek for a second, looking like he was deciding whether to continue. "For a job in Panorama City, maybe fifteen, sixteen years ago. Old woman, got a bunch of jewelry taken, got clobbered on the head. Herbie dimed you as the guy."

I had to inhale twice before I could talk. "Bullshit."

"But about half an hour later the jughead who clubbed her walked into a pawn shop with her jewelry and we just went and picked him up. So your record stayed nice and clean. No arrest."

"Never happened."

"That was one of the things Herbie Mott was," DiGaudio said. "And maybe you ought to know it. Besides being a burglar and a scumbag, he was a pipeline. We busted maybe fifty guys because of Herbie." I started to say something, but he held up a hand. "And Herbie skated. That was the deal, Herbie always skated."

"Like I said." My voice didn't have much breath beneath it. "I didn't know him that well."

He grimaced and waited for it to pass. When he came back, the worn-out eyes were softer than I'd ever seen them. "How many times you been convicted, Bender?"

"Never."

"Charged?"

"Never." I saw where this was going, and it took all I had not to try to get out of the room before we got there.

"Arrested?"

"Never."

"Junior," he said. DiGaudio never called me by my first name. "Just ask yourself, back when I was forcing you to help Paulie, ask yourself how I knew you were a burglar. How every cop in this building knows you're a burglar." He laid his hands flat on the table, one crossed on top of the other, and watched them quiver. "Just think about it."

PART
THREE

"The right way to do burglary," Herbie said, "is backward."

"What do you mean, backward?"

"Before you do it," he said, "do it in your mind. Backward."

I said, "I'm talking to you on the phone, so you can't see that I'm scratching my head."

"Before you go in, see yourself go back out. Before you open anything, see yourself closing it. Before you move anything, see yourself putting it back. Before you leave a fingerprint—"

"Yeah?"

"See yourself getting arrested."

22

The Long Rippling Arpeggio on the Harp

What I didn't want taken away from me was my sense of who Herbie was, who Herbie had been. It felt as though a big part of my life, the part of me that had chosen and then played Herbie's Game, had been built on my sense of who Herbie was; by choosing Herbie's Game I'd locked myself out of several alternative lives. I protected myself against what DiGaudio had said, for the time being, by surrendering to the beating Ting Ting had given me. First I stopped at Doc's and had him improvise a long wire scratcher for the inside of the cast, which had been driving me crazy. He'd tried to talk to me, but I couldn't even hold up my end of the conversation. Then, after half an hour of directionless driving, every possible direction feeling equally meaningless, I went to Bitsy's Bird's Nest, stamping extra hard on the stairs that chirped, took off most of my clothes, ate six aspirin, turned off my phone, and got into bed.

When I woke up, the rectangle of the world framed by the window was dark. Ronnie was sitting on the peacock-print couch, reading something.

"What's that?" I said. My voice felt unused, like it had been folded too long in a drawer. I cleared my throat.

She held the book up. The title was *The Deceived*. "A thriller," she said. "A guy named Brett Battles. He's terrific."

"What a masculine name," I said. "Wonder what he'd be writing if his parents had called him Merle."

"Not to mention Bender." She dog-eared the page while I tried not to wince. "Means *gay* in British slang, did you know that? So your name is, basically, Young Gay."

I said, "It's been brought to my attention."

"How are you feeling?"

"Terrible."

"That kid would have beaten you up no matter what your name was. You could have been Biff Hardcase and you'd still be lying here, swelling."

"It's not that," I said. "Well, okay, it is that. But it's also what Sartre might have called malaise, and I call the heebie-jeebies."

She put the book aside and got up, and I had the pleasure of watching five feet six inches of immaculately assembled womanhood cross the room, with the added savor of knowing she was heading for me. The pleasure of watching even the most interesting woman cross a room is dampened when they're heading for someone else. She sat on the edge of the bed and picked up my left hand, which was resting on top of the covers, and began to massage as much of the hand as she could reach, given the plaster cast, focusing most of her attention on my fingers: taking them one at a time, smoothing them out, lengthening them, giving the tip a sharp tug and then moving on to the next. "Why do you have the heebie-jeebies?"

"Because I don't know what I'm doing. I feel like I'm chasing my tail."

She bent back my thumb and little fingers to open my palm and began to rub it deeply with both of her thumbs. "It's worth chasing."

I said, "Really."

"That was the first thing I noticed about you, your tail." She finished rubbing the center of my palm and blew on it, and every hair on my body stood up.

"Do that again," I said. "Actually, though, the first time you saw me, I was facing you."

"I am such a liar." She reached across and got hold of my right hand, and I rolled onto my side to allow her to sit up straight as she worked on it.

"I've pretty much told you the truth," I said.

"We're different," she said. She'd gotten to the ring finger and she slowed down when she felt the swelling around the middle joint. "Did you get this when you hit him?"

"*Hit* him?" I said. "I never even got close. I probably bent that one of the many times I fell on it. How are we different?"

"You're open, especially for a crook. I tend to parcel out the truth while I try to figure out whether you and I are something real or just another low-level glandular seizure."

"Well," I said, "the way I look at it, it's a low-level glandular seizure, *too*. In addition, I mean, to all the other stuff."

"Let's talk business," she said. She looked very serious, maybe even a little frightened. "What I told you about Trenton—" and there was a knock at the door.

"Go into the bathroom," I said. I meant to leap from the bed, but my leap wasn't on call, and I unfolded myself so slowly I could practically hear my joints. Whoever it was knocked at the door again, and I heard male voices, two of them. "In there," I said, trying to get my legs into my pants. "*Now.*"

"You sound so masterful," she said, "and you look so silly."

"It's just barely possible," I said, zipping my fly, "that this isn't a joke." My T-shirt would do; it was good enough to die in. I grabbed the Glock and handed it to Ronnie as she passed me on the way to the bathroom. "If you hear shots, stay in there with the door closed, and if anybody opens it shoot them over and over."

"Over and over," she said, shutting the bathroom door behind her.

I grabbed a table lamp in the shape of a rooster, the little shade pulled crooked on its head like a drunken Shriner's hat, yanked the cord from the wall, and went to the door. I counted to three to focus myself, put my hand carefully on the door-knob and then turned it and yanked it open, backing up fast and almost pitching the lamp at my caller, which seemed to be an explosion of flowers.

"This is your house?" Ting Ting said, just barely not wrinkling his tiny, decorative nose. He looked at the bathroom door, which had just opened, and his expression cleared. "This is your girlfriend?"

"And this is his gun." She let it dangle from her fingers as though it had been someplace nasty. "Who are you?"

"Um," Ting Ting said. The basket of flowers was half as big as he was.

"He's being diplomatic," I said. "This is Ting Ting. The guy who beat me up."

Ronnie said, "Look at me not laughing."

"Mr. Stinky, he is sorry," Ting Ting said, giving the basket of flowers a little shake in case we'd missed them. "Me, too, very sorry."

"Well, thanks, but how the hell did you find me?"

"I brought him," Louie the Lost said, stepping into the room. "He was blindfolded until he knocked on your door." He took a quick look at my expression and said, "Don't give me that. You want Stinky to stay mad? You want to get shot at again?"

"So," I said, "just to reconstruct. Stinky called you to find out where I was and you volunteered to play peacemaker. And you kept an eye on your rearview mirror all the way over."

"Better than that," he said. "I had Eaglet following me about four cars back. Even Ting Ting didn't know it."

"Eaglet," I said. "Is she outside, too?"

"Yup."

"Is there anybody I know who's not outside?"

"Bring her in," Ronnie said. She grimaced at the giant bouquet. "Ting Ting, I'm so sorry. Please. Put those here."

Ting Ting gave her his high-beam smile and put the flowers on the table in front of the combination birdhouse/ashtray, and began to rearrange the blooms, of which there were a great many. Fussing with them, he had his back to the door when Eaglet came in.

She'd traded the rainbow cape for a peach-colored Indian blouse, circa 1967, covered with bits of plastic mirror that would have made her, if she hadn't been so young, look like a love-in attendee who had just gained consciousness after fifty years beneath a bush in Griffith Park. All she needed was a stick of incense in her hand, a press-on peace symbol tattoo, and a circlet of flowers in her hair. Instead, she had seashells woven into fifteen or twenty long braids. She looked at me, looked at Ting Ting's back, and looked at me again. The shells in her braids clattered. She said, "Who totaled *you*?"

I said, "He did," and Ting Ting turned around and their eyes met, and even I could hear the long rippling arpeggio on the harp.

"Oh," Eaglet said. "My gosh."

Ting Ting said, "Who?" and then lost the rest of the sentence.

"Ting Ting," I said, "this is Eaglet. And vice versa."

Ronnie said, "And you were complaining about *Merle*," but then she broke off and said, "Isn't this sweet?"

There was a long silence, interrupted only by the sound of Eaglet and Ting Ting swallowing, and then Louie said, "Maybe you guys should give them the room."

o o o

"I don't know what I'm doing," I said for the second time that evening. We were in an otherwise empty Chinese restaurant not far from Bitsy's, and I was talking mainly to Ronnie and Louie because Ting Ting and Eaglet were in their own separate book at the end of the table. "I started all this because Wattles asked me to find out who stole the info about his chain, and I took it because of the money and also because the way the locks had been left open made me think it might have been Herbie, leaving tracks, as he used to say, and I could earn the other five K without popping a sweat. But Herbie is dead and Wattles and Janice have vanished, so even though he paid me a first installment, I don't feel particularly compelled to keep looking, especially since I can't find the next link in the chain, this guy named Monty Carlo. I've been keeping at it mainly because Herbie got killed, and number one, he asked me in a letter to figure out who did it, and number two, although he said in the letter that he *knew* who was most likely to kill him, I figured the odds were close to even that he was wrong. That he got murdered because someone hired him to burglarize Wattles's office, and then Herbie either wouldn't give them the information he stole, so they killed him, or they killed him because they didn't want to pay him, or for fun, or I don't know why. And then somebody killed Handkerchief—"

Louie said, "You're shitting me." He looked like something had just exploded in his face.

"I always think you know everything," I said. "I should have told you."

He pushed his plate away. "Killed him how?"

"Same way as Herbie, although maybe not down to the details. Herbie's details were pretty terrible. But they beat him to death."

"Aawww," Louie said. "Handkerchief wasn't that bad."

"That should be on his tombstone," I said. "Handkerchief Harrison: Not That Bad."

Ronnie said, "That's mean."

"Yes, it is." I said to the air, "I'm sorry, Handkerchief," and I meant it.

"So there you are," Louie said. "You're doing it for Herbie."

"And now," I said, my eyes on Louie, "I've been hearing some things about Herbie."

Louie found something to look at in the parking lot. I let him look at it for a minute, and then Ting Ting and Eaglet laughed softly, and I said to Louie, "You're not interested in learning what I've heard about Herbie?"

"People talk," Louie said dismissively, but there was a lot of color in his cheeks. "Especially about the dead. It's easy to talk about the dead. They can't get even."

"You know all about Herbie and me."

"Well, sure," Louie said. He had an open Mediterranean face made more open by an expanse of forehead that registered everything that went through his mind. He was rubbing his forehead as though he had the beginning of a headache, but he was doing it because he'd long known I could read his forehead like skywriting. "Everybody who knows you knows about Herbie."

"No one has ever said anything bad about Herbie to me before."

"Who would?" he said. When it became clear I wasn't going to answer him, he said, "So who did?"

"DiGaudio."

"Oh, well," Louie said, sitting back. "He probably just saw a way to poke a hole in your day. He's that kind of guy."

"He's dying," I said. "It was my impression that he's on a mission to tell the truth while he still can."

"He's a *cop*."

"He said Herbie was a pipeline."

Louie looked across the table at Ronnie, the only person in our group who was eating, although she was eating enough to make up for the rest of us. "Good, huh?" he asked her.

Ronnie said, "Mmmph."

"I need to know, Louie," I said.

Louie gave the tablecloth a sharp tug. "Why? Why do you need to know? When Herbie was with you, he was who he was to you. Why do you care who he was to other people?"

"I have to tell you, that's not an encouraging reaction."

"I mean, come on. All of us, you, me, all of us, we got people who'll say we're terrible. Hell, we got people we been terrible *to*. Why should Herbie be different?"

"He shouldn't," I said. Across the restaurant, the waitress was watching me with concern; I wasn't eating. I gestured to the food with an open hand and smiled to reassure her, then said, "But from your perspective, Louie, just between us, who *was* Herbie, on balance?"

Ronnie put both hands up, a plea for a pause, swallowed, and said, "You said to me once that when you met Herbie, you told him you hated your father, and that Herbie said it would take a long time for you to understand who your father really was. You're doing the same thing to Herbie that you were doing to—"

"Why is everybody so fucking eager to protect me?" Even Eaglet and Ting Ting broke it off and looked at me. "Herbie was a—a *signpost* in my life. *Burning desert this way, Emerald City that way.* I chose, I thought I chose, the Emerald City. But now—"

"You're who you are," Ronnie said. "Nobody made you who you are except you."

"Louie," I said, and paused, trying to find an avenue of approach, and then I had it. Louie had volunteered to front money for me this very week, to pay Eaglet and Debbie, and he was one of the very few crooks I knew who would lend money to other crooks when they were in trouble. "Louie, tell me honestly. How much money would you have loaned to Herbie?"

Louie got up, pushed his chair back, and folded his napkin and dropped it on the table. "None," he said. "You happy now? I wouldn't have loaned him a dime on a hot day if he was ten cents short for a Popsicle. You want to worry about something real? Worry about those two." He nodded toward Ting Ting and Eaglet. "Stinky loves that kid. Loves him like he never loved anybody. The other boys, they were like furniture, but this one— this one, if Stinky loses him and he thinks it's your fault, I'm telling you, Stinky will kill you. No figure of speech, Junior. He'll kill you."

He shoved the chair in, hard, and stomped halfway to the door, his shoulders hunched high, as though fighting a weight. The waitress watched him go, her mouth open. Even Eaglet and Ting Ting were paying attention. Halfway to the door, he turned back around. "Piece of advice, okay? Don't look too close at blessings. You're thirsty and somebody hands you half a glass of water, don't get all bent out of shape about that it wasn't full. Just drink it and say thanks and go do something that makes you feel good."

23
The Monte Carlo Method

I said, "I've already slept. I slept for hours. You sleep."

"Then what'll you do?"

"Go drive around."

"We'll both go drive around." She got up, leaving me alone on the peacock-print couch. "Do you really think Stinky will try to kill you?"

"I don't know why not. He's already tried once."

"I thought he and Ting Ting were a couple."

I got up, too, although I didn't know why. "I'm sure they are, in Stinky's mind. But Ting Ting is a poor, probably *very* poor, Filipino kid who's suddenly living in a mansion. There could remotely, just possibly, be an element of fiscal calculation in his affection for Stinky. I mean, come on, he's *Stinky*. The world's most hydraulically streamlined face, a heart you couldn't find with an electron microscope, and an endless lust for stuff. One long *gimme gimme gimme*."

"I'll bet Ting Ting found his heart." She effortlessly picked up her purse, which I could hardly lift. "What happens if Stinky tosses him out?"

"I suppose he'll move in with Eaglet, which should be interesting. Anyway, she can protect him if Stinky gets vindictive and sends someone to—you know. Louie says she's good with that gun."

"He could teach martial arts," she said.

"Well, by now Stinky should be sitting in the living room, tapping his foot and looking at his watch. Hey, you were going to tell me about Trenton."

"Was I?" She stepped back, putting physical distance between herself and my reminder. "Let's not just drive," she said. "Let's drive to my place. Just in case. I feel like this place is lighted up in fuchsia on Google Maps with the legend JUNIOR'S HERE."

"Fine. Go ahead. I'll, uh, I'll meet you."

"Oh, for Christ's sake. Nothing is less attractive than a mop-ing man."

"Well, then," I said energetically, "how about *this*? You drive and I'll *meet you later*."

"Much better." She went to the closet and took out the Glock and slapped it into my hand. "Me and Eaglet," she said. "Protecting our men."

"From what?"

She opened the door. "From Trenton."

We hadn't been on the road for more than a minute, she a few car lengths ahead of me in her drab little Esoterica or whatever it was, built by the glum mechanics of the former Soviet bloc, when I remembered that I'd turned my cell phone off when I went to bed, much earlier that day. I powered it on, keeping it low in my lap so as not to attract the attention of a cop eager to write a big fat ticket to help offset the city's burgeoning deficit. The screen said, THREE NEW VOICE MESSAGES, and then the phone rang.

Ronnie said, "So as not to waste the time it takes us to get there, why is this Monty Carlo so important to you?"

"Theoretically, Wattles's chain ended in the hit man. I've followed it from Wattles to Janice to Handkerchief to Dippy Thurston, who has now vanished if she took my advice. Dippy handed it off to Monty, who in turn either delivered it to the hitperson or to the person who was supposed to deliver it to the hitperson."

"It's so low-tech it's almost endearing."

The words *low-tech* hung there in the air for a moment, shimmered and then disappeared like a shower of glitter. I said, "Wait a minute."

"Sure."

We maintained radio silence for a couple of blocks, and then she said, "You're somewhere else, aren't you? What are you thinking about?"

"Low-tech," I said. "This morning someone got into my car with a jiggered remote and left a note on my windshield with Kathy's and Rina's birthdays on it."

"There are car thieves who use scanners now. They wait in a parking lot until someone boops his car locked, and the scanner records the frequency of the signal, so they can duplicate it on their own remote and open the car."

"How do you know about this?"

"So soon you forget. Donald, the guy who got me out of either Trenton or Albany and drove me as far west as Chicago, was a car thief. I helped him boost three of the cars we used on that run, and I kind of liked it. It was exciting in a not-very-enlightened way. I keep up with the field, I guess you could say. Anyway, that's the new thing, the boop scanner, but it's not exactly low-tech."

"No," I said. "And those birth dates, getting those wasn't low-tech, either."

"And?"

"And I've been knocking on Monty Carlo's door and he's been ducking me. I suddenly remember that Dippy said he was some sort of brainiac crook. Maybe a hacker?"

"Could be."

"And, who knows? Maybe my attempts to get in touch with him have scared him. He's probably read about Herbie and Handkerchief by now, and Dippy isn't answering his calls, and maybe he figures *I'm* the one who's yanking all those links out of the chain, and he's next. So he's trying to scare me away."

"Or maybe he's the one who killed Herbie and Handkerchief. Maybe he was the hit person at the end of the chain, and since things have gotten out of hand, he's decided to erase the chain."

"Could be," I said.

"But you don't think so. I can hear it in your voice."

"No. I think if he were the killer, he'd have arranged to meet me someplace where he could waste me without a lot of effort. Instead, he's trying to chase me away. And he seems to have a helper who's a kid, a Hispanic boy. Kids are natural hackers."

"A kid?"

"Twelve or thirteen, according to the shopkeeper who saw him go into my car. Skinny, dark-skinned, baseball cap."

"That gets it down to about two and a half million possibilities."

"I need to make a couple of calls," I said. "Do you want to pull over or just go ahead and meet me at your place?"

"I'll stop and pick up some coffee, and replace some of the things that'll be rancid by now, like milk. See you there."

She rang off and I pulled over and brought up my voicemail. First was Rina with information about Edward Mott, Herbie's estranged son, who was currently a salesman at a Toyota dealership in North Hollywood, so who says there aren't second acts in American lives? He'd gone from Hondas to Toyotas, although he hadn't been promoted to floor manager or whatever was above *salesman*. She gave me the address and told me she'd emailed me the URL for his Facebook page so I could see what he looked like, and that I owed her sixty-eight dollars, which seemed high to me.

The second message was DiGaudio, who said, "Your guy will be here tomorrow afternoon at four. Just come in and ask for me." Then he coughed a few times, said, "Ohhh, shit," and disconnected.

The third was from Dippy Thurston. "Just seeing how you are," she said, "and wondering if there was any news." Even her voice was elfin. "This is a throw-away phone and I'm throwing it away, so don't call me back. And don't bother looking for me, either. I'll call tomorrow."

Well, at least *someone* was alive, or had been in the last eight hours. My watch volunteered the information that it was 10:44. I called Rina anyway.

"I don't believe it," she said. "I just this second fell asleep."

"If you were asleep, how do you know it was just this second?"

"The same song is on Spotify."

"What the hell is Spotify? Sounds like an acne treatment."

"It's an Internet music channel. I created a bedtime station called SNOOZE."

"Speaking of the Internet, how hard is it to find a hacker?"

"Too many variables for a decent answer," she said. She yawned. "Is he like a stealth hacker or a showoff? Two completely different types. Stealth hackers are totally hard to trace. They've got names behind names and they're browsing through a whole series of proxies, one proxy strung to another, probably on different continents so they can mimic IP addresses from anywhere in the world."

"If you say so. You want to give it a try?"

"Sure, it's money. What have you got?"

"A name, but probably not a real one. Monty Carlo."

"Gee, you think? Monty with an *e* or a *y*?"

"Y."

"Very brand-name. What else?"

"He's got tattoos."

"Whoa. Maybe you haven't seen any bare arms lately."

"I mean, unusual tattoos. Math. Cosines and stuff."

"Calculus," she said. "Huh, that's modestly interesting. The Monte Carlo Method, spelled with an *e*, is a pretty famous piece of calculus. It's a way of predicting the outcome in a situation with a large number of apparently random variables."

"Do tell." If I said something every time she amazed me, she'd become impossible.

"It was invented in the 1940s by a physicist who was sick and couldn't go to the office, which was like Los Alamos, since he was working on the atomic bomb? Do you remember any of this?"

"The atomic bomb," I said. "These days it sounds almost quaint."

"So he was sitting at home, probably in bed, playing solitaire, and he wondered how he might go about predicting the probability of any specific game's being winnable. What I like about people like this is that he really didn't care how the game would come out or whether he could win or what the odds were. What he cared about was how he might approach a solution."

I said, "My turn to say huh."

"Yeah, huh. So, to continue my story, which I'm pretending interests you, when he got back to the lab, he showed his algorithms to his boss, who named the solution after the famous casino in that little micro-country, and later someone else programmed it into this, like, ice-age computer called ENIAC so he could run it."

"That's extremely helpful," I said. "I wish I'd been making notes."

"It's still used for certain kinds of calculations. Monte Carlo, not ENIAC. ENIAC had about as much power as an alarm clock and it was as big as the Pentagon, and I'm talking about all this because I think I may have heard of this guy, Monty Carlo I mean, not ENIAC. I think he could be right out here somewhere, here in the Valley. Some kid was talking about him."

"He may work with kids," I said. "He sent one, I think, to break into my car."

"Yeah? Scan the frequency on your remote?"

"Why does everyone know about this but me?"

"You know lots of things the rest of us don't," she said. My own daughter, soothing my ego. "Really. Lots of things. Lots and lots." She yawned again, in my ear this time. "Is that it? Can I back go to sleep now?"

"Sure," I said.

"Fine," she said. "This is gonna cost you."

She hung up. I sat in my car, running my own probabilities. If I was right, if Monty Carlo had dug up that info to frighten me rather than to threaten me, I could give myself permission to relax, just a little. Of course, I had no way of knowing whether I was right. There could be a bullet streaking for my head at that very moment.

I ducked, just in case, and then started the car back up and headed for West Hollywood and Ronnie.

24
The Essentials About All of You

The last thing my father said to me before he left for good, with his car idling in the driveway, full of his clothes and books, was, "You'll understand all this when you've grown up."

The last thing I said to Rina before I left her for good, with my car idling in the driveway full of my clothes and books, was, "You'll see. It's not going to be so different."

The last thing Herbie said to me before I left for good, my car idling in his driveway, waiting to take me to whatever long-forgotten thing was more important than spending time with him, was, "See you later, kid."

We'd all been wrong.

People are wrong so often, and things break so easily.

Leaving for good. What a concept.

When I asked at the dealership for Edward Mott, the guy at the front desk said into his microphone, "Eddie, Eddie Mott, come to check-in."

I said, "Eddie, huh?"

"Eddie here, Eddie probably everywhere in the world," the desk guy said. His nametag read MICHAEL, so he had the credentials to turn up his nose at nicknames.

Behind me, someone said in a reedy tenor, "Help you?"

I turned to see a man who looked like the Herbie I first knew, if he'd been freeze-dried for a couple of decades. He was small, although on him it was the kind of smallness that can seem precise and fussy, while Herbie, once I'd gotten to know him, had always seemed to be about my height, even though he wasn't. He had the same receding hair, neither red nor brown, and the same four-pound nose, which the rest of his features had gathered to worship. But where Herbie's eyes had always given me the unsettling impression of being slightly closer to me than the rest of his face, as though he were wearing strong reading glasses, Eddie's were distant and underpowered, the kind of eyes that didn't consider anything very closely and probably didn't remember much of what they'd looked at.

Or they might have been the eyes of someone who just didn't give a shit.

"Eddie," I said. "Can I get a minute of your time?"

The left eye tightened for an instant, just a little pull on the muscles beneath the lower lid, and he said, "Maybe trade it to you for your name."

"Eddie," the man behind the desk said, "the gentleman is looking for a C-A-R."

Eddie reached into his pocket and pulled out a twenty. He slapped it on the desk and said, "Twenty bucks says you're wrong. Want to match it?"

I said to the man behind the desk, "Save your money." To Eddie, I said, "My name is Junior Bender."

He made a sound that might have been a snort. "Well, isn't this a riot? Hope you parked close, because if you didn't you've had a walk for nothing." He crumpled the twenty in his hand and turned to go.

I put a hand on the sleeve of his sport coat. It felt thin and slightly greasy, and it released a faint reek of tobacco. "Eddie.

You can either give me five minutes in your office, or I'll make a stink they'll be asking you about for weeks."

He yanked his arm away. "Stink all you want. Get out of here."

"Do they know about your convictions?" He stopped walking, and I made a note to slip Rina an extra twenty. A man whose job put him in close proximity to half a million dollars' worth of new cars every day wasn't supposed to drive under the influence.

"Those records are sealed," he said. The emotionless little eyes were all over the room. "I was a juvenile."

"They're not sealed very well," I said. "Come on, five minutes. Don't you owe your father that much?"

"I don't owe my father shit," he said.

"Okay," I said. "Then do it because I'll fuck you up with the management if you don't."

The look he gave me brought his eyes alive for the first time; I felt his gaze perforate me and keep right on going. His mouth was screwed up as though he was going to spit, but what he said was, "What a guy, but that's what I should expect. Come on, asshole, let's get it over with."

I followed him past six ethereally gleaming cars, too immaculate ever to have burned gasoline. Separating them from the heat and noise of the day was a curved plate glass window that ran the entire front of the building. Through it, if they'd been looking, the cars would have seen their future: dirty, dented, trailing fumes, packed full of questionable people, jammed grille to tailpipe at one of Ventura's infinite stoplights, and heading mile by dreary mile toward the point where they'd be pulled off the road and chopped for parts.

It didn't take much energy to see the parallels with our own lives, although it took a little more to push it away. I'd managed

to do it by the time Eddie led me into a tiny office, just an anonymous cubicle with a desk, two chairs, and white walls blank
except for an enormous electric clock. The outer wall was made
of glass so the management could make sure he wasn't playing
solitaire or slicing his arms open or weeping helplessly into his
hands when he should be out there selling.

Solitaire. The Monte Carlo Method. Where was Monty
Carlo right now?

"Do it," he said. He was standing in front of his desk with
his hands in his pockets—usually a defensive posture—and
started to jingle some coins. The muscle beneath his eye tugged
once and then again.

"To begin with," I said, "I assume you know about your
father."

"Sure. Got a call from his lawyer, even before the cops told me."

"Guy named Twistleton?"

"A. *Vincent* Twistleton. Uncle Vince."

"Really?"

"Don't be silly. But he might as well have been, since Twist-
eleton was the way my father talked to us. Through 'Uncle'
Vince." He made the first air quotes I'd seen in a decade to set
off *Uncle*. "Easier than face-to-face, I guess, if you can't look
anybody in the eye."

"Talked to you, or to your mother?"

"My mother and I were on the same *side*," Eddie said, his
lips pulling back from his teeth. "The side my father addressed
through his lawyer."

"Really. Well, your dad wrote me a letter—"

"To you personally? Why should that surprise me?"

"He asked me to come and see you."

"And now you've done it. I'm sure you have things to do,
so I—"

"He wanted me to try to make you understand." The words felt surprisingly empty to me, and I realized that some of the things I'd been told about Herbie were making me question what I felt about him. How could I assume that I knew anything about what Eddie's experience had been?

"Oh, I understand," Eddie said. "I've understood for decades. It's not so complicated."

"He thought about you, talked about you, all the time." This wasn't literally true, but I figured, *so what? Maybe it'll make him feel better, if only for now.* "This was his last letter, the one he wrote me, and it's about you."

He glanced up at the clock and then, reflexively, at his wrist-watch, a gesture with years of practice behind it, and said, "I'll bet you that twenty you saved Michael at the desk that it wasn't *only* about me."

"No," I said. "No, it wasn't."

The nod he gave me had a kind of satisfaction that made me want to look away, the satisfaction of someone who's enjoying his pain. "It was mostly about *crook shit*, wasn't it?"

"In a manner of speaking."

"See, that's it, in a nutshell." He was leaning his butt against the desk, trying to look at ease but the hands in his pockets were balled into fists. "Nothing about this is hard to understand. That's the way it always was." He looked down at the floor for a second and then back up at me. "It was just more important for him to be a crook than it was to be a father."

And there it was, like getting hit in the face with a bucket of bolts: the one short, blunt, unequivocal sentence I'd never allowed myself to put together without qualifiers and justifica-tions, the baldest possible description of my relationship with my own daughter, and here was Eddie, the barely-functioning adult casualty of precisely the same kind of treatment. I must have stood there without replying longer than I'd thought because suddenly he was leaning forward, studying me and saying, "Are you okay?"

"Fine," I said, but I was responding to the tone, not the words, because I hadn't actually focused on the words. "Yeah, fine, I'm—"

The electric clock on the wall went *chuck* very softly and the minute hand took another leap.

"Maybe you ought to sit down. Who banged you up, anyway?"

"A chorus boy," I said, still feeling fogged in. "Misrepresenting himself."

Then I was in a chair, and he was sitting on the desk in front of me, although I didn't actually remember either of us moving.

"Sorry," I said. "I—I just got kind of sidetracked." I wanted to talk to my daughter, I wanted to talk to Kathy, but all I could think was, *And say what?*

"Yeah," he said. "I noticed."

I needed to change the subject, but I couldn't manage to change it very much, and I certainly couldn't bring the subject around to Rina. "My own—uhh—my own father left me," I said. "I mean, he left my mother and me."

"Well, of course, he did," Eddie said. "So wasn't it lucky that you got mine?"

"Hold on a minute." I shook my head and rubbed at my face, squeezing my eyes shut and trying to bring myself back into that room with Eddie. "What do you mean, 'of course?' How much do you know about me?"

"Everything that matters, which isn't much, because you don't matter much to me. But I know the *essentials*. I know the *essentials* about all of you."

I parroted, "All of us."

"Well, well," Eddie said. "Lookie here. He's surprised, isn't he?"

"What do you mean, all of us?"

"My father," he said. "It was like the priest's Boys' Town, but for crooks. No, that's not right. It was like—do you read books?"

"When there's no bowling on TV."

"He was Fagin, in *Oliver Twist*, that's who he was. Wanted to make a whole lot of Little Herbies. Actually tried to name me Herbie, my mom says, but she wouldn't let him."

"No," I said, feeling suddenly vicious, "*Eddie* is infinitely preferable."

He jingled his change happily. He'd gotten under my skin. "And you thought you were the only one, didn't you?"

I took a moment, stretching my legs out in front of me just to give myself something to do. "How did you know my father had left my mother?"

"They all needed fathers," Eddie said. "That need was the socket he plugged himself into. He was *Daddy* to everybody except me."

A part of me wanted to say, *Oh, poor you,* but there he was in front of me. The discard left behind by another clueless father, yet one more abandoned adult, trying to act as though it hadn't mattered. So instead I said, "Okay," and got up. "Sorry to bother you."

"Are you going to make trouble for me with the boss?"

"Why would I make trouble for you, Eddie?" I asked, feeling a thousand years old. "We're practically the same person."

The clock went *chuck* again, and once more Eddie looked at it and then at his watch. "Lunchtime," he said. He put a fingertip beneath the twitching eyelid. "Can I buy you a drink?"

"There were three of you," he said, ignoring the little white plastic stick in the glass and stirring his amber drink with his forefinger. We were in an old-style steak place on Ventura—red leather booths, dark wood, and testosterone, the kind of place that should always be called *Bud's*. The waitress had brought him the drink and put it on the table before she even said, "Hi, Eddie."

The drink was a double from the look of it, and light on the water. I said, "Diet Coke, please," and when the waitress was gone, I asked him, "Was I the first one?"

"Second," he said. "The first one was a guy named Chris, who learned what he could from my father and then used it to break in to my father's place and steal everything he could carry, ho ho ho. I guess he left town, but for all I know, my father killed him."

"Your father never killed anyone."

He gave me a long look, up from under his eyebrows, and drank.

"Did he?"

His lower lip popped out, as though the question wasn't worth an answer. "Might have."

I parked that for the moment and said, "Who was the third?"

"Girl," Eddie said, almost spitting the word. "Name of Ellen. She finished off whatever politeness still existed between my mother and him."

"How long did she last?"

"Couple of years." He raised the glass and eyed me over it. "You mean, were you number one?" He laughed, the way I might laugh if someone I didn't like tripped in front of me. "Yeah, if that makes you feel better. You were the favorite son."

The silence stretched out until the waitress arrived with the Diet Coke and said, "The usual, Eddie?" and Eddie nodded.

I asked, "What's the usual?"

The waitress, who was clearly not marking time until her

studio contract came through, said, "Spencer steak and fries, medium."

"You have Caesar salad?"

"We do. Entree-size?"

"Fine. Thanks."

"Want blackened spicy chicken on it?"

"Under no circumstances."

"I shouldn't be jumping on you," Eddie said when she was out of sight. "He disappointed everybody. That's what he did, he disappointed people."

"Are you going to show up for the reading of the will?"

The question seemed to catch him off-guard. "Hadn't thought about it. You think I should?" He tossed back the rest of the drink and then held the glass in the air and rattled the ice cubes.

"It's, I don't know, the last opportunity to show up for him."

"Or to leave him waiting. That's what he did to me, more often than not."

"Seems kind of hollow, doesn't it? It's not like he'll notice. Don't you—sorry if this sounds mercenary—don't you want to know what he left you?"

"I know what he left me. He left me the key to a safety deposit box and whatever is in it, which is probably cash, maybe some jewelry. Right to the end, he's got to be cheating somebody. The box is in both names, his and mine, so he can put stuff in it without me around and I can go empty it out solo without the tax people gathering around. Not that I have the key yet, of course. Probably a reason to go to the will thing." He rattled the glass again, this time earning a glance from the bartender. "Or maybe he'll disappoint me again and leave me a pack of Life Savers. Pitch a perfect game. What's he leaving you?"

"A painting by a guy named John Sloane."

"Pricey?"

"Worth a fortune, probably, but it's not like you could sell it at Sotheby's."

"Probably not."

I took a deep breath and said, "So did he kill somebody?"

He let a good count of five go by before he answered. "He got arrested for a possible homicide once, but it didn't go to a charge. For some reason, almost nothing ever went to a charge. Some cowboy actor from TV."

"No," I said, waving it off. I almost laughed with relief. "Forget it. I was with him. The man was dead when we got there. Scared the hell out of me."

"He took a rug, right? That's what the cops said, it was a big rug."

"Yeah. An old Navajo. But I'm telling you—"

"I know, he was dead when you got there. Did you take anything else?"

"Couple of things, but the rug was what mattered."

A new drink arrived, and Eddie did a two-finger salute to the waitress, who glanced at my mostly-full glass and retreated. "Could he have carried it out himself?"

"I don't know. No, probably not."

He raised the glass in a toast. "So what you actually *know* is that the actor was dead when you got there, but what you don't know is whether my good old dad had been there, say, an hour earlier." He sipped. "And just needed a hand with the rug."

"Life," a friend once said to me, "is a series of disappointments. And that's when it's going *well*."

Back when I was a kid I learned that the best way—for me, anyway—to deal with disappointment, with dashed hopes, with disillusionment, with hitting the wall of life face-first, was to get angry. Getting angry not only put off the moment when whatever it was finally punched a hole in my heart; it also provoked a surge of energy that got me through the immediate aftermath, that kept me moving forward. Even if my action was meaningless, it was better than taking to my bed for days, stewing in adolescent malaise and too male to cry.

So my reaction to what Eddie Mott, DeGaudio, and Louie had told me about Herbie was to get furious. That was infinitely preferable to the paralysis of feeling orphaned or, even worse, knowingly betrayed for a second time. The person who was responsible for all the unwelcome information coming my way, the person who got me into all this, I decided almost arbitrarily, was Wattles. And although Wattles was in Limpopo or someplace equally inaccessible, his office was right where he'd left it, and might yield up an answer or two in his absence.

I had almost two hours before I was due to peer through the one-way mirror in DiGaudio's interrogation room and fail to recognize Ruben Ghorbani, if Ghorbani was really going to be there. Bud's steakhouse, if that's what it was called, was only about ten minutes west of the building from which Wattles spread his fat fingers over his empire of felony.

The guard at the desk didn't look up from his iPad as I strolled past him to the elevators. He was wearing earphones, so two of his senses were off duty. As I passed him I tugged the visor on my baseball cap lower to frustrate the security cameras in the lobby and in the elevators. I knew from my last visit where the cameras were positioned in the hallway on Wattles's floor, and I kept my head down as I passed beneath them, trying to look like someone who was lost in thought.

To my mild surprise, the front door to Wattles, Inc. was unlocked and open by about an inch. I pulled the Glock from under my shirt, listened for a second, and then pushed the door open fast and stepped aside, pressed against the wall just beside the door. There was no reaction—no hail of bullets, no breathy "Come in, handsome," or anything in between. I counted fifteen, listening for all I was worth, using the first skill Herbie had taught me and the one I may have mastered best. Not a sound, not anyone whispering to anyone else or attempting to scurry out of sight, no rustle of nylons, although no one wears nylons any more, no closet door closing, nothing but my own heart, and even that was more felt than heard.

So I went in.

The place had been methodically turned inside out, but there was some evidence that the methodical approach had turned to irritation and then to full-out fury as the search progressed. The closet door was propped open by a cascade of brightly printed cardboard boxes saying TIFFANY LOVES ONLY *YOU*!!! that had spilled out across the carpet. Some of them had been roughly torn open, and protruding from them were bright, fleshy pieces of Tiffany herself. From the random bits on view, it seemed to me that plastic manufacturers still hadn't got skin tone down. As far as I could see, Tiffany's unclothed bits were the bleached dirty-bubblegum pink of flesh-colored bandages.

A couple of Wattles's very good overcoats had been hanging in the closet, and they'd been pulled out and shredded with something razor-sharp, possibly a box cutter. Linings had been ripped out, pockets inverted, lapels slit open.

The Tiffany seated behind the desk was a two-dimensional nightmare, deflated and slashed to ribbons. Her left arm had been almost severed at the shoulder, and the way it hung was too real for me; I didn't want to look at it. I took a quick glance at the inner room, just to make sure I was alone, and then went back into the reception area and locked the front door.

I'd burglarized Wattles's office once, but that was in the middle of the night, and it had been in fast, grab one thing—a blow-up doll named Dora, Tiffany's predecessor—and out again. This was the first time I'd been here alone in daylight. It looked smaller and dingier than I remembered it.

The inner office was intentionally uncomfortable, designed to put Wattles's guests on edge. The furniture had been purchased at the endlessly popular sidewalk discount, except for Wattles's chair, which was an ergonomic marvel covered in the skin of a griffin or something equivalently expensive, with controls that adjusted virtually every part of the body. Bouncing up and down on it, I found a button that heated the lower part of the chair's back—good for Wattles's spine, which was forever pulled out of shape by that gut—and a *vibrate* function that was quite different (I assumed) from Tiffany's more intimate vibrate function, and which worked much better than the Birdy Rub back at Bitsy's.

The point, of course, was that Wattles was the only one who

was *supposed* to feel at home. Everyone else was supposed to be as anxious as I'd been when I was dragged in here. Being off-balance like that probably explained why I'd missed the dinginess of the carpet, the cheap paint on the walls, the muzzy smudge of hand dirt around the doorknobs and light switches. The dust on the bookshelves, on his very up-to-date set of law books.

Was he not doing as well as he pretended, or did he just not care?

I sat in Wattles's chair and tried to look at launching a hit from his perspective. He accepted a contract, undoubtedly in person, undoubtedly somewhere other than this office, took advance payment in cash, and he then chose a hitter. How many times a year would he do this? Not too often, was my guess. He'd be top-of-the line for a hit, considering the care he took to distance himself and his client from the crime, and the amounts of money he had to be shelling out to the links in the chain. Hits, I guessed, were an occasional but profitable sideline.

Wattles thought of himself as an entrepreneur first and a crook second. He had his hand in a lot of things, some of them only marginally illegal, some of them flagrant, but always run from behind a series of screens. While other people did the dirty work, he sat here at the center of a cloud of lime aftershave with his high-rent view of the Valley, intimidating people across his desk, managing misbehavior at a remove, working the phones like a talent agent, slapping away at the keys of—

—of his laptop. The first time I ever met him, when a crooked cop named Lyle Hacker dragged me in here after setting me up to burglarize the home of someone whose house I wouldn't have gone anywhere near for a gazillion dollars if I'd known who he was, Wattles had given as much attention to his laptop as to me.

So where the hell was the laptop?

As I went through the office, I answered some of my own

questions and asked others. The safe—open and with some papers in it, but nothing that put him in the same league as Murder, Inc. *He doesn't do more than four or five hits a year.* The desk, largely empty, most of the drawers thoughtfully left open. *So that means a small pool of hitters.* Nothing behind the books on the shelves. *Talk to Debbie about who he might use. What's she going to do, shoot me?* Use the remote to open the panel on the far side of the room; no secret space behind the flatscreen monitor. *Eaglet is probably less dangerous than Debbie, and she's in love, which might soften her: see whether she knows anything.*

Back in the reception area. Poor Tiffany's desk contained nothing, and I mean not even a paper clip, although I don't know what I thought I might find there. A steno pad? Nail polish? A self-help book? She was a blow-up doll. *Janice and Dippy are gone and Handkerchief is dead; the only other person I know of who was definitely part of the chain is Monty Carlo. Let's poke him again.* I pulled out my phone and called the number Handkerchief had given me. This time, I got the echoing sound of a door opening on a rusty hinge and Orson Welles saying "The Shadow knows," followed by the car crash, which had been extended with a large number of hubcaps rolling across the pavement and then spinning noisily to a stop.

I said, "I'm still here. I'll be here until I talk to you. You've got my number. I have to tell you, though, if you want to keep the advantage and control our meeting, you need to get hold of me because I'm getting closer to you. Every minute. The next person who taps on your shoulder will be me. So call me."

I disconnected, realized I was sitting on the eviscerated latex remains of Tiffany, and jumped to my feet. I instinctively said, "Excuse me," before I could stop myself. She hissed slightly in reply, air flowing in or out of her somewhere. It creeped me out enough to send me back into the other room and Wattles's high-tech chair.

The chain of disconnects, I thought, as I let the unit in the seat massage me. First link, his primary back-and-forth, Janice; second link, a con man temporarily penetrating the veil of reality, Handkerchief; third link, one of the state's premiere pickpockets, with a sideline in magic, Dippy; fourth link, a probable hacker, Monty Carlo.

All of them felons, Janice had said, although now that I thought about it, I didn't remember that Dippy had been convicted of anything that might qualify as a felony. Monty Carlo, presumably, was young, so I made a note to ask Rina to look both for a mess involving Dippy and recent local busts concerning intelligence technology or data theft.

The chair stopped vibrating, and I looked at my watch. Time to get on the road for the Van Nuys station. I got up, and the idea hit me like someone breaking an egg over my head. I said, "Of course," and picked up the chair, flipped it over, and put it on the desk. It took about a minute to figure out that the button that turned on the heat could also be twisted. I twisted it, and the panel popped off. Fitted neatly into a tray beneath the massage unit was Wattles's little black laptop.

26
Bad, Cheap, and Ugly

"Yeah, I'm here, right where you asked me to be," Louie said on the phone. "You're paying me, aren't you?"

He was still a little raw from last night. I said, "Thanks, Louie. Sorry to have been such a jerk."

"You gotta learn to tell when you're lucky," he said. "More guys get screwed up in the head because they're pushing their luck than any other reason. Like marriage, you know? Get crazy about whether the little woman is knocking off a piece every three, four weeks, and break up something you can hardly live without. You find out she did it once and now she can't stand the sight of the guy, but by then she's gone, and you've traded the candy store for a lollipop. Truth," he concluded, "is overrated. What matters is happiness."

"I'll keep that in mind."

"Sure you will." He disconnected. People were hanging up on me lately.

The Van Nuys Police Station is a blank-faced, brute-force building on Sylmar Avenue, and what have we learned, class, about the name Sylmar? Well, you couldn't see the ocean from here, either. The building probably dated from the seventies and had all the charm I personally associate with that decade, which I think of as the antacid the world took to get over the sixties. It was both plain and ugly, but someone had planted some dispirited little trees in front of it to wave their witchy twigs around in the zephyrs of car exhaust.

I parked a couple of blocks away since the designated lot was completely full of crooks, accused crooks, their family members, and their lawyers. It was hot enough that I was just as happy to walk slowly, one eye on my watch. I was two minutes early when I went in and asked for DiGaudio, and Ronnie was already there, sitting demurely on a bench and looking, in that atmosphere, like the sunbeam that pierces the darkness of the treasure cave to finger the gold.

The guy behind the welcoming pane of glass ripped his eyes off of Ronnie and said, with the charm of cops everywhere, "He know you're coming?"

"He did yesterday, when we set it up."

Ronnie came up and kissed the side of my neck, and the cop practically hissed in disappointment and picked up a phone. He said, "Sit."

I sat. It took about eight minutes before DiGaudio pushed his way through the doors. He looked like he'd been dragged to the station behind a truck. His oversize jacket was wet beneath the arms and across the back, his face was dripping sweat, and he had the eyes of someone who'd just looked in a mirror and seen it go black. He'd pulled his mouth over to one side in a kind of tribute to the sheer magnitude of the pain that was staking claim to him. Even the cop behind the glass looked sympathetic.

I got up, but DiGaudio stopped and waved me back down. He leaned one shoulder against the wall and breathed hard at the floor for a minute. When he pushed himself away, he caught the cop behind the glass with his mouth hanging open and he said, "The fuck are you looking at? You got nothing to do?"

"Sorry." The cop moved some papers around on his desk and then moved them back.

"You," DiGaudio said to me, jerking a thumb over his shoulder, toward the door. "Now." To Ronnie, he said, "You the witness, Miss?"

"I am," she said.

He held her gaze for a moment and then said, "I know you from somewhere?"

"I'm impressed. Some time ago, my husband was killed, and you—"

He nodded. "Derek Somebody. Bigelow. Jesus, Bender, you don't waste an opportunity." He pressed a hand to his side and said, "Ahhhhh," and closed his eyes for a moment. When he opened them, he registered Ronnie's expression and said, "It's okay, it's okay. It's nothing I haven't gotten through before."

Ronnie said, "I'm so very sorry."

He blinked so heavily I was surprised I hadn't heard it, then turned and shuffled through the doors with the two of us in tow, and I found myself pierced by a bolt of something—pity or fear or both of them, in a cold and thorny knot, no way to pick it apart and get a better look at it. Instead, I said, "I appreciate this."

"It's not for you," he said. "It's for that nice young lady you got there, Mrs., uhh, Bigelow." He stopped again and said, "Gimme a sec."

We kept a respectful and somewhat cowardly distance from his pain until Ronnie said, "Oh hell. Let me help." She went up and checked her height against his. Then she bent her knees just a tiny bit. "Just put your arm over my shoulders. We'll make everybody jealous."

"Was a time," DiGaudio said, pushing himself off the wall. To my surprise, he let her drape his arm around her and leaned into her. "Was a time," he said again as we began to walk,

"pretty girl like you would have looked at me and seen somebody who was, you know, okay. I never been as good-looking
as Junior here, but I done—I did—okay. With the ladies. Had a
wife almost as pretty as you."

"I'm sure you do," Ronnie said.

DiGaudio said, "Did."

"Well, she was a lucky woman. There's something in you,
something really solid. Women like that. We like it more than
we like some vapid face."

I said, "Vapid?"

"Not really my experience," DiGaudio said, "but nice of you
to say so." He let go of her and stepped away, just barely not
panting. "I can make it. The big part of that one's gone past."

"You're a brave man."

"You got a more comfortable alternative, tell me about it,"
DiGaudio said. "Not *that* one, though, I'm not going near that
one. Too many cops do that. Okay, here we are." He stopped at
a pair of doors leading into a dimmed corridor. "Second window
on the left," he said. "Just take a look and say yes or no."

A small room: a table, three chairs, and a door on the opposite wall. Sitting at the chair nearest the door, with his back to it
so he faced the window, Ruben Ghorbani packed a lot of physical presence. I could feel it even through the pane of glass. He
either sensed us or saw our shadows through the mirror, because
the big face lifted toward us and the green eyes looked almost
straight into mine.

His skin was more deeply pitted than the mug shot had suggested, so rough it qualified as a disfigurement. His hair may
once have been naturally black, but now it was dyed, and the
dye had been applied so long ago that there was a white half-
inch of hair between his scalp and the black. It created a kind of
1950s two-tone effect. The nose was thick and blunt, as though

it had been hit many times, the mouth surrounded by deep lines and pulled down sharply at the corners, the *nyet*-mouth I associated with pictures of Cold War Soviet prime ministers.

But there was also something diminished about him. The steroid-pumped muscles had gone slack and softened into fat beneath his polo shirt, and the eyes, despite their fierce greenness, weren't as energetic as I'd expected. Maybe I'd just built him up too much in my mind. I gave him a long look, trying to seem puzzled, and then stepped away and said to DiGaudio, "No."

He nodded slowly, looking at me as though I'd just drawn an inside straight and it confirmed what he'd known all along: the fix was in. "I'm telling you," he said. "Anything happens to this guy, I'm coming after you."

Ronnie said, "He's not the man."

"'Kay, honey," DiGaudio said to her. To me, he said, "Just so's you know."

"He's on foot," Louie said on the phone. "Heading for the parking lot."

"Okay." I kissed Ronnie and said, "Thanks."

She said, "That poor man."

"We'll talk about it later. I've got to get—"

"You're all heart, Junior."

"I feel terrible about DiGaudio, Ronnie, but there's nothing I can do about him. I *can* do something about Ruben Ghorbani, but only if I get my ass moving."

"It can take the rest of you with it," she said, turning away. I watched her walk away, hoping she'd look back, and when she didn't I did what any guy would do and sprinted for my car.

"He's turning onto Victory," Louie said three or four minutes later as I fought my way into traffic. It was four thirty, the overture to rush hour, and it was starting off with a timpani bang. "Where are you?"

"Behind another Goddamned SUV. It's like driving behind a movie screen for all I can see what's in front of me. Okay, he's signaling to turn right, so that'll clear him out of the way, and in front of him is, Jesus save me, another one. Why are these things legal?"

He said, "You want an answer?"

"No."

"He's heading west, pretty much, on Victory, as west as Victory goes, anyway. He's got his blinker on for a right, might be going to get on the 405."

"North?"

"Yeah. South is a left."

"Stay with him." I zigged the wheel to the left just enough to see around the SUV and nearly experienced a head-on collision with another one, and zagged back into my own lane.

"Nice talk," Louie said.

"Sorry. I thought I was just thinking it."

"So maybe I'm a mind reader. Poor old Handkerchief, huh?"

"I'm going to find the person who did it, and did Herbie, too. And I'm going to neuter the sonofabitch, one nut at a time." Herbie's ball peen hammer, used on Ghorbani in the Angeles National Forest, popped into my mind. Not really the Herbie I'd known.

"You think it's the same per—he's taking the ramp onto the 405 North."

"I'll bet I know where he's going. *Yeah*, I think it's the same person. I think it's some sick mo-fo who gets off on pain. What's he driving?"

"Junker," Louie said. "Old Plymouth Neon. Purple."

I saw daylight to my right and cut into the lane, earning a

disciplinary blare from a horn loud enough for a cruise ship. "I thought the Neon was a Dodge."

"It was a Plymouth first," said Louie. "They started pretending it was a Dodge when they closed down Plymouth. 2001, that was."

"The walking encyclopedia of automotive history," I said, running a yellow and, arguably, getting through it legally. I suddenly remembered the Glock in the trunk and slowed down.

"Kinda sad," Louie said. "He's heading to the left lane, so he's staying on the freeway for a while. First Plymouth hit the street in 1928, did you know that?"

"It will surprise you to know that I didn't." I made a right onto a residential street, heading north toward Sherman Way which, I thought, might be running better.

"First cheap car Chrysler ever made," Louie said. "Chrysler was very hoity-toity, all limousine trade until then. So the first Plymouth rolls off the line just in time for the Great Depression, and it keeps Chrysler alive until people got money again, and how do they show their gratitude? They close it down with a really crap model."

"Not with a bang but a Neon," I said, watching the stoplight go green half a block in front of me and accelerating toward it. "Got any more sad car stories?"

"Anybody who likes American cars," Louie said, "they got a lot of sad car stories. Poor little Neon, such a sad bag of crap. Trying to compete with the Japanese for twenty years and they still hadn't figured it out."

I made the left through the light, and Sherman Way opened up in front of me, traffic blessedly and improbably sparse. Just the other side of the stoplight was the overpass above the 405 freeway and the ramp that would drop me down onto it. "Figured what out?" I said, gliding through the green light, feeling as entitled as a funeral procession and almost as stately. I don't have a license for the Glock. For any of the Glocks.

"Making good cars," Louie said. "After the Japanese started eating their lunch, they, and by *they* I mean Detroit, they made them cheap, they made them small, they made them outta metal so thin that when you hit a hundred thousand miles and it fell apart you could crumple it up like a beer can and throw it away. And in the meantime, people driving Sushis and Konnichiwas are getting a hundred and fifty thousand miles without a tune-up. Fucking tragedy, that's what it was. All the Japanese were doing was what we used to do, make good stuff."

"Where are you now?"

"Past Roscoe, still going north. He's not changing lanes. Thing is, the Brits, you know the Brits?"

"I've heard of the Brits." I merged left and stamped on it. Everyone else was doing 70, 75, trying to put some miles between them and the 5 P.M. tsunami that would stop the whole freeway dead in its tracks.

"The way Brits made cars, they'd break if you scowled at them. Jaguar? *Forget* about it, those things needed five thousand bucks' worth of work every time you put them into reverse. But people bought them, because the Brits made out like it was good breeding to break down, it was *sensitive* to break down, and that was because the car was a thoroughbred, and it had to be a thoroughbred because it *cost* so much. Good and cheap, the Japanese got. Bad and expensive, the Brits got. What we got was bad, cheap, and ugly. Not the best formula, huh?"

"Where are you?"

"What, you're not interested? This is the Great American Decline we're talking about here."

"There have been several," I said. "Where are you?"

"I don't know." He sounded sulky. "Still going north."

"It's okay, I know where he's going."

"You gonna tell me?"

"No," I said. "I'm going to preserve my air of mystery. But I'll tell you what offramp he's going to take."

Ten minutes later, Louie said, "How the hell did you know that?"

Ghorbani was out of sight ahead of me in his purple Neon, but when he'd gotten off at Roxford, I'd felt certain enough about his destination to send Louie home. What with the shooters guarding Kathy's and Rina's house and what I'd already paid Louie, I was most of the way through Wattles's deposit, and since Wattles was in Limpopo and I was absolutely not going to sell those two brooches to Stinky, the only additional money was in my *necessities* box. People don't usually picture crooks worrying about their alimony and child support, but I had never missed a month since the divorce, and I was committed to keeping it that way. There was no way I was going to do anything that might suggest to Rina that she wasn't the most important thing in the world to me.

I'd done that already.

The parking lot for the half-bulldozed shopping center was empty except for the purple Neon, a bruise on wheels, in the slot right in front of the surplus store. I parked in the same space I'd taken before, in obedience to the ancient and mysterious imperative that makes us sit in the same place at the table every night or always choose the left-hand row in a theater, perhaps something as primitive as a few cells in the oldest part of the brain saying *We did this before and we didn't get killed.* I pulled the Glock from the trunk and tucked it into the center of my back. With the righteousness of someone doing something he knows is futile but which is the right thing to do anyway, I pushed the button on my remote and heard the little toot that told me that my car was now locked down and fully alarmed and absolutely defenseless against anyone with a little electronics know-how and twelve dollars' worth of junk from Radio Shack.

When I pulled open the door of the church, seven old folks sitting around an empty table looked hopefully up at me. It was barely five, but no one seemed to be competing for their free time.

I said to the people at the table, "Dr. Angelis?"

"In there," said a lady with very bright blue eyes and immaculately waved white hair. She was wearing fire-engine red coral earrings, and I hoped someone had told her how nice they looked. She pointed a curved index finger, all swollen knuckles, at the dark curtain. The hand didn't shake at all.

The curtain parted, and Dr. Angelis came out. He said, "You're not welcome here."

"I'm sorry to hear that," I said, "but I'm going to talk to Mr. Ghorbani anyway, unless you and Felipe carry me out of the building, and even then I'll just sit on the hood of his car in the parking lot, which would probably dent it." I spread my arms, holding them well away from the sides of my body. "I'm not armed." It was a lie, but worth trying. "You can check."

Angelis closed his eyes and lowered his head, but I thought he was considering rather than praying.

"Tell you what," I said. "You and Felipe take me in there, and put Ghorbani in the bathroom. It locks, right?"

"Of course."

"Fine. Put Ghorbani in there and lock the door. You two stay with me, keep an eye on me, and I'll talk to him through the door.

Five minutes. At the end of five minutes, he can come out or not, and if he does I'll talk to him a little more. If he doesn't, I'll go away. Better still, put *me* in the bathroom and lock the door."

Angelis said, "Felipe's not here." He looked at the floor again. "I have your word?" His voice was soft, but there was no mistaking the will beneath it.

"You do."

"I don't need no bathroom." The words sounded like they'd been spoken in the center of a very large and very empty room. The curtains opened again, and Ghorbani was standing there. He was bigger than he'd looked through glass.

"Ruben," Father Angelis said apprehensively.

"They're going to come sooner or later," Ghorbani said. He had one of the deepest voices I'd ever heard, the kind of sound that might echo for miles over the hills on the seabed. "It might as well be now."

"Who are *they*?" I asked.

Ghorbani said, "Who are you?"

"I'm a friend," I said, "of Herbie Mott."

Ghorbani pulled his face back half an inch, as though I'd tried to slap it. He said, "A good friend?"

I thought for a second and said, "Yes."

"Dr. Angelis," Ruben Ghorbani rumbled, "this man is in pain."

"No," Ghorbani said. He shook his head, and his jowls rippled. "I ain't seen Herbie Mott in years. I ain't seen nobody in years, not from that part of my life."

"Ruben is not the man he once was," Dr. Angelis said.

"Yeah?" I said. "Who is he now?"

"I'm a worthless piece of shit," Ghorbani said, "but I ain't *that* worthless piece of shit."

"The one who did this, he means," Dr. Angelis said, turning a palm toward his face. The three of us were on folding chairs in a little room at the back of the shop. A fluorescent buzzed and flickered overhead, as though debating with itself whether just to give up and go dark.

"And who did you?" Ghorbani said, studying me. He nodded something that looked like professional approval. "Had to be a pro, or else there was three or four of them."

"Well," I said.

"I used to know a couple guys," Ghorbani said, "who could, like, team up for that, hurt you that bad, I mean. Got top money, too."

"It wasn't a couple of guys," I said. I could feel myself blushing. It was hired muscle from the Philippines. What's happened to you?"

Ghorbani said, "I beat up the wrong guy." His smile wasn't so much sudden as it was unexpected.

"Ruben," Dr. Angelis said, "is a minister now."

"Downtown," Ghorbani said. "At the mission on Skid Row."

"They listen to him," Angelis said.

"I still *look* scary," Ghorbani explained.

Angelis swatted Ghorbani on the knee. "You know better than that."

"Grace," Ghorbani said to me. "It comes when you can't see a foot in front of you."

I held up a hand. "Okay. Look." I thought for a moment, and rubbing my eyes seemed to help me organize it. "Herbie wrote a letter, supposed to be given to me if he died—you know—wrong. In it, he said if he got killed, you were probably the guy who would kill him."

"I probably would have," Ghorbani said. "But I kind of lost interest."

Angelis said, "Believe him."

"I do, I guess. But how? What happened?"

Ghorbani leaned back in his chair, which creaked, and closed his eyes. "Couple days after I messed the Rev here up, it was in the papers. Pictures and all." He looked at me. "I seen the picture, which was taken the day after, when things look even worse—"

"I know," I said.

"And I read he was a Rev and that he, you know, he refused to describe me to the cops, both him and Felipe. They wouldn't say nothing about what I looked like. Said they didn't want me punished, he wanted me to be reborn. At first I thought, oh, fuck him, *reborn*, what a bunch of crap." He glanced at Angelis, who gave him a nod of encouragement. "But then the word came back, and when it did, I saw writing on the wall, swear to Christ—sorry, Rev—on the wall in my bedroom, and what I saw was, like—in the Bible?—the words on the wall at the king's feast: *Mene Mene Tekel Upharsin*. I saw *them*. You know what those mean?"

"No," I said.

"They're *weight*." He let the chair come down and leaned toward me as he bit off the final word, his eyes the green of lime leaves. "The shekel, or *tekel*, was the basic Babylonian unit of weight. Like an ounce or something." He had both palms up, cupped, and he raised and lowered them like an old scale. "The *mene* was heavy, like fifty shekels. You following me?"

"Through a fog."

"The *upharsin* was half a *mene*, or twenty-five shekels. I knew that because when I was a kid my parents dragged me to church, made me memorize most of the Old T."

"Testament," Angelis interposed.

"Yeah, testament. So I seen those words in front of me when

I read who the Rev was in the paper, and I knew what I was see-ing was my own weight, the weight I was pulling around. I was seeing that the weight I was carrying was *ancient*, it was as old as evil, and the reason I had all them muscles was to carry that weight, the weight of the bad things I done. It was fucking crush-ing—sorry again, Rev—it was crushing me. Evil was." He looked down at his lap, and I thought for a second he was embarrassed, but when he looked back up at me, the green eyes were shining. "And something had wrote that on my wall. I cried," he said. "First time since I was eight years old, I cried. And it was like the whole earth had been lifted off my back. Like I'd been all bent over in a cave all my life, crawling through this tiny dark cave on my hands and knees under the weight of the earth my whole life, and all of a sudden I could stand up straight, and I was stand-ing in the light. Like a person, not an animal. Then I found out where the Rev's church was and I come down here."

"I will confess," Dr. Angelis said, "that I didn't rejoice when I saw him coming."

He and Ghorbani laughed.

"I stayed here three days," Ghorbani said. "Me and the Rev and Felipe." He pushed a knuckle against his lower right eyelid and blinked away a little moisture. "And that finished it. Never talked to none of them again, the people in the other Ruben's world."

"Bless their souls," Angelis said. "The Lord has infinite mercy."

Ghorbani brought his eyes back to mine. "You want me to talk to this Filipino bruiser? I mean, if *I* could be healed—"

"I think he's beyond help," I said. He and I looked at each other for a moment. "But I know someone you probably *could* help."

"Who?"

"You remember Burt the Gut?"

Ghorbani's face darkened, and for a moment I thought it was probably like looking at the man he'd been before. "I remember him. Don't want to, but I do."

"He's old and sad and lonely," I said. "He's eighty and he hurts all over and he's got a young wife who hates him, with good reason, I guess. Just waiting for him to die." I inclined my head in the direction of the front room. "He's like some of the people out there, except that they've got you and Dr. Angelis and Felipe. He rattles around in this big house with furniture jammed on top of furniture, and the only person he's got wakes up every morning disappointed that he made it through the night."

"I'll call him," Ruben said, looking at Father Angelis, who nodded. "Maybe go see him, if he sounds okay."

"You'd make him happy," I said. I pulled up Burt's number on my phone and wrote it down. Ghorbani put it into his shirt pocket, and I heard myself say, "Don't lose that. He's a sad old man."

"Gotcha," Ghorbani said.

I pushed my chair back but stopped without getting up. "Before I go," I said. "Tell me why you wanted to kill Herbie."

"Worst fall I ever took," Ghorbani said. "It put me away for three years. I got pounded pretty good in the jug, damn near every day, until I beefed up. Worst thing in my life. So anyways, what they got me for, I did it to protect Herbie. And Herbie ratted me to the cops."

Ratted is just about the worst word in the crook's dictionary. Ruben Ghorbani wouldn't be unique, or even unusual, if he offed someone who sent him up for hard time. I knew half a dozen people who didn't think of themselves as killers in spite of the fact they'd aced a rat.

I was listening to Ghorbani's words ricochet around in my head as I came out of the church, hip-deep in the shadows of the other buildings, the sun well on its way west, plowing its path to the ocean that you couldn't see from Sylmar. I hit the broken pavement of the parking lot, running a finger along the dust on Ruben's purple neon and thinking about Herbie, and I almost had my hand on the door of my car before I saw the person in the passenger seat.

I backed up, reflexively reaching for the gun at the base of my spine, but before I grabbed it the person leaned forward to look at me, and I saw it was a kid in a baseball cap, not more than thirteen or fourteen. He smiled and wiggled four fingers at me in a cheery little wave.

Before I did anything else, I took a slow, deep-breathing 360-degree turn to survey the lot. No cars other than Ruben's and mine, no one on the sidewalk, no one lurking in any of the doors to the remaining shops. No one anywhere I could see.

The kid in the car mimicked me, looking around everywhere, and when he turned his back I saw the long, straight, black pony-tail hanging out of the opening at the back of the cap, saw the bright red ribbon tied around it to hold it in place.

A girl.

When she turned back to me and smiled again, I realized she wasn't Latina. She was Asian, either Chinese or Korean. She had a sharp face, a fox's face, with a tiny, pointed nose, the nostrils looking almost too narrow to breathe through, the cheekbones swelling above the delicate jaw to create a V-shape that was emphasized by the upward tilt of the eyes. She lifted a hand, palm down, and paddled with her fingers, meaning *come on*.

I looked around the parking lot again and then opened the door—which was, of course, unlocked—and got in.

She said, brightly, "Hi."

I said, "Who the hell are you?"

"Anime."

"Anna May?"

"Anime," she said. "You know, like the Japanese cartoons?"

"I know what *anime* is. Anime what?"

"Anime Wong."

I said, "You're kidding."

She drew a question mark in the air, backward, so I could read it. "Why? Why would I be kidding?"

"Fine," I said. "Now, beyond the dubious name, who are you?"

"I'm your guide," Anime Wong said. She couldn't have been more than fourteen.

"To where?"

"Shut up and she'll tell you," said the man behind me, who had been jammed down between the seats. Something cold parted my hair and touched my skull. "Forget about your gun," he said, sounding like a hood in a 1930s movie, "and stop looking in the mirror. Just keep both hands on the wheel and go where Anime says. Are you capable of that?"

I said, "Sounds manageable."

"If I have to shoot you," he said, "she knows how to drive, and she'll have the wheel before you've had time to kiss your ass goodbye."

Anime Wong's eyes widened, apparently at the news that she knew how to drive.

"I see," I said. "And how about I jam the accelerator down with both feet and just take us across the center line? She going to whisk you out of the way of the oncoming truck after my spirit has departed?"

"*Mon*ty," Anime said, with the massive patience only a teenager can pack into a couple of syllables, "just park it, okay? Jeez, look at him. Even *you're* scarier than he is."

"Give me the gun," Monty Carlo said.

I said, "No."

Anime Wong snickered.

Monty Carlo said, "So . . ." and let it trail off.

I said, "Is there someplace we really have to go? The tree house or something? If not, do you guys know where there's some good Mexican food? I haven't eaten since breakfast."

I waited. The guy in the backseat didn't brush his teeth enough, and he exhaled a kind of mossy vapor. I was analyzing its components when the gun, or whatever it was, stopped prodding my neck, and Anime said, "Out the driveway and make a right."

28
The Ponytail Gang

"Where were you going to make me go?" I said, once we were in traffic. There was no reply, and he was still sitting too low in the back for me to see him in the mirror without making a big deal out of it.

My question was still unanswered three-tenths of a mile later. I said, "Did you actually *have* anyplace in mind?"

He said, and he sounded like he was sulking, "I don't plan on that level."

"Really. What level do you plan on?" No response. I might as well have been talking to myself. Anime shot me an amused glance, and then Monty cleared his throat.

"Subaqueous," he said.

I waited for more, but it wasn't forthcoming.

Anime said, "Monty doesn't always speak English"

I said, "So I gather."

About half a mile farther west, Monty said, "Talking is old media." He sat up a little, and I saw a high forehead with long brown hair pulled tightly back, perhaps in a ponytail. Maybe I was in the clutches of the Ponytail Gang. "Talk is never precise, and when it *is* precise, it's usually untrue. Information gets re-prioritized by the brain or muddled by qualifiers or misshapen by emotions when it's said out loud. Or it's misheard. Not a problem in coding, not a problem in math. They can still be wrong, but they're precise. And they're rarely untrue. *Untrue* is just one form of *wrong*, right?"

"Wrong, right," Anime parroted. She was poking at numbers on a Samsung smart phone with a screen big enough for *Lawrence of Arabia*, and she put it to her ear and waited. "Hey," she said. "Lilli." Somebody obviously said something on the other end because Anime nodded. "Bonito's," she said into the phone. "About five minutes. *Tout suite*, whatever that means. Okay, we won't pick you up." She put the phone in her lap. "Lilli can walk," she announced.

I said, "Is that a dramatic development?"

"No, silly. She just lives close to the restaurant."

"How did you guys know I was going to be there today?"

"When you were here before," Anime said, "I paid the guy who runs the surplus store fifty bucks to call us if he saw your car again. And to tell you I was a boy. But the *real* question is how we followed you there the first time."

Monte said, "*Anime*."

"But that'll have to wait," Anime said promptly, "until we've decided how much you can know about us." She looked at the road ahead and gestured grandly. "Drive on, my good man."

Monty Carlo turned out to be almost as short as Anime, who was shorter than Rina, who was agonizingly aware that she was short for her age. Sure enough, his hair was yanked into a painful-looking ponytail, and there were threads of gray in it although I put him in his early thirties. If Anime had a fox's face, Monty had a possum's. I don't mean to suggest it was sleepy-looking: just pale and weak-eyed and sharp-snouted, with a sparse mustache above a straggle of pointed teeth. An ill-advised soul-patch that might have escaped from a saxophonist sat off-center below his lower lip. He had the furtive edginess of someone who had spent a large part of his life being surprised by everything that happened and had retired to a small dark room to get away from it all.

As we eased into the booth at Bonito's, which was clean and smelled promising, I could barely take my eyes off Monty's arms. Beneath the short sleeves of his polo shirt, circa 1970, with the little alligator and all, they were densely scrawled with symbols, what I thought I remembered as square root signs, lots of Greek Sigmas, parentheses, curves, something that looked like the elongated, sloping "f" that indicates *forte* in music, and dozens of others, none of which meant anything to me. Sometimes the symbols were integrated with letters and numbers in long horizontal arrangements that looked a little like traditional equations, sometimes they were arranged in blocks. I couldn't have read them under any circumstances, but in Monty's case the tattoos spiraled up and down his arms so that only part of each grouping was visible at any time.

He saw me looking and held up an arm, parallel to the table so I could see it better, making me feel like I'd been caught cheating on a test. "The language of God," he said. "According to Richard Feynman, anyway."

"No wonder my prayers go unanswered."

He leaned toward me, and it felt aggressive. "Calculus doesn't lie. Want to define the atmospheric effects of a sunset or the glinting of light on waves at the beach? This is the only way to do it."

"Don't get him started," Anime said. Her eyes shifted past me and lit up. "Hey, Lilli."

"Hey," A new girl—new to me, anyway—slid into the booth next to Anime, swinging her hip to bump Anime a few inches farther in. It was a friendly bump, followed by an arm thrown over Anime's shoulder. "This is him?" she said, sounding disappointed. She was Anime's opposite, plump, blonde, with rounded features and eyes the bleached blue of a hazy sky. The eyes looked like she hurt easily.

"I suppose I am," I said. "You're Lilli?"

She gave me a half-second of judgment. When she spoke, there was a coolness in her voice that complemented the warmth in Anime's tone. "I am. How old are you?"

"How old are you?" I asked.

"We're fourteen," she said, apparently meaning her and Anime. Anime confirmed it by nodding, and leaned her head on Lilli's shoulder. Lilli patted Anime's cheek and said, "It's a shitty age."

"I'm sorry to report that I haven't found a really good one yet," I said. To Monty, I said, "I wasn't expecting Campfire Girls."

"I could out-think you," Lilli said, "with my frontal lobe running Windows Vista."

"That's not the point. The point is that what I have to talk to Monty about is something that people keep getting killed over, and I'm not going to bring you into it."

"They're already in it," Monty said.

"Then I'd like to shove your face in," I said.

"Do it," Anime said. "His nose and mouth stick out too far."

Monty had lowered his head slightly, and the look he gave me wasn't the look of someone who would be afraid to emerge from the security of a dark room. "You don't know anything about us," he said. "And you're not going to learn anything. This was a mistake." He put his hands on the table, getting ready to slide out of the booth. "Move," he said to me.

"I'm going to *eat*, Monty," Anime said. "And so is Lilli. If you leave, you'll go crazy worrying about what we told Junior, since we're just kids and all that and we're not as smart as you are, which you tell us all the time. Anyway, he's driving. What're you gonna do, hitch? Hey, Maria," she said, looking up.

"Anime," the waitress said. "*Como estas? Salsa fresca*, extra chips, *carnitas* with corn tortillas for you." She put a basket of chips and two bowls of salsa on the table, pointed at the one nearer to me, looked at me, and fanned her mouth. "For Lilli, California Vegan burrito and rice, no beans, and for Genius here—" She nodded at Monty. "*Carne asada*, beans, no rice, sissy watered-down salsa, and for the tall, handsome stranger?"

"If that's me," I said, "what do you like best?"

"*Sopes*, we make the best except for my mother. My name is Maria." She was a very tidy package, if that doesn't sound too much like objectification, with eyes as black as olives but a lot more expressive.

"I'm Junior, and the *sopes* will be great. And, *por favor*, more of the *salsa picosa*."

"You will remember it forever," Maria said. "Coke, tamarind juice," she said, pointing at Anime and Lilliput, "Corona for the genius, and you want?"

"Black coffee."

"Done." She was gone.

"*Well*," Anime said, packing the syllable pretty full. "No chit-chat. Do you get much of that? I mean, you're nice-looking, but nothing to cut my wrists over."

Lilli said, "Swell talk."

"I need to finish what I was saying," I said. "At least two people have already been killed because of this, and I don't want to put you kids in the line of fire."

Lilli said, "Been killed because of what?"

"That's what I mean," I said. "Do you two know *anything* about the chain old Monty here is part of?"

"Yes," they both said.

"Okay," I said. "Tell me about it."

"Some crook—" Anime said.

"—wanted Monty to set up—" Lilli said.

"—some kind of scam," Anime finished. "So he passed this envelope along."

"It wasn't a scam," I said. "It was a hit."

"I figured," Lilli said, "for that much money."

"How much?" I asked Monty.

He wasn't liking this at all. "Forty-five hundred for me," he said. "But what's your interest?"

"Do you know who the chain started with?"

"Of course he doesn't," Anime said.

"If he did," Lilli said, "why bother with the chain in the first place?"

"How many links back do you go?" I asked Monty.

He didn't want to answer. He moved his fork around and then shook some salt on the table, pressed his forefinger to it, and licked it off. "Just one. Just Dippy."

"And how many after you?"

He shook his head. "I'm it," he said. "I'm the delivery boy to the technician."

"How do you know?"

He picked up more salt and put his finger back in his mouth. "Your turn. Who got murdered?"

"A con man named Handkerchief Harrison, who was link number two, not counting the guy who started the chain. And a burglar named Herbie Mott, who broke into the office of the guy who organized the chain."

"To steal what?"

"A piece of paper with the names of the people in the chain written on it."

Lilli looked at Anime, her eyes enormous and her cool forgotten. "Holy shit."

"The guy who started this," Monty began. He licked his lips. "He *wrote it down*?"

"He's getting old."

"And someone stole it. Why did he steal it?"

"My guess? He wanted to know who was in the chain."

He looked quickly at Anime and Lilli, who were looking at me. "Did the people who killed him, did they, ummm, did they get the list?"

"I don't know. I didn't think so, but then Handkerchief got killed."

"Why didn't you think so?"

"Because—" I looked at the girls, who both had their mouths open. "Because they tortured him but he died of natural causes— a heart attack, I think. They would have killed him. So I think he died before he gave them what they wanted."

"Tortured," Lilli said. "Awesome."

"He was a friend of mine," I said, "and I don't think it was so fucking awesome."

"You're friends with a *burglar*?" Lilli looked like I'd just admitted that both of my parents were dog walkers.

"*I'm* a burglar," I said.

"Old media," Monty said again. "Burglary is old media." He looked down at his left arm and used his right index finger to trace one of the problems or equations or whatever they were. Without looking up, he said, "Then that's why you're involved? Because of your friend?"

"I was being paid to figure out who stole the piece of paper," I said, "until my client, the guy who started the whole thing, disappeared. No, I don't think he's dead, but listen to me, especially you two. He's hiding, and he doesn't scare easily. His number one back-and-forth, who also doesn't scare easily, is missing, too. Herbie is dead, Handkerchief is dead, Dippy is hiding, and here you and the girls are sitting in Bonito's, big as life."

"Whoa," Anime said. "It's kind of exciting."

"Drinks," Maria said, slapping various things on the table. "You want a shot in the coffee, stranger?"

"Sure," I said. "It's been a long day."

"Already in," she said. She popped my deltoid muscle with a sharp knuckle. "For you, free."

"Wow," Anime said, watching her go. "I hope you're not married."

We look online for money that isn't glued down," Monty said. He was in the front now as I drove, the two girls leaning against each other in the back seat like a couple of puppies. "Then we move it a dozen times in an hour or two until we've got it someplace we can put our hands on it without leaving fingerprints."

"For example."

"You're going to turn left two streets from now. Example: most states run a fund that holds money from abandoned safety-deposit boxes. Someone dies or moves away and doesn't keep up payments on the box, and sooner or later, the bank empties the box and holds the stuff for a certain amount of time, according to law, and then they turn it over to the state, which monetizes it—"

"Monetizes."

"Sells it," he said impatiently. "Turns it into *money*, you know money?"

"Money," I said. "Kind of old-media, isn't it?"

"The proceeds sit there in what's called a suspense account for however many years it is until the state no longer has to accept a claim on the box, and then that money goes into the state's general fund, so it can be spent on vote-buying and pork projects. A lot of money, some of those funds have hundreds of millions in them. Most states have crappy software. Getting in is as easy as sneaking into a movie."

"If you're Lilli and me," Anime said.

"We hit half a dozen of those."

"You and these girls."

"Who do you think? Okay, the turn's coming up."

I made a left onto a residential street: nice one- and two-story houses set well back, mailboxes standing at attention at the curb. "How much can you get out of something like that?"

Monty said, "You don't want to take so much that all the alarms go off. You want them to think the discrepancy might be on their end, a rounding error or something. For a while, anyway, at least until you've got the money in your hands."

Lilli said, "Lots."

Anime said, "Lilli and I have made eighty grand so far this year."

Lilli said, "Each."

"It's been a good year," Monty said, sounding modest.

"How much have *you* made?"

"Somewhat more," he said, "but I have other business interests."

"Then why did you accept forty-five hundred to set up a hit?"

"Show you in a second. Here, slow down. There, on the left, see that mailbox? The one shaped like the house behind it?"

"It would be hard not to."

"Well, *that's* what I had to do: see that mailbox. The message Dippy sent me said, 'Forty-two comma three.'"

I said, "Is there a punch line?"

"A year ago I got a postcard in the mail. It had fifty addresses on it, each numbered. That mailbox is address number forty-two. I've done this five times. The addresses haven't been used in numerical order: it's been like random—twelve, four, thirty-eight, you get it. All the addresses are within a ten- or twelve-mile radius, all in single-family-home neighborhoods with mailboxes set out front where the delivery person doesn't have to get out of the truck to stick the mail in. All I had to do was find address number forty-two, right there, and then drive by at three A.M.— that's what the *three* stood for—and put the envelope into the mailbox. Then I went home and got into bed, forty-five hundred dollars richer. My guess is that the envelope was picked up about two minutes later."

"What was in the envelope?"

He turned and looked at me for at least thirty seconds. "Why do you think I know?"

It was my turn to look at him, and I slowed the car down to do it, until he blinked and turned to the girls in back. "Take him to the office, or not?"

Anime said, "Sure."

Monty said, "Lilli?"

Lilli said, "I guess."

Monty shrugged and said, "Two to one."

29
The Hobgoblin of Small Minds

Oui, STORE WHAT YOU WANT, the sign said. The words, topped by a four-foot high plastic Eiffel Tower, gleamed mustard-yellow above a dark, short block of body shops, tire shops, and metal-plating businesses, all closed and lighted at this hour mostly by a crescent moon a quarter of the way up. The little pollution zone ended abruptly in a row of back fences that blocked the noise and hid the ugliness from the modest houses on the other side.

"*Oui*?" I was driving through the sliding gate. "Kind of obscure for a storage joint."

"I bought it," Monty said. "The person who built it was French."

Anime said, "*Really*? How *surprising*."

"And it's not worth changing. It's around four point seven percent of my income."

I said, "*Around* four point seven?"

"Okay," Monty said, "Four point seven two five, maybe six."

Anime emitted a ticking, mechanical sound from the back seat, and Monty made a waving motion with his hand, indicating *go right*. "Around this building here."

The building was one of five parallel structures that I could see as we pulled in, all low and flat-roofed, maybe two double garages wide and six long. Corrugated, segmented slide-up doors, a king-size twentieth-century industrial variant on the roll-top desk, had been inset at even intervals, six on each side of each building. Cold, waxy light came from low-wattage fixtures placed high on the wall above and between the corrugated doors. A few of the bulbs were out, so most of the property was moonlit, which was to say, dark. The entire facility was protected by a nine-foot fence of vertical metal bars that bent outward at the top and had been filed into points. I rejected instantly the notion of climbing it, or anything like it, ever.

"Third door," Monty said. "You can pull up to it."

I did, and Monty was out before I'd stopped moving. He darted in front of my headlights, something bright glinting in his hand. They turned out to be keys, which he used to undo two locks on the latch that secured the door.

"Nice locks," I said. "Assa Abloy."

He popped the locks and hit the hasp with the key. "*This* is what people forget. They spend a fortune on a lock and the crook cuts through the hasp."

"I know," I said. "I am the crook of whom you speak."

"Carbon steel, the hasps," he said. "I replaced every one of them."

"That's a lot of work," I said.

"This building only. The others are just storage units." He bent down and yanked on the door, which whispered upward with none of the rumble and clatter I expected. A moment later we were inside, and the door glided back down. Only then did the lights go on. When they did, I nearly gasped.

All the internal walls had been removed, only weight-bearing posts indicating where they'd been, to create a single, enormous room. Work stations, perhaps ten of them, had been set here and there, all chrome and thick glass, each equipped with its own laptop. Monty pushed a button, and all the screens began to glow.

The back wall was a junk-food eater's fever dream: vending machines of every imaginable kind offered soft drinks, chips, candy, ice cream, even bottled water. The vending machines were lined up on either side of a small but expensive kitchen: sink, stainless steel counter, vented four-burner stove, microwave, and a double-wide refrigerator-freezer unit, also in stainless. At the far end of the room, all the way to my right, was a sheetrock wall unit with three doors in it.

"Bathroom," Anime said, following my gaze. "Bedroom, bedroom."

"Bedroom," I said.

"For all-nighters," she said.

Lilli said, "Look at his face," and laughed.

"Not what you think," Anime said. "None of that."

"They like each other," Monty said. "I've got a partner, too."

"His name is Brad," Anime said. She gave me very level eyes. "Do you have a problem?"

"No," I said. "There's not so much love in the world that we can afford to toss any of it away." I took a few steps into the room as the air conditioning kicked in. I said, "I know a woman who's married to an oak tree. She bought the property because of the tree, she built her house around the tree so every room opens onto it, and she lives there, just her and her tree. Probably doesn't make for exciting breakfasts or a lot of small talk, but it's the love she wants, oak tree love, and she's glad to have it."

Anime said, "That's nice."

Lilli said, "He made it up."

"I did," I said, "but I meant it." To the left, four leather easy chairs had been pulled into a circle, the area lighted by vertical steel halogen lamps, 1930s futura-style with modern wiring. I sat in the fattest one. "Mexican food makes me sleepy."

Anime went to a vending machine and pushed a button.

Something racketed into the slot below, and when she came over to the chairs she was peeling plastic off a Butterfinger. "Tell us what you think is happening."

"First, you tell me a few things. How you know when a chain is coming and that you're part of it, how you know how much you're going to get paid. Given the fact that everyone in the chain is a crook, there has to be a way for each of you to know how much money you're supposed to get."

From the kitchen area, Monty glanced at Anime and then at Lilli. After a pause just long enough to be awkward, Anime shook her head impatiently and jumped in. "We get an email, or Monty does, sent to an address we almost never use except for, umm, oddities. The email is based on the world's most common spam, a message from a supposed-to-be-Canadian pharmacy, offering a deal on erectile dysfunction pills. A hundred million of them go out every day."

Monty, who had the refrigerator open, said, "The email usually announces a two-day sale, with dates, like the fifth and the sixth, and those are the days you're supposed to get and pass along the envelope. The discount tells us how much we'll be paid, in units of a hundred, so forty percent off means four Gs. Forty hundreds totals—"

"I know," I said.

He smirked, a smirk so little that I knew he didn't think I'd seen it all the way over here, and took out a bottle of *Wham-O!*, a highly caffeinated drink sweet enough to gag a bee. "If the discount has an exclamation point after it, it means units of one thousand, so forty percent would mean forty thousand. Got it?"

"Your turn," Anime said, displaying chocolate teeth.

"Fine. I think that three or four days ago, whoever picked up the envelope Monty left in that mailbox went out and killed someone. Someone else, maybe a friend of the victim, got mad about that and thought it might be nice to get back at whoever whacked his friend and, while he was at it, whoever supplied a helping hand. For some reason, that person, the hittee's friend, had a hunch about the identity of the guy who put together the chain, the guy who hired me. And I think the victim's friend commissioned Herbie to break into the office of the guy who hired me—"

"The guy, the guy, the guy, the friend," Monty said. "This would be a lot more coherent if you used the name of the person who hired you." He dropped down into the chair beside Anime's. Lilli had seated herself at a workstation beneath a life-size color poster of Selena Gomez wearing something wet, and was apparently paying no attention to us, hitting the keys as fast as Rina did.

"No. He paid me, half in advance, and one of the things he's buying is that I don't use his name. I'll call him Roger, if you want. To take it from the beginning, a client paid Roger for the hit, and Roger set up the chain. The message went down the chain, the hittee got whacked, some friend or associate of the hittee hired Herbie to break into Roger's office to find something that would associate Roger with the hit, and Herbie found the piece of paper with the chain on it. Then the hittee's friend or friends went to Herbie to pick up the paper, and Herbie refused to give it to them—"

"Why?" The last inch of the Butterfinger was poised in front of Anime's mouth, but her eyes were on me.

"Maybe they didn't want to give him his money. Maybe he looked at the piece of paper and realized what it was and tried to hold out for more. Maybe—" I broke off and swallowed.

"Maybe?" Lilli still hadn't slowed her keying.

"Maybe he—maybe he thought he could get more money for it by double-crossing his client and selling it to someone else," I said. "Herbie's Game. *One* of Herbie's Games. He went out of his way to make it obvious that Roger's office had been burglarized, left the safe open and everything. Maybe left it that way—like a blinking sign saying, *You've been robbed!*—because he wanted to try to sell the list of names back to Roger at a higher price."

Anime said, "Would he do that?"

"I'm learning that there wasn't much he wouldn't do. And the people who hired him to steal it tortured him, but they got overenthusiastic, and he died. And then I get confused."

"About what?" Monty said.

"Okay. There were several people who might have wanted to kill Herbie, one in particular, a guy named Ghorbani. Herbie even named Ghorbani in a letter he left for me with his lawyer. So I thought, well, just maybe Herbie's murder didn't have anything to do with the chain. Are you following this?"

"I think so," Anime said.

"It's not complicated," Monty said impatiently. "You've got essentially one question. Was your friend killed by the people who want the names in the chain, or by this other guy with the Persian name? What's so hard about that?"

Anime said to Monty, "Sometimes I hate you."

I said, "This is what's hard. The day after Herbie was killed, the second person in the chain, Handkerchief Harrison, was murdered. Beaten to death, and very unpleasantly, according to the papers. Sounds like the same person who killed Herbie, and Ghorbani was a steroid rager, so it looked right. But I just found out, five minutes before you picked me up outside that church, that it wasn't Ghorbani."

"You're a hundred percent certain?" Anime said.

"I think it's immensely improbable."

"Probability," Monty said. "When we say 'probability,' what we *think* we're doing is making an objective assessment of the variants of what might happen, or might *have* happened, within a situation, but we always distort it with what we *want* or *hope* happened, which is a completely different kind of integer. The Monte Carlo method—"

"I'm not using the Monte Carlo method," I said, admiring my calm. "I'm using my gut, which told me even before I learned that Ghorbani was out of the picture that the people who killed Herbie also killed Handkerchief. So that leaves me with a question. If those people didn't get the list from Herbie, *how did they know about Handkerchief?* And that's why I've been worried about you and Dippy and the first person in the chain, Roger's back-and-forth."

Monty was making invisible marks on the thighs of his trousers, writing out something only he could read. "Was Handkerchief—is that really a name?"

"It's what everyone called him the whole time I knew him. He probably had eight or ten names."

"Was he the kind of person people would want to kill?"

"Absolutely. He was a con man who didn't draw the line at widows and orphans."

"Maybe it *is* a coincidence," Monty said. "Coincidence is just a relatively remote probability. Or maybe you're wrong, and they did get the list of names from Herbie."

"Both possible," I said. "But I don't believe either of them."

"Belief," Monty said, in the same tone he'd used for *probability*.

"So to get anywhere, I need to know who the hit was set up to kill," I said. "Operating on the assumption that this is revenge, I need to know who's being revenged. What was in the envelope you put in that mailbox?"

He tilted his head back and looked down his weasel nose at me. "How do you know I opened it?"

"I don't think you did," I said. "I think Dippy opened it, and you reopened it."

He almost smiled for the first time all evening. "You saw her onstage."

"I did. The best bit in her act was the trick where the woman writes on a playing card and puts it in her purse, and later Dippy pulls it out of her husband's pocket in a sealed envelope."

"You're skipping the highlight," Monty said. "It was subtle but it was the best part of the trick. The woman writes her husband's name on the card and puts the card in the envelope, in front of all of us, and addresses the envelope—the night I watched, it was 'to Bob'—and then she seals the envelope and puts it in her purse. She keeps the purse throughout the trick. When Dippy pickpockets the husband's jacket, out comes the envelope the wife addressed, and when she opens it, inside is *another* sealed envelope, a new one, and that's what's got the card in it. There's nothing Dippy can't open."

"So you opened it, too. And inside it was?"

"This is going to disappoint you," he said. "A phone number." He wrote on his thigh again. "This phone number," he said, pointing at his trousers, which were blank. "Lilli, can you give me a pad and a pencil?"

"Sure," she said. "I'd hate for you to have to get up while you're not doing anything."

When he had the pad, Monty wrote a number on it and handed it to me. His numerals were back-slanted, precise, and European, with crossed sevens. "This number is no longer in service," he said, parroting a phone-company recording. "It was a throw-away phone, probably used only one time, to receive the call from the hitter, and tossed a day or two later. My guess is that the name of the victim and maybe a couple of identifiers were in the voicemail message that answered the phone. Once it had rung and been answered, it probably got dropped off the end of a pier."

"So we don't even know the hitter's name," I said. "Much less the victim's."

There was no sound except for Lilli's keyboard. I got up and yawned. "Come on," I said. "I'll take you back to your car."

"Sort of a letdown, huh?" Anime said.

"Yeah." I looked down at Monty, who was still tracing invisible digits on his pants. "Unless you've got another car here somewhere, you need to get into gear."

"Thirty thousand," he said, getting up. "That's how much the hitter got."

"Not bad," I said. "Not absolutely first-rank, but not cutrate, either."

"C'mon, Lilli," Anime said. She reached both arms out and stretched. "Caught your yawn," she said to me through her own yawn. "This has been kind of exciting."

Lilli rolled her chair back. "I think we might be able to get past South Dakota's firewall."

"Tomorrow," Monty said. To me, he said, "They're the wizards. I can find the money and I know how to make it jump around, but I haven't got the chops to get it away from the states."

"This is how we found you the first time," Anime said. "You used your name on your first voice mail to Monte, and Lilli tracked down your address, where you don't live any more, and found a back door into your Visa card, which you were using at that stupid motel. We also had your license plate, so we picked you up at the motel and followed you from there."

"I still don't approve," I said, knowing how old I sounded and not caring. "These girls shouldn't be committing felonies."

Monty said, "Coming from you—"

"I know," I said, "but consistency is the hobgoblin of small minds."

Lilli got up and joined us at the door, and Monty turned the lights out and leaned down to pull the door up.

"What's a hobgoblin?" Anime asked. "I mean, how is it different from a regular goblin?"

"If any goblin can be said to be regular," Lilli said. Then she yawned, too.

"I always heard consistency was the *refuge* of small minds," Monty said as we stepped out into the darkness. The moon floated in the sky, a little yellow slice of eternity, casting no judgment on the modern ugliness of the street it was decorating.

"Yeah, well people say *gild the lily*, too," I said, "when it's actually *paint* the lily." I heard the door snick its way down behind me, and Anime and Lilli, stepping forward to get out from under it, were suddenly almost touching me.

Anime said, "Shut *up*, it isn't paint the lily."

"You two," I said, hearing the locks snapping into place, "you smell just like my daughter."

"How's that?" Lilli asked, sounding suspicious.

"I knew you were married," Anime said over her. "Poor Maria," and then someone slammed the cast on my arm with what felt like a bat, and chips flew off it and Lilli said, "*No*," and over her I heard the shot and then the second shot, and Monty went down sideways, slamming into Anime and pushing her into me. By then I had the gun out and I was running for the fence, running toward the muzzle-flash as Lilli and Anime began to scream behind me, but I knew I was wasting my time because the fence was going to stop me and he was already on the run and too far away to hit, tall, skeletal, sloping, in that black suit that looked like it had been stolen by an undertaker from a corpse: Wattles's hitman, Bones.

**PART
FOUR**

"Okay," Herbie said. "I remember, a long time ago,
I remember talking to you about Robin Hood. Do you remember?"

"Sure," I said.

"Well, forget it," he said.

"Why? Why should I forget it?"

"The Merry Men," he said. "Bunch of crooks in green tights. And
they'll lay down their lives—is that what you say, *lay down their lives*?"

"I don't say it," I said. "But maybe back then—"

"Lay down their lives for each other. Because they're friends. One for
all and all for one and all that."

"That's the Three—"

"I don't care who it is. Doesn't exist. Never did. I'm telling you,
kid, *don't fall for it*. There ain't no honor among thieves."

30

Like Being Run Over by a Car Made of Wool

"He's going to need some blood," Doc said, rolling down his sleeves. We were in his upstairs hallway, outside the guest bedroom he used for minor surgical procedures. Wadded up on the hardwood floor, looking like the carpeting in a slaughterhouse, was the shower curtain I'd ripped out of the bathroom in Monty's office so I could prevent a bunch of incriminating DNA from soaking into the seats of my car.

"Can you get it?"

"I can get anything except type hh," Doc said. "The Bombay phenotype. Lucky for him he's not from Bombay. He'd be all alone in the emergency room. Only people with genetic roots in Bombay have hh blood."

"The things I learn from you," I said.

"He got off easy. The bullet went through the outer thigh, missed the femoral artery, just nicked the bone. Still got young, pliable bones, almost no splintering. Doesn't say much for the other guy's aim. But you have to know, Junior, this is going to cost. I'm going to have to get a blackballed nurse to stay with him all day, the blood's expensive if you get it the way I have to, and then, of course, there's me."

"The kids' pockets are jammed," I said. Anime had grabbed

an amazing amount of cash, afraid that someone had called the cops and there might be a search.

Doc gave me a suspicious frown. "Why? How do girls this age come to have so much money on them?"

"They're hackers," I said. I flexed my newly naked left arm, still splotchy-white from the plaster of the cast, a sharp, flying piece of which had sliced Lilli. My arm felt cold the same way my jaw had when, long ago, I'd shaved off an ill-advised beard. "And they're making a fortune."

Doc said, carefully, "*Hack*ers."

"With computers."

Doc blew out a lungful of sheer relief. "Glad to hear it."

"I suppose." I sounded a little sour, but there wasn't anything I could do about it. "I need something else. Tuinal."

"Rainbows, huh? I used to need them myself. Take enough of them, it was like being run over by a car made of wool. How many?"

"A full jar. A hundred."

His eyebrows shot up. "Not for anyone I know, I hope."

"Definitely not. But the guy they're for, he'll make good use of them."

"For the record, I'm morally opposed to this," Doc said. "And they're expensive. Maybe twelve hundred bucks."

"I'll hit the girls up for it. How long?"

"Tomorrow. Anything else? Raw opium? *Salvia divinorum*? Some of the Oracle of Delphi's special laurel leaves?"

"No, but thanks. For everything." I put a hand on his shoulder and took it off again. For all his apparent affability, Doc wasn't a touch-me guy. "Lilli's good to go, huh?"

"Three stitches, real pretty ones if I do say so myself, but she's going to hurt when the Novocain wears off. She's a tough one. Never cried, didn't flinch at the needle, watched me take the stitches like I was sewing a handkerchief. They're interesting kids."

"They both break my heart," I said.

"I'll go to Anime's," Lilli said from the back seat, where she was lying down. "My mom won't care." We were in the parking lot of a 7-11, and Anime was working loudly on a Slurpee. Lilli had a Dove Bar. I could smell the dark chocolate. Except for the scream when she'd been cut, Doc was right about Lilli's toughness: she'd taken it all silently.

I said, "What are you going to tell her about your arm?"

"A dog bit me."

"That high?"

"Okay," Lilli said, as though to a small child. "It was a giraffe. She won't even notice. I could grow a mustache and she wouldn't notice."

Anime, sitting next to me, made a little waving gesture, palm down, meaning, *Leave it alone.*

"So," Anime said, hardly changing the subject at all, "*are* you married?"

"Divorced, but, you know, not available."

Anime slurped, and Lilli cracked through the chocolate coating. With her mouth full, she said, "I liked the woman who loved the tree. It sounded calm."

"Well, I'm glad you like calm, because you're going to get a lot of it while Monty gets better. I don't want you anywhere near the office until this is over. You both have computers at home?"

There was a long pause, which I interpreted as disbelief that I would even have asked the question. Finally, Anime said, "We can't work from those computers, though. They're not masked the way the ones in the office are."

"North Dakota will wait," I said. "They're not going to

upgrade their software in the next few days. And I'll give you something to keep you busy. Lilli, under the seat Anime is sitting in, there's a black laptop. I want to know what's on it."

"Got it," Lilli said. "So that's how long you think it will be? Just a few days?"

"Yeah."

"Until what?" Anime said.

"Until everyone who might hurt you is dead."

This was a different silence, one that stretched out as I started the car and was broken by Anime saying, "That sounds, you know, definitive."

"When you finish with that laptop, I need more help. I want you to comb every news source in the country for recent gunshot victims."

"You're kidding," Anime said. "That's like the population of California."

"Parameters. Two shots, no more, probably at close range. Within one to two days after Monty dropped off that envelope. Not gang killings or drug killings or crazy guys in movie theaters or any of the trash-opera murders you see on the *Huffington Post*. It'll almost certainly be one victim, an adult. The cops won't name any suspects. It's possible that he or she will have been popped with a small-caliber gun, maybe through the ear or the back of the head. It'll be somebody interesting, probably someone with vague criminal ties, somebody you have the feeling there are questions about."

"You want us to go into police databases?"

I said—and it took some effort to believe I was having the conversation—"Not from home."

"What data do you want on the victim?" Lilli said, sounding a little more energetic.

"Whatever you get. But at a minimum, name, age, occupation,

location, details of the crime, a thumbnail of what's known about him or her."

"Picture?"

"If there is one."

"By when?" Anime asked.

"Get me whatever you've developed by tomorrow—do you have school tomorrow?"

"I've been *shot*," Lilli said.

I gunned the engine to make sure I had her attention. "No, you haven't, and don't talk like that or you'll wind up in the center of a circle of cops. Schools have to take that stuff seriously. You were cut and you had stitches." Suddenly, I felt like Fagin, and then immediately corrected myself: I felt like Herbie, indoctrinating two new apprentices. "Okay," I said, "I don't want to encourage you to skip school—"

The girls sighed heavily in unison, the hopeless sigh of adolescents faced with yet another clueless adult.

"—but if you do, give me whatever you've got by two tomorrow afternoon and then go back to it. Give me more rather than less. You never know which fact is going to jump out at me."

"Until everyone who might hurt us is dead, huh?" Lilli said. "That's cool with me." She sat up and threw the stick from the Dove bar out the window, and I told myself not to get out and pick it up. "Let's go home," she said. "To Anime's."

Over the next twenty minutes, Lilli had yielded up a couple of clenched moans as the shots wore off. I had driven north and east from Doc's house toward the girls' neighborhood, and we were getting close. "I need you to tell me some stuff," I said. "You said all the emails were addressed to Monty. Can you think of any way the people in the chain would know about the two of you?"

"No," Anime said. "Just the email and those envelopes."

"Did you ever meet anyone? Dippy, for example?"

"Uh-uh. I've never even heard her last name. Monty only ever met her like twice."

"Three times," Lilli said. She sounded like her teeth were clenched.

"Nobody's ever been around," I said. "No one ever came by."

"Nothing like that," Lilli said. "No one except us has ever been in the office."

"Except you," Anime said, "and the man who shot at us tonight."

"It was pretty dark," I said. "I don't know what he could see. He probably wouldn't recognize you again, even if he saw you in broad daylight. And I know no one's been following us since Doc's because I've had an eye on the mirror. So he probably can't find you even if he's supposed to."

"I suppose that's encouraging," Anime said. "I'm not used to being shot at."

"Well, look. I want you to stay together for the next few days, and keep your eyes open—I mean wide open. Don't go out any more than you need to. If you see *anything*, anyone who seems to be watching you, anyone who pops up in two or three places, you call me immediately, and I don't mean in ten minutes or when you get around to it, do you understand?"

"We can take care of ourselves," Lilli said.

"No, we can't," Anime said. "What could you do from wherever you'll be?"

I said, "Here's the drill. If you think you see someone, you get into a place with a lot of people in it—a restaurant or a library, someplace where you can sit for a while—and call me. Then just stay there. I'll call back in a minute or two to tell you who's coming for you."

"*Coming* for us? You mean, like a superhero or something?"

"It'll be a shooter," I said. "A woman, probably. Or it'll be me."

"My, my," Anime said. She folded her hands in her lap and crossed her ankles, the perfect little lady. "A woman shooter. Life is so interesting."

"Time is it?" Louie said in the frog-voice of the recently awakened.

"I was going to ask you," I said.

"Hold on," he said. "I'll call Stinky and ask him. He'll be real happy to know I've got you on the line."

"Jesus, I forgot about him." I was on Highland, climbing the gentle hill of the Sepulveda Pass. There was almost no traffic.

"Don't forget about him again. He's called me five times today. Where's Junior, where's Ting Ting, where's Ting Ting, where's Ting Ting, where's that motherfucker Bender? If I was you, I'd find out where Wattles went, and go stay with him for a while."

"Stinky's upset."

"Crying, a couple of times."

"Well, shoot. I don't like Stinky, but that's not good."

"Can I make a suggestion? You're showing pity, and pity says you're a good guy, but fear will keep a good guy alive. I'd put my energy into fear if I was you." He put his hand over the phone and said, "It's just that asshole, Junior." When he came back, he said, "Alice says hi."

"Okay, I'm frightened. Do you know where Bones lives?" I checked the mirror for the fifteenth time. Nobody back there.

No transmitter on the car, either. I'd slid beneath it to look just around the corner from Anime's apartment house.

"Near some cemetery, people say, but there's a lot of them and I don't know which one. Must be he likes cemeteries. Quiet neighbors, he likes the view. Like a banker probably likes looking at money."

"And he can probably hit the dead when he shoots at them." I told him what had happened.

Louie made the appropriate sympathetic noises and said, "He's cheap labor, bottom of the barrel. People use him for the first try. If he makes the shot, fine. If he gets killed, fine."

"How much?"

"Twenty-five hundred, a thousand if his stash is low. A hundred if it's empty."

"Not thirty thousand."

"Not."

"Who would I go to, if I wanted to find him?"

"You would go to me," Louie said, clipping the words. "And you would go to me at a reasonable hour."

"How much time would I give you?"

"As long as it took," Louie said. "But, me being me, it would probably take less than a day."

"Starting now?"

"Starting after my first cup of coffee, tomorrow around nine. And look out for Stinky. I'm telling you, he's half crazy." He disconnected.

I looked at my watch, which I should have done before I called. Time had been compressed since Monty got shot, and I was startled to see it was quarter past one. The moon was now in the final third of its glide, dipping gracefully to the west, the pockmarks on its crescent face unusually sharp-looking through Los Angeles air, and they made me think of Ruben Ghorbani.

Conversion. The fire of God, the pure clean light of heaven, burning out the impurities. The Word blowing through him, the wings wrapped around him, the weight lifted from him. Weight is so often associated with sin. Witches sinking in seventeenth-century ponds, the *Quran's* ounce of evil, Marley's chains, devils cast down to the earth and straight through it, angels feather-light on the wind.

I'd never seen sudden redemption up close before. I suppose I wrote it off as spiritual fiction. I've always believed that the way people behave over time makes fold-marks on their character, like frequently-creased paper, and even if you can smooth them out temporarily somehow, those fault lines will crumple people back into their old shapes, their old behavior, under pressure. When I'd thought of salvation at all, I'd thought of it as a nightly stage effect mounted under bright light in the sweating tents of false prophets who headed nonprofit religious corporations. The hammer-like touch of God, the fall backwards into the arms of the waiting acolytes, the empty wheelchair, the crutches cast aside, the foresworn evil, the upraised hand of the man in the white suit, proclaiming the presence of the Lord—the only one who gets in free—while he counts the house.

But what had happened to Ruben was, or seemed to be, real.

People change. Everybody says it but nobody believes it. I think that's because most of us can't really imagine other people as being much different from ourselves, and we feel—even after we've successfully changed our behavior—that our flaws, our stagnant pools and errant spirits, are still down there, running things. Our behavior is a new overcoat, persuasive, well-fitted, and attractive, but beneath it we believe we're the same equivo-cal mess we've always been. Why should we think other people are different?

I'd believed most of my life that people's basic character was set by the time they were five or six, but I had a feeling Ruben Ghorbani wouldn't agree with me.

To the extent that we *can* change, I've always felt that the best method is to picture ourselves as better in some highly specific way and then try to become that. Acting on it, I punched in a speed-dial number, and when Ronnie answered, I said, "I love you."

"Careful, big boy," she said. "You don't know what's on the other side of that door."

"I just want it on the record," I said. "I don't want to have to tiptoe around it any more. It's only a window-breaker the first time you say it, and now that's over with."

"Where are you? I can't have the man who loves me rattling around somewhere, getting into trouble."

"Ten minutes away."

"Barring catastrophe."

"I already got shot at tonight," I said. "I think I've had my taste of catastrophe for the evening."

"If you'd been hit, *that* would have been a catastrophe. Who did it?"

"Bones, that zombie who came to the door with Wattles."

Ronnie said, "Oh," and I could practically hear her thinking. "Do you think this was a forceful way of telling you you're fired?"

"I think it was an accident that I was there at all. What it looks like to me is a continuing effort to kill everybody in that chain."

"But Bones is Wattles's guy, isn't he?"

"He's freelance. My feeling is that Wattles might use him as a threat—he has a nice Halloween presence—but I *think* Wattles would trust an actual whack to someone who could hit something. There were four of us there tonight, and Bones didn't get a good hit in from point-blank range. Way off-center and way low. Managed to graze one guy's leg with one shot, and the other somehow missed both me and the girl standing eight inches away from me."

"Really," Ronnie said.

"She's fourteen. She's a nerd."

"That was pure habit," she said. "What I said just then, that was a reflex. I should slap myself. You got shot at and you're okay. You just told me you love me."

"I did."

"Well, come home," she said. "Let's see what we can do with that."

I confess. I accelerated.

32

The Only Pros in the Room

Ting Ting blinked into the light, looking like someone who'd just seen the sun for the first time. The sun was, in fact, sitting on my shoulder from his perspective, low in the sky behind me this early in the morning, and I imagined it had been years since he'd been up at this hour. Stinky rarely went to bed before the paper landed on the lawn.

I said, "Hi."

He screwed up his eyes at me in obvious pain, and then he stood aside and shielded them with his hand and said, "Come in." As I passed, he said, "Arm better?"

"Miracle drug," I said.

He pushed the door closed against the sunlight and looked at his watch. "Yipe," he said, using the rare singular form. "Eaglet, she sleeping." He was shirtless and barefoot, wearing loose pajama pants, apparently silk, that had slipped low over his nonexistent hips. He seemed to have a surplus of slenderness, if that's possible, and his skin was the kind of gold that we of English and Irish heritage can get only at the risk of basal cell carcinoma. All in all, I thought as I followed him down the entry hall, once you got past the fact that he could kill you with a blink, he was a positive variant on the usual run of humanity—compact in an environmentally friendly, essentials-only kind of way, shiny, and graceful. I could see why Stinky wanted him back and Eaglet wanted him here.

The hall had been painted a pale gray to bring out the warmth of the floor, a highly-finished, light-bouncing bamboo. The hallway opened, a few yards down, into a bright living room, obviously full of window, probably looking south to the sea. Eaglet lived in an upper-middle-rank condominium on a palm-lined street in Santa Monica that I figured at a million two if she'd bought it and seven thousand a month if she was renting. Crime in general may not pay, but murder does.

The place was bare in an intentional way; it wasn't that the people who lived there didn't have stuff, it was just that they liked space better. In place of the lava lamps and Fillmore West posters Eaglet's personal style had led me to expect, there were good Japanese woodblock prints, mostly birds and flowers, that were framed in matting of muted colors set inside bamboo frames that picked up the pale hues of the floor. A gorgeous set of cedar *tansu*, matching Japanese chests from the Meiji era, late nineteenth-century—possibly authentic, but if not, extremely good fakes—were stacked to create a ziggurat effect against the right-hand wall, and on each of the horizontal surfaces rested a dark gray clay vase bearing a single tall stalk of tuberose.

"Smells good," I said.

Ting Ting wrinkled his nose and waved his hand under it as though the fragrance were too heavy for him. "Eaglet like." he said.

"You don't?"

"Have too much in Philippines," he said, pronouncing it *Pilippines,* as he led me into the living room. "My home, Palawan, have too much. Smell, smell, smell, everywhere."

I sat on a low leather couch, one of a matching pair facing each other over a long table, a four-inch-thick slab of teak, probably ripped illegally from one of the remaining Cambodian hardwood forests. On the table was yet another vase, this one celadon-green, with two white lilies in it, and at a precisely casual diagonal was a gaily-colored magazine that turned out to be the latest issue of *Guns & Ammo*.

"I need to talk to both of you," I said.

"She sleeping," Ting Ting said again, but then he lifted his head and looked past me, and his eyes caught fire.

"I'm up," Eaglet said, coming into the room. She was holding a floor-length floral wrap closed with her hands, and when she let go of the edges to retrieve the ties, I got a long pale flash of thigh and hip. When I raised my eyes from the leg to her face, she was looking directly at me, hard-eyed as a marketer gauging a product's impact, and for the first time I felt like I was seeing the person who pulled the trigger.

The recognition passed between us, a snappy little electrical arc in the air, and we were, for an instant, not just Eaglet and Junior, but the only pros in the room. Ting Ting was gaping at her almost as fervently as he had the night they met.

"Doesn't he blow your mind?" Eaglet said, retreating back to the 1960s. "He's so cherry it hurts."

Ting Ting said, "Cherry?"

"Perfect, it means you're perfect," Eaglet said. "Do you want coffee, Junior?"

"I always want coffee."

"Jammin'," Eaglet said. "Honey, would you—"

"Sure, sure," Ting Ting said. To me, he said, "You no sugar, right?"

"Right. And thanks."

When Ting Ting was in the kitchen, Eaglet leaned toward me and said, in a pleasant tone, "If you fuck this up, I'll come after you, and don't think I won't. I love him all the way to the center of his clean little bones."

"I wish you every happiness."

"He is soooo cherry. It's like he was created an hour ago." She sat on the facing couch, not giving me any skin this time, and said, "Anything before he comes back?"

"Yes. When did you do your last hit?"

She raised an eyebrow. "That's kind of personal."

"Humor me."

"In Solvang," she said. "The day Louie called me to come down and sit in front of your house. That's why I was late. Who's on watch now?"

"Debbie again, and nice of you to ask. Who was the target?"

"Are you wearing a wire?"

"Don't be silly."

"Well, if I *had* hit someone," she said, rolling her eyes, "which, of course, I *haven't*, it would have been an accountant who was on the run after poking holes in a union pension fund."

She watched me as I looked at it from every angle I could think of and failed to find a connection. "Have you turned anything down in the past eight or nine days?"

"I'm just starting out," she said. "I'm like a starlet, just a kid from the sticks, not a top-liner like Debbie. My phone doesn't ring all that much."

I looked around the expensive room. "That's not exactly an answer."

"No," she snapped. "No other offers."

"Do you hear much scuttlebutt?"

She shook her head and the beads braided into it—it was beads that day—rattled. The sound brought to mind a stick being dragged over a bleached-white rib cage, not a cheerful association. "I'm not on the party line yet," she said. "Debbie's the girl you want for that."

"She won't talk to me about it."

"Then she's smarter than I am. Anything else before Sunshine comes in?"

"Do you really love him, or is this just for fun?"

She looked into my eyes for at least ten seconds before she said, "I'd eat him alive if I could, just to have him with me all the time."

"Do you know, or have you heard of, a guy named Bones?"

The name *Bones* produced a blink. "A zombie, right?"

I said, "That's a fair description."

"Black suit, white socks. Weirdest eyes ever. I met him once, at a party Debbie took me to." She extended a tapering hand and used the tip of her index finger to push the magazine a couple of degrees closer to parallel with the table's edge, but she wasn't focused on it. Her eyes were on a spot on the table about halfway between the magazine and me. "He's not like anybody back home in Mill Valley, that's for sure. He's got cold air around him all the time. Shaking hands with him was like reaching into the refrigerator. I won't lie to you, he spooked me. What about him?"

"Nothing. I ran into him glancingly last night. Just trying to see how he fits in. Do you know where he lives?"

"I don't want to know where he lives. Fits into what?"

It was my turn to look at one thing and think about something else. I looked at Eaglet, which was easy enough to do, and tried to figure out, as complicated as things had gotten since Bones showed up, whether there was any way she could be involved in the whirlpool around Wattles's chain. What I finally said was, "Something I'm working on."

She sat back, arms crossed. "Good to swap info like this. A free and frank discussion."

"I'm not swapping info. I'm asking you about something that's already killed two people and almost killed four more last night, with no sign of stopping there. I'm in the process of trying to eliminate you from the list of suspects."

She said, with her eyes hooded, "Do tell." We regarded each other like a couple of dogs trying to decide whether to bare our teeth or wag our tails, and Ting Ting bustled in with a tray. He'd put on a short-sleeved shirt.

"Have only instant," he said. "Herbal for you, Sweetie."

She picked up the cup, and all the tension went out of her face. She looked like a teenager. "Smells almost as good as you," she said.

Blushing all the way to his bare forearms, Ting Ting said, "She like to smell me."

"I think you smell pretty good myself," I said.

Eaglet said, "He's taken," and laughed, but there was a lot of gravel in the laugh.

The coffee was strong enough to dissolve the cup, and I swallowed twice and felt my pupils expand. "You guys need to think about Stinky."

Eaglet said, "Fuck him," and Ting Ting gave her a quick, startled glance.

"He tried to kill me a few weeks ago," I said, and hearing the words stopped me in my tracks. "Ting Ting," I said. "Did you meet the person he hired?"

Ting Ting looked from me to Eaglet and back again, and a dusky flush bloomed on his cheekbones. Eaglet gave him a tiny nod, and he said, "Did."

"Who was it?"

"Girl," he said shyly. He swallowed. "Name Debbie."

I sat there as Eaglet began to laugh, a much merrier laugh than the last one. It sounded innocent, young, and carefree.

"She likes you, our little Debbie does," she said. She wiped her eyes. "Missed you twice, didn't she?"

I smiled back at her, but all I could think of was what she'd said about Bones: *He's got cold air around him all the time*, and it made me wonder whether Ting Ting hadn't been better off with Stinky. People who kill people for a living, no matter how well they imitate humanity, are different from people who don't.

"When he goes after you, Stinky's not going to send someone soft-hearted," I said, and a surge of malice made me add, "He's going to send someone like you."

She shrugged it off. "Probably more experienced but with less talent."

"Well, here's the issue. When one person gets shot at, sometimes other people get killed."

Ting Ting said, "I talk to Mr. Stinky. I feeling bad already."

"No," Eaglet said.

"I said I talk to Mr. Stinky," Ting Ting said, with some muscle in his tone. "You are not telling me no."

I said, "I'd do it on the phone if I were you."

The look I got from Ting Ting made me remember his left foot. "Mr. Stinky not going to hurt me. Mr. Stinky love me."

I said, calmingly, "He's pretty upset."

"Maybe," Eaglet said to me, her eyes narrow, "you're the one he wants to kill."

"Too," I said. "He wants to kill me, too."

"You wrong," Ting Ting said. "You both wrong. Everything okay. Mr. Stinky, Mr. Stinky want me to be happy."

"Fine," I said. "But on the phone, okay?"

33
Natural Selection Favors the Timid

I'd been operating on an assumption, something I try not to do. In my one and only straight job, selling overpriced shoes in a shop that catered to teens—a job I'd quit right after I met Herbie—my boss had asked me why I'd done something, and I'd said, "Well, I assumed—" And he had pointed a tutorial finger toward the ceiling and said, "*Assume* makes an *ass* of U and *me*," with the tamped-down certainty of someone reciting a mantra or explaining why he put his faith in one idiot candidate instead of another. In non-straight life, I'd learned a variant on my boss's credo: assumptions cannot only make an ass of you and me; they can also make either or both of us dead.

So even though I was already back on the Valley side of the hill when I made up my mind to try to verify my assumption, I decided to take the trip anyway. It required the long, curving drive through Malibu Canyon, but I figured I'd use the time to organize my thoughts. When that failed, I pulled out the phone, in flagrant violation of the vehicular laws of Southern California, and did some checking in.

"We're just sitting here," Anime said. Her mouth was full. "We both skipped today. Lilli is taking aspirin like it's popcorn."

"Am *not*," Lilli said in the background.

"So *many* people get shot," Anime said. "Hold on." I listened to her chew for a moment and then heard a gulp that sounded like a sinkhole opening. "We're already at almost a hundred, and that's just the day before yesterday, but a lot of them are the kinds you told us to skip."

"I should have told you," I said. After all, Wattles had said at Bitsy's that the victim had been shot three days earlier. "Go back between five and seven days ago."

"Lilli will get on it when she's not popping pills. Hey, we looked at your friend's computer?"

"Is that a question?"

"We looked at your friend's computer, period. It's like it's still in the store even though it's four years old. Almost nothing on it. He uses Internet *Explorer,* if you can believe that, but the browsing history is almost empty. There's an email account that needs a password, and that seems to be the only place he ever went."

"Probably what he used to send you the Viagra ads."

"Gee, you really think so?" she said, and I could almost hear her eyes rolling. "We never even *thought* of that. And Windows history is mostly Hearts and Spider Solitaire."

I thought back to those moments I'd spent on Wattles's lumpy couch, waiting to learn my fate, and got just a touch angry at the idea he'd let me sit there sweating while he was putting a red eight on a black nine.

"Here's some good news," Anime continued. "Monty is feeling better and your friend Doc says he's got your rainbows, whatever that means."

I heard Lilli say, "Omigod, look at *this* one," and I hung up so Anime could get a look at whatever atrocity had just streamed into that fourteen-year-old girl's bedroom. Ahh, technology.

The Malibu tunnel was coming up, a black hole for cellular reception, so I dropped the phone into my lap and coasted through, and when I came out on the other side, there was a sheriff's big black-and-white tucked partway into the chapar-ral, just waiting to bust a ticket on someone. If I had DiGaudio with me, I thought, he'd force me to pull over so he could chew out the cop. If you're looking to ticket cell phone users, why do it at the end of a tunnel?

The thought of DiGaudio brought an unexpected twinge. There are people, whether you like them or not, whom you have to credit for being absolutely and exclusively who they seem to be. If DiGaudio were in a coloring book, he'd require only one crayon, LAPD blue. He wasn't a crook, he wasn't a thug, he wasn't even much of a bully, in spite of my long-held conviction that most cops were bullies in high school. DiGaudio was a cop who cared about the job, a cop who'd become a cop for the right reasons.

I never would have believed it, but I was going to miss him.

"Your friend is doing nicely," Doc said, without bothering with *hello*. "Your rainbows are here, the full hundred. You owe me seventeen hundred bucks."

I said, "Whoa."

"If you'd wanted something more current, Roofies or some-thing, I could have gotten you an Indian knockoff. But with Tuinal, the Indian knockoff is all there is these days, and they're using it to get all those discounts back."

"I suppose that's a kind of justice."

"Monty, or whatever his real name is, will be ready to go home day after tomorrow."

"So the girls said. He discussed calculus with you yet?"

"He's stronger on integral than he is on differential."

"Boy, I noticed that myself," I said. "I had to bite my tongue to keep from laughing."

"Seventeen hundred," Doc said. "And another four hundred for the blood, and I'll be totaling up the rest of the charges later today." There was a red car in my rear-view mirror, and in spite of my conviction that no one would ever use a red car to tail anyone, I pulled over and let him pass. Just as I was about to pull back on, I saw the cherry lights, and I waited for the sheriff to pass me, too. You don't break the law in a red car, either.

When I was moving again, I said, "Doc, with a clientele that's pretty much all crooks, does anyone ever stiff you?"

The silence stretched out until I said, "Well, it's a good thing the girls have the money," and hung up.

Louie didn't say *hello* either. Instead, he said, "How'd you get our girl so pissed off?"

"I presume you mean Eaglet." The road was straightening out, and I'd twice caught a glimpse, between the hills, of the flat blue sheet of the Pacific. "I told her and Ting Ting that they were going to have to talk to Stinky."

"Well, she's not going to show up today, that's how pissed off she is."

I passed the Sheriff as he took that slow, six-testicle John Wayne walk all cops use, pacing off the distance from his black-and-white to the driver's door on the red car, like he was on his way to the OK Corral. "Have you got someone else?"

"Yeah, but he'll be a little while getting there. Debbie will stay for a couple extra hours until he makes it. Try not to get any more people mad at you, these folks don't grow on trees. You know, if it wasn't for Ronnie, I think old Debbie would make a move on you."

"Did you know," I asked, "that Debbie was who Stinky sent after me?"

He didn't even pause for breath. "I know most stuff," he said.

"And you didn't feel that was anything worth discussing?"

"She missed, right?"

Another long curve and the Pacific opened up below me, doing its cute little frilly act on the sand to hide the fact that it was the biggest, most implacable thing on the planet. The air, which had given me such a good look at the moon's craters the previous night, was still miraculously transparent, and the horizon looked sharp enough to slice a ship in two. "Just, you know, might have been something to mention."

"Phooey."

"Did you hire her for Stinky?"

"I might have made a recommendation."

"But it didn't occur to you—"

"If he'd hired someone else, I mighta told you. But he hired Debbie like I said he should, and I figured if I told you, you might have ducked the wrong way. Look, someone wanted me to find someone to take you out. I hired someone who wouldn't do it, I checked with her to make *sure* she wouldn't do it, and I didn't blow it by telling you because you would have stormed up there and Stinky would have figured it out and found someone else to hire a hitter for him. Right?"

It was a little tortuous, but it made sense. I said, "Well."

"I know you're driving," Louie said, "but later I want you to call me back and gimme a round of applause."

"What about Bones?"

"Hollywood. Near the Hollywood Forever Cemetery."

I'd heard of it but never seen it. "Where's that?"

"Right behind Paramount. Or you could say Paramount's in front of it since the studio bought the land from the cemetery, and I've been asking myself ever since I learned that whether there are bodies buried there."

"There are bodies under every studio in town."

"Mister Metaphor. Craziest cemetery in the world. They show movies there at night, they stream funerals on the Internet, imagine that. Live funerals for strangers, right in your living room. Whole fucking world is buried there. Douglas Fairbanks, Peter Lorre, Tyrone Power, Rudolf Valentino, Cecil B. DeMille, Jayne Mansfield, that chick Phil Spector shot—uh, Lana Clarkson—Mel Blanc, you know, the guy who was the voice for Bugs Bunny; the kid who was Alfalfa in the old 'Our Gang' movies—"

"How do you know all this?"

"There's some gangsters want to get in, but the place is drawing the line. I mean, come on, they let in that sonofabitch Harry Cohn? A guy people hated so much that when the place was jammed for his funeral somebody said, 'Just goes to prove it. Give the people what they want and they'll always show up.'"

I said, "How about that," but there was no stopping Louie in mid-vent.

"They let in *Bugsy Siegel*, back in '47, but they won't take a crook now? What, we didn't have laws then? Discrimination, plain as the nose on your face."

"Have you got an address?"

"I told you, right behind—oh, sorry. You mean Bones. Working on it. Right now I got someone says he's in one of those apartment houses, you know, from the fifties."

"That narrows it way down."

"Hollywood's not really my territory," Louie said. "I'm doing pretty good. More later." He hung up.

Malibu Canyon spilled me out onto the Pacific Coast Highway, and I disengaged the gears in my mind and let it wobble loosely from one thing to another. I discovered something interesting. Whichever hill I tried to let it roll down, it kept ending up in front of Bones.

What was he doing at Monty's storage place last night? When I looked back over the past few days, it seemed like everyone I knew was being followed wherever they went, and no one was spotting the tail, not even me. And I was pretty good at it, after all these years, even if I had missed Monty and the girls. Bones had *not* followed me, I knew it. Or, if he had, it was time for me to go back to my first and only boss and try to get that job back. Maybe the shoes weren't so silly-looking now.

I set the phone on speaker and put it back in my lap. PCH has more cops on it, mile for mile, than any other stretch of road I know. Ronnie answered on the first ring, skipping the hello like everyone else. "I *knew* you'd have to call. How could you not, after all that?"

"It was memorable," I said. "Like when I was seventeen."

"You coming home for lunch? We could skip eating."

"I'm in Malibu, and I've got a few more things to do after I finish here. Sorry to be so prosaic, but I need to know something. How positive are you that you were being followed the night you wound up at Cantor's?"

The turnoff was coming up and I hit the turn signal. It had blinked a couple of times before she replied.

"Pretty sure. But you know, I'd be kind of embarrassed by now if I'd been wrong, with you sending the cavalry to pick me up and everything. I mean, I *thought* there was somebody back there."

"But you're not a hundred percent."

"I suppose not. We were both pretty jumpy at that point."

"No problem. It was better for you to call when you were wrong than to not call when you weren't."

"Sorry?"

"Well, I know what I meant. Here's my turn, I've got to hang up."

"Listen," she said, "come home for dinner and we'll skip that instead of lunch."

The road to Herbie's place wound up the hill above the highway, probably following—like the streets in the hills of Tarzana—the track of an old arroyo. There were always cars parked on the first few blocks because it was close enough to walk to the beach if you were crazy enough to cross PCH on foot. I drove past the address, checking each car for I didn't actually know what—for some indication that might mark them as anything but random. When I was two blocks above the condominium complex I eased into a parking spot and sat there for a few minutes, waiting to see whether anyone had been behind me.

I smelled the sage on the hillside, watched the sea crinkle and smooth itself and throw off the gold sparks that calculus can apparently explain, and listened to the hum of traffic below. No one came up the hill, so I got out of the car and hiked down the grade until I reached the walkway that would take me to the rear of Herbie's place.

I didn't feel any eyes on me, although I was starting to question my ability. I took what I hoped was a casual look around and followed the walkway around the building.

Stretched across the broken door and vibrating in the ocean breeze was the usual yellow crime scene tape. I'd half expected the place to be boarded up, but it wasn't, which was a good thing because my picks were stuck in the bush I'd left them in, about halfway back up to the car. If you're going to be caught where you don't belong, it's much better not to be holding a deck of picks or to be armed, which is why the Glock was in its hidey-hole in the trunk. I'd be in trouble if the cops found the Glock, but at least I wouldn't be up on a charge of armed burglary. Having a gun on you, even when the place you're hitting is empty, is enough to knock the charge up to first-degree, and that's the charge we're all most eager, we nonviolent crooks, to avoid.

Crime scene tape is obviously supposed to keep people out, but it's never exerted much of a repellent force on me. It marks a crime scene, right? Who's more comfortable in a crime scene than a criminal? Putting up crime scene tape to keep us out is sort of like a supermarket trying to turn away shoppers by putting a sign that says FREE FOOD.

So I put on my food service gloves and eased the big double-thick baggies over my shoes, parted the ribbons of tape, listened for two or three long minutes, and went in.

The place had been picked over but not ransacked. Objects of obvious value, including the John Sloane painting that was at least putatively mine, had been removed neatly. My guess was that the orderly ransacker was A. Vincent Twistleton in his role as protector of Herbie's legacy. There was certainly no sign of any sort of hurry. Drawers and cabinet doors were closed tightly, sofas were intact with their cushions unslit, and a few "shinies," which was what Herbie called objects that looked valuable but weren't, sat in their usual places, where he'd put them as burglar bait. Burglars, generally speaking, aren't any more sympathetic to the needs of other burglars than straight people are.

I had a few hiding places in mind.

Up until now I'd been relying on my assumption that Herbie's natural death—before his tormentors could kill him themselves—meant that he hadn't told them where the piece of paper with Wattles's chain on it was. If I was right, then I was pretty sure I knew who was behind most of what was going on. If I was wrong, I had no idea. Well, actually, I did have an idea, but it was too new and too raw for me to be comfortable with it yet.

Nothing is easier to hide than a piece of paper. If Herbie had been creative about it, there wouldn't have been a chance in the world of my finding it. But—and okay, this is another assumption—I didn't think Herbie believed he had any reason to hide the paper. He certainly couldn't have known that Wattles would call me—out of all the crooks in the world one of a very small number who would have thought of Herbie the moment the burglary was described. No, I was betting that Herbie thought the paper was safe in plain sight, or in relatively plain sight, right up to the moment his clients arrived at his door, probably hours earlier than the time that had been set.

Let's say he'd had thirty or forty seconds after the doorbell rang, maybe sixty. The teapot still had water in it when I arrived, so the visitors hadn't been gone more than, say, an hour. Herbie wasn't an early riser; a lifetime of night work had turned him into someone who rarely got up before ten. I'd seen no half-empty coffee cup when I arrived the first time. My guess was that he was either in bed or in the bathroom when they showed up. The bathroom had doors that led both to the bedroom and the hallway, so that gave me an obtusely angular path to look at first. I felt I could skip the bedroom since the people who killed him had been in it so long they would have looked everywhere, so the most likely places were from the bathroom door to the office, where the paper was most likely to have been, and beyond the office to the front door.

I started with the master bath. My first two guesses—taped to the back of the toilet and in the hanging light fixture in the room's center—were wrong. Nothing at all behind the toilet and nothing but a few dead moths in the light fixture, in spite of the fact that the old adage still holds true: nobody looks up. I took a quick survey of the office and saved it for later because there were too many places to look, and headed to the living room. I'm aware that under a carpet seems obvious, but I knew what Herbie's visitors didn't, which was that in the living room there was one corner where the wall-to-wall wasn't tacked down. I did find twenty-two hundred-dollar bills there and I took them, planning to give them to Doc. But no chain.

My next hiding place was also a bust, because it was missing. Herbie had a nice nineteenth-century desk in the living room with a top plank that slid out and doubled the size of the desk's surface. The feature wasn't obvious, and it would have been a snap for Herbie to pull out the top plank, put the paper on the plank beneath, and then slide the top plank back again. And maybe he had, but there was no way for me to tell because the desk was gone, almost certainly with the other stuff that A. Vincent Twistleton, whom I really should have called by then, had spirited away, out of the reach of people like me.

I was standing there, staring at the four dimples in the living room carpet made by the legs of the vanished desk, when I heard a man's voice.

It was coming from the direction of the dining room, probably from just outside the broken glass door, and that meant that my exit was cut off. The front door was an equally unattractive option, since, if whoever it was hadn't come alone, it was likely that his companion was sitting out there in a car, idling at the curb. The place had only two doors.

And I could think of only one place to hide.

The centerpiece of Herbie's office was his desk. It was a massive piece of mahogany from the 1940s, and it sat up against the wall, just to the left of the door that took you into the room. The drawers were long, and there was a row of pigeonholes at the back of the work surface, which meant that the well, or whatever the hell you call the place where your knees go, was extra-deep. I heard the man's voice grow louder as I tiptoed up the hall, and I figured he'd ducked under the tape just as I had and was in the house.

I pulled back Herbie's chair as quietly as I could and crawled into the well. Then I pulled the chair back into place, obscuring the well and making it darker, and crowded myself into the smallest area I could, pressed against the back of the well.

The man was on the phone. I heard him say, "That's where I am," and then a pause, and he said, "Nothing doing. Where? Okay, okay, hold your horses."

It wasn't a voice I could put a name to, but it seemed familiar somehow. It was low and sounded short-tempered, and its owner walked heavily. I got a mental picture of a guy who was wide and close to the ground, and also carrying a gun. I know the gun was an assumption that would have had my old boss raising an instructive finger, but since all I had was a choice between two assumptions—he was strapped or he wasn't—it seemed to me safer to choose the former.

"Nope," he said, and the voice seemed to come from the living room. "Not here, either. This is bullshit."

I was inclined to agree with him. I concentrated as hard as I could, trying to send him the message *bullshit bullshit bullshit* and wondering whether Handkerchief could have given me a tip or two. I was immediately rewarded by his saying, "Bullshit, bullshit." And just as I was congratulating myself, he said, "Okay, then, the office."

I am not a brave person. I stay alive by not being any braver than I have to be. If I were an insurance salesperson I would disqualify all applicants for policies who described themselves as *brave* or *relatively brave* or even *intermittently brave*. I believe that most people are cowards because they inherited it, and the reason they inherited it is that natural selection favors the timid. A few feet beneath the surface, the earth is interlaced with the bones of the brave. The valiant's more prudent comrades march home, their uniforms unbloodied, to fix watches, drive nails, and raise children. The brave molder where they lie.

I know that I don't talk much about courage. In my description of how Ting Ting tore me to shreds and picked his teeth with the splinters, I left out the fact that I was terrified. I am frequently terrified, and more power to it. And, of course, at that moment in Herbie's house, I wasn't armed. What all that meant, as Mr. Short Wide Deep Voice tromped down the hallway toward the room I was cowering in, was that I found a way to make myself even smaller. And a very sound strategy it seemed, too.

"Yeah, I'm doing it," he said, and I realized belatedly that he and his partner, who was almost certainly outside at the wheel of a car, were doing the same thing I was. They were looking for Wattles's chain. And since these were virtually guaranteed to be the two who had hurried Herbie toward his heart attack, my primary assumption had been correct: they hadn't found the piece of paper.

Which meant, in turn, that I probably knew at least part of what was going on and who was behind it. Now all I had to do was live through the next ten or fifteen minutes so I could act on it. It was, I realized, a moral imperative: to avenge Herbie and untie a remarkably complicated knot, I had a responsibility right at this moment to be as cowardly as possible.

I could handle that.

Handkerchief Harrison used to claim that he had a kind of perfect pitch for voices. Once he heard one, he could pick it out of a room full of chattering people and mimic it, too; the voices of his various identities, a braid of three or four borrowed voices. I'd been paying more attention to voices since Handkerchief told me that, and I usually knew when I'd heard one before. And cowering under Herbie's desk, I stretched my budding talent to its extreme and realized that I'd heard this man's voice at some point in the recent past.

And here he was. Mr. Short Wide Deep Voice came into the room, muttering mutinously, and the first thing he did was yank

Herbie's chair out of the well, which had an interesting impact on my heart rate. He stood in front of me, moving things around on the desk as I stared at the bottoms of a pair of plaid Bermuda Shorts and muscular calves so hairy I could have climbed up them hanging onto the fur. Below the shorts were a pair of yellow socks sticking out of black, scuffed loafers. This was a style of dress I was pretty certain I'd recognize, but I didn't, although there was something familiar about his stance. And then two things happened: he pulled the drawer of Herbie's desk all the way out, and he dropped his phone, which landed in the center of the well, not three feet from me.

He said, "Balls," and ignored the phone to focus on the pulled-out drawer. I had been looking up at the underside of the drawer, and now that it had been yanked free, I could see the bottom four or five inches of a knit shirt in a green so vile that people would have thrown rocks at it even in Ireland. A shower of stuff landed on the floor as he flipped the drawer over to see whether anything was taped underneath it—paper clips, pens, reading glasses, packets of Kleenex, a couple of those pink rubber erasers I didn't think people used any more. He yelled toward the phone, now at the bottom of a pile of office trash, "Told you. You watch too many movies. Anybody with a TV is gonna be too smart to tape something under a drawer, for Chrissakes." He slammed the drawer home and then spread his feet, preparatory to bending down to pick up the phone.

And grunted. And said, "Damn back," and lifted a foot and kicked the phone about six feet away, toward the window. Then he called to it, "That's it. I'm taking a leak." The feet went to my right, toward a door I had thought was a closet, and as I listened to it open I expected him to swear again and turn around, but instead there was a pause followed by a stream of water and a sigh. I hadn't even heard him lift the seat.

He didn't flush, either, the pig. Nor, to my disappointment, did he catch himself in his zipper. What he *did* do was come back into my field of vision, six or eight feet away—giving me a quick glimpse of some pendulous pectorals—and kick the phone again, toward the door this time. He vanished from sight to my left, toward the hallway. I heard him kick the phone again, bouncing it off the hallway wall, booting the phone in front of him as he went, and I figured out what he was going to do: maneuver the phone to the top of the two steps down into the sunken living room, go down the steps, and pick it up there, where he wouldn't have to bend so far.

I was sopping wet. I listened for the grunt as he finally stooped for the phone and then I heard his awful shoes as he crossed the dining room's hardwood floor toward the back yard. In the silence of the house, I sat there, weak and wet, and waited until I was sure he wasn't going to come back in, and then I backed out as quickly as I could and double-timed it to Herbie's bedroom, where I yanked open he door, intending to peek between the curtains, just to confirm what I thought I knew, given the sound of the man's voice and the partial glimpse I'd had of him: the identity of the person driving the car.

Pulling the door open like that, without thinking, was a mistake. It had been closed tightly, probably by Twistleton and his troops, and when I opened it, the stench almost took my feet out from under me. With no circulating air, the damp carpets had stayed damp, and the blood had gone way, way south. I backed up to slam the door but instead I stopped and forced myself to breathe deeply three or four times, just putting a seal on the fury in my heart.

That was what was left of Herbie, and someone was going to pay.

The door closed almost too easily, and I stood there, looking at its blemish-free surface and waiting for the spots in front of my eyes to clear. I heard a car accelerate down the hill and still I stayed there, trying to breathe regularly and clear my head. When I felt a little clearer, I turned and crossed the hall into the office, both to search it more carefully and to clean up the mess that Mr. Short Wide Deep Voice had made. At the very least, to flush the damn toilet.

So I spent a couple of minutes on my hands and knees, picking up the crap he'd spilled on the carpet and shoveling it into the drawer. Then I turned to put the drawer back and found myself looking through the open door into the bathroom.

I couldn't figure out at first what had caught my attention, so I softened my gaze and tried to see all of it at once. My eyes went over all the shapes and surfaces and settled on the toilet-paper roll. It was full enough to protrude out from the little inset in the wall the roller occupied, and it seemed warped, as though the paper had gotten wet and swelled unevenly as it absorbed water. I said, out loud, "Oh, for heaven's sake," and got up and went into the john and gave the roll a spin.

The tissue unspooled onto the floor, and out fell a single sheet of paper, folded vertically into equal thirds. I opened it and saw Wattles's printing, all block capitals. I read it with no surprise, but with disappointment: the name of the hitter wasn't on it. That, Wattles figured he could remember.

I tore the list, the thing that started all this, into little pieces and flushed them along with the goon's urine, the smell of which suggested that he ought to cut back on the asparagus. I went out into the hall and put my hand flat against the open bedroom door, spreading my fingers and just feeling its cool, smooth surface.

I said, "Goodbye, Herbie."

34
The Famous Three Reasons

"So you're the man." A. Vincent Twistleton treated me to a wide view of a splendid set of choppers, breathtakingly white although they may have gained in whiteness through contrast with his face, which was very dark indeed. I couldn't see his eyes through the wire-framed sunglasses, but as I failed to respond the smile went a little professional and he extended a brown, long-fingered hand across the desert of his desk and said, "Give."

"Sorry?"

"The pic, the proof. Something that says you're really Herbie's top guy."

"Was I?" I pulled out my wallet and leafed through four driver's licenses until I came up with the one with my real name on it, and I handed it to him, our fingers just barely meeting across a desk half the size of a skating rink.

Twistleton pushed the shades down on his nose and looked over them at the stack of licenses in my hand. His eyes were a startling blue; I never expect blue eyes in black people. "How many people are you?"

"Only one at a time," I said.

He laughed, a low collection of consonants and glottal stops that sounded like someone bowling a strike. "Lawyer's answer," he said, looking at the license I'd given him. "Looks good. Of course, they probably all look good." He dealt my license back to me with a practiced flip of the wrist and it stopped obediently at the desk's edge. "Still got it," he said. "You think you can lose it if you ever really had it?"

I said, "I hate to be stuffy, but I don't know what *it* refers to."

"If we're going to be literal," he said, "I was talking about me, and I was referring to a skill I just demonstrated, a finely honed manual dexterity that I developed doing thousands of hours of small-scale mechanical assembly work as I put myself through college. Dexterity that also translated into a certain flair with a deck of cards. If we're being figurative, I was referring to the skill each of us nurtures most and maybe even cares about most. In your case, according to Herbie, that was a sort of burglar's sixth sense."

"Herbie said that about me?"

"Herbie said a lot of things about you, all of them good." He swiveled his chair to look out the window at a view of Century City, or perhaps I should say *the* view of Century City, since they all look alike. He was a big man, a couple of inches taller than I was, with a football lineman's shoulders and a burgeoning, contented-looking gut straining at his $200 shirt. As huge as the desk was, the office made it look small. "You always answer a question with a question?"

"Was it you who removed most of the valuables from Herbie's place?"

He used the tip of a blunt index finger to push the glasses back up over his eyes and turned his head toward me. "You've been there? Inside? Through the crime scene tape?"

"I have."

"And may I ask why?"

"You may."

He waited. Then he turned the chair back around to face

me, shook his head, blew heavily through his nostrils, and said, "Why?"

"Herbie asked me to figure out who killed him. I thought I might find something that would help me answer that question."

"I thought Herbie *knew* who was going to kill him."

"Yeah? You read the letter he wrote me?"

He leaned forward, resting his elbows on the desk and lowering his head like a bull that's considering using his horns. "I didn't have to read the letter. Herbie and I talked about it, and he said he knew who was most likely to come after him."

I said, "He was wrong." Twistleton kept the specs trained on me, and I said, "That man experienced a conversion on the road to Damascus."

"Then you don't know who killed him."

"That's not what I said."

"You really should have been a lawyer."

"Not only should I have not been a lawyer, but I live my life in such a way as to give employment to as few lawyers as possible."

He was determined to put up with me, so I got the grin and the bowling-strike laugh again, but it didn't have much support. Then he put away the white teeth and said, "Yes, well, that seems to be consistent with the prevailing opinion. And yet here I am, the living exception." He shook his head, I wasn't sure at what, although it may have been an amused fondness for himself. Lawyers can get that way. He said, "A *real* conversion? Because I've got to tell you, I can't count the number of convicted murderers who have found Jesus while their cases were on appeal."

"Real enough for me."

"But you *do* know who killed Herbie."

"Ninety-five percent. When I have one more piece of information, it'll be certain."

"Will that be before the will's read on Saturday?"

"Why Saturday?"

"It's going to be a somewhat unorthodox reading. It'll go down better if there aren't a lot of extra lawyers, officers of the court, around. So, will you know by Saturday?"

"How would I know?"

"Listen," he said, leaning back in the chair so forcibly it squeaked. "Have I done something to upset you? If you were always such a jerk, Herbie would have mentioned it."

"I don't know how your day is going," I said. "But the last thing I did before I came here was spend a minute that felt like an hour standing in a bedroom that reeked of my friend's blood, breathing it in. On purpose. Because I wanted to get mad. I succeeded, which probably makes me less vulnerable to your charm than I would usually be."

Twistleton said, "I'm angry, too."

"Then take off the shades so I can see your eyes, and talk to me."

He took them off. The blue eyes surprised me all over again. They were a pale, transparent blue, but there was no looking in through them. A. Vincent Twistleton had kept his guard up for a long time. He said, "It matters whether you figure it out before the will is read because it will be a mess if the person who did it is a legatee."

"Gee," I said. "A mess."

"Is it possible that you won't know before then?"

"It might be. Just out of curiosity, how would my identifying the murderer simplify the what-do-you-call-them, the bequests?"

He spread his huge hands, looking like someone who was being reasonable but saying nothing.

"I see," I said. "You think I'm going to—*remove*—whoever it is, don't you?"

"Well, well, *well*," he said quickly, "we have moved far afield, haven't we? I am, I'll remind you, an officer of the court." He lifted the sunglasses in his hand. "These are my officer of the court glasses." He put them on the desk, pulled his hands away from them and made a little motion, shooing them away. "You are, aren't you?"

"Aren't I what?"

He gazed toward the ceiling, a man requesting patience from above, and put the glasses on again, low on his nose. "Herbie made an enormous difference in my life," he said. "I don't want to give anything of his, even temporarily, to someone who harmed him. Coffee?"

"Sure, thanks. Black."

He pushed a button on the desk and said, "Joe? Two coffees, one black and one for me. And some donuts."

"Sorry, sir, donuts are gone," someone who was presumably Joe said.

Twistleton closed his eyes and pursed his lips. He had long, luxuriant eyelashes, long and thick enough to make a shadow on his cheeks. "Please," he said, "tell me this is not a problem I have to help you solve."

"No, sir."

"Good." He released the button. "He's still afraid of me, Joe is. I asked him to go down and get my car a couple of days ago, bring it up to the front of the building, and he took off like he'd been shot out of a gun. About eight minutes later he came back in and asked me for my keys."

I said, "I usually go get my own car."

He grinned at me. "Herbie said you were a pisser."

"How did he make an enormous difference, I think that was the phrase you used, in your life?"

"Mmmmm," he said. "This isn't something I usually talk

about. In fact, Herbie may have been the only person I did talk to about it." He looked around the office, as if seeking something that would prompt him, provide an opening. "I wasn't exactly born to this."

"I sort of got that. All that precision mechanical work."

"I never met my father. My mother, single, like a lot of moms in South Central, supported three kids by working two jobs for a total of four hundred dollars a week. I make a hundred times that, more or less. When I was twelve, I set my eye on that figure, a hundred times what my mother made, and I went twenty hours a day to get it." He rocked in the chair a couple of times. "And for quite a while it didn't look like I was going to get it."

"And this leads to Herbie?"

"It did, but it takes a minute or two. I got into a pretty good firm, worked longer and harder than anyone in the history of the company, and became a really expert white man. I dressed white, sounded white, thought white. If the dominant race had six fingers, I would have had an artificial one sewn on. If they'd had chrome foreheads, I would have had a chrome implant."

"Just for the money?" I asked.

He smiled again, the smile of someone who's been caught and doesn't care. "No. There was power, too, of course. As a kid I didn't have any power. My mother didn't have any power. We lived at the whim of others. If one of my mother's employers had let her go, we'd have been homeless. So power was part of it, too."

I said, "Makes sense."

He sat back and gave me an assessing look. "Are you actually interested in this?"

I said, "I am." I was still looking for what Herbie had seen in him.

"Fine. School was awful, typical South Central in those days, rundown building, not enough books, too many kids, and most of the teachers were there because they couldn't get themselves sent anywhere else. But then there was third grade, and third grade was Mrs. Ridgely. Thanks to my mother, I was reading way ahead of grade level. Until third grade, my teachers were too busy to notice, just trying to manage the classroom. By first day in Mrs. Ridgely's class, I was reading at junior-high level and writing about the same. The minute we sat down that morning, she had us take fifteen minutes to write about what we wanted to get out of school. The kid next to me was done in about one minute, and he took his paper up and put it on her desk. That started it. Every fifteen seconds, someone would get up and drop their page on her desk."

"While you beavered away," I said.

He gave me a stainlessly white grin. "I guess I tuned everything out, because as I was finishing up I felt eyes on me and the whole class was watching. Mrs. Ridgely was at her desk, her glasses pushed down on her nose, looking over them at me. I got kind of flustered, I guess, because I left my last sentence unfinished and took the paper up to her. She just watched over those glasses, and when I got there she pushed them up and read my name on the front page and said, 'Vince or Vincent?' I said, 'Vincent.' Even in third grade I knew I wasn't a Vince.

"She said, 'Well, Vincent, you must want quite a lot.' Then she looked down at the page and her eyebrows went up as she read the first few words—I mean, I guess that's why they went up, because when she looked back at me her eyes were narrow and she was chewing her lower lip. She said, 'We'll have to see what we can do for you.'

"I said, 'Thank you,' but I didn't think she'd really do anything."

"What did you write?"

"Idealistic kid stuff. My mother had taught me that language was the most powerful weapon. I used a lot of words to say I wanted to learn to read and write well enough so I could help people. Ask a hundred kids what they want to do in life, and they'll say *help people*. It's enough to make you wonder why most of them turn out the way they do."

"And what did she do for you?"

He held up an index finger and touched it with the opposite one. "First thing she did was put me near the kids who could barely read but wanted to, and I helped them, right there in class." He touched the next finger. "Second thing she did was design a whole year's worth of study, just for me, reading seventh grade books, and not just textbooks, either, but novels and even nonfiction. Third, at the end of the year she passed me off to the dreaded Miss Willis. This was still the era of 'Miss' and 'Mrs.' Anyway, Miss Willis had quit being a nun for reasons that everyone wondered about, but she was still capable of taking a ruler to the back of your hand when she thought you needed it." He laughed a little and rubbed at his left eye. "This was, of course, a less enlightened age when you could still rap a kid's knuckles without going to jail. Miss Willis picked up where Mrs. Ridgely had left off and handed me in fifth grade to Mr. Lee, Mr. Johnnie Lee. Mr. Lee was famous in the school because for years he used his summers to go down south and get hit on the head by cops and bitten by police dogs. Had a big pink scar in the center of an actual dent on the left side of his forehead." He took a deep breath and let it out. "Some brave people back then."

I just nodded, not wanting to slow him down.

"So Mr. Lee showed me a piece of paper and said, 'Do you mean this?' and when I looked at it, it was the thing I'd written for Mrs. Ridgely. I said I did, and for the rest of the year Mr. Lee talked to me about the law and gave me books about lawyers.

The one I remember best was *To Kill a Mockingbird,* but William Jennings Bryan and the Scopes trial stood out, too. So, to condense things a bit, I skipped sixth and seventh, went into eighth before my voice had begun to change, and wound up in pre-law at UCLA at sixteen. By then, I could practically hear the trumpet fanfares in my ears." He raised his hand, miming stairs. "I was going to come out of South Central and *climb.*"

"And you have." I said.

"Well," he said, his face tight, "this isn't exactly what I had in mind. I started out in advocacy law, but it burned holes in me. The system was so big and so slow, and people's lives were so short, and I'd go home and not sleep and not eat, actually banging my head against the wall at times, and a few years later, when I got an offer from these folks, I took it. I got to do some pro bono cases I cared about, and I still do them, but the office game got into my blood, and I decided to play it for all I was worth. And, yeah, I made a little progress. I talked white and I watched baseball and even played a little golf—whitest game ever invented, who but a white man would come up with a sport that requires a hundred acres of mowed lawn? Played golf, talked baseball, dressed right, worked eighty hours a week, but it wasn't really happening, I wasn't getting there. I was stalled, doing and being everything I thought these folks wanted in a prospective partner and not making the progress I felt I deserved."

He swiveled the chair and looked out the window at Century City, all money and no taste, until he'd exhausted the view's interest value and then turned back to me. "I'm telling you this because of Herbie, of course. I'm not in the habit of going Chaucerian on people, boring them with my tale while I run up the billable hours."

"I'm interested," I said. "A guy in my position doesn't hear a lot of lawyers' life stories."

"Herbie," he said. "Along came Herbie. He was up on a bunch of charges, all related to a single offense, but they were junk. One cop just wanted to put him down, and he wasn't overly scrupulous about how he was going to do it, so it was easy to pick it apart. A kid—Joe, out there, for example—who'd read the law books carefully could have gotten him off, even if he was literally guilty of some of it. So I got him off, and we celebrated by going out and drinking. We smoked, too. Those were the days."

"How long ago?"

"Twenty-one, twenty-two years."

I nodded. Just before I became Herbie's apprentice.

"And about three in the morning and a gallon of gin down, he said to me, 'You know, you'd do a lot better if you weren't just a mirror.'"

I said, "A mirror."

"He said I was giving my bosses themselves back, in a mirror. He said it was the wrong thing to do, for three reasons."

"The famous three reasons," I said. "Herbie had three reasons for everything."

"First reason," Twistleton said, "they actually didn't believe I was like them. They were white, right? Deep inside, they knew I was just mimicking them, and you know what? It made them uneasy because in their souls they were sure I wasn't really *any-thing* like them. Who knew? Maybe one day I'd snap and come in wearing African robes and calling myself *A. Vincent X.* How could they promote me when *that* was in the cards?"

I felt myself smile. "And the second reason?"

"The second reason, Herbie said, was that I wasn't having any *fun.* You can rub away at work until you either disappear or you rule the world, he told me, and you'll never get what you want. Because even if you think you want money and power, what you really want is to have *fun* having money and power. And when people focus only on the money and the power, by the time they get it they've forgotten how to have fun. And that, he said, is when you develop Donald Trump Mouth."

"He used to talk to me about Donald Trump Mouth."

"And the third reason was that I wasn't using my biggest advantage, which was that the other people in the company were afraid of me. They were all good liberals, all voted Democrat and contributed to the United Negro College Fund, they were all proud of having hired me, but if they'd seen me coming at night on a dark sidewalk, they would have thought about crossing the street. They wouldn't actually have *crossed* the street, of course. They were too enlightened for that. They would have stayed on that sidewalk, possibly praying silently, and when we passed each other, they'd have said *Hi* or something, maybe lowering their voices to sound more formidable. When they were past me they would have resisted turning to look over their shoulder, and they would have silently congratulated themselves on that. Take advantage of that, Herbie said. Scare them a little. *Push* them. Make them cross the street."

"And it worked."

"It did. A little aggression, a little attitude, a willingness to say no to cases that affronted my sense of social justice and to tell them *why* I was saying no, no golf at all, ever, and those shades, which created quite a little stir among the staff when I started to wear them all the time. Plus, of course, eighty hours a week and being smarter than most of them, and here I am. And you know what? Even if I hadn't gotten here, it was so much damn fun that I still would've been grateful."

"Well," I said, "he changed my life, too. I'm just not sure how grateful I should be."

"That's up to you," Twistleton said. "Unless your relationship with him was a lot different than mine, he didn't force you to do anything. He just helped you to be more of what you were anyway."

"I guess."

"He said sometimes he felt more like your father than your friend."

The word *father* almost made me flinch, I'd been hearing it and thinking about it so much lately. "It felt that way to me, too. Of course, that was before I knew he was kind of a serial father. Did you ever deal with the cops on his behalf?"

Twistleton's eyebrows had constricted at the words *serial father*, and they didn't relax when I asked the question. "What does that mean? I don't *deal with cops* for anyone, but what in the world could you possibly mean?"

"I have it on good authority that he ratted people out. On a continuing basis."

"I see," Twistleton said, just as the door opened and a very thin, nocturnally pale young man in a monumentally inexpensive suit came in with a tray containing two cups of coffee and a mountain of donuts. The kid crossed the carpet as though he thought it might be mined, and when he got to Twistleton's desk, he hesitated about putting the tray down.

"With the exception of my calendar book, the entire desk is empty, Joe," Twistleton pointed out. "I'd say that the spot you're looking for is a place both Mr. Bender and I can reach without having to get up and walk to it."

"Yes, sir," Joe said, his face flaming. His ears stuck out like handles, and they were as red as the lantern on the back of an old caboose.

"Lot of donuts," I observed.

"Joe overachieves," Twistleton said. "Don't you, son?"

"If you say so," Joe said, putting the tray down.

"I like Joe," Twistleton said to me as though the kid weren't in the room. "He's got a first-class mind and he's a born organizer. You know what, Joe?"

"I don't, sir, no," Joe said.

"You'll have this desk one day. Not until I'm gone in a blaze of glory, of course, but you'll have it. Or one just like it. And then you'll give the next Joe a hard time even as you envy him or her for being so young and not knowing yet how much everything fucking costs."

I said, "Why don't you share with Joe the three reasons he's not making the progress he should be?"

"Good idea," Twistleton said. "We'll talk one of these days, Joe. Do you drink?"

"A little, sir," Joe said.

"Well, we'll work on that. Grab a couple of donuts and beat it."

When Joe was gone, Twistleton popped the cap off his coffee and picked up a donut. "Yes," he said. "Your mentor, your adopted father, the best friend you ever had in your life, Herbie Mott, *yeah*, he shopped some guys to the cops. It was part of the deal that got him off those charges I just told you about. But it wasn't just that, just filing a few tips with the police. For two decades, from the first time I worked with him until the day he was killed, he had an understanding with the law. He worked both sides of the street, and very skillfully, too." He took a bite, and powdered sugar sifted down onto his lapels. "So," he said, "it looks like you'll just have to learn to live with that, won't you?"

35
Vacation Videos of the Damned

I felt like I'd spent the past few days looking at the video of some stranger's awful cruise. One face I didn't know after another, one mask after another, masks I didn't know how to penetrate. People who did things I hadn't done, committed crimes I hadn't committed, had consciences I couldn't plumb, went places—emotional and physical—I hadn't been: a tour of the circles of hell, but in better weather. Vacation videos of the damned, I thought. And every now and then the camera would hit the floor and the person who'd been holding it would disappear, beaten to death or shot at and wounded, and someone else would pick it up and point it someplace new. In the background at all times, partially hidden by the motion and the occasional violence, I could see, half-exposed and transparent, the face of someone I thought I'd known well, but looking very, very different.

I was parked behind the chain link fence that separated the parking lot from the acre of dark earth with its orderly green rows. New plants have a brighter green, a more optimistic green, than plants that have learned, to their surprise, that they're not always going to get watered on time and that once in a while the plant next to them, the one they thought of as their best friend, is going to get yanked up by the roots, leaving nothing to mark its existence except a dry little dimple in the dirt.

The fence went all the way around, which explained, I supposed, why no one had stolen all the plants out of hunger or sheer meanness. The garden was intact, waiting for the return of its caretakers. Those women and girls pulling weeds had been the most optimistic thing I'd seen since Wattles barged into our room at Bitsy's Bird's Nest, dragging his goddamn chain behind him. It seemed to me, sitting there, that the world—or perhaps just my world—was short on beauty and kindness.

And then I pulled myself up short and took another survey, this one beyond the perimeter of the fogged-in Valley of Perpetual Self-Pity. Kathy when she'd opened her arms to me on the night after Herbie was killed; Rina holding down her end of the couch, taking my emotional temperature and putting a figurative cooling hand on my brow; Louie the Lost telling me how he drove Alice to the garden in his meticulous Caddy so she wouldn't get her own car dirty; Ronnie on the night I got home after telling her I loved her on the phone.

My God, I thought, that was just last night.

So I was wrong. My life had more, probably, than the share I'd earned of beauty and sweetness, even if it was tempered with the occasional cold faceful of sheer evil. It was time, I guessed, to do something about the evil, or at least the evil of the moment which, as the Bible tells us, is always sufficient to the day, whichever day it is. Even though evil seems to be an ever-present constant, we're usually strong enough to take on a specific day's allotment. And I could do that now. Even if I didn't have all the pieces, I had enough.

I got out of the car and went around to open the trunk to get the Glock, and there it was, the cheap jewelry box. It had been in there ever since I left Stinky's place, bleeding and humiliated by Ting Ting. Okay, it wasn't urgent, I thought, picking up the box, but perhaps that was the very reason to do something about it. I couldn't hurt, much less kill, anyone by learning a little more about its contents. As an added benefit, I wasn't likely to get hurt or killed myself. It might even occupy me while I waited for that last piece of information.

I leaned against the car and looked for a number among my contacts, and the phone rang. ANIME, it read.

"Hey, truant," I said,

"Lilli and I have been talking," she said. "Way too many people get shot. This world is full of guns. The person who did the shooting—no, I mean, the one we're trying to find, the, um, the victim of the person Monty left the money for?"

"I'm following you."

"Well, he or she, the shooter, got the envelope out of that mailbox, right? Right here in the Valley. And Monty said the pay was thirty thousand, right?"

"Right and right."

"So, I mean, come on. Somebody who can set up a chain like that one, someone who can pay thirty thou, well, if that person wanted somebody killed in, geography's not my subject, *Chicago*, wouldn't he or she have gotten someone in Chicago?"

"Maybe. We crooks, we mostly know crooks in adjacent ZIP codes."

"Not us. We know people just like us in China and Taiwan and Germany."

"Well, you live in a different world. Listen, let me interrupt you for a minute, okay? I want you to think about quitting this thing with Monty."

She said instantly, "Why should I care what you want me to do?"

"That's a good question, and there are three reasons why." I was surprised by how easily the old formula came to my lips. "One, I have only your best interests at heart. Two, there's no way I can benefit from what I want to say. And three, I'm older than you and you should shut up and listen."

"So there's two good ones and that last one," she said. "Hey, Lilli, Junior wants us to quit ripping off the states."

Lilli, in the background, said, "Call the newspapers."

My eyes ranged over the planted acre. I could hear in the background, at a constant level like the sound of running water, the sound of cars on the Ventura Freeway, half a mile south of me. "You could get caught," I said. "The kind of thing you're doing gets less safe by the minute, and I mean that literally. The governments, state and local, they're spending a fortune on this. Those people you think you know in China or wherever it was, for all you know by this time tomorrow they'll be working for the government or they'll be in jail and someone else will be sitting at their computer, pretending to be them and trying to bring you down."

"We know all that."

"I really don't think you should be a crook at all, but if you have to be, you should think about some area that's not changing so fast. Burglary, to pick an example, it hasn't changed in centuries."

"Are you volunteering to show us how to be burglars?"

I rested my elbow on top of the car, which was about as hot as a white car gets. "No, not at all. That's not something I'm going to do for anyone."

"Okay. My turn. I'm sure you like burglary and that you're, you know, talented at it. But I'm fourteen years old, okay? And I've got almost two hundred thousand dollars stashed, in cash, in a bunch of shoe boxes, and every penny of that plus everything else I make in the next couple of years, which should get me to a million easy, is going to put me through MIT in six years on a cash basis, and I'll come out with two degrees and fearsome skills and I won't owe anyone a penny. I'll be set for life."

I was shaking my head as though she could see me. "No one is ever set for life."

"Oh, please. I know, people get cancer and die in car accidents or marry the wrong person or blah blah blah. But the things I can control, I'm going to control them."

"And if you get caught?"

"Then I'll be able to afford a really good lawyer. And anyway, like you say, the government will probably try to hire me."

"I'm not going waste any more time arguing with you. But remember this, will you?"

"Wait while I plug in some memory. Okay, go."

"If you get jammed, or you suddenly don't know what to do, either you or Lilli, if it gets spooky, if you think maybe you need help or you should disappear—well, you've got my phone number."

There was a silence, and then she said, "That's really nice of you. You're, like, not like an adult sometimes, you know?"

"I'll take that as a compliment."

"That thing about knowing crooks who are mostly in the neighborhood?" It was a sentence fragment, but she turned it into a question.

"I remember," I said. "I was the one who said it."

"Well, wouldn't that be true about whoever paid for the hit? Isn't he probably here, and that's why he knows about the guy who set up the chain, and isn't the person who got killed probably somewhere around here, too?"

"It qualifies as a hypothesis."

"Good, because we've been working on it. In a few minutes, Lilli is going to text you the names of five people in the LA area who got shot in the last five to seven days and who fit that—that list of things you gave us, about being interesting and the cops not knowing much about them and all that."

"I'll look for it. Will you think about what I said to you?"

"No," she said. "But thanks for saying it."

o o o

"This is Anthony," said the man on the other end of the phone. He sounded like he was on tiptoe, like he thought he might be talking to the president, and the customers he dealt with—movie stars and self-important multi-millionaires—undoubtedly felt it was appropriate.

"Tony," I said. "It's Junior."

"*Anthony*," Tony said, and I could almost see him sneaking looks around the store and covering the phone with his hand. "And I don't buy from you guys no more. I'm on Beverly Drive, okay? Next door to a fur shop. I buy from people who actually *own* stuff."

"I'm not looking to sell you anything. I just want to ask you for an opinion."

"No," he said. "You describe it, I'll want it, and that'll just get me upset."

"I think it's junk," I said.

"Sure, sure. You always had an eye for junk. Herbie taught you better than that."

"Liberation jewelry—"

"Nice stuff, but faked a lot. If it's real, in great shape, eighteen, twenty. That's retail. If you've got the legend—who owned it, maybe a picture of her, and if she's got a title that people would kneel to, like duchess or princess, maybe twenty-five."

"Well, I've got a nice one, and—"

"Not interested," he said. "Not unless you can come up with a provenance, and I mean iron-clad. Liberation jewelry, that's not junk. People ask questions about it."

"I've got two of them. One is the one you've seen pictures of, right out of Cartier. The other one is a kind of Incredible Hulk version, made out of wire and nail polish and—"

"From the same person?"

"Well, I got them from the same person. In the same box."

He said, "Yeah?"

I stood there and listened to him think. He said, "You know the story?"

"Whose story?"

"The person who had it, the person who made it."

"No."

"Well," he said. Then he cleared his throat and then he cleared it again. "Tell you something you never thought I'd say to you," he said. "You should probably give it back."

I said, "Give it back," but he'd hung up, and as he did, my cell phone buzzed to announce a text. I brought it up, and I was looking at this:

Norman Wishert, cops say he was a loan shark

Eladio (cool name!) Amador (even cooler!!!), a mechanic who chopped cars to send to Mexico

"Austin Willie," real name William Estes, gambler banned from practically every casino in the world

Yoo-Mi Song (Anime says should be Song Yoo-Mi), ran a string of bars in K-town that were getting busted for hooking. Seriously, you-me????? LOL

Manny, real name Manfred, Spoon (not cool name!), no details but "well known to police," the papers say. Duh. With a name like that, what was he supposed to do? Couldn't run for office. Vote for Manfred? I don't think so.

"Austin Willie," I said the moment she answered. "Think he got that from Willie Nelson?"

"From who?" Anime said.

"I give up," I said. "The things your generation has been denied."

"We've got computers," she said. "You guys had like electric frying pans and hammers and stuff."

"Get me more on Austin Willie. All you can. And one more thing, fast as you can do it. I've got someone on my own list who's using an alias and I need a real name."

"Better be an unusual name."

"It's not that common." I gave her the name. "Start with IMDb, the Internet Movie Database," I said. "And I want the mother's name, too. Maybe a birth certificate."

"Birth certificates have gotten pretty tough," she said. "Since 9/11, those things are like twelve layers deep."

I said, "On 9/11, you were one year old."

"Everything's present tense online," she said. "Happens every day, as far as I'm concerned. Anyway, if I can find a birth town I can probably find a birth announcement and that'll have the parents' married name and then I can find a wedding announcement and that'll have the wife's maiden name."

"Jesus," I said. "Is my money safe?"

"As long as we like you."

"And you do?"

"Lilli, do we like him?"

I heard Lilli say, "But of *course*," in a Dracula accent and Anime said, "You might want to keep your balance under ten thousand."

"I need all of this soon," I said. "I don't want anyone else to get killed."

36
Rainbows

Louie struck out.

"All I know is what I already told you," he said. "The guy who gave it to me isn't answering the phone, and he only went there once, like anybody would go more than that. So it's what I said. Bones has a view of Hollywood Forever and he lives in a crappy apartment-house."

It sounded like a total waste of time until I got there. Hollywood Forever is bordered by Santa Monica Boulevard on the north, Gower on the west, and Van Ness to the east, respectively. To the south it butts right up against Paramount, as Louie had told me, so that left me with only three streets. Santa Monica Boulevard was all businesses, and the other two were a mixture, with a few post-production facilities that had fastened themselves limpet-like to Paramount. The only apartment houses of any description that had a direct view of Rudolf Valentino's final resting place were clustered together on the east side of Van Ness.

Four buildings, to be precise, lined up like giant bricks, narrow end facing the street. Faded aqua and watermelon and plum over stucco, once probably eye-catching, flat-roofed, two stories, with louvered windows that suggested no air conditioning. Maybe twelve, fourteen units in each. I drove by twice, the heavy late-afternoon traffic allowing me to take my time. It was ideal; I could look practically as long as I wanted without standing out.

No driveways, which probably meant that there was a back entrance. I made a right on Santa Monica and another on the first street to the east, and there it was, a single driveway behind the apartment buildings, but there were four more behind the ones I'd seen, making eight buildings in all, the complex running the full distance between the two streets. Eight buildings times fourteen apartments gave me too high a number to go from one to the other knocking on doors, even using my well-creased issue of *Watchtower*.

At the far end of the driveway, in a doleful patch of scrub grass and some of those awful flowers that look like big pom-poms or the front ends of poodles, a group of Hispanic kids were playing noisily and in Spanish, trying to avoid a big sprinkler pipe standing in the middle of the grass. I parked in someone's spot, grabbed the paper bag I'd picked up at Doc's, and got out of the car. I was getting some attention from the kids because, parking being what it was in that area, those spaces were probably defended with violence when necessary.

The game, which had involved a lot of pushing and falling down, plus some crying, frittered to an end as I approached. Ten brown eyes watched me come, their owners ranging in age from five to ten or eleven. They backed up and sidled a little closer together as I neared them.

"Hey," I said.

No one said a word, and in a couple of faces I could practically see the words *Never talk to strangers* zip through their heads, probably in Spanish.

"*Habla Inglés?*" I asked.

One of them, a bigger girl, said, "No," and the quicker-witted ones laughed, since the word is the same in both languages.

"I'm looking for a friend," I said. One of the little ones began to pick his nose with total concentration, but the others just looked at me. "*Un amigo de*, uh, me," I said, pointing to myself. "*Un hombre.*"

Now a couple of the kids were snickering, and I mean openly, not politely behind their hands.

"*Es*, uhhh, big," I said, holding my hand higher than my own head. "*Y muy*, oh, boy, thin." I mimed a very narrow person, my hands close together.

"*Flaco*," one kid said helpfully, and another said, more or less in English, "Eskinny."

"Yes," I said, "*Si*. Eskinny, I mean *flaco*. Y, uh, *vestido*?" I tugged at my shirt as I said the word, and two kids nodded. "*Es, es,* uh, *negro*." No one said anything, but a couple of the kids' eyes went watchful.

"Looks, um, like this," I said, having failed to find the translation, and I raised my shoulders almost to my ears. "And, uh, y ojos azul. Azules?"

The littlest kid, the one who'd been picking his nose, said, "*El monstro*," and a girl promptly kicked him in the thigh, and he started to cry. One of the other kids gave me big honest eyes, pumped full of childish innocence, and said, "No, mister. Nobody like that here."

I said, "Fine, sorry to bother you," and the girl who'd spoken first said, in unaccented English, "No problem," and I turned to go back to my car, seeing out of the corner of my eye one of the boys race off toward the buildings on the left. I gave him about fifteen seconds to get where he was going and then turned and charged after him, the paper bag in my hand making a chittering sound, like a maraca. The kids saw me coming and emitted a unison scream so high it probably would have brought rain if it had been cloudy, but by the time it trailed off into a babble of high voices and two languages, I was around the corner and I saw the boy on the second story, standing in front of a door and looking down at me with huge eyes.

I waved him away from the door he'd just knocked on, taking the stairs three at a time, and as I hit the walkway that ran in front of the second-floor doors, the one he'd been standing in front of opened inward, and I dove at it, the boy scurrying backward and bumping his back hard against the iron railing. The door, closing again now, hit me on the shoulder, but I shoved my way through and saw Bones backing away from me, the shoulders bunched even higher, looking even tighter, his hands slapping at his pockets. I was reaching for the Glock when I heard what he was saying.

"Please don't hit me, don't hit me, don't hit me, please don't—" He ran out of pockets and his legs bumped the edge of the couch behind him. He stopped, his lips still saying the words although he'd run out of voice, his hands swinging like pendulums at his sides.

I yanked the door closed, just missing the boy's nose. Bones jumped at the sound, the eyes with their strange blue whites wide, wide open. He said again, "Don't hit me." He licked his lips and looked all around the room, as though he'd never seen it before.

I said, "I'm not going to hit you, Bones." Pushing the cheap locking button in the center of the doorknob and throwing the chain, I leaned against the door, fighting for breath.

"I know you," Bones said. There was a greasy sheen to his face, and from the smell of him it was clear he hadn't showered in many days. "I saw you."

"Last night, right?"

His eyes slid past me to the wall and scanned it for information, and his lips formed a few voiceless syllables before he said, "With Wattles." He squinted into the past and added, "Girl."

"Yeah, Wattles, girl. Sit down, sit down."

He turned and looked behind him, which required him to twist his entire torso and seemed to hurt. Then, very gently, he lowered himself onto the couch. He moved as carefully as a glass figurine that had suddenly come to life and found itself on a very high, very narrow shelf above a stone floor. He bent his knees to lower himself and spread his fingers wide on the cushions, and this time I did bring the Glock out, thinking he might be digging for a gun, but all he did was push his hands carefully into the couch and use them to take most of his weight as he eased his long body into a sitting position. When he was all the way down he sighed as though he'd crossed a chasm on a tightrope and rested his hands in his lap.

"You don't remember me from last night?" I said.

He said, "You?" He looked at the gun in my hand and pulled his head back as though he'd just registered it.

"Who sent you?"

He leaned against the cushions behind him and closed his eyes. "I missed."

"Not by much."

He brought his hands up in front of him, and I watched them tremble. "My hands shook. I'da got you but my hands shook."

"Really," I said. "Just out of curiosity, what happens if I haul off and hit you?"

"My bones break." The eyes were moving beneath the closed lids, as though he were reading something written on them.

"Why's that?"

"Disease," he said. "*Osteogenesis imperfecta*. Means my bones break easy. I can break an arm lifting something that's too heavy."

"Never heard of it. What about gun recoil?"

"Have to be careful." He opened his eyes and blinked slowly. "Shoot two-handed, small caliber."

"Still. Why do something that could break your wrist?"

"Growing up," he said. "When kids know your bones break, they break them. Nasty little fuckers, kids."

"So you carried a gun?"

"I got a knife in fourth grade. No gun until high school." His eyes went to the ceiling and stayed there, as though he were expecting it to clear away any moment and let the sun shine in.

While he was occupied, or whatever he was, I looked around the apartment, which had been efficiently darkened by tinfoil taped over the windows. Basically two rooms: out front, the hybrid space common to so many cheap apartments in which the living room is separated from the clutter and smells of the kitchen only by a chest-high counter that—*voila!*—becomes a dining room with the addition of a couple of stools, in this case stools with pillows plumped onto the seats; and, in the back, a bedroom, a dim slice of which was visible through the door in front of me, a bathroom certainly attached to it.

The floors were very thickly, even spongily, carpeted, and other than the carpet nothing at all was underfoot: nothing to trip over, nothing to slip on. Over and above Bones's body odor, the place smelled of old socks with a high, raggedy note of fried fat. The temperature was in the high eighties, the air completely still.

"So you don't like kids," I said. There were two cheap over-stuffed armchairs, no hard edges, against the wall behind me, and I pulled one up to the table in front of the couch and sat. The table was wood, and bubble-wrap, perhaps two inches thick, had been taped all the way around its edges. I rattled the bag a little and put it on the table, and his eyes snapped to it.

"No. Little shits, all of them."

"Interesting effect," I said, indicating the bubble-wrap. He was still looking at the bag, and when he pulled his eyes off it, I could almost hear the sound of a suction cup being pulled free. He glanced at the bubble-wrap and shook his head a very little, as though he wanted to clear it. When his chin moved to either side, his shoulders went with it and his eyes ricocheted around the apartment. His pupils, surrounded by the indigo whites and the ale-brown irises, were pinholes.

I said, "What are you looking for?"

"Oh," he said, and he ducked his head in a gesture that I could only read as shyness. "Nobody ever comes over." He looked doubtfully at the tinfoiled windows behind me. "The place looks different when somebody else is seeing it."

Whatever I'd expected, this wasn't it, and before I could stop myself, I'd said automatically, "I think it's nice."

Something odd happened to Bones's mouth: the corners pulled outward, as though he was going bare his teeth, but then it went back to normal. It might have been meant as a smile. He said, focused again on the bag, "Thank you."

"Really," I said helplessly, locked in my mother's *polite* mode. "I like it. Carpeting's great."

"I can fall down," he said, "without breaking anything."

"See?" I was desperate. "Umm, form follows function and all that. So, not to change the subject, you don't like kids, but the kids outside, they—"

"*Los Niños,*" he said. The smile, if that was what it had been, was gone. "I pay them. They like money."

"So if you hate kids so much, why did you shoot at the adults first, last night?"

"Bigger," he said. "Easier to hit. And I figured you had the guns. Thought I could put you down and come in close to get the kids." He must have seen something in my eyes because he gave a rigid little shrug and said, "Hey. You asked."

I had to look away. I was examining the rest of the room, bubble-wrap taped to every corner, waiting for my heartbeat to slow. He swallowed loudly enough for me to hear him, and I realized I had picked up the gun in my lap.

As long as I was holding it, I let the barrel drift toward him. When I met his gaze he closed his eyes.

"Was it Wattles who sent you?"

Now he crossed his arms. With his eyes squeezed shut, he said, "Please don't hit me. Don't shoot me."

"Why would Wattles send you?"

Nothing.

"*Did* Wattles send you?"

He ducked his head, giving me a look at hair that looked like fat could be squeezed from it. "I can't tell you."

Putting the gun back in my lap, I picked up the bag and shook it. The rattling sound opened his eyes.

"Wattles," I said, but I might as well not have been there. As far as he was concerned, the bag was floating in mid-air all by itself. I opened it and pulled out the white plastic container.

His jaw dropped. He leaned forward with a grunt, spine rigid, and said, "That's 'bows."

"Rainbows it is," I said. I gave the container a quick little up-and-down for the sound effect.

"A *whole jar*?" he said in the voice of someone who has just recognized the Virgin Mary in a piece of toast.

"Yeah. Hundred of them."

"I've never—" He wiped his chin with the back of his hand, his eyes not leaving the container. "I've never seen a whole jar before."

"Wattles," I said.

"Rainbows," he said.

I fumbled with the adult-proof cap while Bones fidgeted. By the time I had it off, only to confront an internal seal of that odd aluminum foil that's elastic enough to push to the bottom of the bottle without its breaking, he was muttering. I used my teeth on the foil like I always do, and shook some into the palm of my hand: at a glance, a dozen. "How many of these have you taken at once?"

"Twelve?" he said, looking at my hand.

I dropped three on the table and handed him the rest. He was swallowing by the time I said, "Water?"

He swallowed again, as though one of the gelcaps had stuck in his throat, emitted a sort of *kack* sound to clear it, swallowed again, and released a tremendous sigh. Then he sat back, and said, "Wattles."

"Why did he send you?" I asked again.

Bones had closed his eyes again, very, very slowly, and I had the feeling he was preparing himself for the gradual change in climate, the very beginning of the capsules' effect sliding in, like a cooling trend, beneath the heat and chatter in his mind. I was about to ask again when he said, "Wanted them dead."

"Why?"

His eyes opened halfway and went to the pill container. "Scared. Thought someone would . . ."

"Would."

". . . would come up the chain. Kill him."

"Who? Who would come up the chain?"

"Up the chain," he said. "People who were pissed about the hit."

"Me, too? He wanted me dead?"

He did that tortuous head-shake, the shoulders moving with it, and I realized that at some point in his past, his upper vertebrae had been fused. "Didn't know you'd be there."

"Who else does he want dead?"

He pressed his lips together like a child with a secret he won't tell.

"Tell me, or I'm leaving. With all the rainbows."

He looked at the three capsules on the table, orange on one end, blue on the other, a dirty purple where they overlapped in the middle. I had to admit they were kind of pretty, although I doubted they looked as good to me as they did to Bones. I pushed them toward him, and he tossed them back like jelly beans and dry-swallowed them.

"Kill everybody," he said. "Everybody in the chain."

"But not me?"

He shook his head again. "He didn't say you. He said he was—" He closed his eyes. "*Disappointed* in you. That's why he came back. 'Cause you didn't fix it."

"What about Janice?"

"He didn't say a name like Janice." He scratched the heavy, oily hair, licked his lips, and looked at the container. "I really took twenty. Before, I mean."

I pulled the container closer. I wanted him unconscious when I left, but not dead. Too loaded to use the phone, too straight to die. "And have you? Killed the other people in the chain, I mean?"

"No. You guys were first."

"And you missed us."

He said again, "My hand shook."

We sat and looked at each other, or rather I looked at him and he looked past me as though I were a pile of dirty clothes. He said, softly, "Ohhhhhhhhh," and his eyes widened in what looked like appreciation. "Fast," he said. "Haven't eaten."

"Since when?"

He looked at me as though I'd asked him a trick question. "Yesterday?"

"You really did twenty before?"

"Thirty," he said, the lie as thin and transparent as air.

Someone knocked on the door.

I pulled the Glock out again and used it to wave him down although he'd made no move to get up. His eyes were on the white plastic pill container. I picked it up and went to the door, pills in one hand and gun in the other.

"Who's there?"

A high voice said, "Me."

I looked back at Bones and his mouth widened again. "Behave," I said to him. I put the pills in my pocket, shifted my gun into my left hand, undid the chain, and opened the door.

The tallest of the girls stood there, backed up by three boys and the littlest kid, the one who had called Bones *El Monstro*. They all looked pretty jacked up, wide-eyed and skittish, but they were there, bless them, knocking on the door that had closed behind God-knew-who so he could do God-knew-what to their money source.

I said, "Hey," and they said nothing. "We're just talking, just friends, *amigos*, huh?" I pulled the door further open so they could see Bones on the couch. "See? Say 'Hi,' Bones."

Bones raised one hand and waved slowly, as though he was under water.

I had a sudden idea. "Do you guys know he's not eating?" I asked them.

The second-larger boy said, "He don' eat never," in accented English.

"Well, he needs to eat. Once in a while, bring him something if you've got extra, okay?"

"Did you?" This was the big girl, and her tone was accusing. "Did you bring him something?"

"Yes," I said. "A bag of candy. You bring him something later, okay?"

She looked from Bones to me and back again. "Okay," she said. She added, meaningfully, "We'll come back." She turned to go and the others trotted behind in a herd, the setting sun gleaming off the dark hair on their round heads.

I closed the door. "When you were little, how did the kids at school know you were sick?"

"Because of these," he said, pointing an index finger in the general direction of his eyes. "And because I moved so careful. Anybody could tell."

"The blue in the eyes—is that the disease?"

"Sure."

"Must have been tough."

"Not after I got the knife. And then the gun."

His speech was a little on the furry side, and he was sitting about ten degrees left of vertical, so the pills were obviously making themselves at home. I sat down again, opened the jar, and shook out eight more. "You said twenty, right?"

"Thirty," he said. He looked at the pill bottle and said, "A jar, a jar is one hundred. Enough to take them all the way out. I never had enough to take them all the way out."

"Well, we'll see how good you are," I said. "Maybe this will be Christmas." I put the eight capsules on the table, and he snatched them up and popped them with surprising precision. I said, "You didn't kill anyone else."

"Killed a lot of people," he said.

"But not this week."

"Uh-uh."

"Not anyone in Malibu."

He stuck his tongue out to reveal two capsules glued to it. He pulled them off between his fingers and then separated the two shells of one capsule and poured the white powder onto his tongue. He was popping open the other one when I repeated, "Not anyone in Malibu."

"No," he said, his mouth white at the corners.

"You ever hear of a guy named Herbie Mott?"

"Don't know." He let his head loll back against the wall. "Not good with names."

"Handkerchief Harrison?"

He laughed exactly once, a low sound like "Hungh," and said, "Funny name."

"He was a funny guy," I said. Bones's eyes drifted closed.

"When did Wattles tell you to kill the people in the chain?"

Bones said, "Huh?"

I reached over and patted the back of his skeletal wrist, and he snatched his hands back and his eyes snapped open, although they were trained on a spot four or five feet above my head. I raised a hand and brought it down slowly, and his eyes followed it. When he was looking approximately at me, I repeated the question.

"Today?" he said.

"You shot at us last night."

"Then," he said, and his eyes started to close again, but he fought them open again. "Then yesterday." He squinted at me and shook his head as much as his fused neck would allow, and said, "You leaving the 'bows?"

"Yes."

"'Kay. 'At's good."

"Did he call you? Wattles, did he call you?"

"No." He started to slide slowly to the left.

"Then how did he tell you—"

"His house," Bones said. He was lying on his left side now, both feet still on the floor. "Girl called me. Said to go to his house." His eyes closed so heavily I knew he wouldn't open them again for quite a while.

The girl, I thought, was my sweetheart Janice. I sat there for about ten minutes, listening to him snore. He hiccupped a couple of times, and I waited to see whether anything would come up, but his system seemed to be accepting the shovelful of Tuinal. I got up and went into his kitchen.

I was standing there, trying to choose a course of action, when he said, quite clearly, "Brazil." I jumped a little and looked over at him, wondering what fragment of Brazil his consciousness had snagged on, and kind of hoping it was mag-azine-bright, warm, full of color, and child-free. His mouth was wide open and he was snoring again. One stiff arm had slid off the couch, and his hand was palm-up on the soft carpet, open and vulnerable.

What to do? I worked myself through several theoretical eth-ical positions quite quickly and when I was finished, I couldn't think of a single really serious objection to letting him kill him-self. He'd said himself that he'd like to take the rainbows *all the way out*, and if that meant what I thought it meant, I didn't see many reasons to interfere. It wasn't like he was doing anything except killing people and poisoning himself.

And then there were the *other* people to think about, the unknown others he'd kill if I took the rainbows with me and left him there to sleep it off. Keeping them in mind, I went to the sink and took some paper towels off the roll that was standing beside it. I wrapped my right hand in them, and used that hand to turn on the water. With my left, I grabbed another wad of towels, got them wet, and squeezed out the excess moisture. Then I toured the apartment, wet-wiping everything I had touched, and by the time I'd finished doing that, I'd decided on a course of action.

I wiped the bottle of Tuinal and shoved it into the pocket of Bones's awful black pants, where he'd feel it as soon as he was sentient, or close to sentient. I gave it a farewell pat and picked up the paper bag, into which I jammed all the paper towels I'd used. Covering my hand with my shirt, I turned on every light in the apartment.

When I pulled up the lid of Bones's right eye, the eyeball barely moved. But he kept snoring and his pulse was strong, so I tucked the gun inside my shirt, unlocked the front door, and left it wide open behind me, carrying the full paper bag exactly as I'd carried it in. If anyone was looking, I'd arrived with something and now I was leaving with it. It was dusk outside, shading into dark, and the bright rectangle of Bones's open door plus their promise to bring him food would, I was pretty sure, draw the kids, and they'd find Bones alive, or at least today's version of alive. He'd probably kill himself in the next twenty-four hours, but not right after five children saw me go into his apartment.

Even as I struggled with the emotional aftermath of my decision, that seemed to have quite a bit to recommend it.

37
Simple Subtraction

Despite all of Monty's fancy algorithms, in the end it came down to simple subtraction. It was really just a question of who was left. The fact that the victim of Wattles's hit had turned out to be a gambler iced it, even before Anime called me with the name I'd asked for. And the name tied the final knot.

But as neat and final as the knot was, the puzzle it solved comprised only one part of the problem. Wattles was the other part, and since Bones's apartment was near Paramount, the shortest route to Herbie's killer took me right past Wattles's house in Benedict Canyon.

Of course, Benedict was at a crawl at that time of night, a little before seven, jammed with all the people who work on the LA side of the hill and sleep in the Valley. The sun was about thirty minutes down, and between the hills, as I inched northward up the canyon, I caught glimpses of the red glow in the west, punctuated by the silver gleam of Venus as it followed the sun down.

Wattles had never been a friend, but I'd never really thought of him as an enemy, either, and I supposed I'd been right about that since he hadn't specifically told Bones to kill me. Still, it was hard to work up much sympathy for him at this stage, and

I couldn't think of a reason to bother trying. This whole thing had to come to an end.

I pulled past his driveway and made the next right, about fifty yards downhill. Most of the houses here were tucked behind gates and invisible from the street, but that didn't mean they couldn't see me; security cameras sat on the fences, pointed at the members of the hoi polloi who were misguided enough to pay a call. I was stopping on this street precisely because there was a camera just like these above Wattles's gates.

But I knew something Wattles had no idea I knew. I'd trailed Janice to his house the second time she'd hired me on his behalf because I like to know whose money I'm taking and where to find him or her if it turns out to be a setup. I'd driven past the house as the gates opened to admit her and then parked around the corner, pretty much where I was now, and about ten minutes later I'd learned that Wattles put a little too much trust in the steepness of the hill on which his house sat. The fence on either side of the gate went only about twenty feet up before it gave way to a ficus hedge, dense and scratchy, but permeable to someone who doesn't mind getting all scraped up and tearing his clothes.

There was a lot of poison oak up there, and it was getting too dark to be comfortable about spotting it, but I couldn't use a penlight, since I had no idea who might be on the lookout. This was a bad beginning, since I'm highly allergic to poison oak. But after a few moments standing about six feet up the hill from the street, just out of sight of the traffic, my allergies became an academic question because I heard a shot.

The shot put me in an interesting position. I very much doubted that Wattles had just committed suicide; it was impossible for me to imagine him feeling either the guilt or the fear that might lead him to put the gun barrel in his mouth. That left four alternatives: a) someone had done it *for* him, and he was dead; b) someone had tried to do it for him, and he was alive; c) he had tried to do it for someone else, and the other person was dead; or d) he had tried, etc., and the other person was alive. Alternatives b) and d) would make themselves apparent in a moment, I figured, because there would be at least one more shot.

And there it was. Or, rather, there they were: one, followed closely by another one. This actually complicated my position, rather than simplifying it, since the way things were turning out, it seemed likely that I'd wind up finishing off the survivor, if there was one. It's one thing not to have, as Herbie sometimes said, a dog in the fight. It's quite another thing to be cheering for both dogs to lose.

Nevertheless, I ran up the hill, through clumps of stuff that bore a disconcerting resemblance, in the dark, to poison oak. I tripped once and went facedown in the center of one of those clumps, but I was immediately up and running again, as much to get away from it as to arrive anywhere in particular, since I had no illusions about my ability to make a difference in what was happening at Wattles's house. Even if, by some miracle, I burst upon the scene at the moment when a decisive and survivable act on my part would make all the difference in the outcome, I wasn't sure I was actually up to choosing a side, much less going all heroic.

The hedge bristled at me, spiky-looking and dead black, since all the light was behind it, pouring through the big windows of what was, if I remembered correctly, Wattles's dining room. My face and hands weren't covered against all the sharpness in that tangle, so I pulled on the food-service gloves, stretched my sleeves down over my hands, and used my forearms to force a head-high path through the hedge. It made a lot of noise and seemed to take a long time, but eventually I was through it. For a moment, after the darkness of the climb, I had to squint against the light through the big window, so it took a few heartbeats before the window's surface resolved itself into a Jackson Pollack abstract: frantic, kinetic drips and splashes of color, and the color was all red. My eyes went to the one identifiable form, a scarlet handprint in the lower right corner.

Instinct shoved judgment aside and sent me running for the door, but then it banged outward and Dippy Thurston was propelled through it, as though shot from a gun. She was wide-eyed and screaming and splattered from head to toe with blood, even her hair clumped and clotted with it, and when she saw me she came at me at a run, her arms spread as though she expected me to pick her up and carry her away, but instead I waited till the very last moment, stepped to the side, stuck out a foot, and shoved at the small of her back. Dippy went down, hard.

She'd had the breath knocked out of her, but she started to roll over, so I stepped onto the center of her back and put my gun against her neck. I said, "Don't move."

"Junior," she panted. "He's—he's trying to kill me. He's right behind—"

"I'll take my chances," I said. It took me less than five seconds to find the little Barbie gun sticking out of the pocket of her jeans. She kicked out at me, and I put all my weight on the foot in the middle of her back and stepped over her, leaving her legs thrashing empty pavement.

I put my own gun back under my shirt and stuck Dippy's into her ear. "Is Wattles dead?"

She stopped moving. After a moment, she began to cry, big gulping sobs. "I don't know," she said. "You have to help me. He's crazy, he just went crazy trying to kill me."

I pulled the gun away but kept my weight on her back, and sniffed the barrel. "How many shots did you fire?"

"Two." She sniffled. "Can I get up?"

"Is he dead?"

"I think he's in there, waiting to kill me. He probably saw you. He'll—he'll shoot us both."

"Whose blood is all over the window?"

She said nothing, and her body went still.

"Whose blood is on you?"

"Please," she said. "You're hurting me."

I said, "Good. Where's your fat friend?"

"I don't know who you—"

"The guy you pretended to kick out of your house the day I was there. The one who searched Herbie's place this morning."

She said, "Herbie? I don't—"

"The one who held Herbie's arms still while you poured boiling water into those gloves."

For a long moment, I thought she wouldn't answer. Then, in a completely different voice, a voice as calm as the one that tells you to be careful stepping onto a moving sidewalk, she said, "He's at home."

I pivoted around so I could keep my eyes on the windows. "What's his name again?"

"Frank. Frank Lissandro."

"Your boyfriend? Husband?"

She said nothing. No one seemed to be moving inside the house, but there was a *lot* of blood on the dining room window, and I supposed there could be someone crouching there, looking at me without my being able to see him. I said, "Frank's at home?"

"That's what I just said. You have my gun, you have your gun. Let me up."

"Who was Willie Estes to you, other than your uncle?"

"How do you know—?"

"He was a card shark, and a card shark is just a close-up magician with a deck of cards. Your name, Thurston, is obviously a stage name; Thurston the Great is most magicians' favorite magician, even if he did work more than a century ago. So I had someone look up your real name and then your mom's maiden name, and there it was, *Estes*. As I said, who was he to you?"

A long sigh. I prodded her with the gun barrel, and she said, "Everything."

I said, "It would take very little provocation for me to shoot you through the head right now. Explain to me why I shouldn't."

"Get your damn foot off my back."

"Austin Willie, right? That's the first time I've heard the Texas in your voice."

"So? It took me long enough to get rid of it."

I looked around. We were in the parking area, black asphalt ringed by rose bushes, about six feet from the hedge I'd come through. Wattles's 1980s white Rolls Royce was parked next to the dining room door. In the carport, up the hill about twenty yards to our left, was what seemed to be a vintage Cadillac, maybe 1967, all gleaming tail fins. The moon was up, but not so bright that it dimmed the light that was streaming through the bloody dining room window. The light seemed to be confined mostly to the dining room, though; the light leaking through the windows in the living room, to my right, was pale and washed out. At a guess, I put the house, low and white, at about 6,000 square feet. The prospect of searching it for old Frank wasn't very appealing.

I stepped back, keeping my eyes on the door into the dining room, thinking it might be better to make him come to me. "Sit up. Do you have another gun?"

"Nope."

"Anything? Because when you're standing I'm going to pat you down—"

"I'll look forward to it."

"—and if you've got anything, I'll break one of your arms."

"Am I wrong about this," she said, "or is this something personal?"

"It is. Austin Willie was, what, your mother's brother?"

She rolled over onto her back and pushed herself into a sitting position. For just a moment, her eyes went to the windows, which was all I needed to know. "He taught me everything," she said. "He taught me magic, he taught me dipping. He taught me how to live."

"He was a dip?"

"Not a pro, just a sideline. But he could do anything with his hands. He could deal a five-card hand with every card coming from a different part of the deck, and nobody would even blink. If it wasn't for him, I'd be living in some trailer park in west Texas, killing scorpions and getting beat up every Friday by my husband."

"So you were married. Before old Frank, I mean," There was, as far as I could see, no movement inside the house.

"Three years, two broken noses, a broken jaw, and one fist-in-the-stomach abortion's worth. And some teeth." She smiled at me, but it was just a display. "Implants," she said. "When Jason—every guy born in the seventies was named Jason—when Jason was done with me, I could spit out chunks of watermelon with my teeth pressed together. Uncle Willie took care of my teeth."

"And Jason?"

"Took care of him, too. Uncle Willie pret' near beat him to death," she said, all Texas. "He *woulda* beat him to death, but he got tired and finished him off with a gun. Uncle Willie and I put him under, 'bout two miles from the trailer park, and we took off."

"You can stand up now, and put your hands on top of your

head. Lace your fingers together and turn your back. Don't even think about running. How'd you get the blood all over you?"

"Splashback," she said. "I guess Wattles had high blood pressure."

I maneuvered her between me and the windows and, standing behind her, patted her down. She said, "Whee," when I got to her hips. I stepped back and knotted her short pony-tail in my hand, pushing the barrel of her gun against the base of her spine, dead center between her shoulders.

"So Wattles is dead."

She said, "And then some."

"What did he tell you?"

"Name of the shooter who got Uncle Willie." She shrugged, felt the gun, and stopped moving. "No one I ever heard of."

"Who was it?"

"Don't even remember. Danny something,"

"And the client?"

"Some other dude I never heard of. Someone who lost his boat to Uncle Willie in a game of Texas Hold'em and then found out he got sharked. From what Wattles said, Uncle Willie middle-decked him the whole game. So," she said, and she sighed. "All for nothing. Couple of nobodies."

"Anyone who thinks God doesn't have a sense of humor isn't paying attention," I said.

"Yeah?" She looked at the house again. "You want to explain the joke?"

"I'm thinking about killing you for the same reason you killed Wattles and Handkerchief and Herbie. Because Herbie did for me the same things Willie did for you."

"Then you understand," she said, letting her voice soften. "When I heard that phone message, my blood turned solid. I thought I'd die."

I was looking past her head, scanning one window at a time and not getting a very good view through any of them. "Which message?"

"On the number the hitter got, the one they were supposed to erase. I wrote it down when I opened all the envelopes, and then, two days later, I learned Uncle Willie had been shot, and I dialed it, even though I knew there was no chance that I'd—" She swallowed. "That I'd passed along the money to kill my own Uncle. But there it was: 'Hi, you've reached William Estes.' And it said he'd be at this address in North Hollywood for the next three days, which told the hitter, this guy Danny, where he was and how long he had to do the job." She began to turn to face me, but I yanked her hair against the movement, and she stopped. "You have to know how I felt, I mean you *obviously* know how I felt, because that's why you're here, because you feel the same, right? I was just trying to get whoever did Uncle Willie. I didn't know for sure that Wattles was the start of the chain, so I hired Herbie Mott to hit the offices of four guys who might be it, and Wattles was his second stop. He saw the paper with my name on it and went home."

Leaving everything unlocked, I didn't say, so he could scare Wattles into paying more for it than Dippy would. I said, "Is your friend inside?"

She turned her head slowly against my pull on her hair, giving me the elfin profile, now speckled with blood. "I told you, he's home. I came alone. I thought Wattles would let me in if I was alone, and maybe even talk to me."

I said, "Uh-huh."

"He might have told me without having to get all mangled. Why not?"

"You didn't care," I said. "The point was to hurt him. Just like it was the point with Handkerchief. There was nothing

Handkerchief could have told you. He didn't know where the chain started."

"You've gotta understand," she said. She put a hand on my arm, and I shrugged it off and took a step back. "Willie was everything. Everybody who helped to kill him had to go. And Wattles, he not only ordered the hit, he *put me in the fucking chain*. You *must* understand. You and me, we're in the same position. You could be me."

"No," I said. "There's that boiling water and those gloves."

"He wouldn't tell us where the paper—" Her voice trailed off.

"Come on," I said. "Stay in front of me, and don't try to be clever. Right now I'd shoot you for a nickel and then I'd probably give the nickel back. So just move."

"Where?"

"Inside," I said.

"You don't—you don't want to go in there."

"I know, but I'm going." I was angry enough to shove the gun barrel against her spine, hard. "Look at us," I said. "Revenge is so *stupid*."

"It is, I know that now. I feel the same way. Please, let's just leave."

"Inside."

"But you just said that revenge was—"

"Yes, I did, and I meant it. But I'll tell you, Dippy, me feeling bad about myself doesn't mean I feel any better about you. Get in there."

I kept her hair in a tight knot as we neared the door, but my eyes were all over the place, checking window after window. It distracted me to the point that, when she suddenly stepped up, I almost shot her.

"Holy cow," she said. "I felt that. Two steps here."

"I'm right behind you," I said. "No reason to shout."

"Sorry," she whispered.

"You afraid Frank won't hear you?"

"I told you, he's—"

"Fine. Now listen. You open this door slowly. Take the handle in your right hand and pull, and hold it open as you go through. Don't do anything cute with it. There's going to be a moment when I have to let go of your hair to take the door, but if you try to run I'll shoot you straight through the neck as many times as it takes to bring you down. Clear?"

"Yes."

"Good. Here goes."

We got the door open and up the two steps, and I had her ponytail in my hand again before we were inside. Going through the door, I smelled it, and I said, "Jesus Christ."

"Yeah," she said. "Stinks, don't it?" She'd regressed to pure Texas.

I said, "Stop."

Hanging from the ceiling was a heavy rococo chandelier with about forty small candle-light bulbs in it. It was obviously on a rheostat that was turned up high, because the room was dazzlingly bright. There were big gouges in the wooden floor made by the legs of the massive dining-room table, which had been dragged over to the window. Wattles was spread-eagled in the center of the table, his wrists and ankles tied to the table legs. There was blood everywhere, and from one corner of the table rose a byzantine squiggle of smoke with its base at the tip of a soldering iron that had fallen over. The room smelled like a barbeque.

"It looks worse than it is," Dippy said in that same flat Texas voice.

"You, um, pulled the table over to the wall why?"

"You know why," she said.

"I want to hear you say it."

"So I could plug in the soldering thing."

"Kitchen," I said, and I followed her.

The kitchen was bright, too. It had been ransacked for knives and other useful implements, and they'd left the lights on, so it was easy to see that no one was there. The pantry and the utility room were empty, too. The utility room opened into the back yard, and the chain lock was on, so no one had gone out that way.

"Turn around," I said. "Living room."

Dippy led me back through the bright kitchen and the dazzling slaughterhouse of the dining room and toward a wide doorway that opened into a large, dim room. Just as we passed through it, from behind me Wattles made a loud rattling noise deep in his throat and Dippy, panicking, tried to pull away. At the same time, I saw movement to the right and I yanked Dippy around in front of me again as Frank rose from behind the couch, which he'd pulled away from the wall, and leveled a gun at me. I felt the impact twice as the shots banged against the walls and ceiling, the shells pushing Dippy back against my hand, and I emptied her little gun at the center mass of Frank's body. He fired again, and Dippy shuddered and went down as Frank folded in half over the back of the sofa, facedown on the cushions with his legs still on the floor behind it. Then I guess his legs let go because he was dragged up the back of the couch, leaving a red smear on the upholstery, and he disappeared behind it with a sound like someone dropping an armload of books.

Dippy was on her back, one arm thrown outward as though to catch something. Her eyes were open in an expression that looked like surprise, as though she'd just recognized someone at a distance. She wasn't breathing. I pocketed her gun and pulled the Glock and eased my way across the room. Behind the couch, Frank had both hands clenched across his middle and he glared up at me, and I stood there and watched the intensity evaporate and the eyes roll back, and when I absolutely knew he was dead, I still leaned down and felt for his pulse.

And didn't find it. I have no idea how long I stood there. What brought me back to myself was the ticking of an antique pendulum clock on the wall above the couch. I found myself astonished that it was only a little after eight o'clock.

It took a minute to put Dippy's gun back into her hand. The crime scene told a story even a rookie could read: a falling out between killers, each shot with the other's gun, powder burns on both hands, all the wounds entering from the front. I hadn't left much of anything as far as I could recall, but even if I had, my DNA still wasn't on file.

So I was free and clear. I held that phrase in mind, *free and clear,* like a mantra as I backed out of the living room. I repeated it over and over as I slowed for a look at the huge cut of meat that had been Wattles just to confirm that he was dead even though I'd heard the rattle of his final breath, and I repeated it as I went through the back door. I followed the thought like a guiding light while I fought my way downhill in the dark. I took it hand over hand like a safety rope that led me to my car, and it didn't desert me until I'd climbed in and pulled the door safely closed behind me.

And then I burst into tears. If you'd asked me who I was crying for—whether it was for Herbie or Wattles or Dippy being brutalized in that trailer or Handkerchief or Bones getting beat up in those schoolyards or Eddie Mott and me—the two abandoned boys—or even my own failures to be there for Rina, I couldn't have told you. I couldn't have said whether it was for the chain of revenge that Dippy had followed to get to Willie's murderer, or the one I'd followed to get to Herbie's, or the new one that Dippy's death might set into motion. I just know that I sat there at the wheel, crying like I hadn't cried since the day my father left for good.

38

Duff

The first person I saw in the little circle of chairs drawn up in front of A. Vincent Twistleton's desk was Ruben Ghorbani, who looked as surprised to be there as I was to see him. Next to him was the pastor, Father Angelis, who gave me a sliver of sanctified smile as I came in.

Also present were Eddie Mott and a woman who had to be his mother. From the way Herbie had talked about her, I half-expected her to have scales and a forked tongue, but she was a nice-looking woman in her late fifties, slightly faded and a little worn away, as though she'd been washed too hard and too many times. There were also a couple of mugs I knew in passing, but even if they'd been strangers it was obvious from the look of them that they were in Herbie's Game. The bigger one made me the moment I walked in and gave me an assessing look, as though I were more competition for Herbie's treasure.

On the desk in front of Twistleton were some envelopes. Behind him, leaning against the window and hard to see clearly with the light behind it, was the John Sloane painting.

"Good," Twistleton said. "We're all here." He rubbed his hands together and then flexed his fingers as though he were about to play an especially difficult bit of Liszt. "I'm not going to be formal, because Herbert Mott wasn't a formal guy, and we're departing from procedure by having some of the material aspects of the bequest here in the room, to be handed out as we go, but nobody here should be confused about whether all this is legal and binding, because it is. Oh, and the bigger pieces will be available for pickup beginning on Monday."

He gave us a lawyerly eye, one eyebrow raised in a way I've always wanted to be able to do myself. When no one shrieked or fainted or argued with him, he nodded.

"Good." He picked up the only piece of paper on his desk. "Herbie Mott wrote this himself, and it's short and informal, but it's legal."

He leaned back in his chair, which squeaked, as I tried to get a better look at the Sloane.

"'My current legal name is Herbert Arthur Elgar Mott,'" Twistleton read. He looked up. "I've always found four names to be reassuring. Is something wrong, Mr. Bender?"

"No," I said. "Just looking at the painting."

"You'll have lots of time to look at it later. So, da-da, da-da, Herbie wrote, '—and I am as sane and healthy now as I've ever been. This is what I want to do with my stuff. To my only son, Edward Elgar Mott, I leave the envelope numbered one, which contains a list of the furniture he gets plus the key him and me talked about, and I'm sure he'll be happy with it.'" Twistleton picked up a standard number-ten envelope that did indeed have a whopping number 1 printed on it in about 60-point type and handed it across the desk to Eddie. "I am bound to say," Twistleton said, "that I have no knowledge of what this key opens or what impact it might or might not have on the value of Herbie's estate, but I'm sure your tax people, if you decide to consult them, can get everything straightened out."

"Sure," Eddie said, folding the envelope and putting it into his pocket.

"'To my former wife, Eloise Chandler Mott,'" Twistleton read in his ripest voice, "'I leave the envelope numbered two, which is full of engagement and wedding rings I've been collecting for a while. In case any of you are thinking, *Herbie's rules said no engagement or wedding rings*, let me remind you that according to my rules, a ring that ain't being worn ain't a link between two people any more, it's just a piece of jewelry.'"

Twistleton handed the envelope, thick manila this time and obviously heavy, to Eddie's mother, who took them with the expression the phrase *mixed emotions* was coined to describe. "I'm happy to tell you, just within the confines of this room, that the assessors Herbie informally consulted put the value of the stones and metals in here at a little better than a hundred and fifty thousand dollars."

Eddie's mother said, "And I earned it."

"'To Ruben Ghorbani, if he didn't kill me—'" His eyes went to Ghorbani. "Do I need to explain that, Mr. Ghorbani?"

"No," Ghorbani said, looking embarrassed.

"Fine, so . . . 'To Ruben Ghorbani, if he didn't *et cetera*, with apologies for the worst thing I ever did, I leave envelope number three, which has ten K in it for every year he spent inside and my wishes that it could have been more.'"

"Thirty K?" Ghorbani said, taking the envelope.

Twistleton shook his head. "I don't know, Mr. Ghorbani. I have no idea how many years you spent inside, whatever that means." He held up a hand to cut Ghorbani off. "This is one of the reasons I'm afraid that we've vastly undervalued the estate."

"Aahhh," Ghorbani said. "Gotcha." He gave the envelope to Angelis. "Anyway," he said, "it's going to a church."

Whatever it was that was signaling me from the picture, I hadn't identified it yet.

Twistleton said, "I'm sure Mr. Mott would be very pleased

to know that. To continue, 'To my colleagues, Wide Fritzi Hummell and Merk Forbush, I leave—'" He pushed his sunglasses down on his nose and said, "Which of you gentlemen is Wide Fritzi?"

Wide Fritzi, who had earned his nickname one calorie at a time over multiple decades, raised a dimpled hand.

"Thank you. Mr. Mott goes on to say that he leaves you and Mr. Forbush, respectively, envelopes four and five, which contain, for you, Wide Fritzi, what Mr. Mott describes as his tools, and for you, Mr. Forbush, his map to the stars' homes, annotated with the brand names and locations of, it says here, 'many major locks.'"

"Bitchen," said Merk Forbush.

I sat up. I'd spotted it, and it told me everything I'd been afraid of.

"'And finally, to my friend and companion, my second son, Junior Bender, I leave the painting *Ninth Avenue Evening* by John Sloane, with my fervent hope that he can find a way to beat the tax man on the—'"

"It's duff," I said. My heart was pounding so heavily I could see my shirt bouncing at the bottom of my field of vision.

Twistleton said, "Excuse me?"

"It's a phony. It's not even a good phony."

"I assure you—" Twistleton began.

"It's a Chinese copy," I said. "It's painted okay, but whoever did it doesn't read English. Mr. Twistleton, will you read the sign on the building in the upper left corner of the painting?"

Twistleton said, "Burlesque."

"Would you spell it, please."

"Certain—oh. *Oh.* Oh, my." Twistleton leaned back to take in the whole canvas and then forward to scrutinize the letters. "Yes, I see. B-U-R-L-E-K-S." He shook his head sharply. "No, no, that won't do, not even accounting for phonetic spelling, which I gather was a bit of a rage when Sloane was painting. But perhaps it's Sloane's mistake?"

"I've been looking at it for years. It says—it *said*—'Burlesk'— E-S-K."

"My, my," Twistleton said. "How distressing. Well, there's no sense in your claiming it if, as you say, it has no value. Could cause tax problems for nothing. We'll keep it here, just in case the estate tax people—Where are you going?"

"Home," I said. "I guess I should have known."

"Known what?"

"That it wouldn't be straight. Not with all I've learned about Herbie this week."

"Don't leap to conclusions," Twistleton said, but by then the door was closing behind me. In the outer room, Ronnie, who hadn't felt like she belonged at the reading, looked up from one of those magazines you only see in offices—*Façade* or *Country Lawns* or *Gentile Living* or something like that—and said, "Through?"

"I certainly am."

The hallway door opened, and Joe came in. "Here you go," he said, handing her something.

"What's that?" I said.

"Keys," Joe said. "I brought your car around to the front."

"Thank you, Joe," Ronnie said. She gave him a smile that drove him back a step.

In the elevator, she said, "What's wrong?"

"Nothing new," I said. "Skip it."

"Skipped it is," she said, and we rode the rest of the way down in silence, which lasted until she opened the door of the car, when she said, "What's that?"

I looked into the back seat. On the floor, leaning against the seat, was a large rectangle of a familiar size, wrapped in brown paper and twine. Whatever it was that had been pummeling my heart backed off and went looking for somebody else to bother.

"It's a present from Herbie," I said, feeling the smile take charge of my face. "And an incredibly elaborate tax dodge."

39
If She'll Have Me

"He's not here," the cop on the other end of the line said. "Didn't come in today."

"Is he—I mean, I know he's sick, but is he all right?"

The cop said, "Compared to what?"

"Right. Okay, look, do me a favor. Does he call in?"

"Sometimes, sometimes not. He a friend of yours?"

I said, "I guess he is. Listen, if he calls in, ask him to call Junior." I gave him my number, and he wrote it down with a slowness that surprised and even angered me; if there's one skill you'd think a cop would have, it'd be writing down a phone number.

I hung up. Ronnie and I were in a booth at Musso and Frank, the first place we'd ever eaten. We'd spent a nice evening being ignored by waiters who'd had decades to perfect the skill. In between being unseen and unheard, we'd been served the food that almost makes it worth it.

Ronnie sighed happily and studied the wreckage of dishes on the table. She said, "Restaurants were illegal in Paris until after the revolution, and then there were hundreds of them. They changed the city's whole culture. Balzac practically lived in them. Do you know he sometimes ate a hundred oysters at a single sitting?"

"He was making up for Proust," I said.

"Balzac was before Proust."

"I know," I said. "But it seemed like such a literary remark, I was hoping it would impress you."

She looked at the cell phone in my hand. "Why do you want to talk to that cop?"

I shrugged. "Just tidying up, I guess."

My phone rang. Before I could say anything, he said, "DiGaudio."

"How you feeling?"

Ronnie looked up. She was tearing the last piece of bread in half, not to share it but just to give herself the pleasure of picking it up twice.

"You're not stupid, Bender. Don't waste my time with stupid questions."

"Right." I inhaled to loosen the band around my chest. "You had Herbie once as a person of interest in a murder."

"Yeah?"

"An actor," I said. "Up in the hills."

"I know who you're talking about. Mott was only ever on the edge of one murder I know of."

"Was he guilty?"

"Are you shitting me?" He sounded almost like the old DeGaudio. "If the sonofabitch was guilty, we'd have—oh," he said, the energy deserting his voice. "I get it. No, no, there's no way we'd let a guy, just because he's a pipeline, float on a murder one charge, which is what that woulda been, murder during the commission of a felony. No, we got the guy pretty quick, and he'd have gotten the chair if there was a single full pair of balls anywhere in Sacramento."

"Got it," I said. "Thanks."

"You really cared about him, huh?"

"I guess I did."

"Well, here's a piece of advice for you, from someone who's realized he's not gonna have time to fix any of the ways he fucked up his life. You sitting down?"

"Yeah."

"Okay, I'm only gonna say this once. You never really know anybody. Cops, we learn this real fast. You get a guy who kills twenty-three people and feeds them to his fish, and when the news trucks come along, people who knew him for years are shocked. 'Such a nice guy,' they say. Every time, you see it over and over. Or, I don't know, take that homeless guy who kicked in the door where all those kidnapped women were chained to the walls. You know what I'm saying?"

I said, "Probably."

DiGaudio said, "You meet somebody, right? You don't need to say yeah, you meet somebody and you think you get to know them. This could be anybody, your best friend, someone you forget in a week, your wife, your father. Doesn't matter. When I say you get to know them, what I mean is that you see the bits and pieces they want to show you, and at a certain point you go, *Well, fine, that's Herbie* or whatever the name is, and you put that version of whoever it is into a package and you seal it, like a loaf of bread, and you put it in the fridge. And from then on, when you think about Herbie or hang around with him, you don't see Herbie, what you see is whatever you wrote on that package: Sourdough Rye or Sweet Potato Raisin or whatever. What you see is just the guy you knew he'd be. You with me?"

"Right here."

"So that's the first problem. You don't know anyone for shit. And here's the second problem. People change all the time. Every day they get up and they change. You probably figure you understand all there is about that knockout you tried to pass off as a witness, even though you don't really know her any better than you knew Herbie. And already she's not the same girl she was when you met her. She changes every day, day after day. And she always will. You gonna marry her?"

"Maybe. If she'll have me." I could feel Ronnie's gaze without even looking up.

"Well, by the time you do, she'll be a different person. Name'll be the same, same nice face, but inside, uh-uh. So here's the moral, Junior. You listening?"

"I'm not doing anything else."

"However people are to you, that's how they are. Herbie was great to you, then I gotta tell you, unless you know he secretly did you dirty, Herbie was a great guy. Whatever he gave you, you still got it. You'll have it until you fuck it up yourself, and when you do, you know what?"

"What."

"It won't be Herbie's fault."

He went silent, and I let it stretch out. I had nothing to say except *thanks*, and I didn't know how he'd take it.

"So here we are," he said at last. "I guess this is it, huh? Well, I gotta tell you, Junior, it's been interesting knowing you."

"Goes for me, too."

"Ease up," he said. "You got a long way to go, if you're lucky. Just fucking ease up." And he hung up.

Ronnie said, "If she'll have me?"

I said, "Figure of speech."

She put an elbow on the table and rested her chin on her palm. "If she'll have me?"

"Well," I said, "all things being equal, would you?"

"All things are never equal. If they were, we'd spend our lives trying to get from Point A to Point A."

"Right," I said. "I mean, no. They're not."

"But if they were," she said.

"If they were?"

She lowered her eyes to the tabletop and looked at it as though the remnants of the meal were a code of some kind. "But they're not."

"I need to say something to you."

She looked up at me again and swung her legs up onto the cushion of the booth, leaving her shoes under the table and giving me a clear shot at her elegant toes. Today she'd painted every third toenail and it made me think of a piano. She said, "Fire away."

"That whole thing," I said, "that thing about Trenton and Newark—"

"Albany," she said. "I think."

"Whatever it is. Youngstown, Ohio, I don't care. Whatever it is, please do me a favor."

She sat there and waited for me.

"Don't tell me until you're good and ready."

She said, "I can live with that."

40

The Beautiful One

It was a little after eleven when I let myself into the very nice house in the Beverly Hills Flats. The place was dark and the BMW SUV hadn't been in the driveway, which was the pattern: the woman who lived there rarely came home before midnight, so I went in through the back, feeling fine.

Maybe it was because my heart was light. Maybe it was because I knew exactly where I was going and what I was going to do, and there was no question that I'd be in and out within two minutes.

Whatever it was, I didn't follow two of Herbie's rules. I didn't listen first and I didn't think it through backward.

So I really shouldn't have been so surprised when I was just about to open the drawer in the bedroom and the woman said, "I am pointing a gun at your back."

I slowly extended my arms, fingers spread wide, and rotated them so she could see that my hands were open.

"In my other hand is a cell phone," she said. She had a faint accent that, I thought, was French. "I am going to take my eyes off you just long enough to do a speed-dial that will connect me with the police. If you move, I will shoot you."

I said, "May I turn around?"

"Why not?" she said, and an edge came into her voice. "I

would like to see the face of a man who forces his way into other people's lives and takes from them the things they love. Please. By all means. Show me your face."

I turned, quite slowly, keeping my arms wide apart. She was in her fifties, beautiful in a kind of lit-by-sunset way, a fine pair of eyes below high-arching brows and the kind of bone structures that makes plastic surgeons despair.

"Disappointing," she said. "Just another uselessly pretty American face. This is the land of the pretty face. Not the beautiful face or the interesting face, but the pretty face. Just hold still."

I said, "Why do you think I'm here?"

"It's obvious. You're here to steal from me. First the other one, now you."

"The pocket of my shirt, the one on the left. Can you see it?"

"Be quiet. I am phoning now."

"It has a box in it."

She lifted her chin, and it made her look like a woman who had given orders from childhood. "What is this to me?"

"The box belongs to you."

She started to say something but stopped.

"Very slowly," I said, holding up an index finger, "I'm going to put this finger at the bottom of the pocket, from the outside, and push the box up so you can see it."

She said, "No. This is not amusing. Stop. I said, stop."

But I slowly brought the hand around and pushed the box up until most of it was visible over the pocket's edge. "Do you recognize it?"

She said, "Yes," but it was mostly an exhalation.

"It has both of your brooches in it," I said. "The pretty one and the beautiful one." I took it out, still moving slowly, and popped the top off with my thumb so I could tilt the box down for her to see inside it.

"Oh," she said, but actually the word escaped her, and she looked surprised when she heard it. She brought up the hand with the phone in it and put it over her mouth. "Why do—why do you have them? What I mean to say is, what are you *doing* here?"

"I'm bringing them back," I said.

"You took them?"

"I did."

"Then why are you bringing them back?"

"A long time ago," I said, "someone taught me some rules about stealing things. One of them was to be on the lookout for something that might be the one thing the person I was robbing couldn't live without. And when I thought I recognized it, not to take it."

"The one thing—"

"The one thing that, if it was still there, the person who was robbed would say, 'At least they didn't get *that*.' And I think I broke that rule here."

She said, "Please put the cover back on the box, and put the box on the bed nearer to you."

I did as I was told, and the gun stayed on me the whole time, steady as a beam of sunlight.

"Now go over to the other bed. When you get there, you may sit."

It wasn't until I'd seated myself that I realized how weak my legs had been.

"Tell me," she said. "Which was the beautiful one?"

"The one that was made by hand."

She had been leaning against the frame of the open door, and when I said that, she slowly sank to a sitting position, with her knees up, the gun still pointed at me. "Do you know what it is?"

"No," I said.

"Or what it's worth?"

"Quite a bit," I said. "I got beat up pretty badly because I wouldn't sell it."

She leaned forward a bit to look at me. "Really. And why wouldn't you sell it?"

"I didn't like the guy."

"Why did that matter?"

"I don't know. Yes, I do. Because he talked about selling it to someone who collects Nazi memorabilia."

"Then you *do* know what it is."

"I know what the Cartier is, liberation jewelry. The other one—"

She gave a smile that was all in the eyes. "The beautiful one."

"Yeah, that one. I have no idea."

"There are only ten or twelve of them that anyone knows of. From time to time, a woman who owned one of the Cartier pieces would be arrested. Even those of high rank could be dragged down into those filthy basements. My *mémé*, my *grand-maman*, was one of them. After they lived through what was done to them in the basements, they were either sent to a prison camp or they were shot. One of the first to be imprisoned was a very, very high-ranking lady, the *Duchesse* d'Aubert. They came for her in the morning and found her in her dressing gown. She had been about to paint her nails, and she had decided, as a joke, to paint them the colors of the French flag, red, white, and blue. Nail polish in many colors was new then, and it amused her to paint the flag with them. It was probably good for her she hadn't done it when the troopers arrived because the Gestapo would not have been charmed. Does this not interest you?"

"Why do you ask?"

"You keep looking toward the window."

"My fiancée," I said, using the word for the first time in my life, "is outside in the car, and I wish she could hear it."

"You can tell it to her. I'm not yet enough of a democrat to invite your fiancée inside my home." She reached into a pocket and came out with a pack of cigarettes. "Excuse me," she said, "European vice." She shook one free and lit it with a slim silver lighter. "So, *la Duchesse*, and in her pocket the nail colors, yes?"

"Yes."

"She was too great a lady for the Germans to keep. Her family looked down on the former royal family of France as *arrivistes*. When they released her, she gave the colors to another lady, who gave them to another lady, who, well, you can guess." She took another drag off the cigarette and blew the smoke away, out the door, taking her eyes off me for the first time. "When a woman was sentenced to be shot, the other ladies would make her her own liberation jewelry. They unwound wire from bedsprings or even from wristwatches, they used bits of wood or cork or chips of cement for the bird's body. Then, on the morning, they would pin it inside their clothes and go face the rifles. To be liberated."

I said, "But you got this back."

"You're quick," she said. "It was August of 1944. The Allies were practically in the suburbs. The cells were emptied by officers who hoped someone would testify in their defense. My *grand-maman* went home and took with her the brooch her friends had made for her to wear the next day, when she was to be shot. She also took the nail colors, which she returned to the *Duchesse*."

"Was there much left?"

She shook her head.

I said, "Are you going to call the police?"

"Why?" she said. "Because you returned to me something I had lost?"

I said, "Thank you," and got up.

"The person who taught you this rule about what not to steal?" She hadn't gotten to her feet. "He is a friend?"

"Yes," I said. "He was."

"Very well. Please go out the front door. I don't want the neighbors thinking I have young men creeping in and out of the place."

"May I tell you something?"

"But of course."

I said, "You need better locks."

Afterword

This book began life as *Liberation Jewelry*, a novella of (theoretically) 30,000 words, which I undertook in response to a request from the folks at Soho that I "knock one out" during an otherwise idle week or two. Problem is, it's harder for me to write short than it is to write long, and the more-than 100,000-word book you're holding is evidence of that fact. Also, Wattles barged in, and that complicated things.

The first thing I wrote was the burglary that opens the book, the scene in which Junior nicks the two brooches, the Cartier and the amateurish one. When I wrote it, I had no idea where the second brooch came from or why it was there. I'm embarrassed to say that I do this kind of thing all the time. It's a part of my process that I indulge on faith, without understanding it. I think of planting these open questions as a kind of mystery for myself, something I have to solve before I get to the end of the book. Almost invariably, these things not only get worked out, but they also become important to the story.

In this case, there was virtually no suspense about whether the mystery brooch would work out because about eight days into the writing of the book, I mentioned the two brooches to my agent, Bob Mecoy, and he instantly came up with the explanation that you probably just read. When I hung up the phone,

I felt like I'd tripped over a ten-pound emerald. That piece of information shaped about half of the book, so thanks, Bob.

It may be disappointing to some of you to know those hand-crafted liberation brooches didn't actually exist. The Cartier version did, though, and it was both sold and worn under the noses of the Nazis, which was pretty gutsy in itself.

In this book I killed off some peripheral characters (as a favor to those of you who skip to notes like these without reading the story first, I won't name them). One of the things that happens when you write a series is that you gradually accumulate a small army of peripheral characters, and *they all want to get into every book*. It's hard enough to make up a story without a platoon of underemployed characters standing just offstage, shifting impatiently from foot to foot as they wait to be called into the light, so I've thinned them out a bit. Two of them are gone for good (and I already regret one of them) and the other is in that peculiar fictional dusk where I don't know whether he's alive or dead and probably won't until he lurches through some doorway when I least want him.

Lots of good music went into the writing of *Herbie's Game*. I made a playlist of about nine hundred songs by reasonably new-to-me artists such as MS/MR, Jack's Mannequin (and its frontman, Andrew McMahon), The Boxer Rebellion, passEnger, Amanda Shires ("Detroit or Buffalo" became Ronnie's theme song), John Fulbright, Langhorne Slim, and Alabama Shakes. Also on call were more familiar names: The Hold Steady (and *its* frontman, Craig Finn), John Hiatt, Neko Case, Tegan and Sara, The National, Steve Earle (burning the Walmart down!), Jon Fratelli, Vampire Weekend, The Dodos, Over the Rhine, Arctic Monkeys, Franz Ferdinand (a new album after only *four years*!), and a bunch of reasonably obscure Rolling Stones songs from their first three albums.

And this is a good place to say thank you to all the people who have written to suggest new music to me. I listen to all of it, even if it doesn't make it into a writing playlist. Send more! And finally, thanks to all of you who have said such nice things about Junior.

Please continue to let me know what's up via my website, www.timothyhallinan.com. As far as I know, I've responded to every piece of reader mail in the past couple of years. And who knows? You might write something that would lift my spirits on one of the three days a week, on average, that writing is less fun, and less productive, than doing my own dental work. More than one book has been saved by a letter—and this is true not only of me, but also of most of the writers I know.

While I'm thanking people, I want to start a round of applause for the people at Soho Crime for breaking every rule in the publisher's playbook to put out the first three Junior Bender novels in seven months, while going to the wall in their support. So let's hear it for publisher Bronwen Hruska; my indefatigable if occasionally fractious editor, Juliet Grames; marketing marvel (and all-around well-read guy) Paul Oliver; and gifted enablers Meredith Barnes and Amara Hoshijo. And, of course, cover artist Katherine Grames, whose jacket design for this book was the first one I ever saw that I didn't want changed in any way, however minuscule. Gratitude also goes to three tireless beta readers, Everett Kaser, Alan Katz, and Ellie Korn, who caught dozens of errors.

As always, thanks to Munyin.

Other Titles in the Soho Crime Series